D0129436

Tru
Detective

Norah McClintock

illustrated by

Steven P. Hughes

ORCA BOOK PUBLISHERS

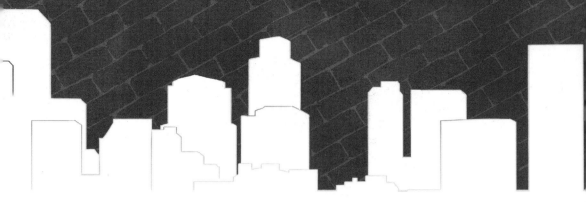

Library and Archives Canada Cataloguing in Publication

McClintock, Norah, author
Tru detective / Noah McClintock ; illustrated by Steven Hughes.

ISBN 978-1-4598-0379-4 (PBK.).—ISBN 978-1-4598-0380-0 (PDF).—
ISBN 978-1-4598-0381-7 (EPUB)

1. Graphic novels. I. Hughes, Steven, 1989-, illustrator II. Title.
PN6733.M29T78 2015 j741.5'971 C2014-906657-0
C2014-906658-9

First published in the United States, 2015
Library of Congress Control Number: 2014952051

Summary: In this chilling graphic novel, Truman, the prime suspect in his girlfriend's murder, struggles to find the truth.

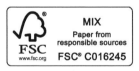

MIX
Paper from responsible sources
FSC® C016245
FSC www.fsc.org

Orca Book Publishers is dedicated to preserving the environment and has printed this book on Forest Stewardship Council® certified paper.

Orca Book Publishers gratefully acknowledges the support for its publishing programs provided by the following agencies: the Government of Canada through the Canada Book Fund and the Canada Council for the Arts, and the Province of British Columbia through the BC Arts Council and the Book Publishing Tax Credit.

Cover and interior artwork by Steven P. Hughes
Cover design by Chantal Gabriell and Steven P. Hughes

ORCA BOOK PUBLISHERS
PO Box 5626, Stn. B
Victoria, BC Canada
V8R 6S4

ORCA BOOK PUBLISHERS
PO Box 468
Custer, WA USA
98240-0468

www.orcabook.com
Printed and bound in Canada.

18 17 16 15 • 4 3 2 1

To HR, my tru love. —NM

To Rachel. —SH

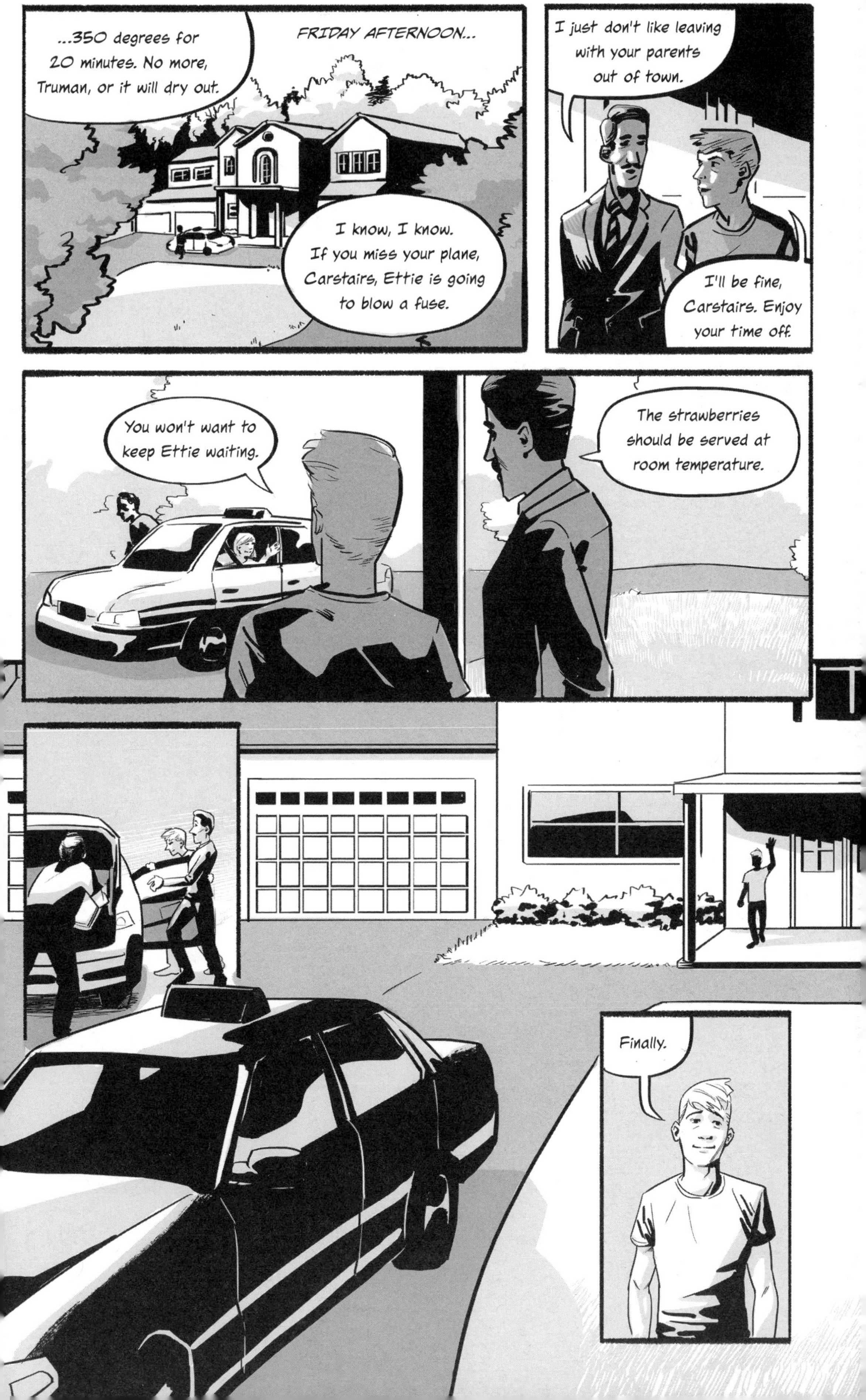
FRIDAY AFTERNOON...
...350 degrees for 20 minutes. No more, Truman, or it will dry out.
I know, I know. If you miss your plane, Carstairs, Ettie is going to blow a fuse.
I just don't like leaving with your parents out of town.
I'll be fine, Carstairs. Enjoy your time off.
You won't want to keep Ettie waiting.
The strawberries should be served at room temperature.
Finally.

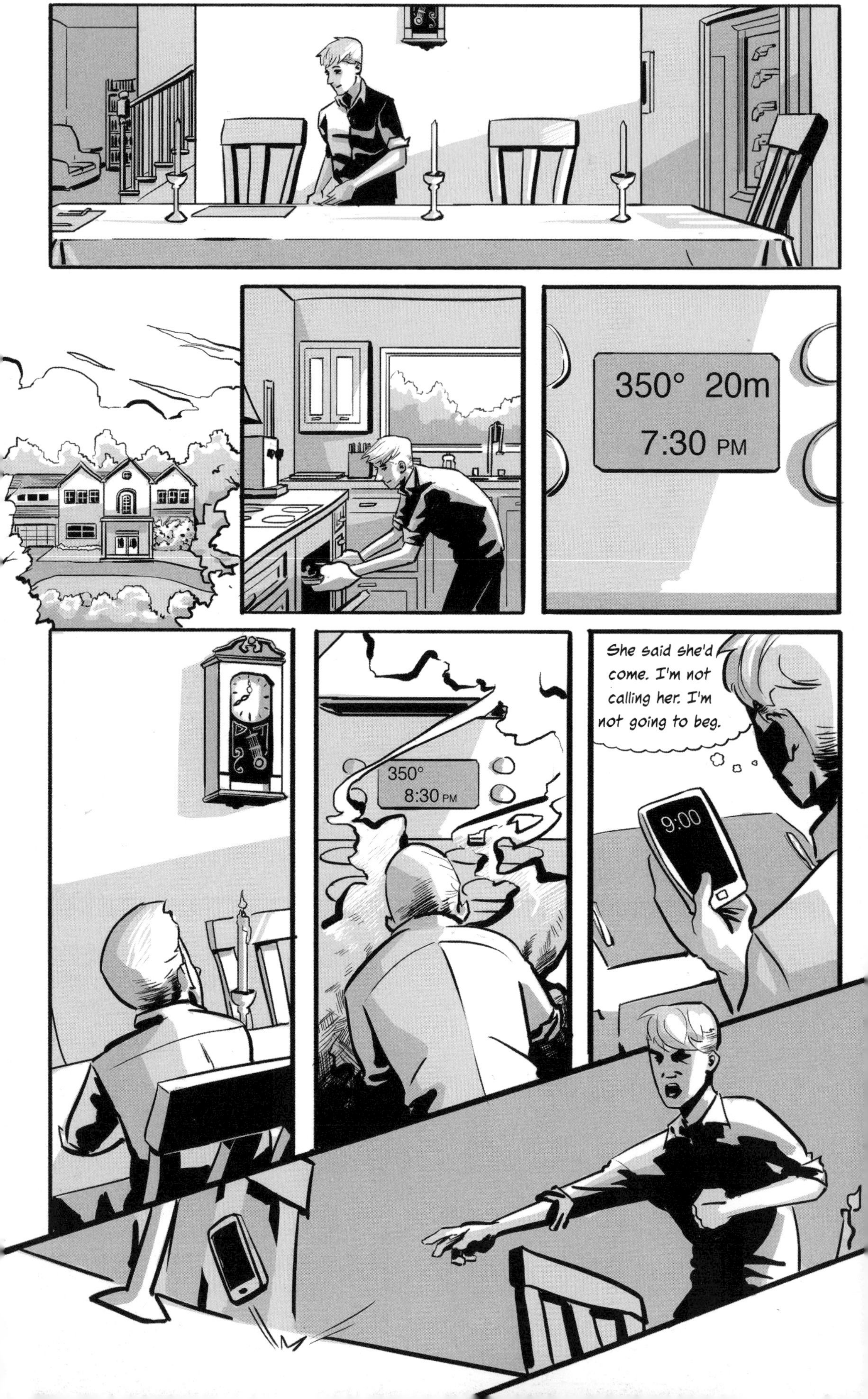
350° 20m
7:30 PM
350°
8:30 PM
She said she'd come. I'm not calling her. I'm not going to beg.
9:00

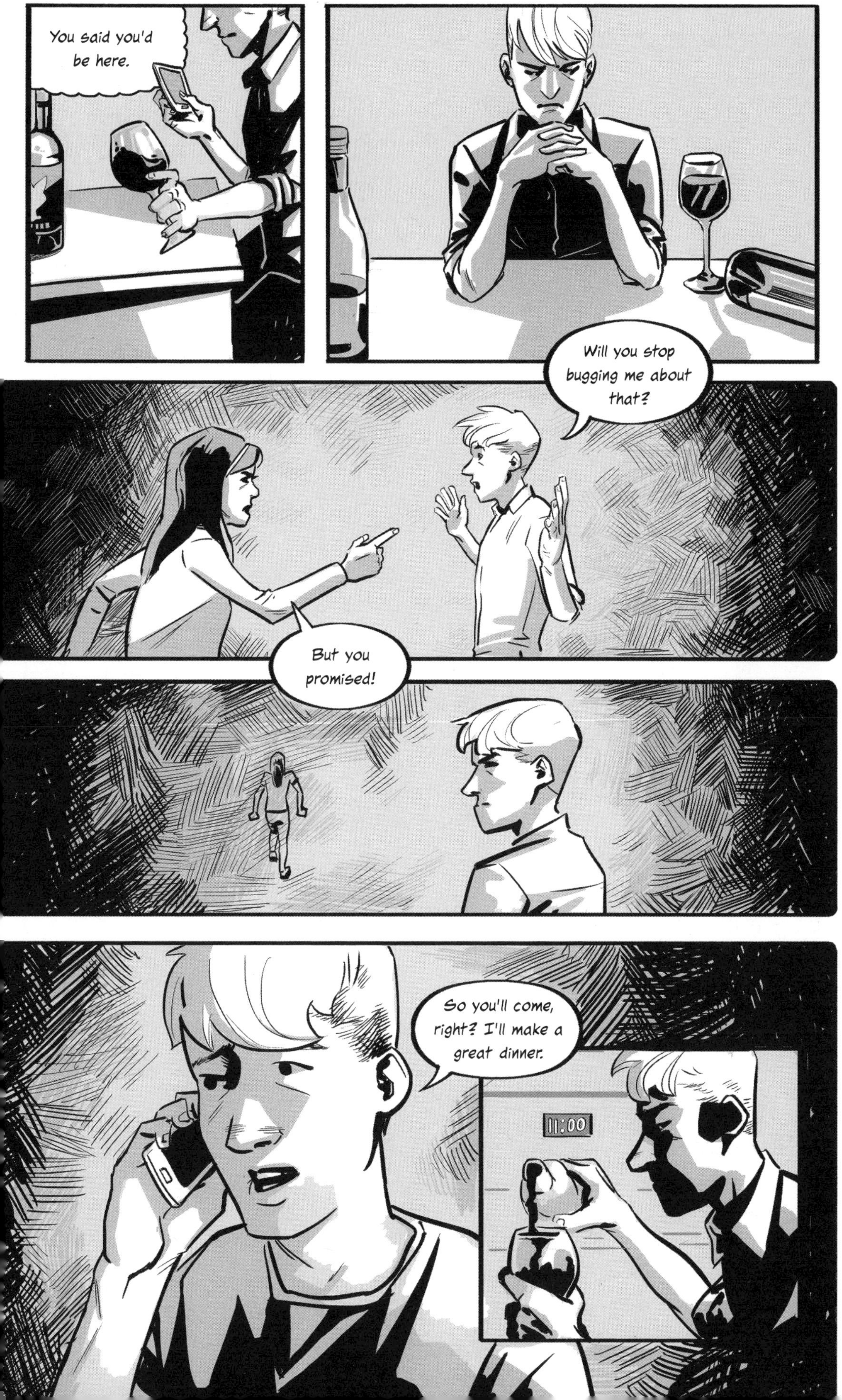
You said you'd be here.
Will you stop bugging me about that?
But you promised!
So you'll come, right? I'll make a great dinner.
11:00

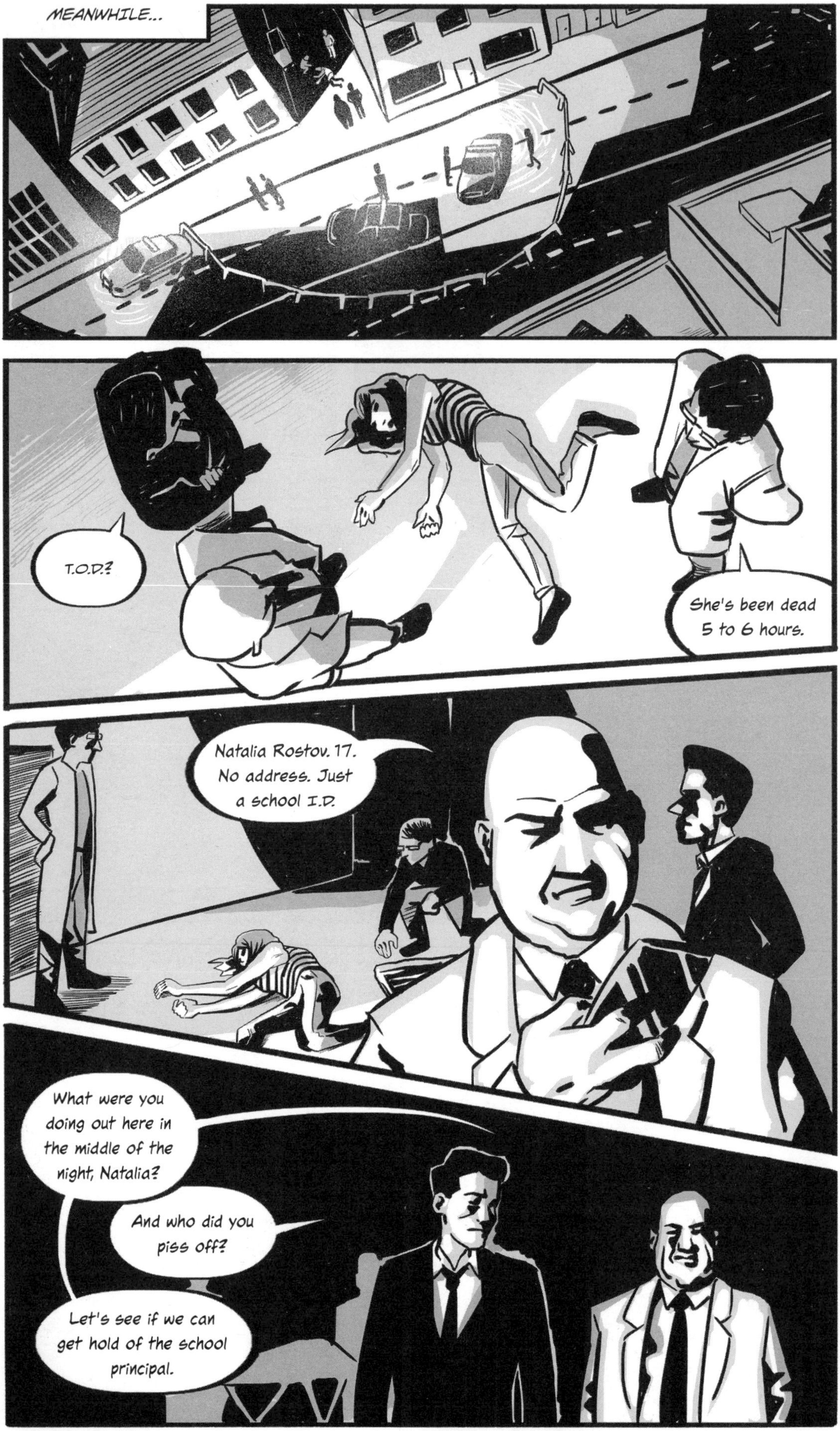

MEANWHILE...
T.O.D.?
She's been dead 5 to 6 hours.
Natalia Rostov. 17. No address. Just a school I.D.
What were you doing out here in the middle of the night, Natalia?
And who did you piss off?
Let's see if we can get hold of the school principal.

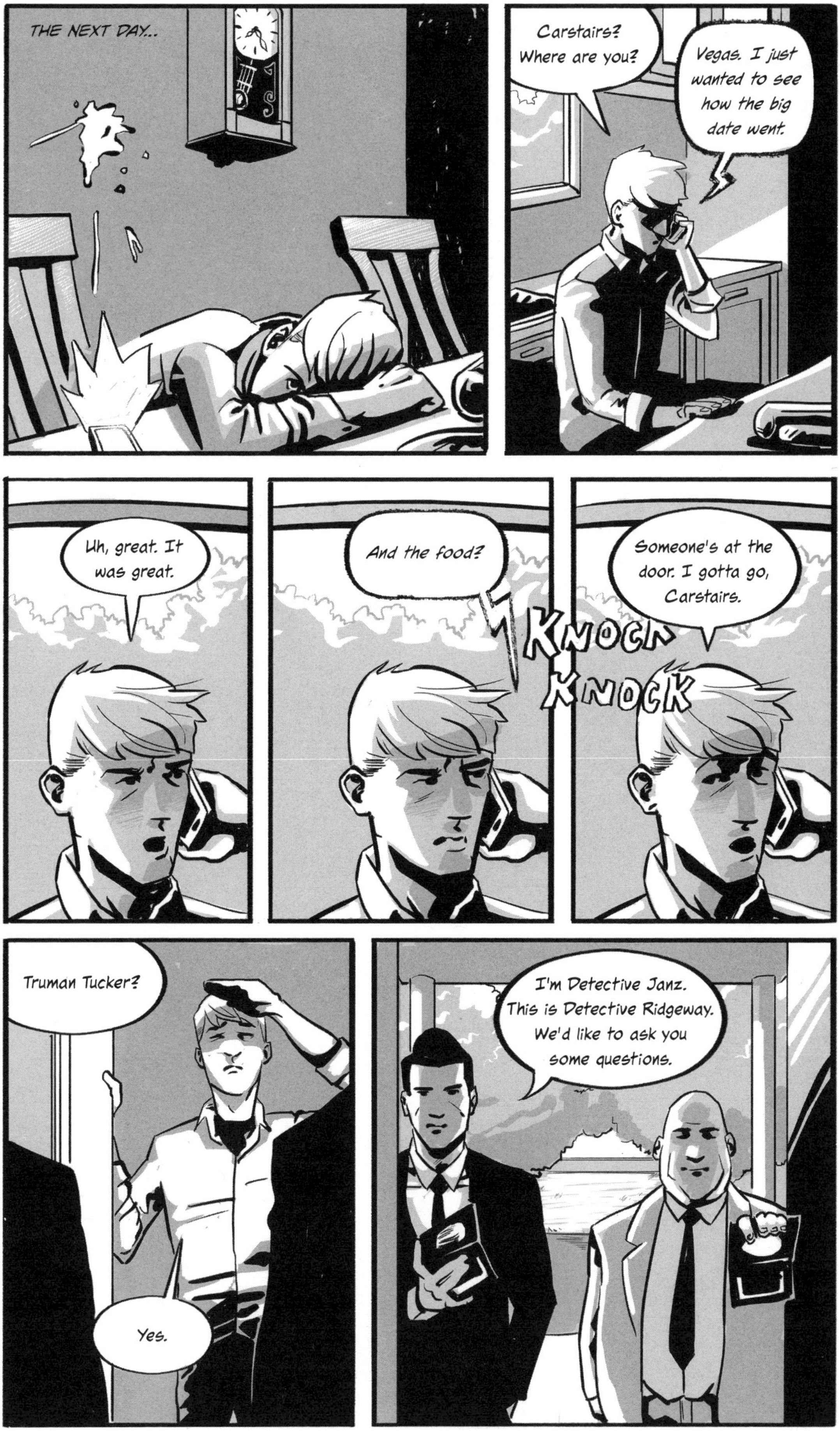
THE NEXT DAY...
Carstairs? Where are you?
Vegas. I just wanted to see how the big date went.
Uh, great. It was great.
And the food?
KNOCK KNOCK
Someone's at the door. I gotta go, Carstairs.
Truman Tucker?
Yes.
I'm Detective Janz. This is Detective Ridgeway. We'd like to ask you some questions.

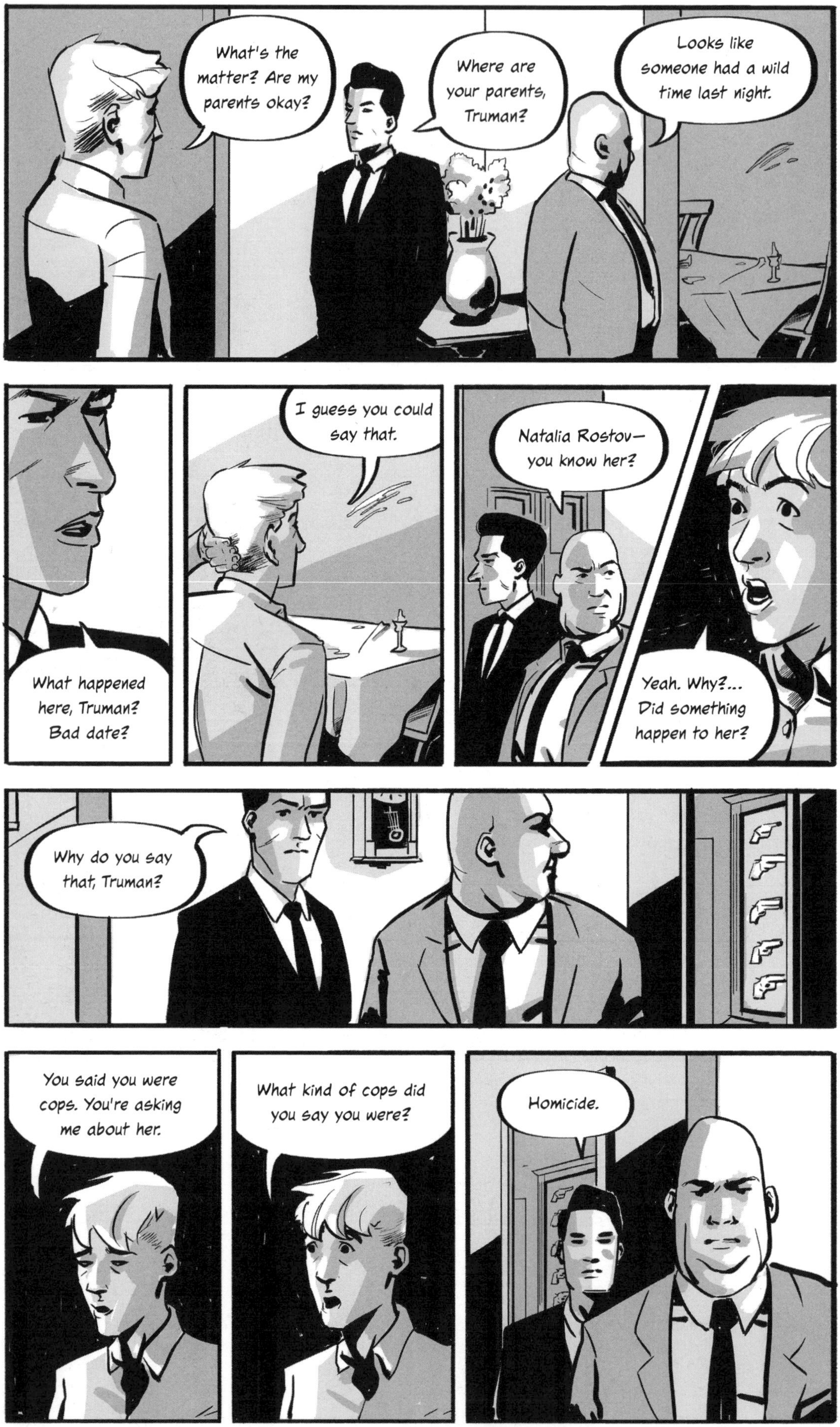
What's the matter? Are my parents okay?
Where are your parents, Truman?
Looks like someone had a wild time last night.
What happened here, Truman? Bad date?
I guess you could say that.
Natalia Rostov—you know her?
Yeah. Why?... Did something happen to her?
Why do you say that, Truman?
You said you were cops. You're asking me about her.
What kind of cops did you say you were?
Homicide.

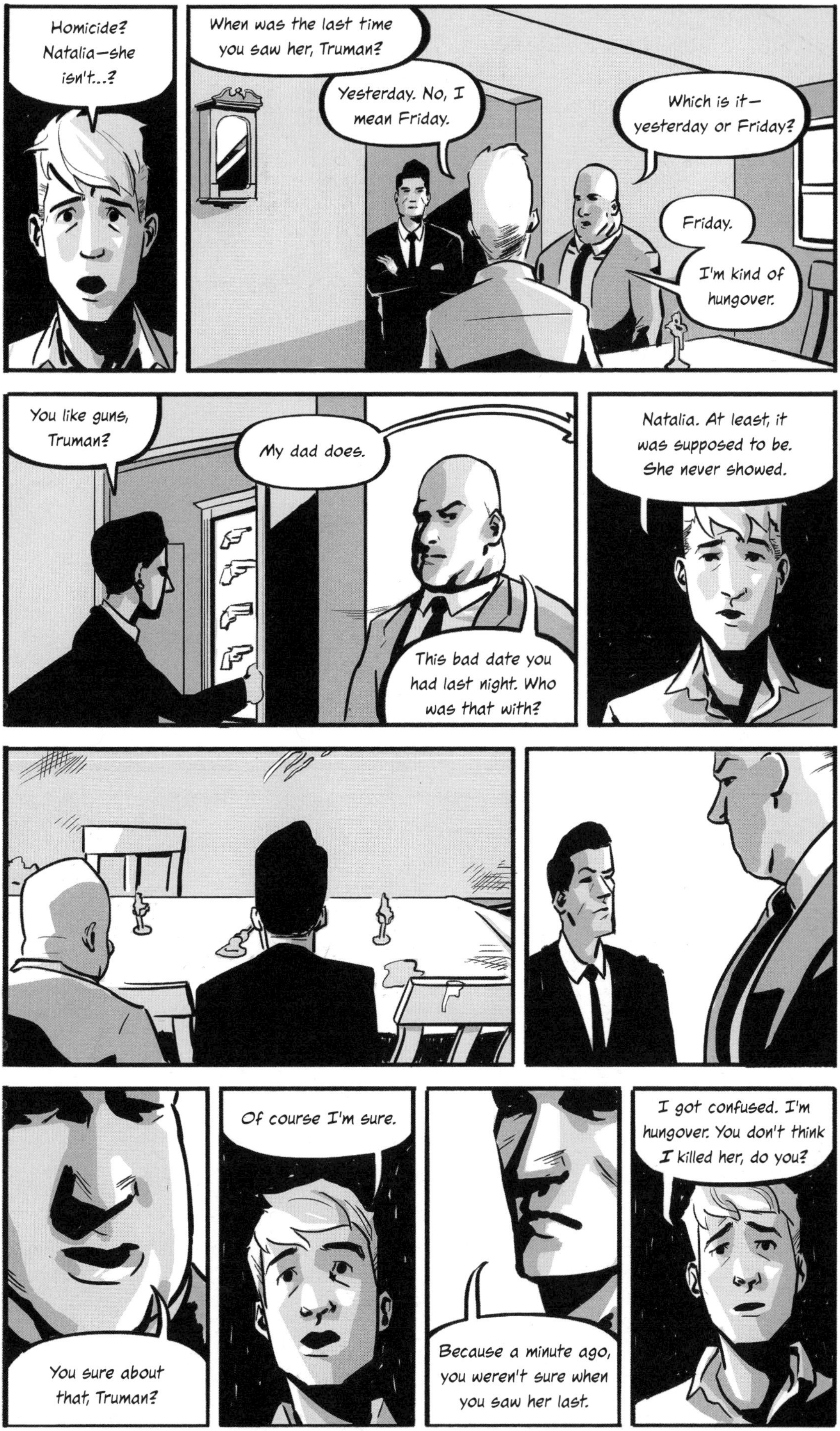
Homicide? Natalia—she isn't...?
When was the last time you saw her, Truman?
Yesterday. No, I mean Friday.
Which is it—yesterday or Friday?
Friday.
I'm kind of hungover.
You like guns, Truman?
My dad does.
This bad date you had last night. Who was that with?
Natalia. At least, it was supposed to be. She never showed.
You sure about that, Truman?
Of course I'm sure.
Because a minute ago, you weren't sure when you saw her last.
I got confused. I'm hungover. You don't think I killed her, do you?

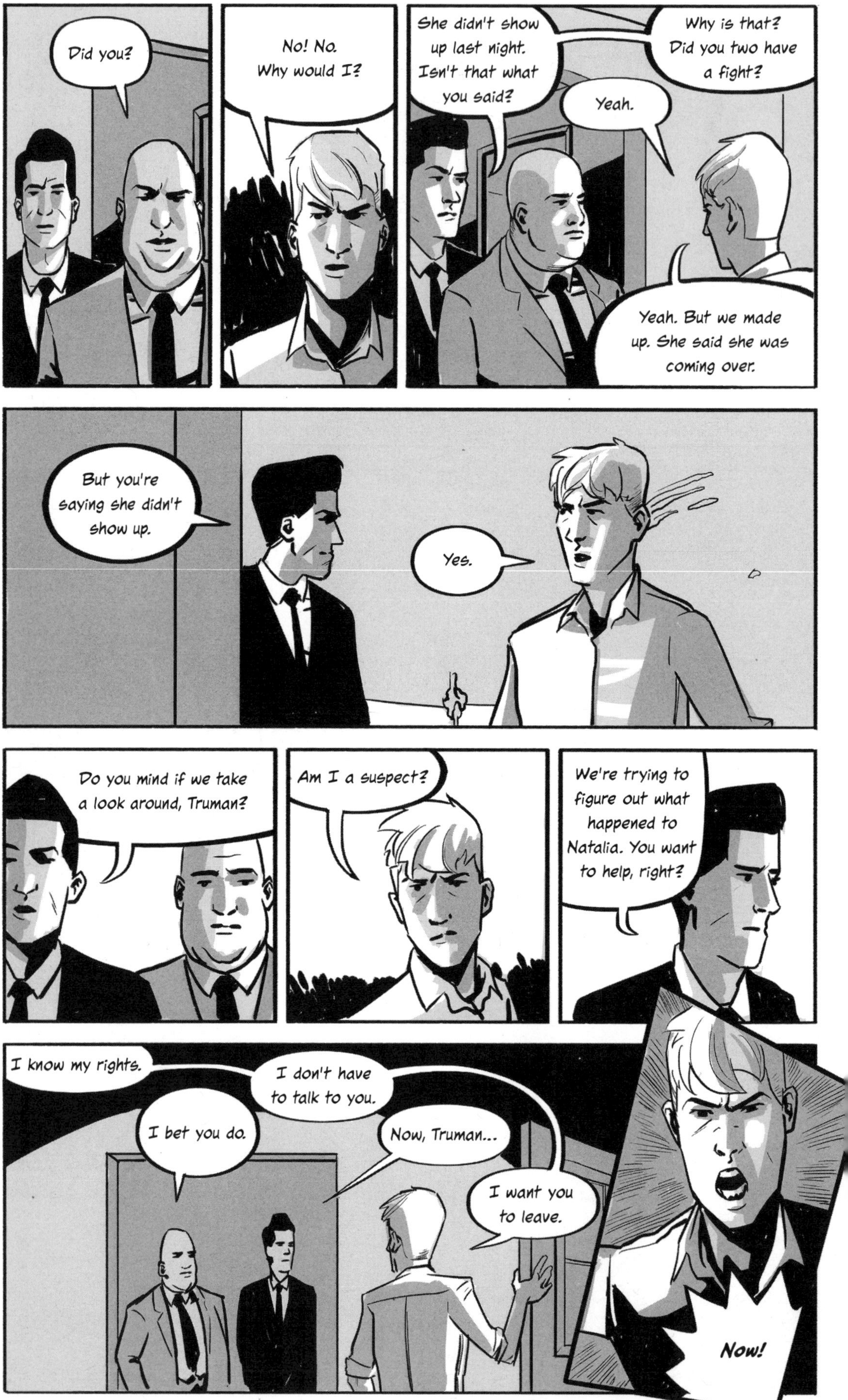
Did you?
No! No.
Why would I?
She didn't show up last night. Isn't that what you said?
Why is that? Did you two have a fight?
Yeah.
Yeah. But we made up. She said she was coming over.
But you're saying she didn't show up.
Yes.
Do you mind if we take a look around, Truman?
Am I a suspect?
We're trying to figure out what happened to Natalia. You want to help, right?
I know my rights.
I don't have to talk to you.
I bet you do.
Now, Truman...
I want you to leave.
Now!

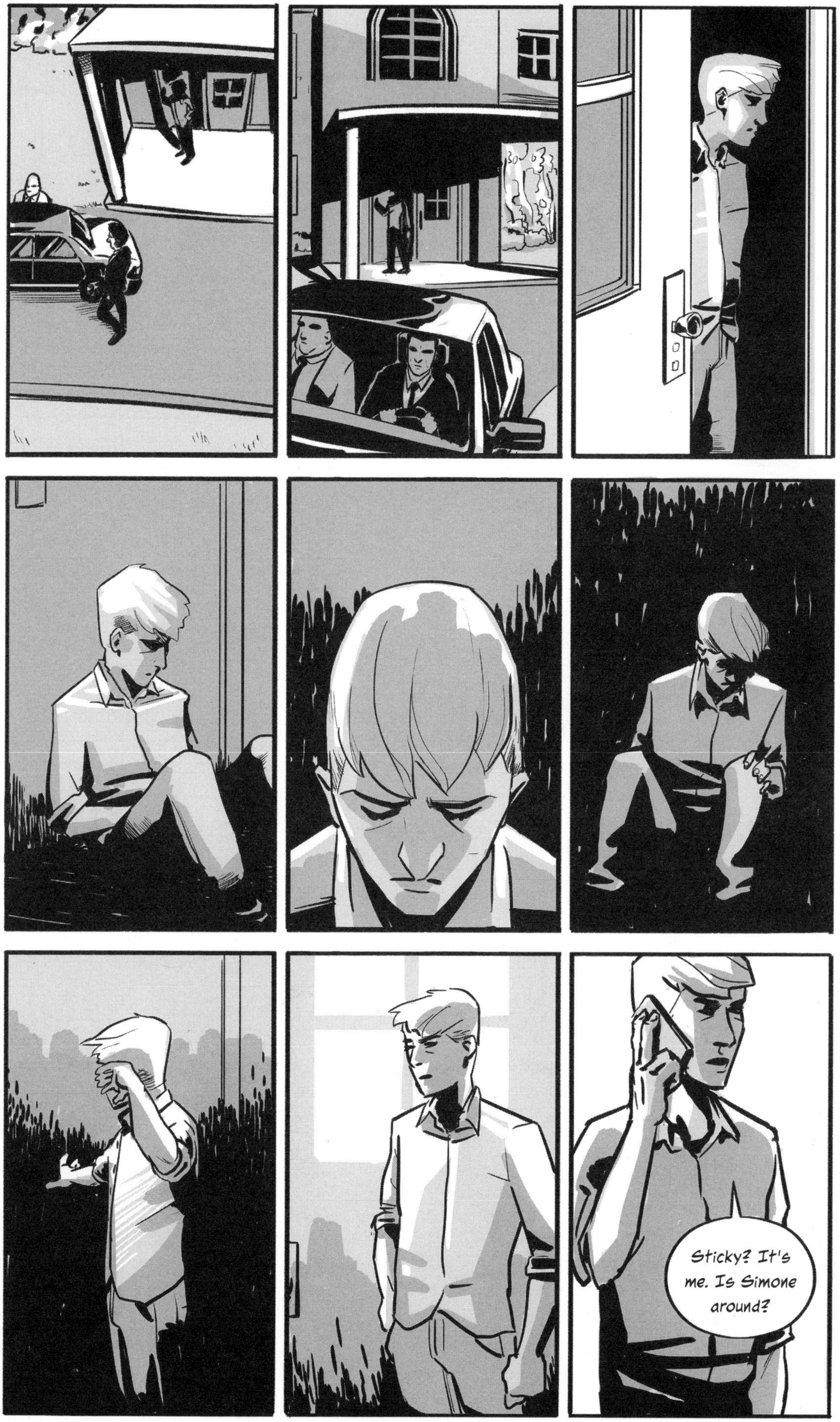
Sticky? It's me. Is Simone around?

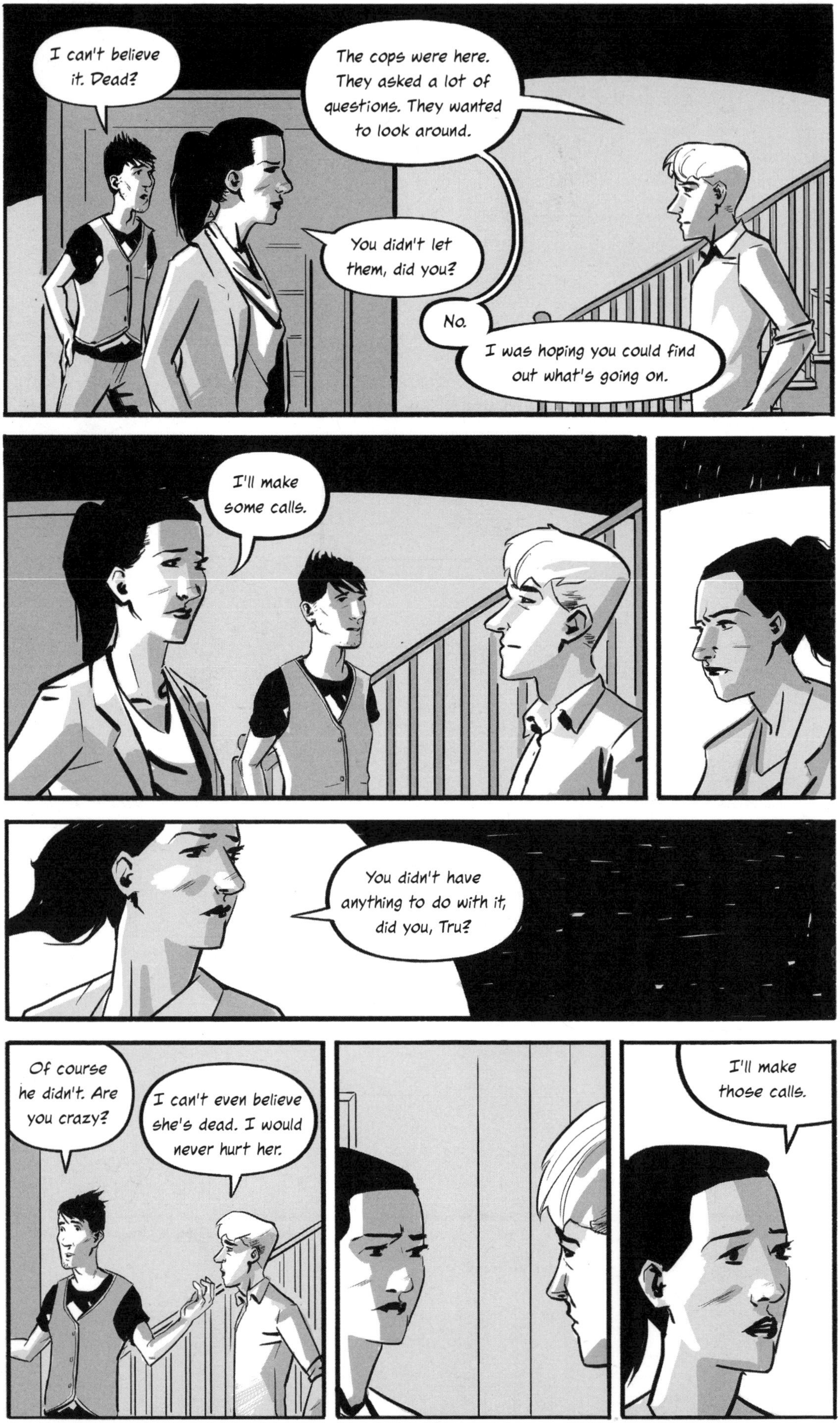
I can't believe it. Dead?
The cops were here. They asked a lot of questions. They wanted to look around.
You didn't let them, did you?
No.
I was hoping you could find out what's going on.
I'll make some calls.
You didn't have anything to do with it, did you, Tru?
Of course he didn't. Are you crazy?
I can't even believe she's dead. I would never hurt her.
I'll make those calls.

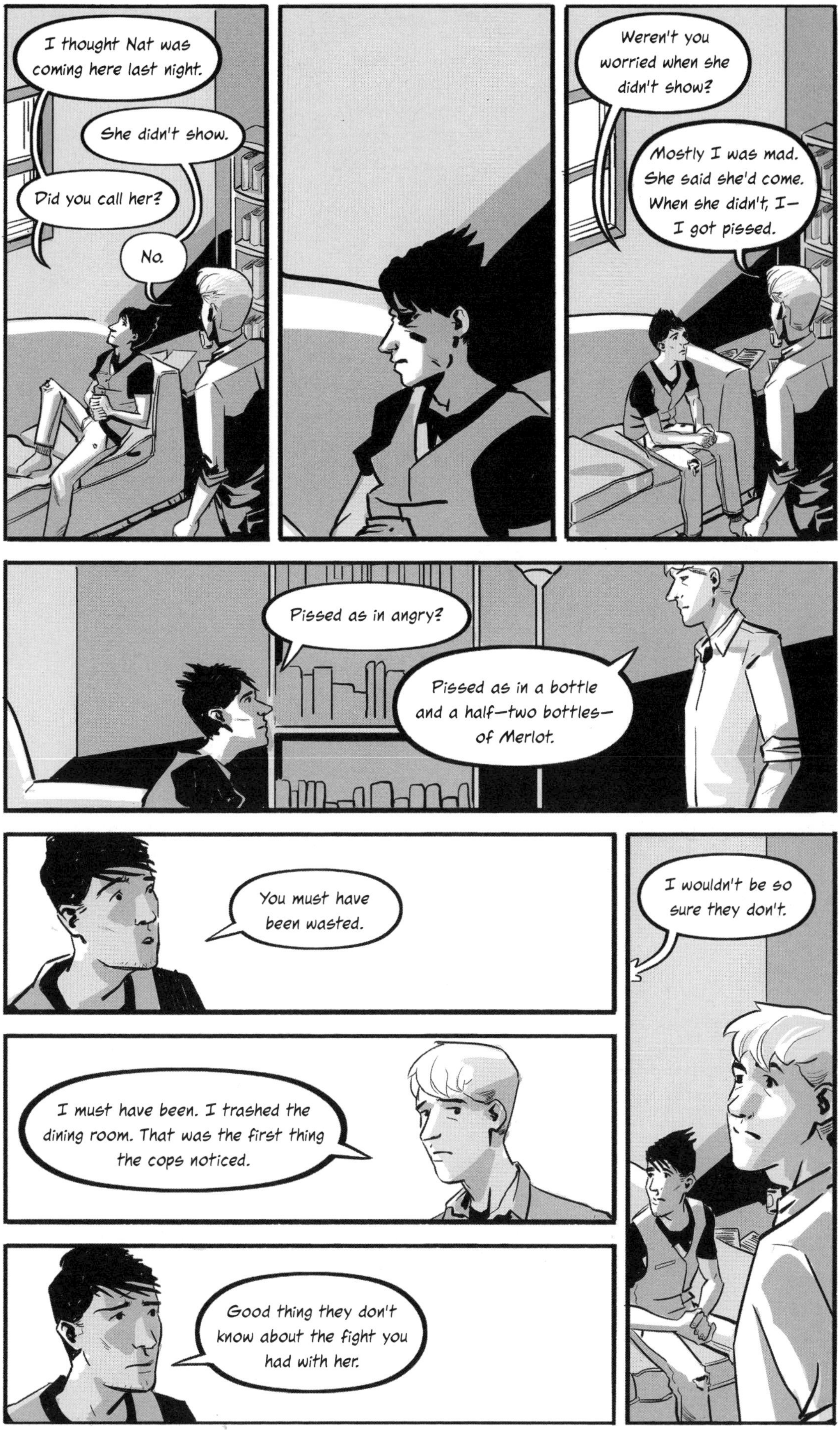
I thought Nat was coming here last night.
She didn't show.
Did you call her?
No.
Weren't you worried when she didn't show?
Mostly I was mad. She said she'd come. When she didn't, I—I got pissed.
Pissed as in angry?
Pissed as in a bottle and a half—two bottles—of Merlot.
You must have been wasted.
I must have been. I trashed the dining room. That was the first thing the cops noticed.
Good thing they don't know about the fight you had with her.
I wouldn't be so sure they don't.

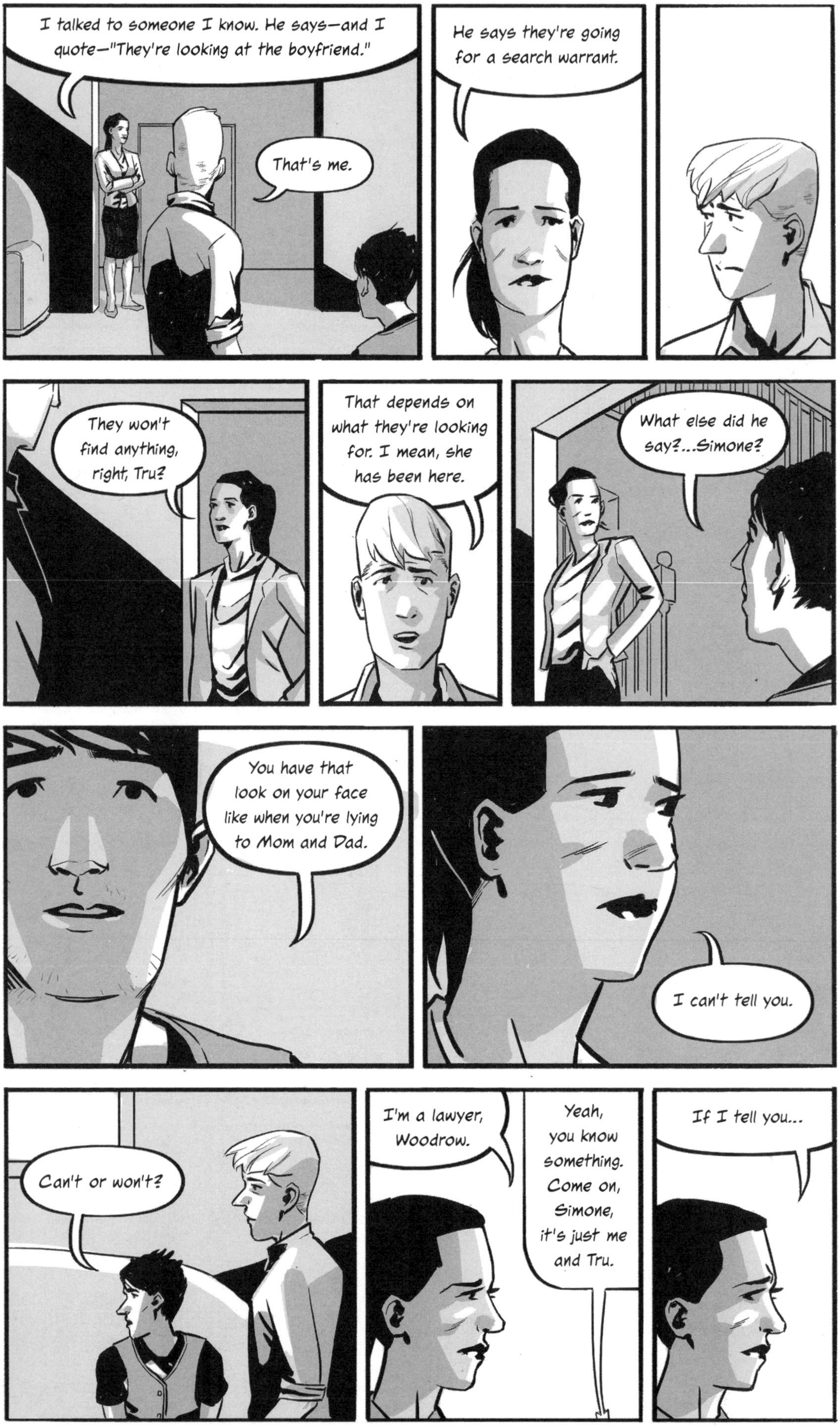
I talked to someone I know. He says—and I quote—"They're looking at the boyfriend."
That's me.
He says they're going for a search warrant.
They won't find anything, right, Tru?
That depends on what they're looking for. I mean, she has been here.
What else did he say?...Simone?
You have that look on your face like when you're lying to Mom and Dad.
I can't tell you.
Can't or won't?
I'm a lawyer, Woodrow.
Yeah, you know something. Come on, Simone, it's just me and Tru.
If I tell you...

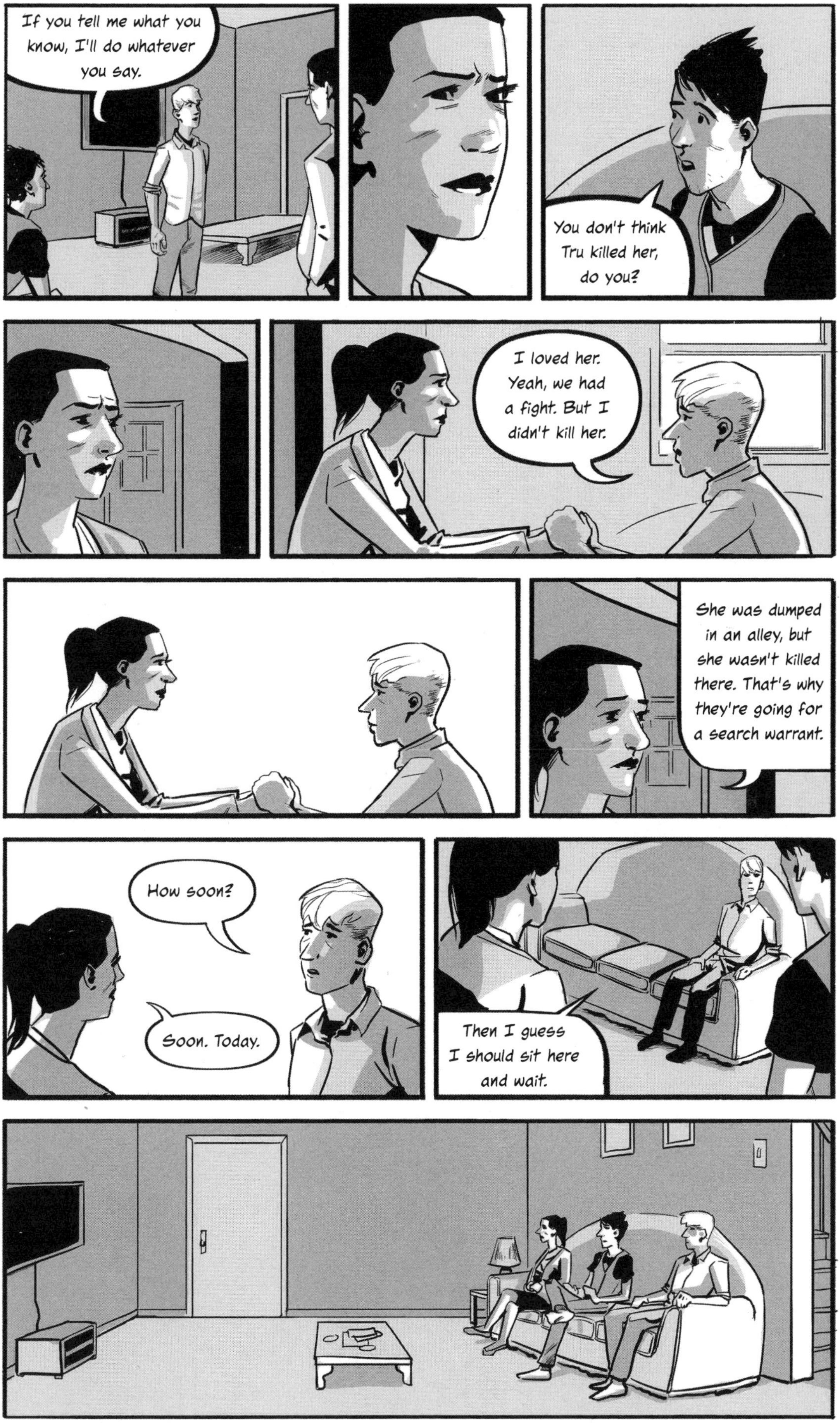
If you tell me what you know, I'll do whatever you say.
You don't think Tru killed her, do you?
I loved her. Yeah, we had a fight. But I didn't kill her.
She was dumped in an alley, but she wasn't killed there. That's why they're going for a search warrant.
How soon?
Soon. Today.
Then I guess I should sit here and wait.

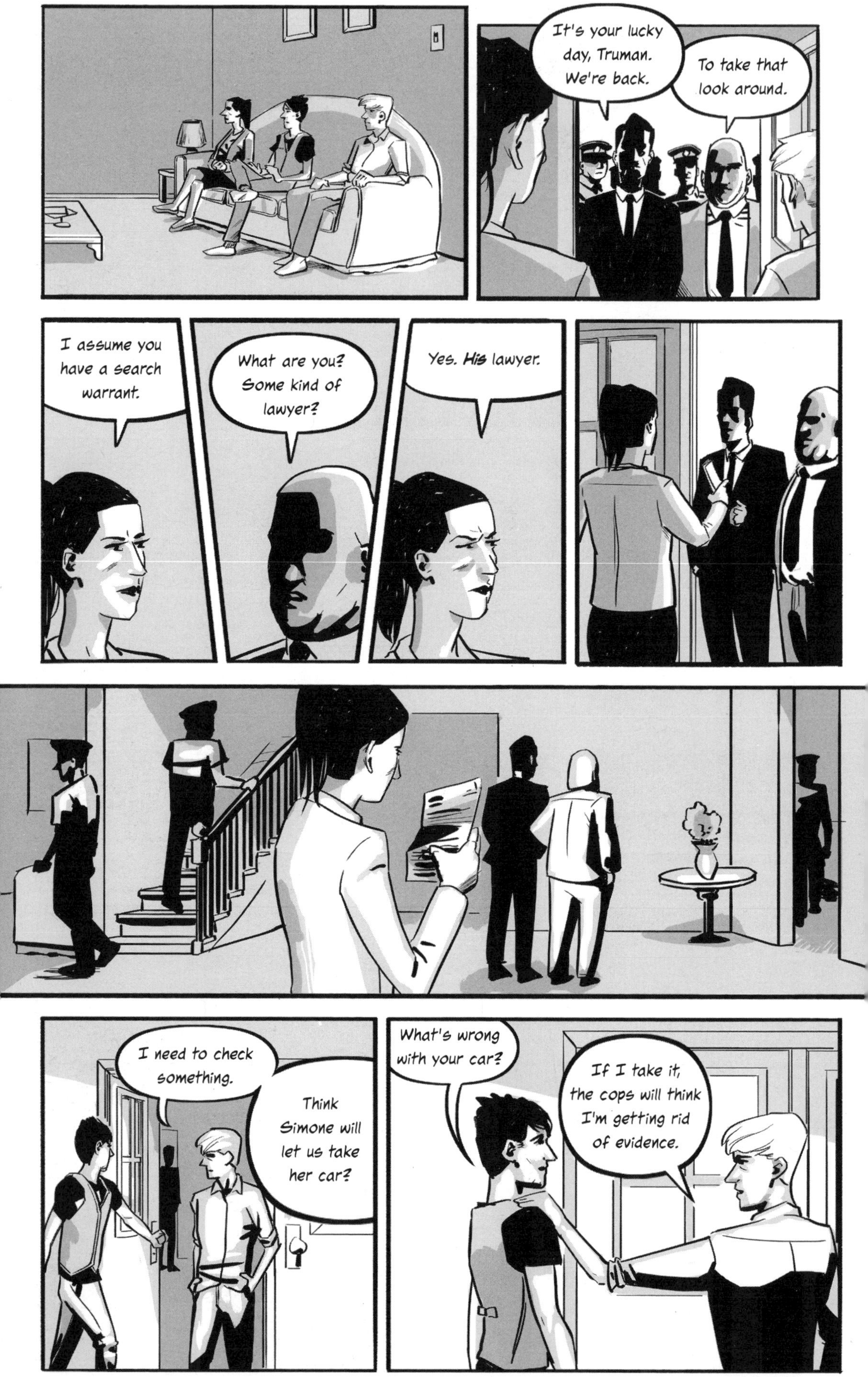
It's your lucky day, Truman. We're back.
To take that look around.
I assume you have a search warrant.
What are you? Some kind of lawyer?
Yes. His lawyer.
I need to check something.
Think Simone will let us take her car?
What's wrong with your car?
If I take it, the cops will think I'm getting rid of evidence.

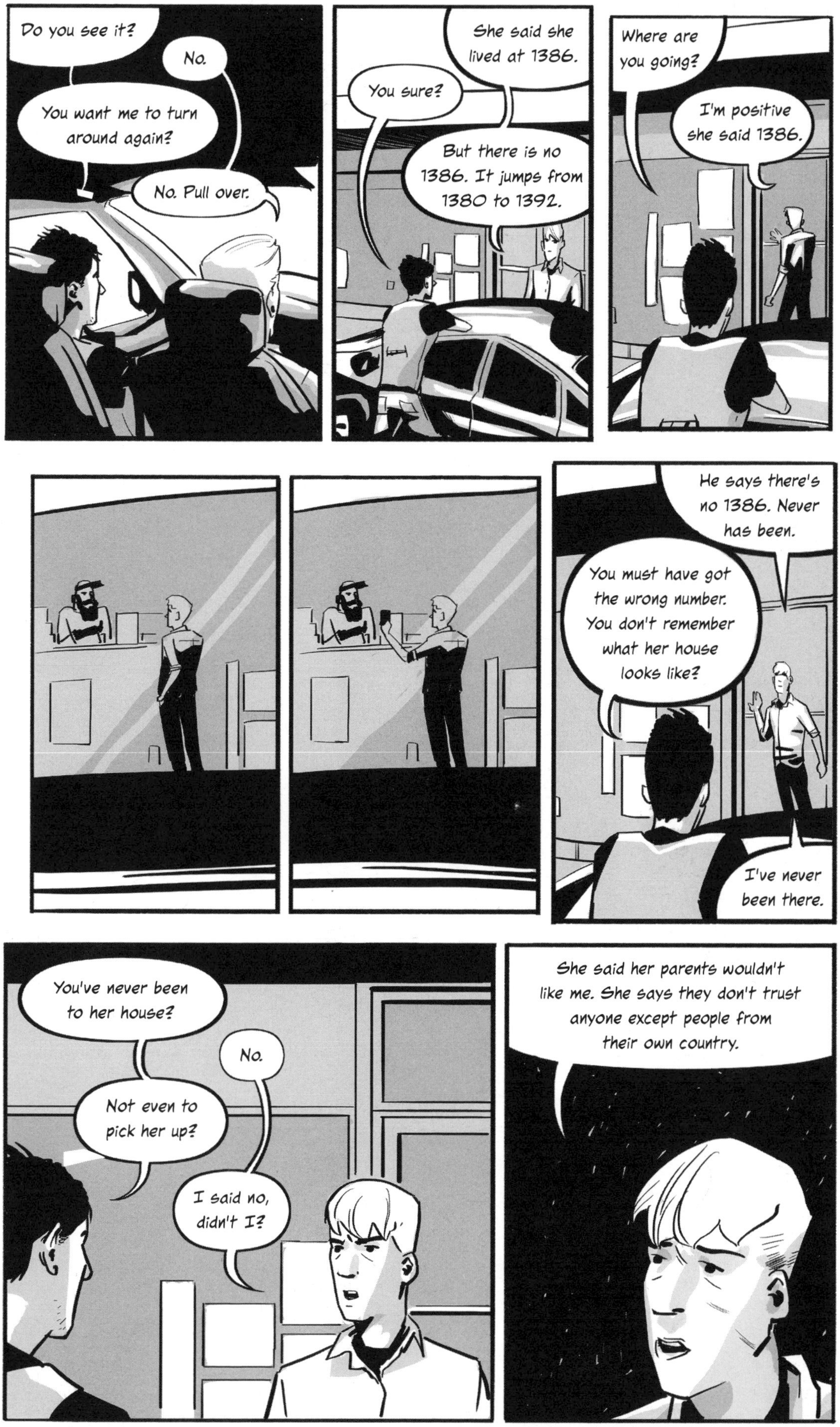
Do you see it?
No.
You want me to turn around again?
No. Pull over.
She said she lived at 1386.
You sure?
But there is no 1386. It jumps from 1380 to 1392.
Where are you going?
I'm positive she said 1386.
He says there's no 1386. Never has been.
You must have got the wrong number. You don't remember what her house looks like?
I've never been there.
You've never been to her house?
No.
Not even to pick her up?
I said no, didn't I?
She said her parents wouldn't like me. She says they don't trust anyone except people from their own country.

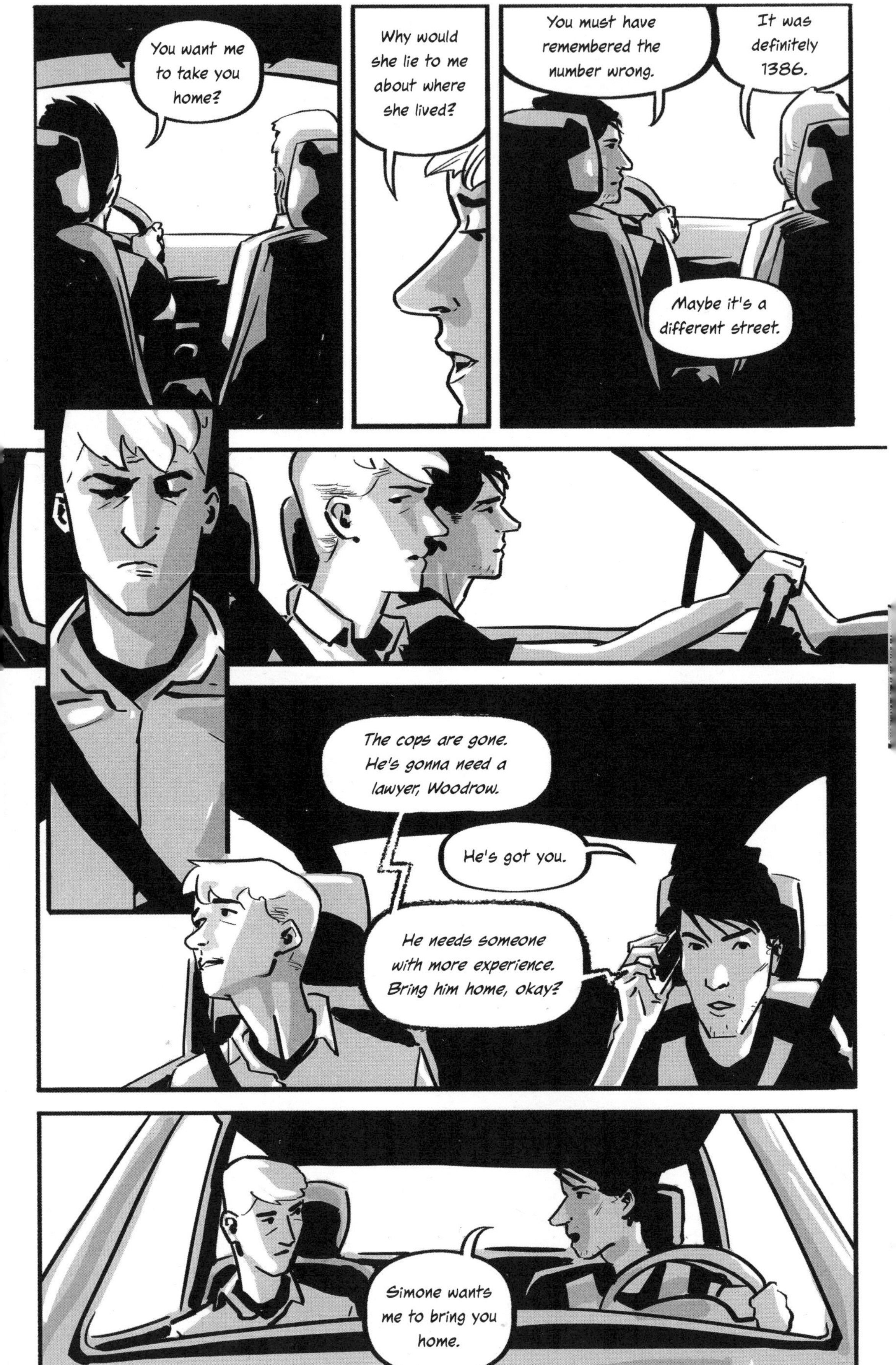

You want me to take you home?
Why would she lie to me about where she lived?
You must have remembered the number wrong.
It was definitely 1386.
Maybe it's a different street.
The cops are gone. He's gonna need a lawyer, Woodrow.
He's got you.
He needs someone with more experience. Bring him home, okay?
Simone wants me to bring you home.

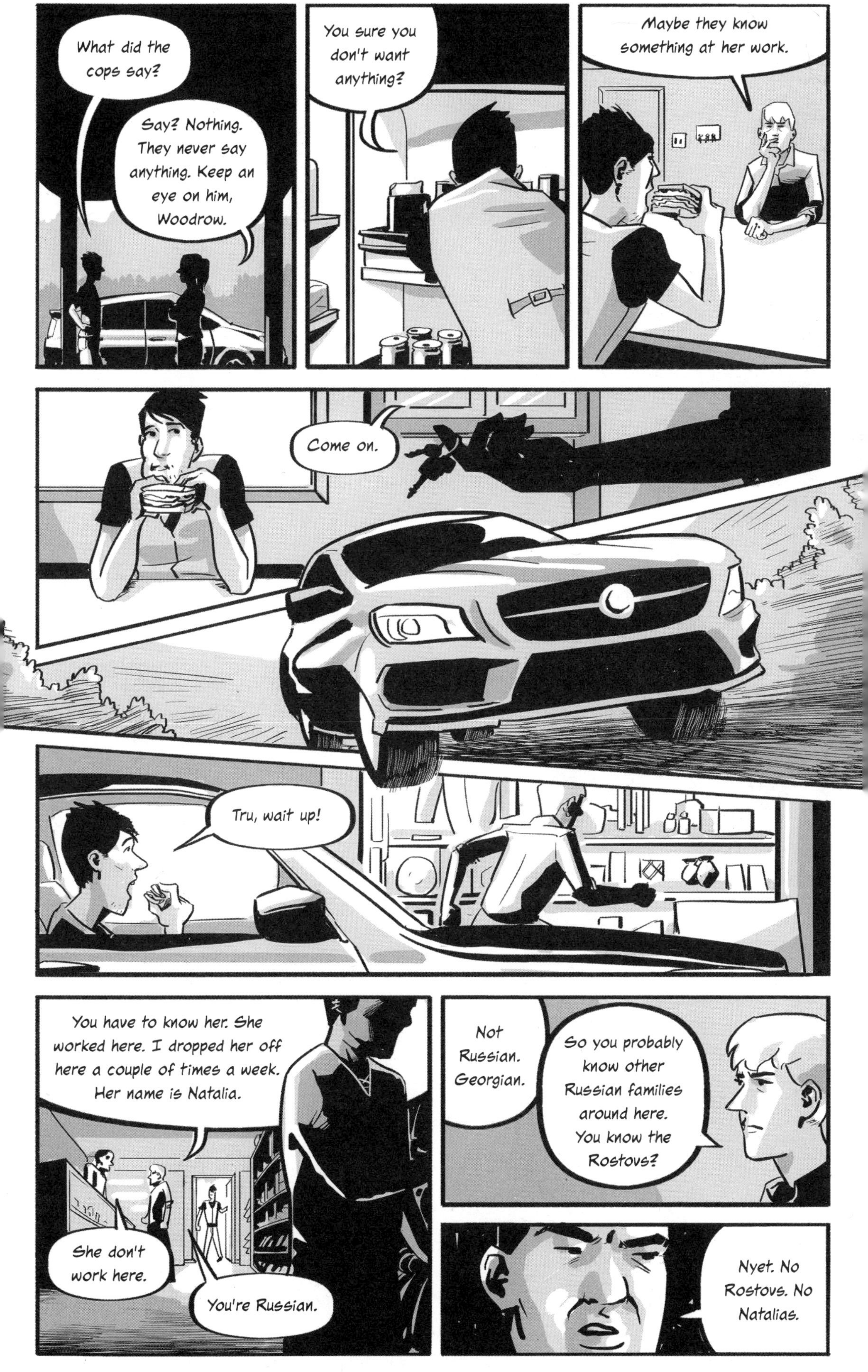

What did the cops say?
Say? Nothing. They never say anything. Keep an eye on him, Woodrow.
You sure you don't want anything?
Maybe they know something at her work.
Come on.
Tru, wait up!
You have to know her. She worked here. I dropped her off here a couple of times a week. Her name is Natalia.
She don't work here.
You're Russian.
Not Russian. Georgian.
So you probably know other Russian families around here. You know the Rostovs?
Nyet. No Rostovs. No Natalias.

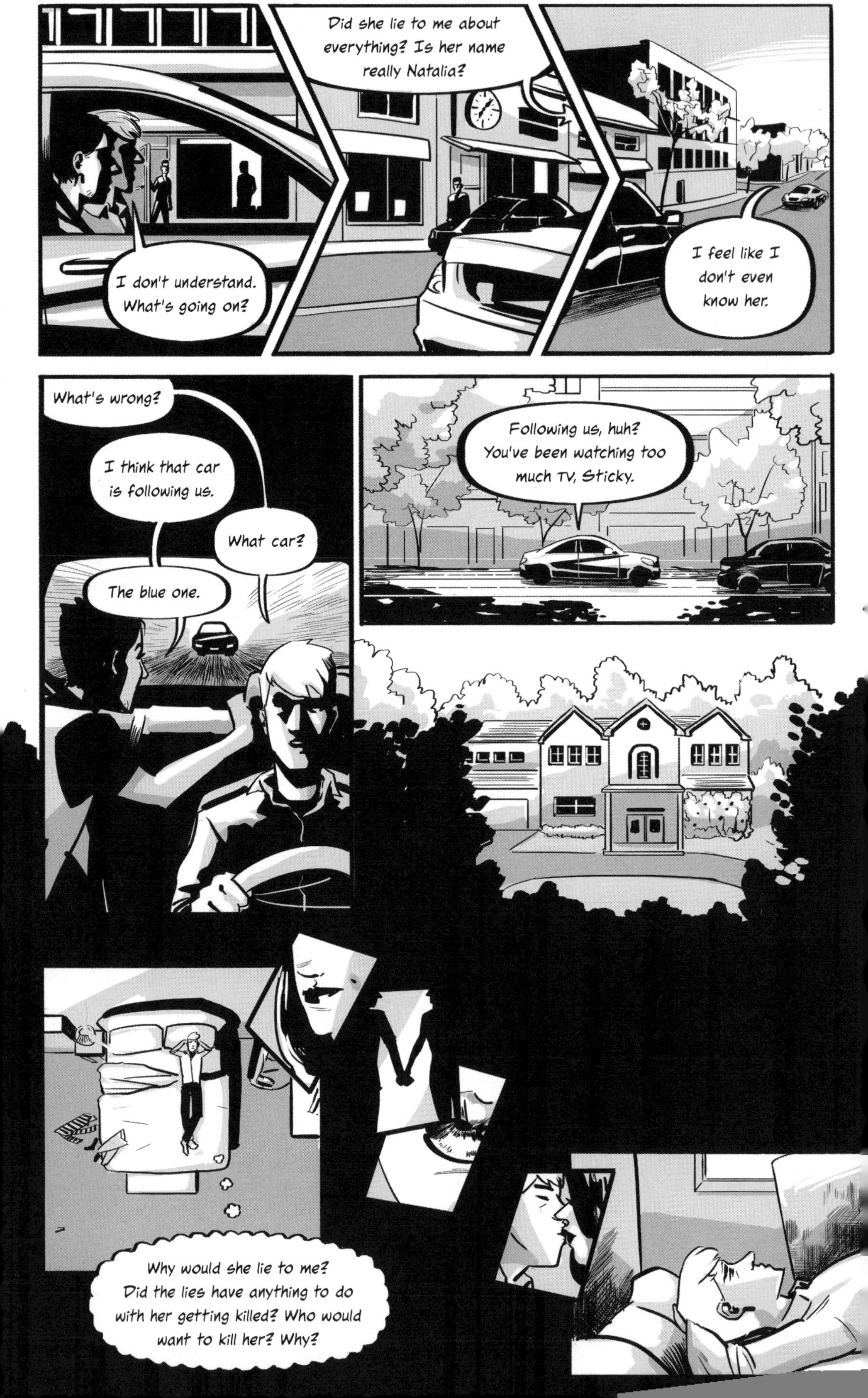
I don't understand. What's going on?
Did she lie to me about everything? Is her name really Natalia?
I feel like I don't even know her.
What's wrong?
I think that car is following us.
What car?
The blue one.
Following us, huh? You've been watching too much TV, Sticky.
Why would she lie to me? Did the lies have anything to do with her getting killed? Who would want to kill her? Why?

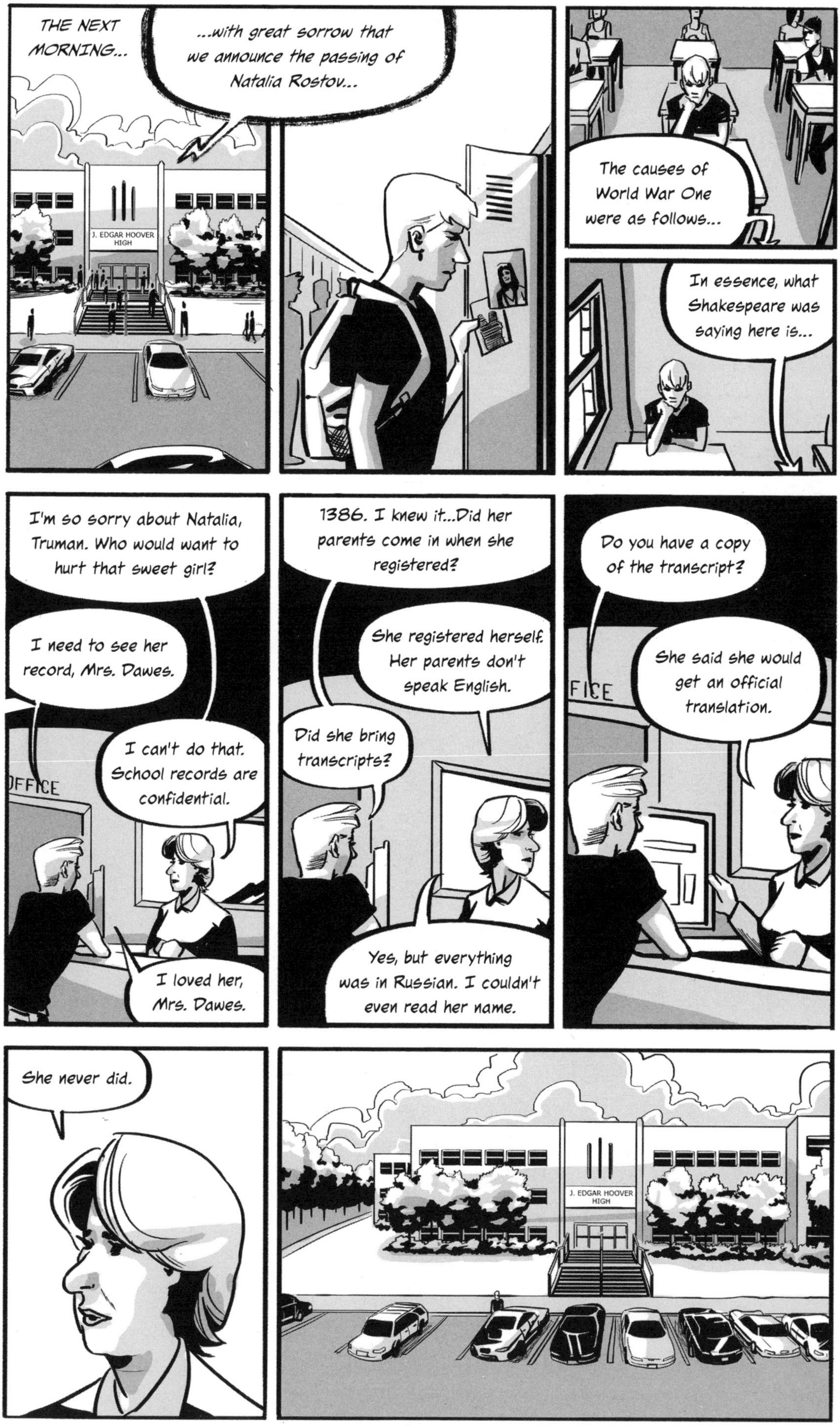
THE NEXT MORNING...
...with great sorrow that we announce the passing of Natalia Rostov...
J. EDGAR HOOVER HIGH
The causes of World War One were as follows...
In essence, what Shakespeare was saying here is...
I'm so sorry about Natalia, Truman. Who would want to hurt that sweet girl?
I need to see her record, Mrs. Dawes.
OFFICE
I can't do that. School records are confidential.
I loved her, Mrs. Dawes.
1386. I knew it...Did her parents come in when she registered?
She registered herself. Her parents don't speak English.
Did she bring transcripts?
Yes, but everything was in Russian. I couldn't even read her name.
Do you have a copy of the transcript?
FICE
She said she would get an official translation.
She never did.
J. EDGAR HOOVER HIGH

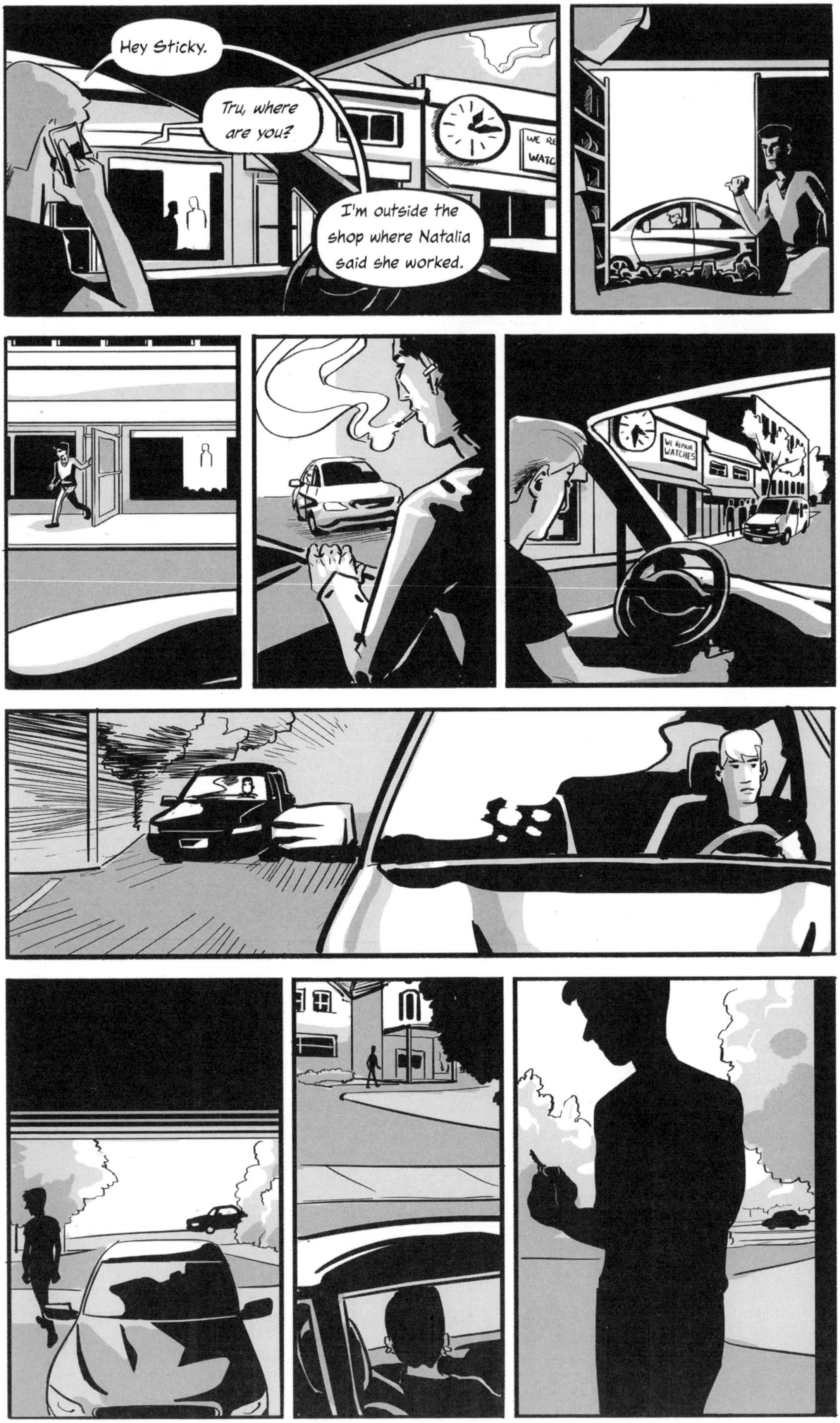

Hey Sticky.
Tru, where are you?
I'm outside the shop where Natalia said she worked.
WE REPAIR WATCHES

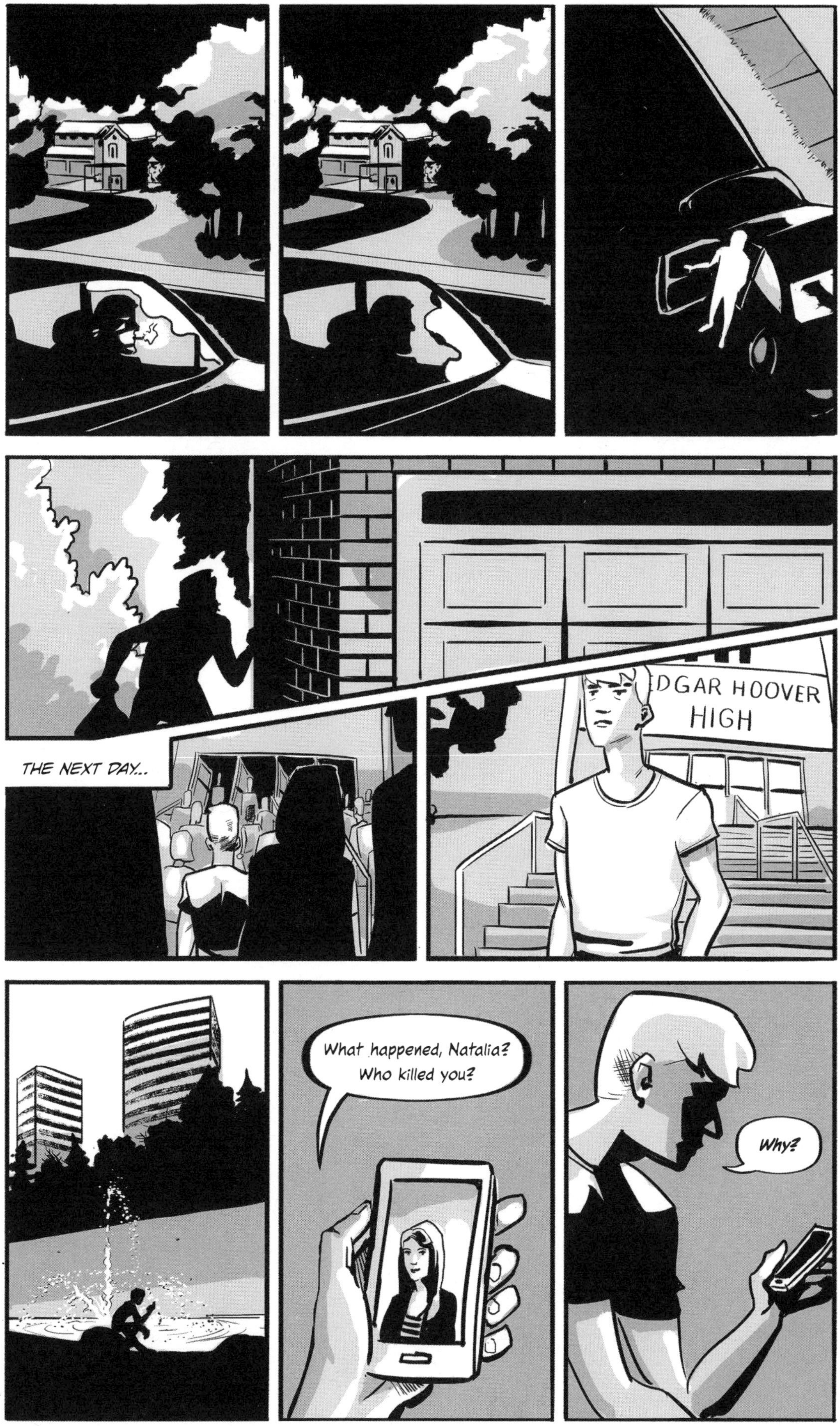
THE NEXT DAY...
DGAR HOOVER
HIGH
What happened, Natalia? Who killed you?
Why?

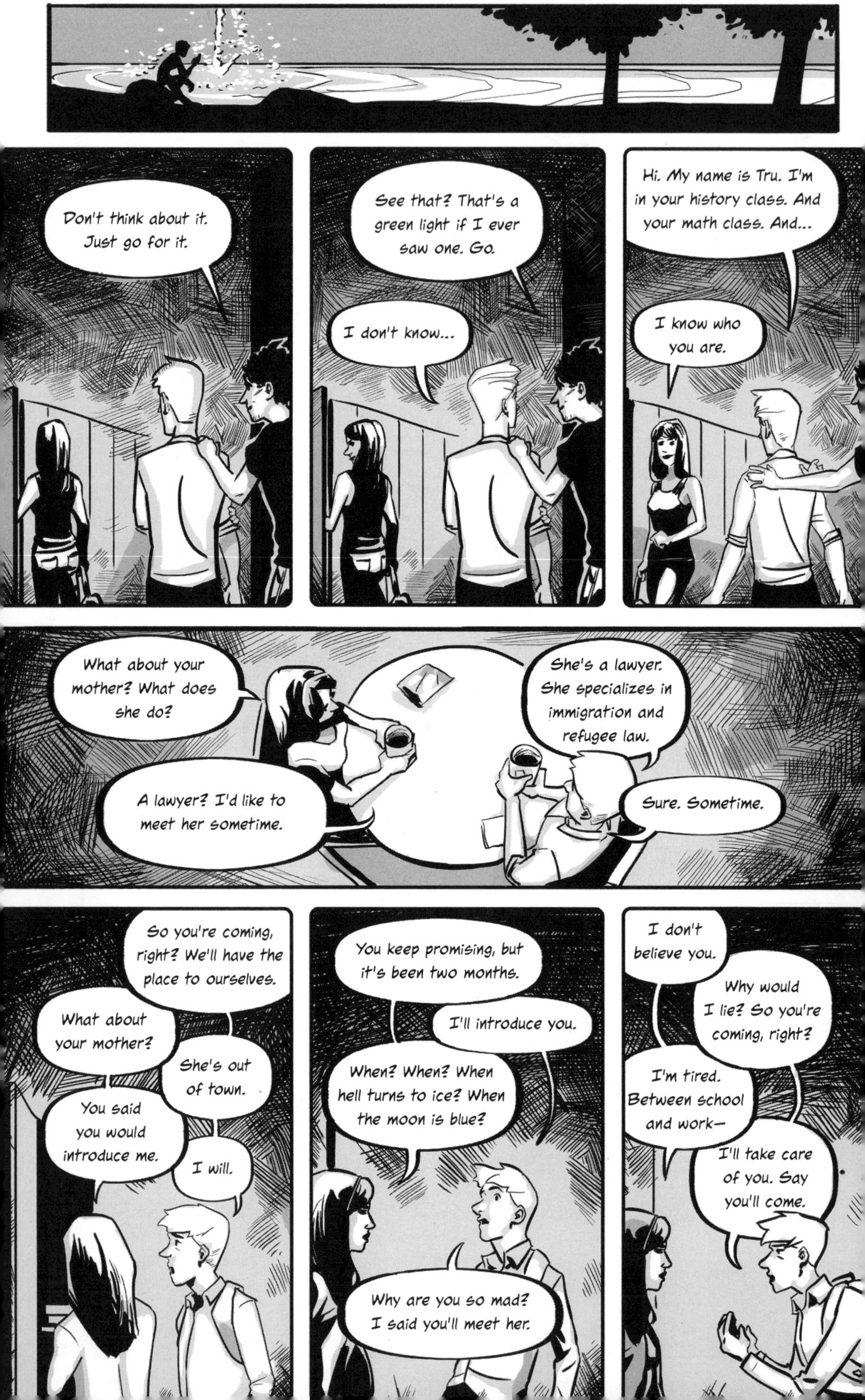
Don't think about it. Just go for it.
See that? That's a green light if I ever saw one. Go.
I don't know...
Hi. My name is Tru. I'm in your history class. And your math class. And...
I know who you are.
What about your mother? What does she do?
She's a lawyer. She specializes in immigration and refugee law.
A lawyer? I'd like to meet her sometime.
Sure. Sometime.
So you're coming, right? We'll have the place to ourselves.
What about your mother?
She's out of town.
You said you would introduce me.
I will.
You keep promising, but it's been two months.
I'll introduce you.
When? When? When hell turns to ice? When the moon is blue?
Why are you so mad? I said you'll meet her.
I don't believe you.
Why would I lie? So you're coming, right?
I'm tired. Between school and work—
I'll take care of you. Say you'll come.

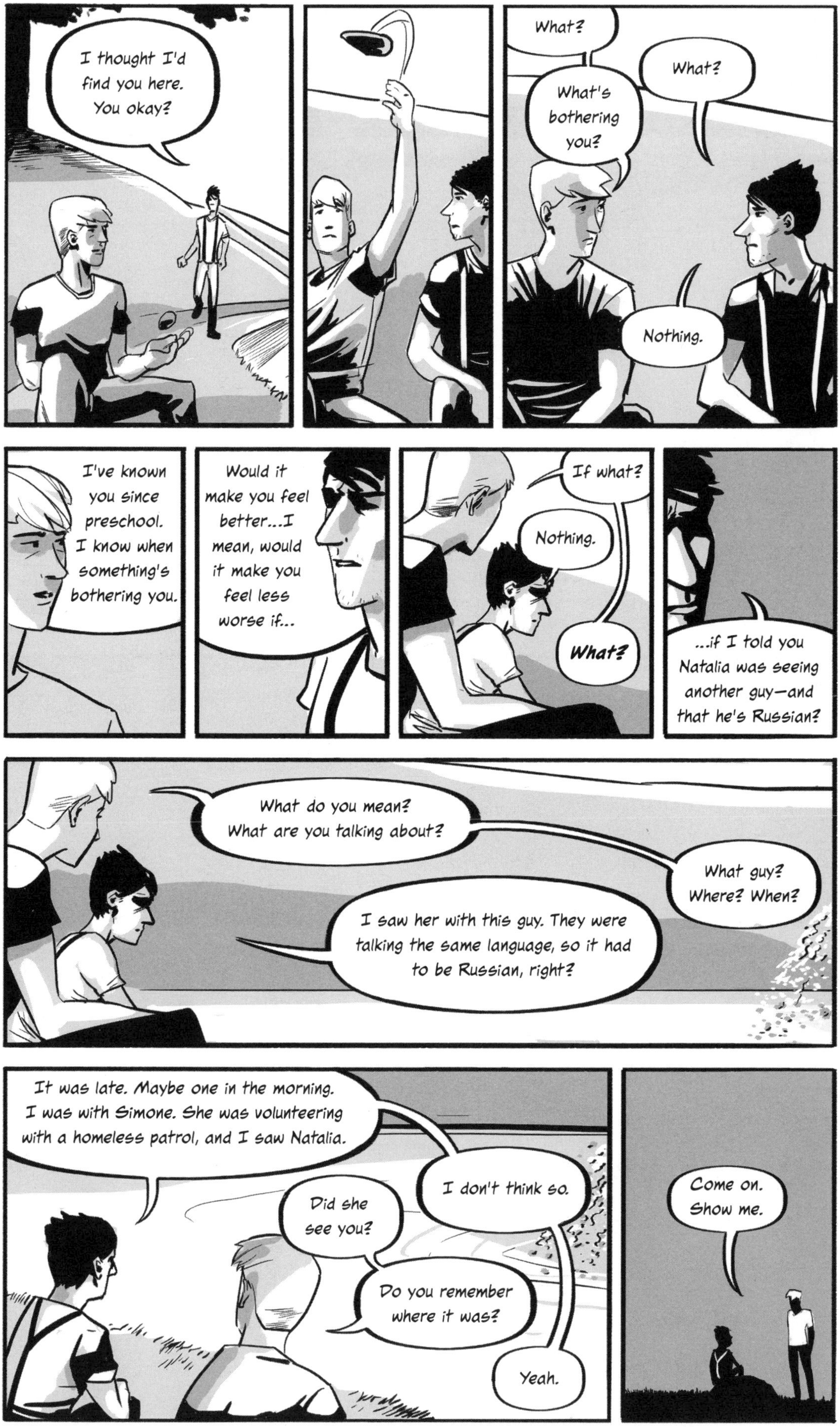

I thought I'd find you here. You okay?
What?
What's bothering you?
What?
Nothing.
I've known you since preschool. I know when something's bothering you.
Would it make you feel better...I mean, would it make you feel less worse if...
If what?
Nothing.
What?
...if I told you Natalia was seeing another guy—and that he's Russian?
What do you mean? What are you talking about?
What guy? Where? When?
I saw her with this guy. They were talking the same language, so it had to be Russian, right?
It was late. Maybe one in the morning. I was with Simone. She was volunteering with a homeless patrol, and I saw Natalia.
Did she see you?
I don't think so.
Do you remember where it was?
Yeah.
Come on. Show me.

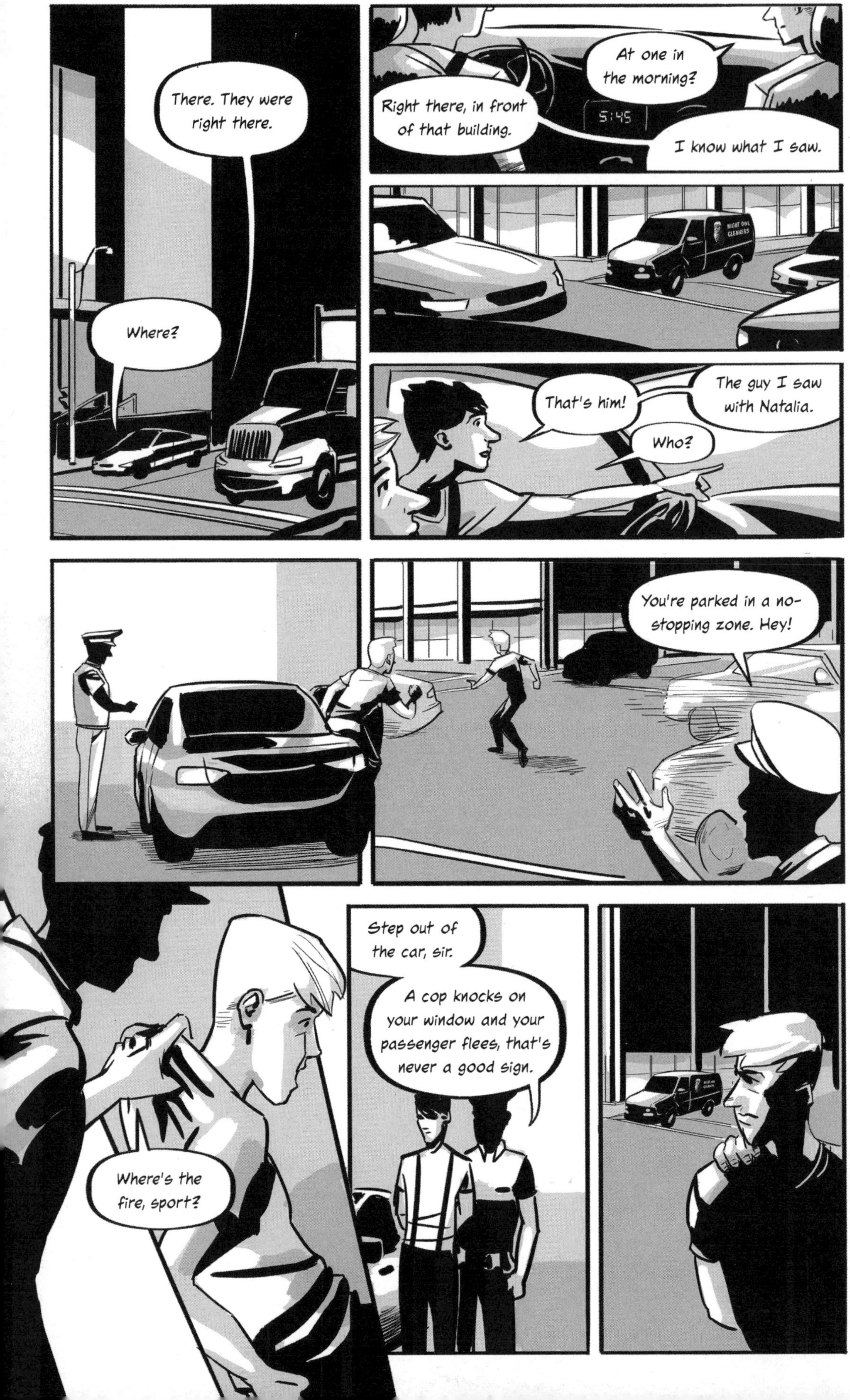
There. They were right there.
Where?
Right there, in front of that building.
At one in the morning?
5:45
I know what I saw.
NIGHT OWL CLEANERS
That's him!
The guy I saw with Natalia.
Who?
You're parked in a no-stopping zone. Hey!
Where's the fire, sport?
Step out of the car, sir.
A cop knocks on your window and your passenger flees, that's never a good sign.

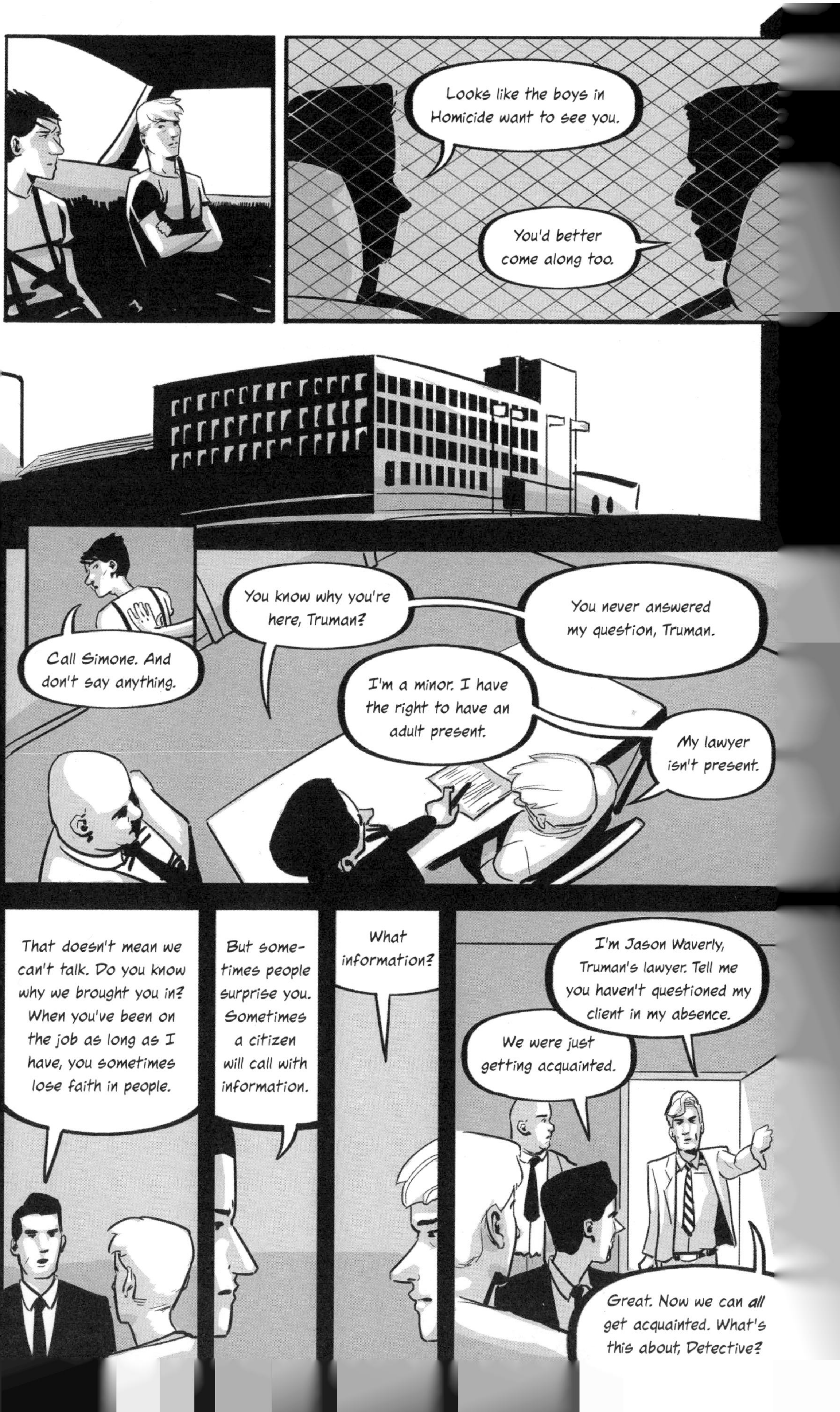

Looks like the boys in Homicide want to see you.
You'd better come along too.
Call Simone. And don't say anything.
You know why you're here, Truman?
You never answered my question, Truman.
I'm a minor. I have the right to have an adult present.
My lawyer isn't present.
That doesn't mean we can't talk. Do you know why we brought you in? When you've been on the job as long as I have, you sometimes lose faith in people.
But sometimes people surprise you. Sometimes a citizen will call with information.
What information?
I'm Jason Waverly, Truman's lawyer. Tell me you haven't questioned my client in my absence.
We were just getting acquainted.
Great. Now we can *all* get acquainted. What's this about, Detective?

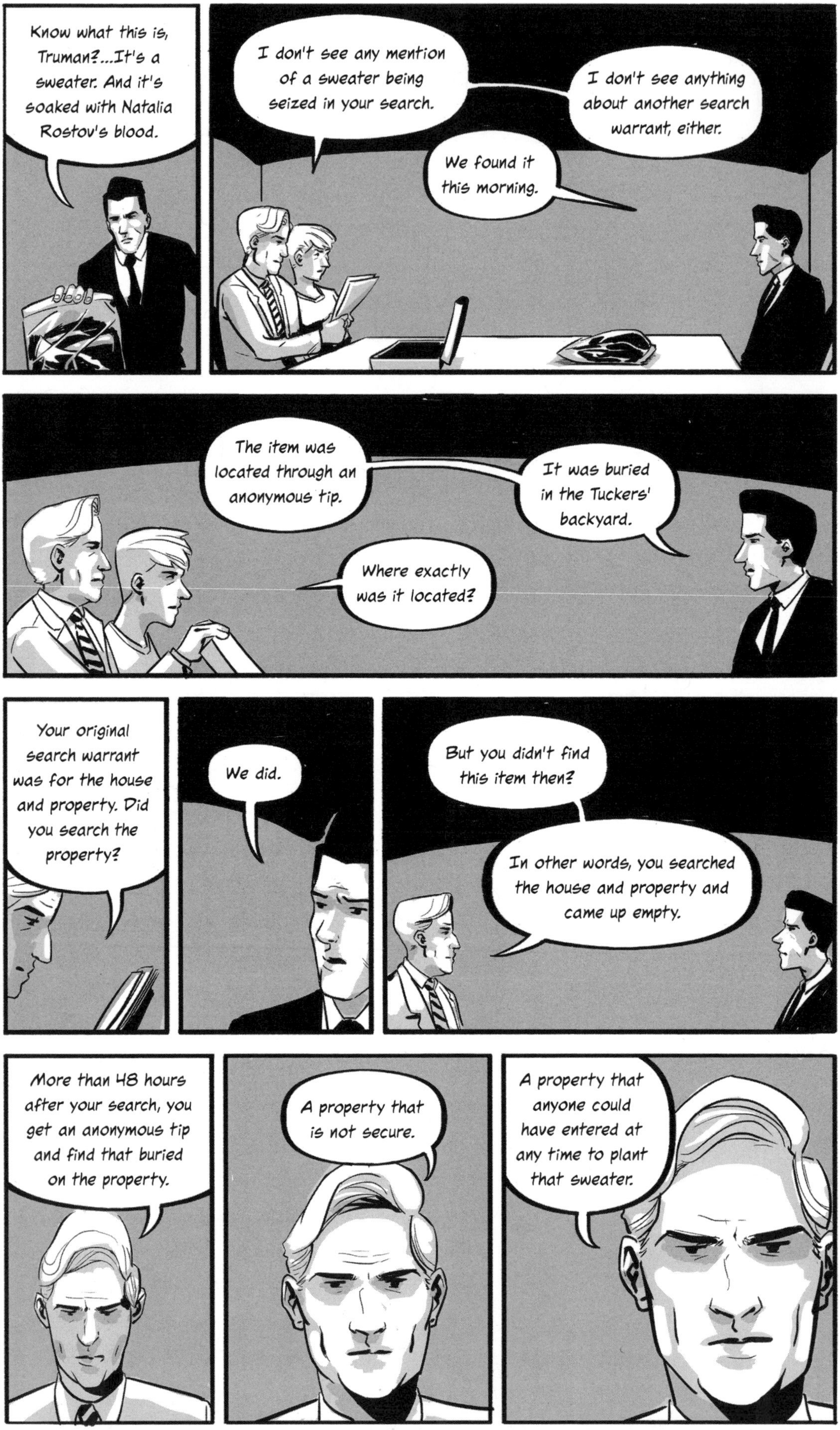
Know what this is, Truman?...It's a sweater. And it's soaked with Natalia Rostov's blood.
I don't see any mention of a sweater being seized in your search.
We found it this morning.
I don't see anything about another search warrant, either.
The item was located through an anonymous tip.
It was buried in the Tuckers' backyard.
Where exactly was it located?
Your original search warrant was for the house and property. Did you search the property?
We did.
But you didn't find this item then?
In other words, you searched the house and property and came up empty.
More than 48 hours after your search, you get an anonymous tip and find that buried on the property.
A property that is not secure.
A property that anyone could have entered at any time to plant that sweater.

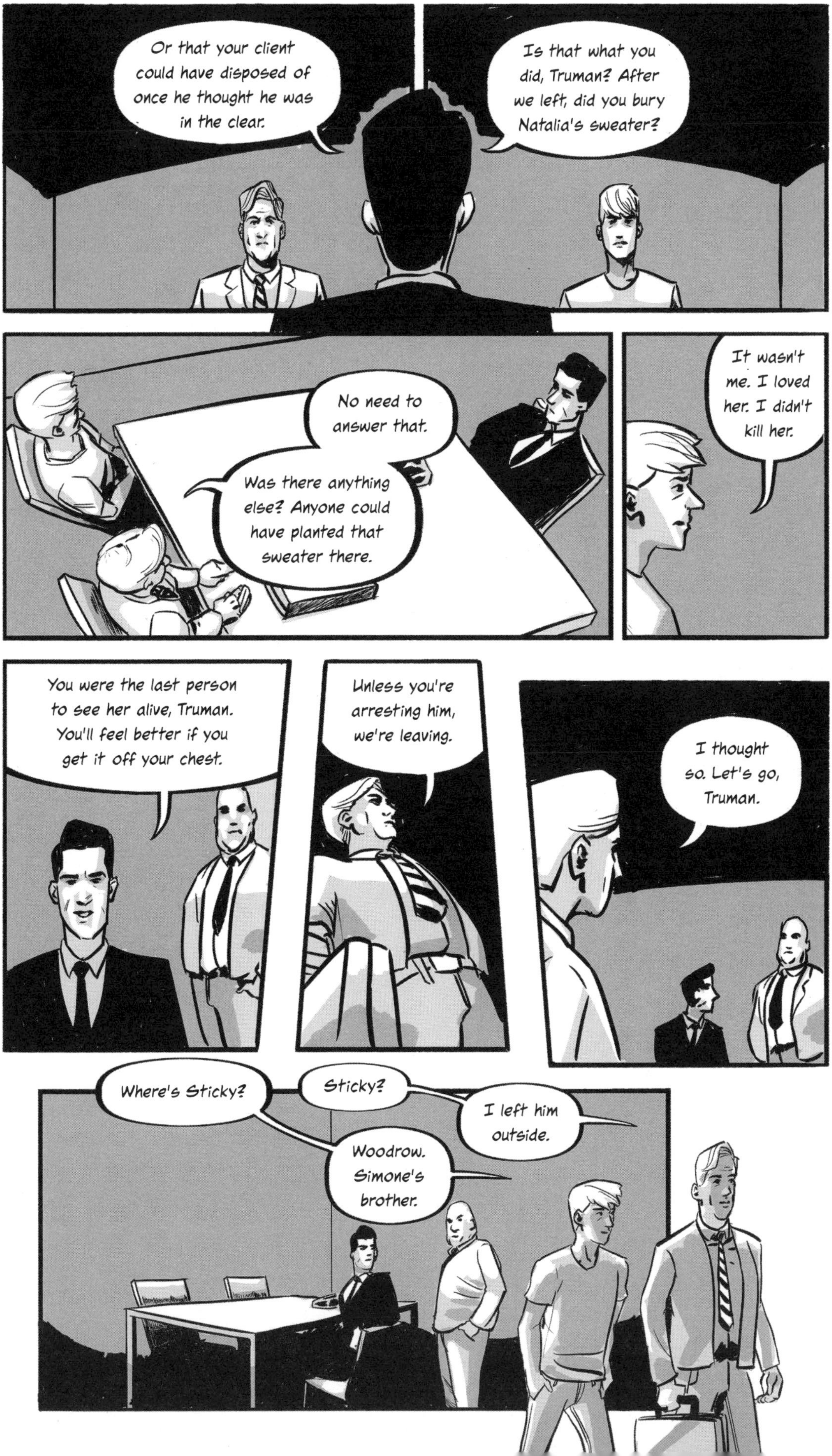

Or that your client could have disposed of once he thought he was in the clear.
Is that what you did, Truman? After we left, did you bury Natalia's sweater?
No need to answer that.
Was there anything else? Anyone could have planted that sweater there.
It wasn't me. I loved her. I didn't kill her.
You were the last person to see her alive, Truman. You'll feel better if you get it off your chest.
Unless you're arresting him, we're leaving.
I thought so. Let's go, Truman.
Where's Sticky?
Sticky?
Woodrow. Simone's brother.
I left him outside.

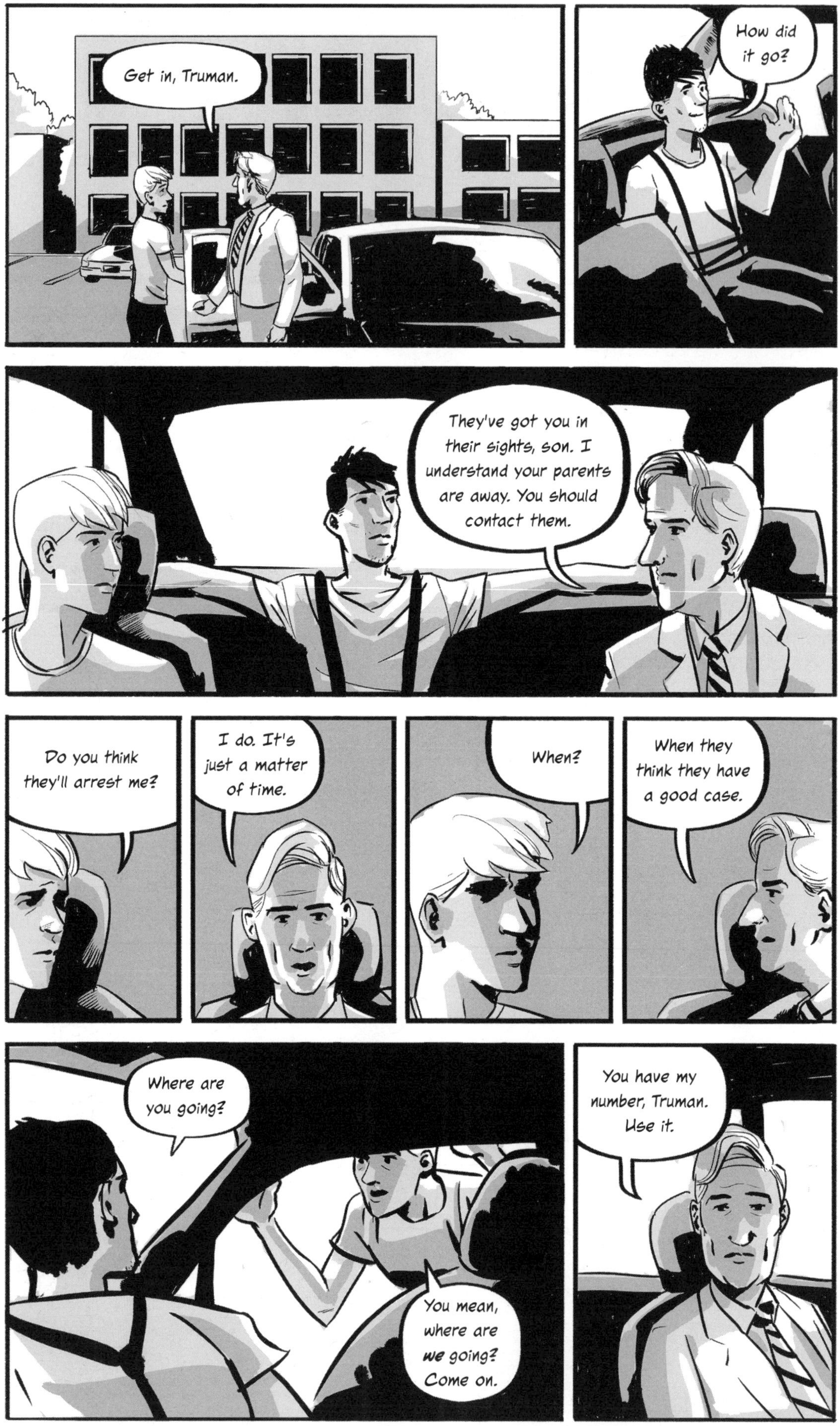
Get in, Truman.
How did it go?
They've got you in their sights, son. I understand your parents are away. You should contact them.
Do you think they'll arrest me?
I do. It's just a matter of time.
When?
When they think they have a good case.
Where are you going?
You mean, where are *we* going? Come on.
You have my number, Truman. Use it.

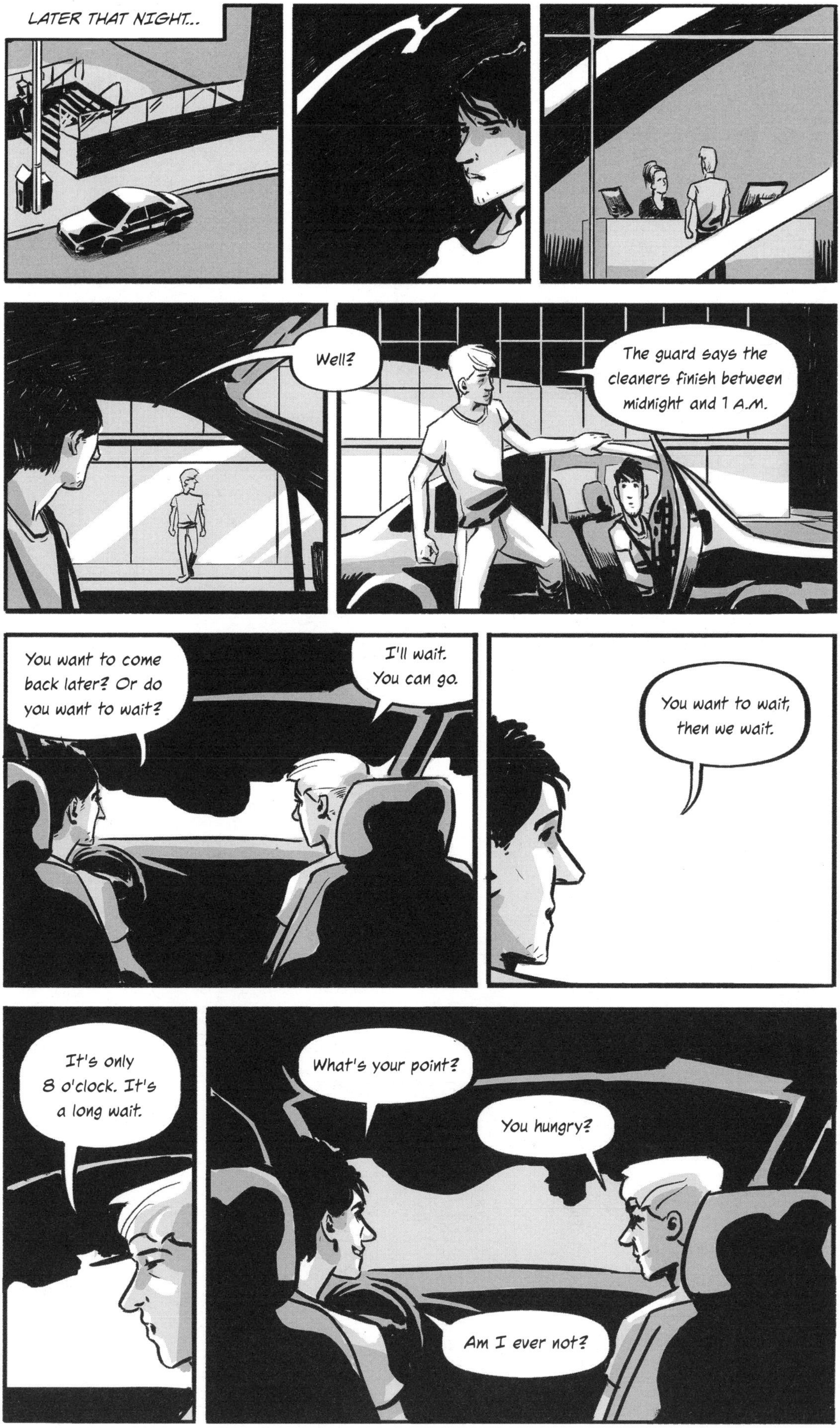
LATER THAT NIGHT...
Well?
The guard says the cleaners finish between midnight and 1 A.M.
You want to come back later? Or do you want to wait?
I'll wait. You can go.
You want to wait, then we wait.
It's only 8 o'clock. It's a long wait.
What's your point?
You hungry?
Am I ever not?

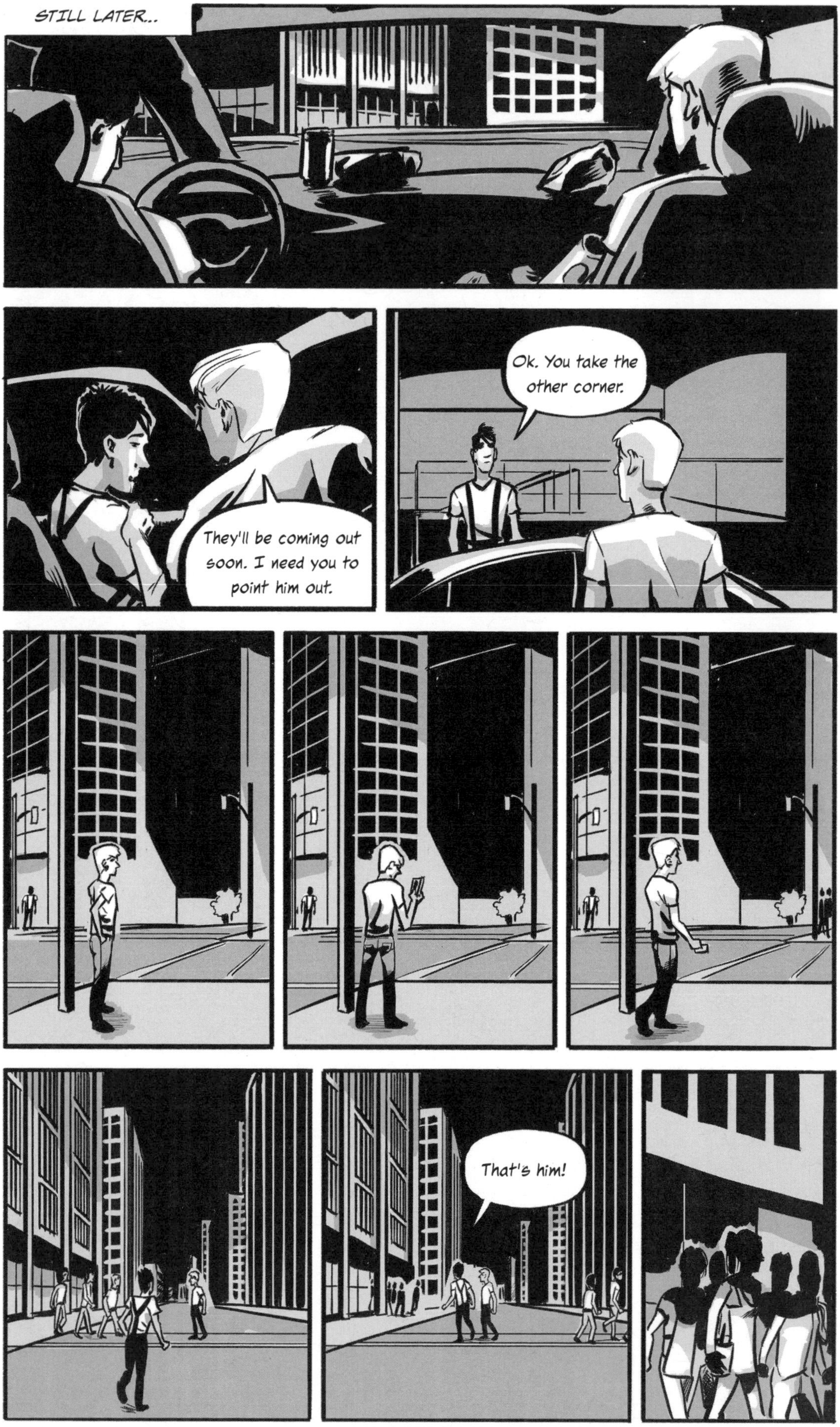
STILL LATER...
They'll be coming out soon. I need you to point him out.
Ok. You take the other corner.
That's him!

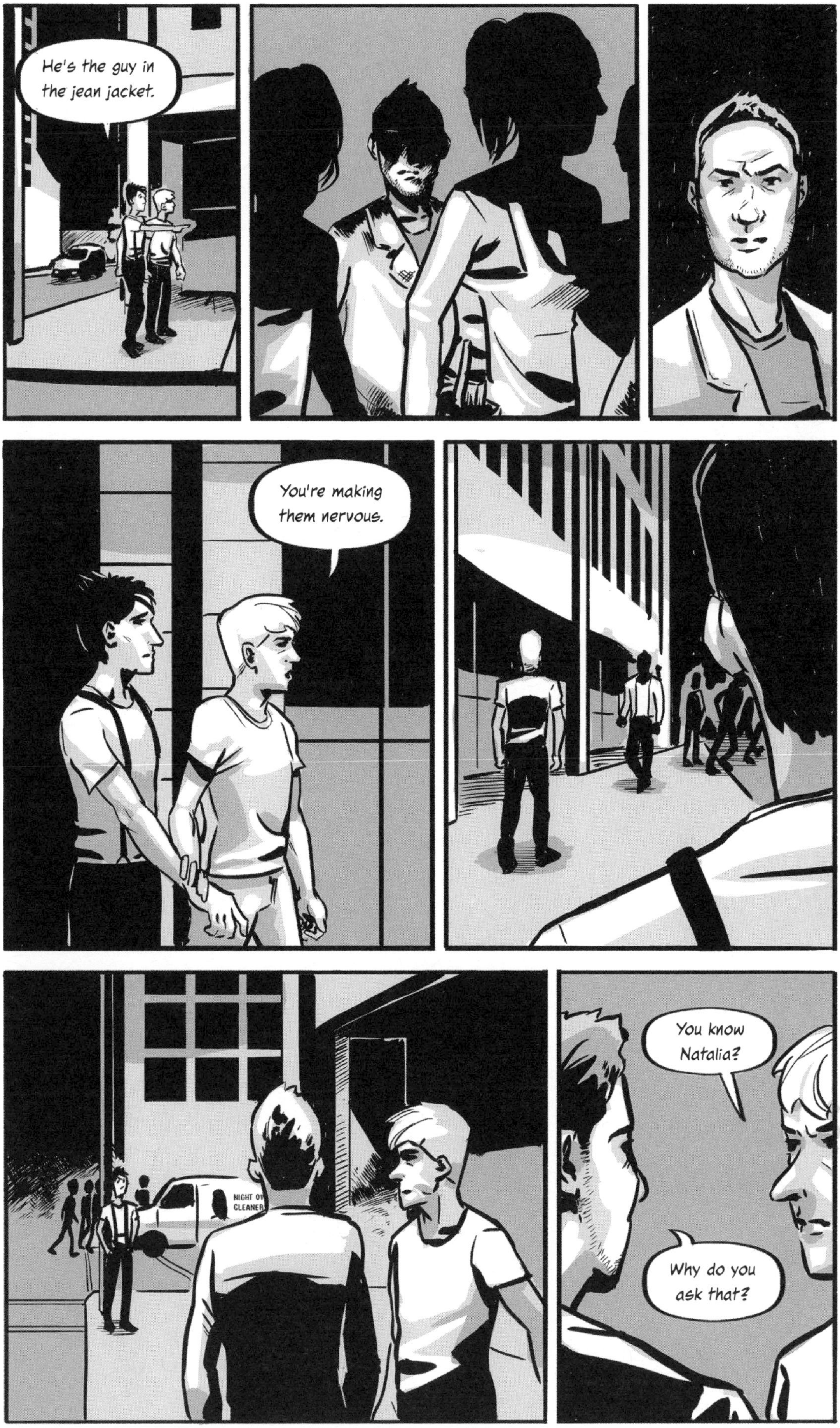
He's the guy in the jean jacket.
You're making them nervous.
NIGHT OW
CLEANER
You know Natalia?
Why do you ask that?

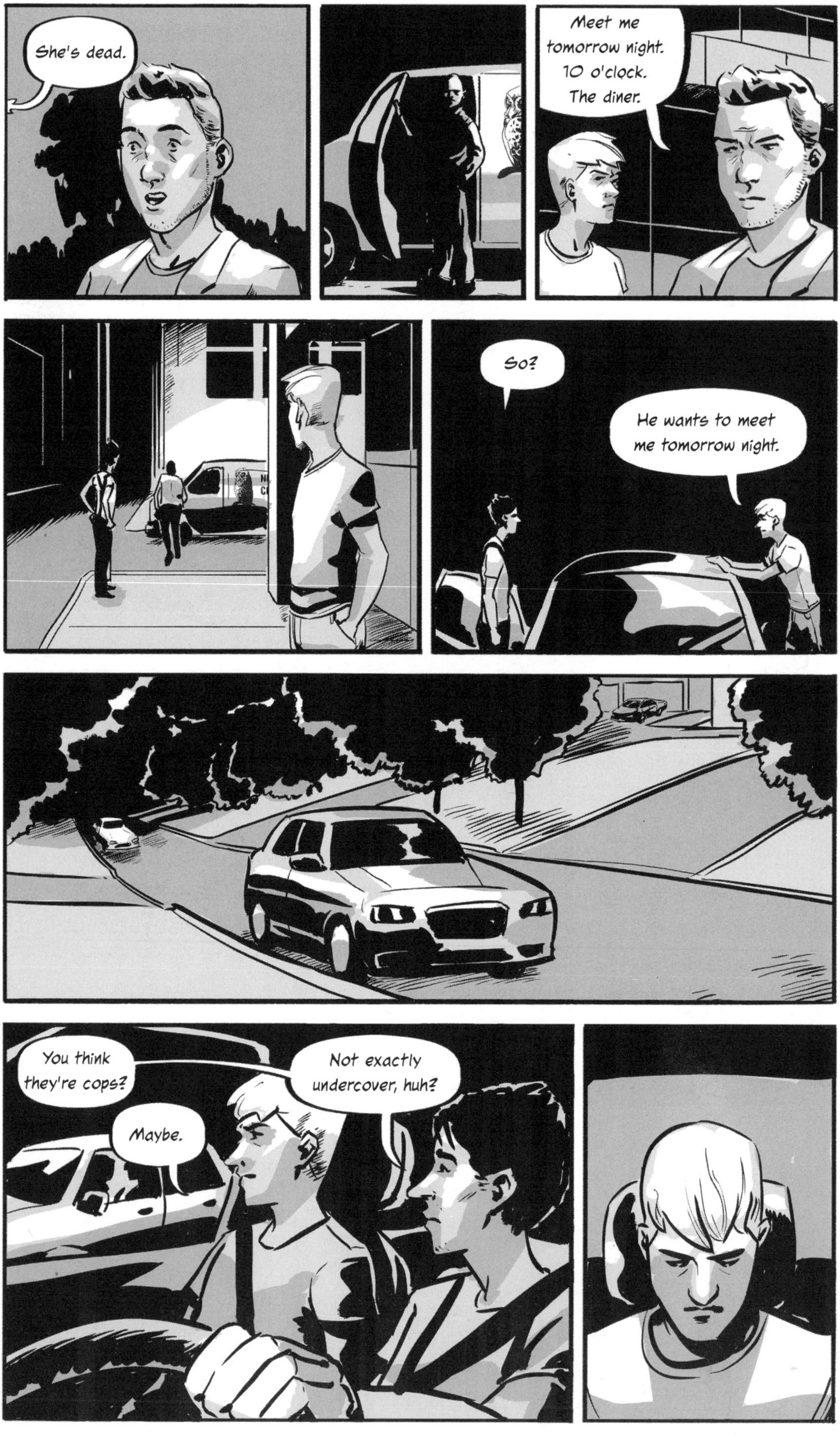
She's dead.
Meet me tomorrow night. 10 o'clock. The diner.
So?
He wants to meet me tomorrow night.
You think they're cops?
Not exactly undercover, huh?
Maybe.

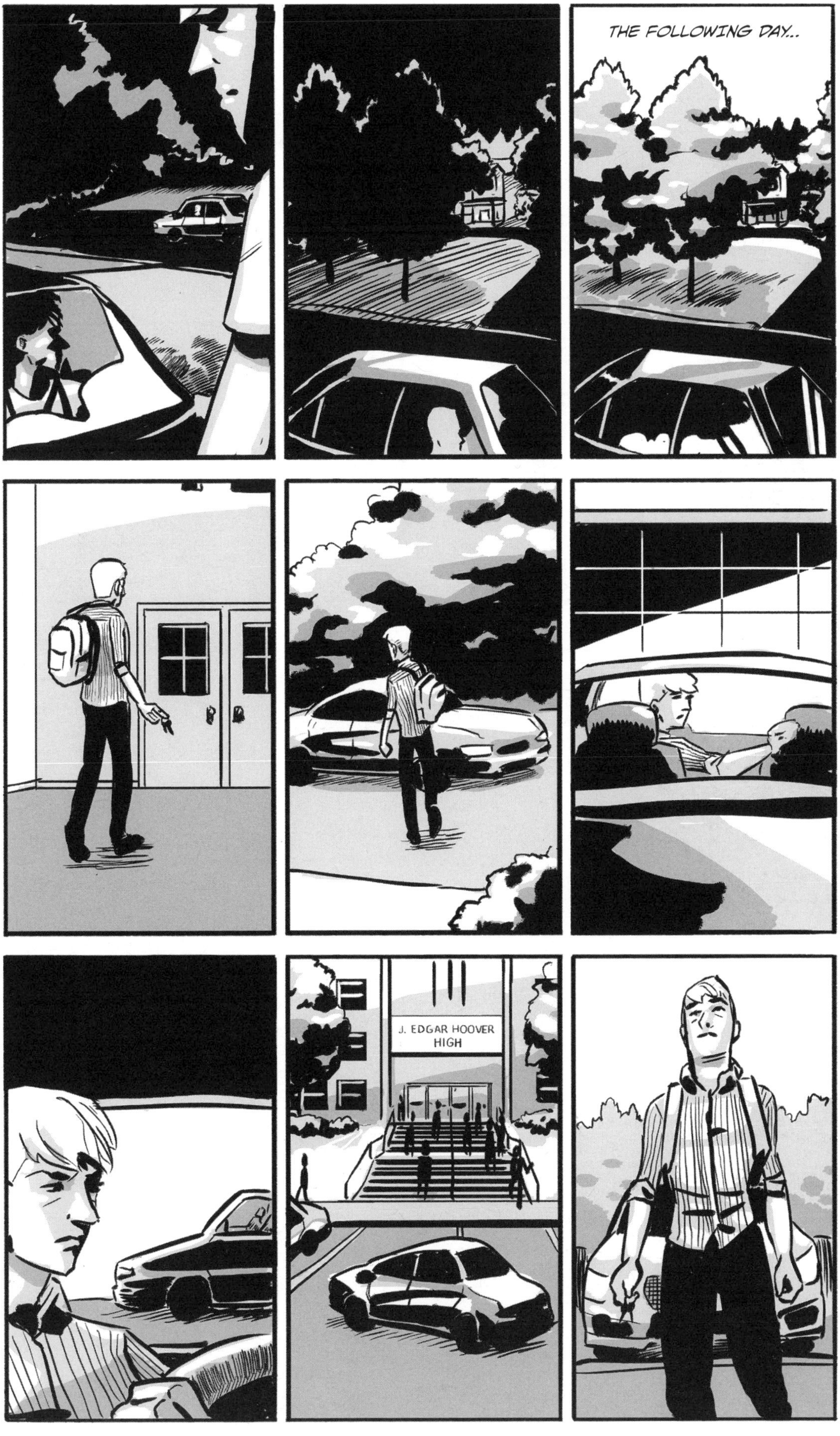

THE FOLLOWING DAY...
J. EDGAR HOOVER
HIGH

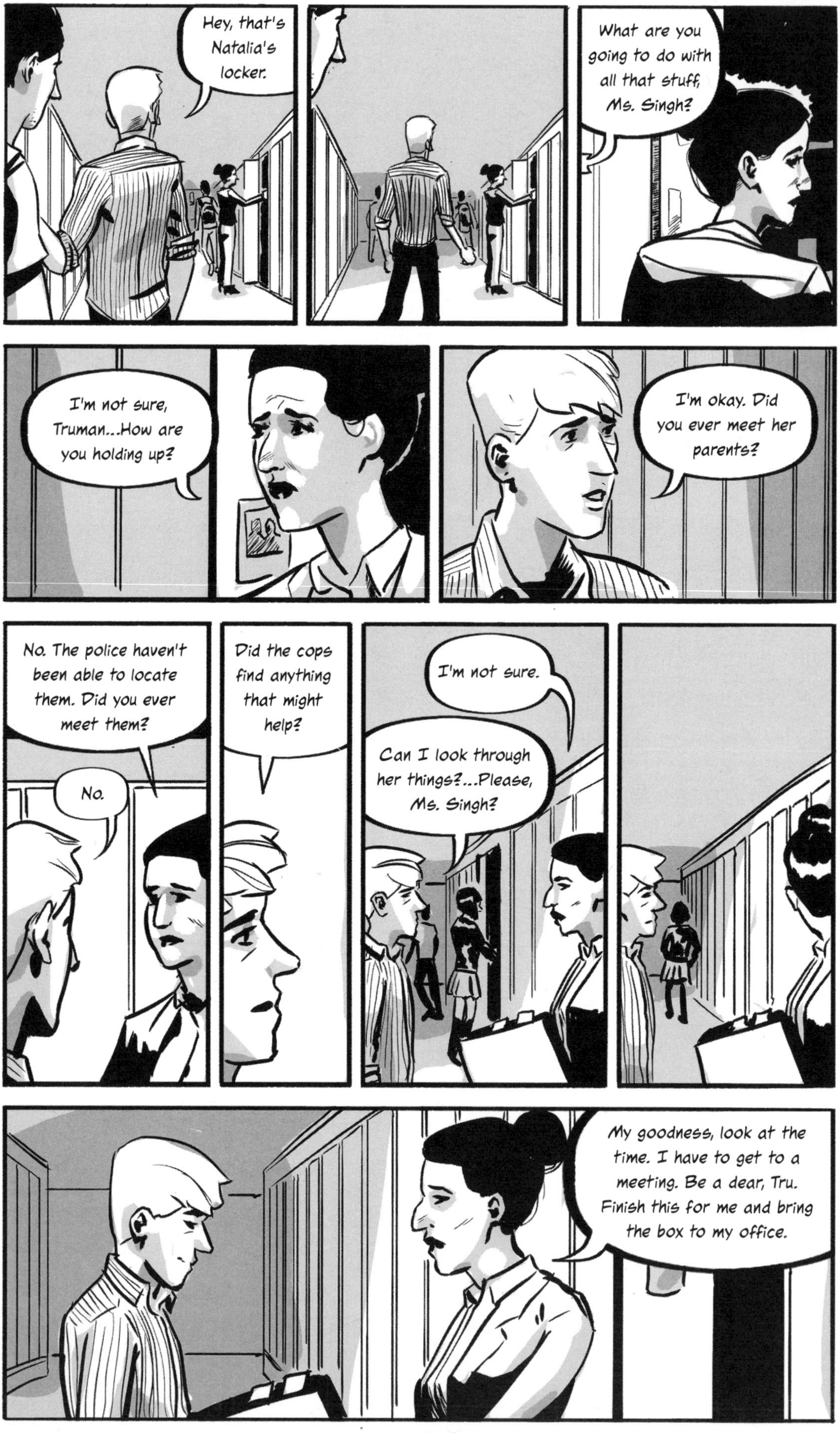

Hey, that's Natalia's locker.
What are you going to do with all that stuff, Ms. Singh?
I'm not sure, Truman...How are you holding up?
I'm okay. Did you ever meet her parents?
No. The police haven't been able to locate them. Did you ever meet them?
No.
Did the cops find anything that might help?
I'm not sure.
Can I look through her things?...Please, Ms. Singh?
My goodness, look at the time. I have to get to a meeting. Be a dear, Tru. Finish this for me and bring the box to my office.

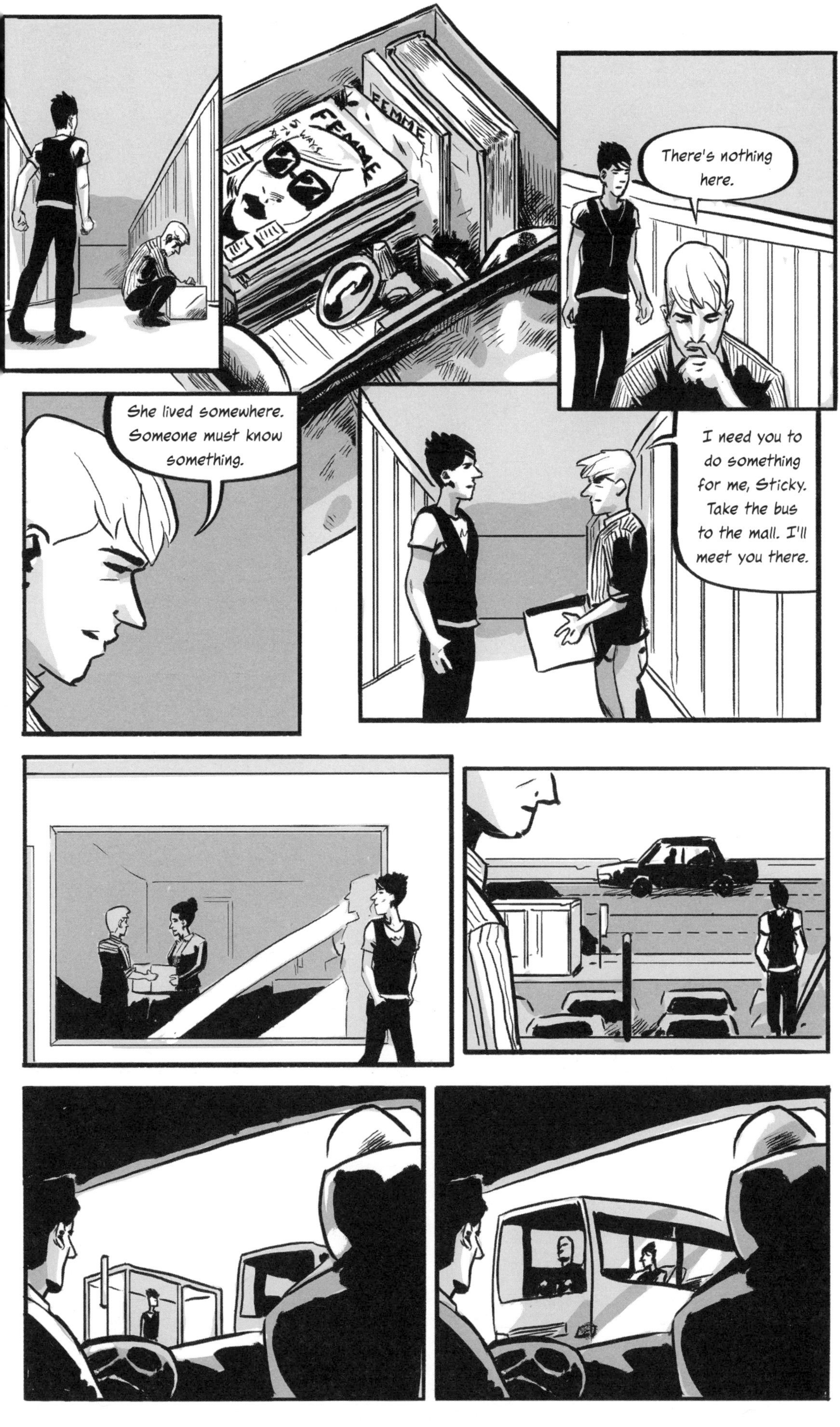
FEMME
5 WAYS
FEMME
There's nothing here.
She lived somewhere. Someone must know something.
I need you to do something for me, Sticky. Take the bus to the mall. I'll meet you there.

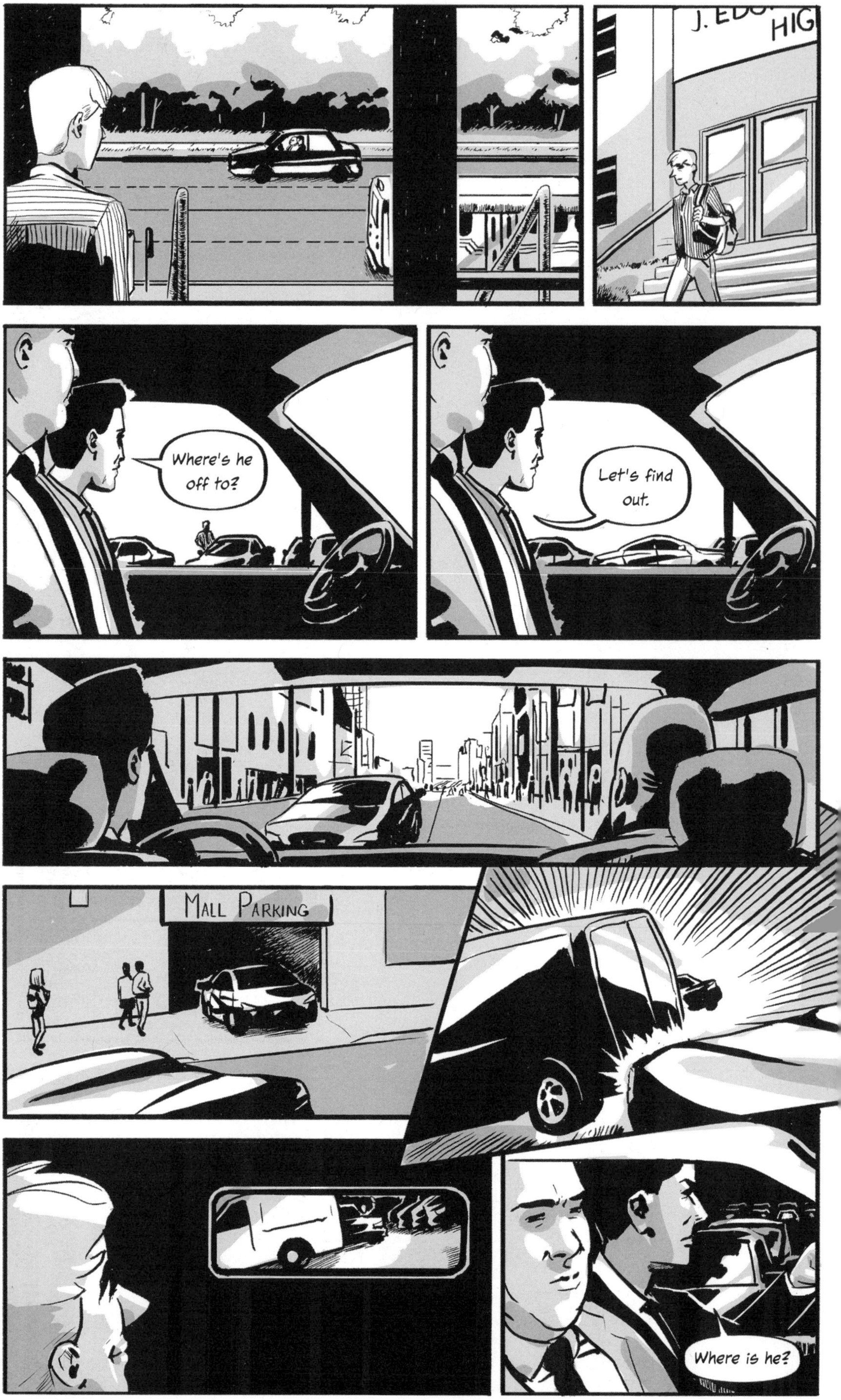
J. EDG
HIG
Where's he off to?
Let's find out.
MALL PARKING
Where is he?

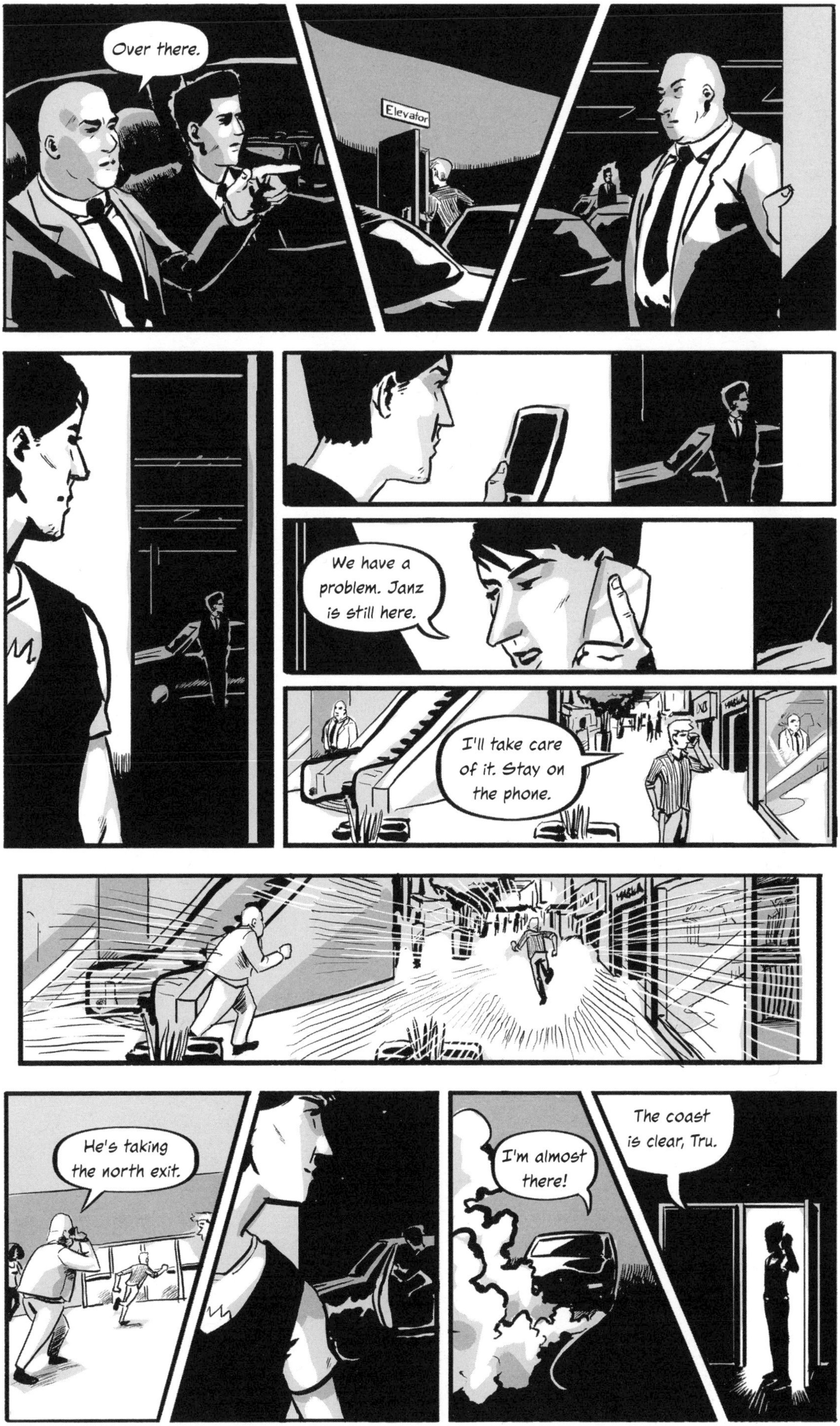
Over there.
Elevator
We have a problem. Janz is still here.
I'll take care of it. Stay on the phone.
He's taking the north exit.
I'm almost there!
The coast is clear, Tru.

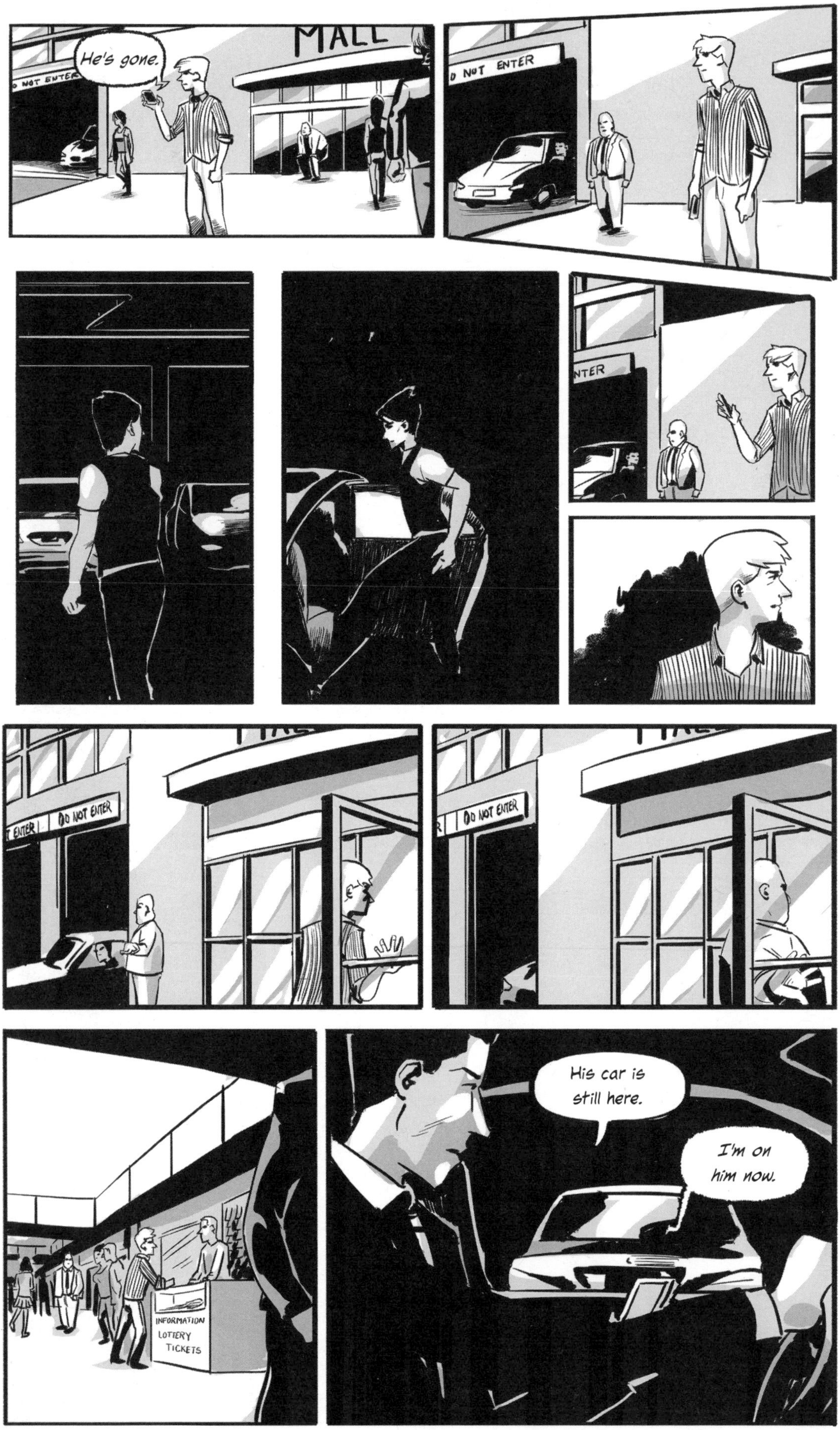
MALL
DO NOT ENTER
He's gone.
DO NOT ENTER
NTER
T ENTER
DO NOT ENTER
R
DO NOT ENTER
INFORMATION
LOTTERY
TICKETS
His car is
still here.
I'm on
him now.

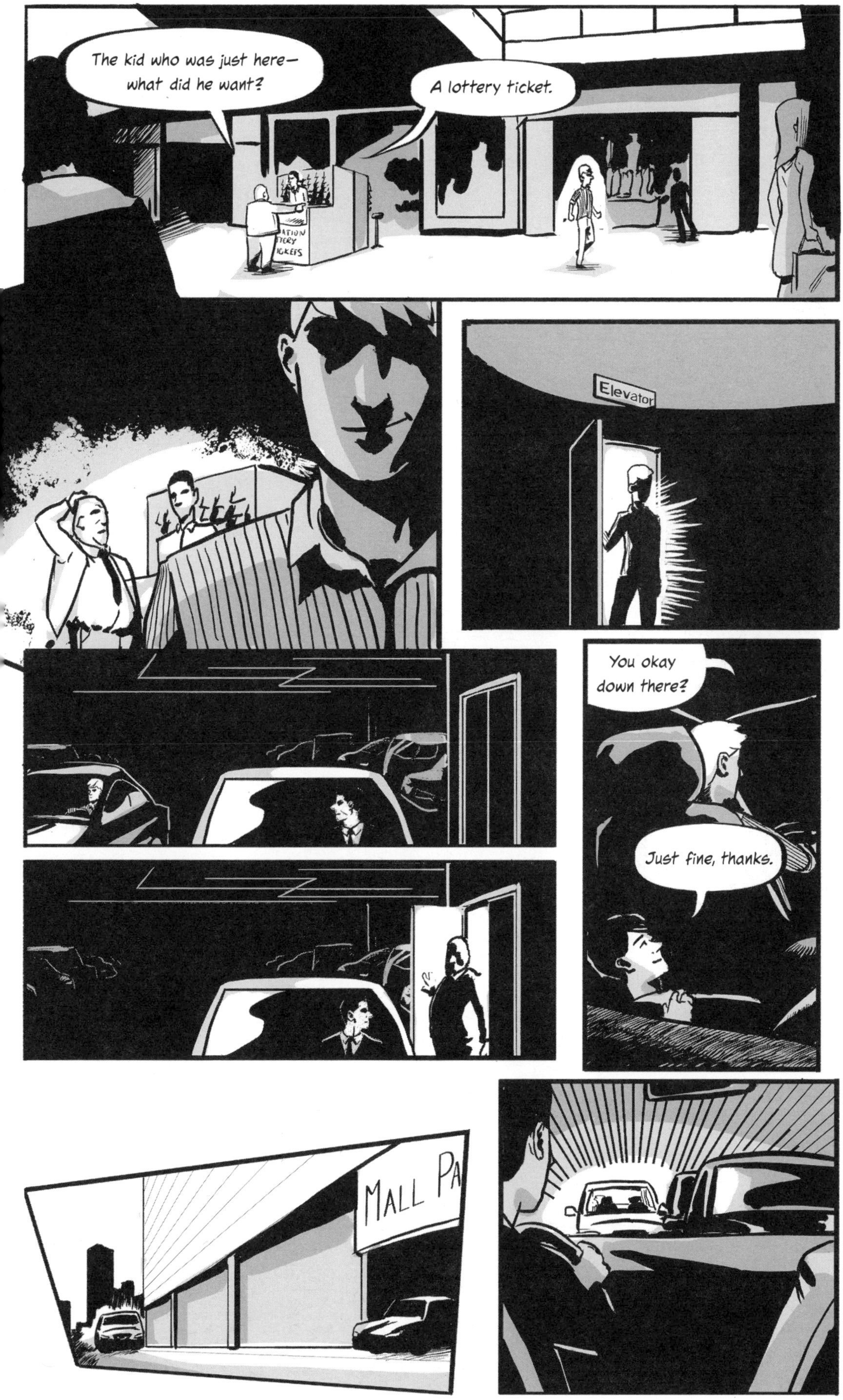
The kid who was just here—what did he want?
A lottery ticket.
Elevator
You okay down there?
Just fine, thanks.
MALL PA

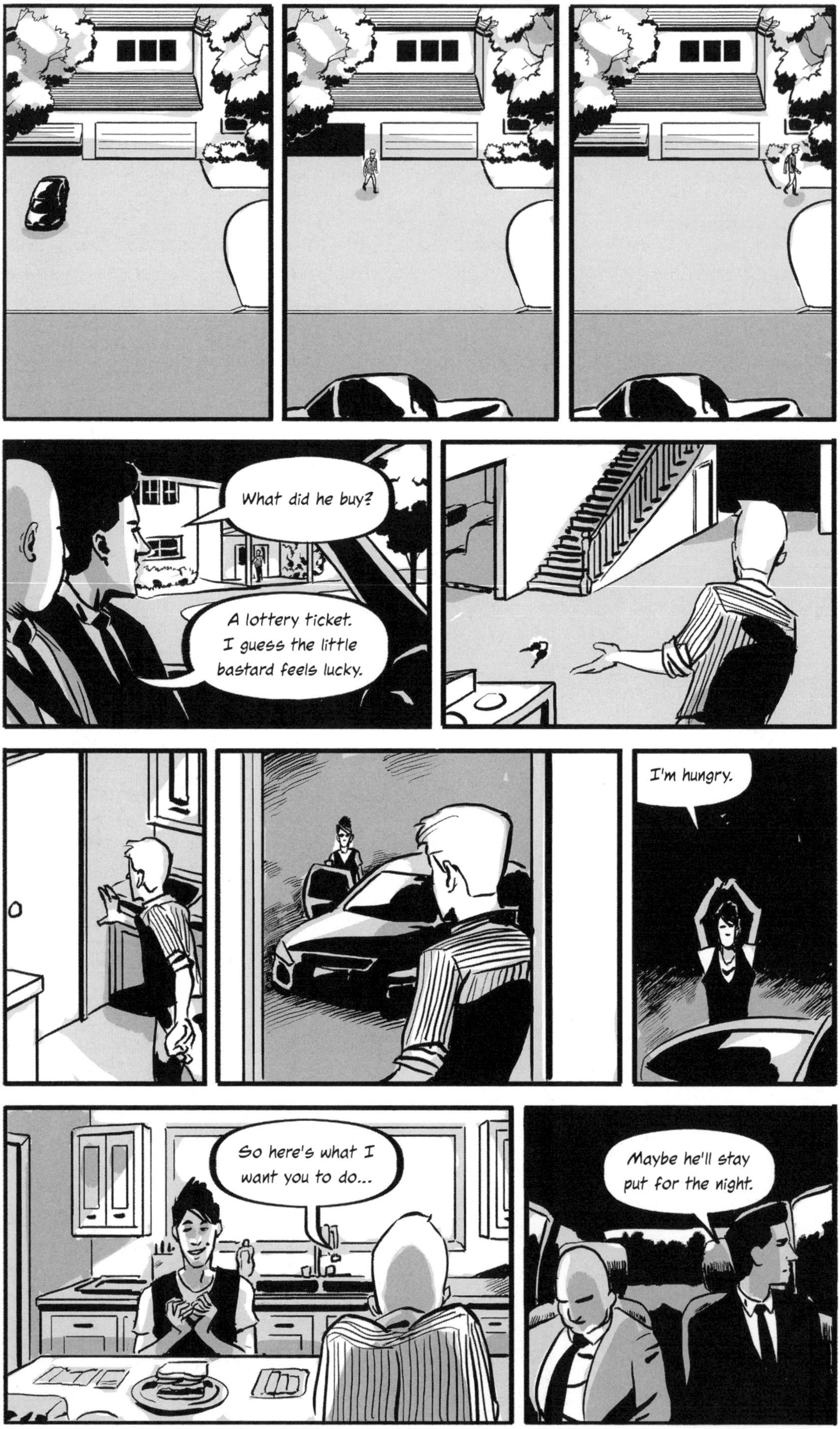
What did he buy?
A lottery ticket. I guess the little bastard feels lucky.
I'm hungry.
So here's what I want you to do...
Maybe he'll stay put for the night.

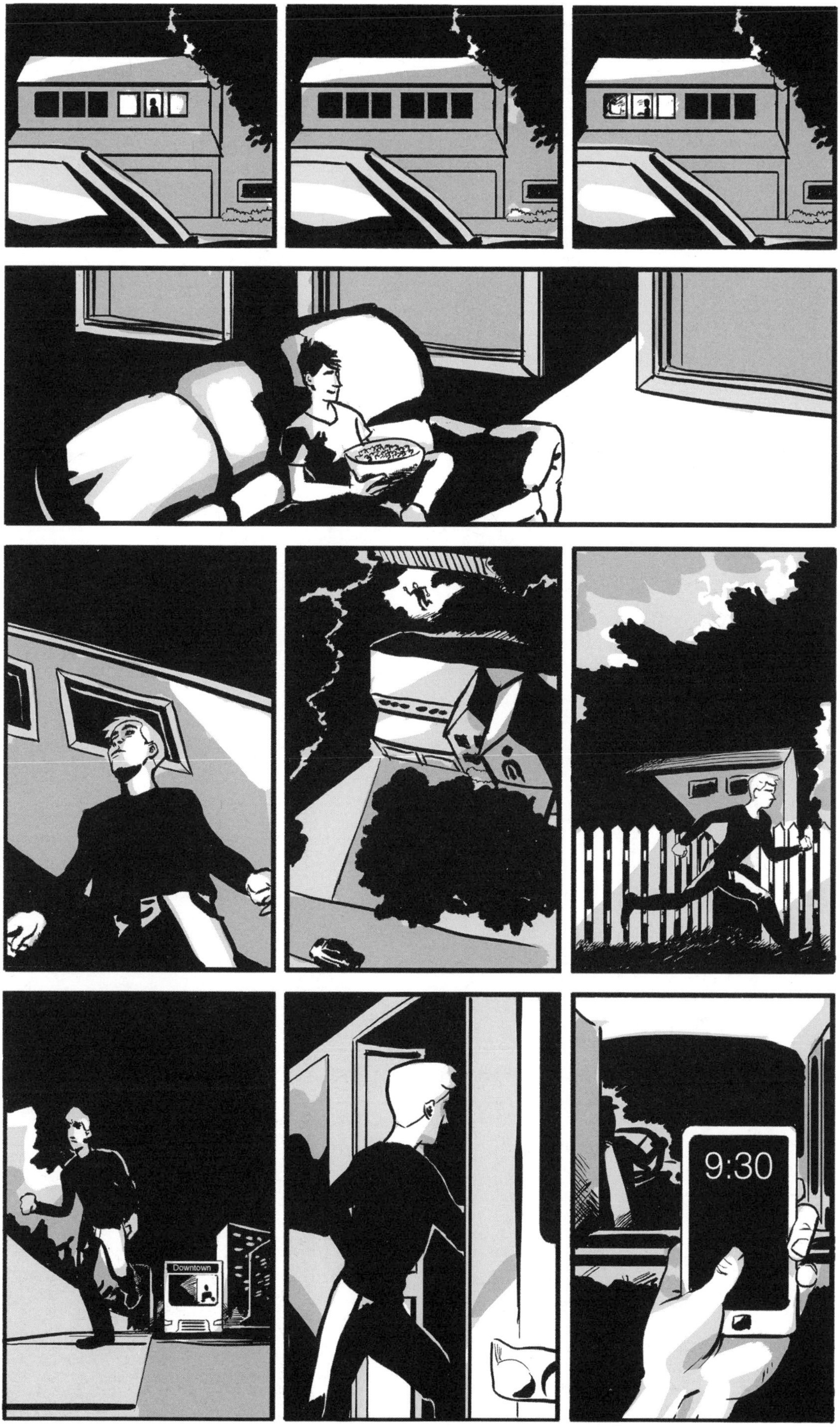
Downtown
9:30

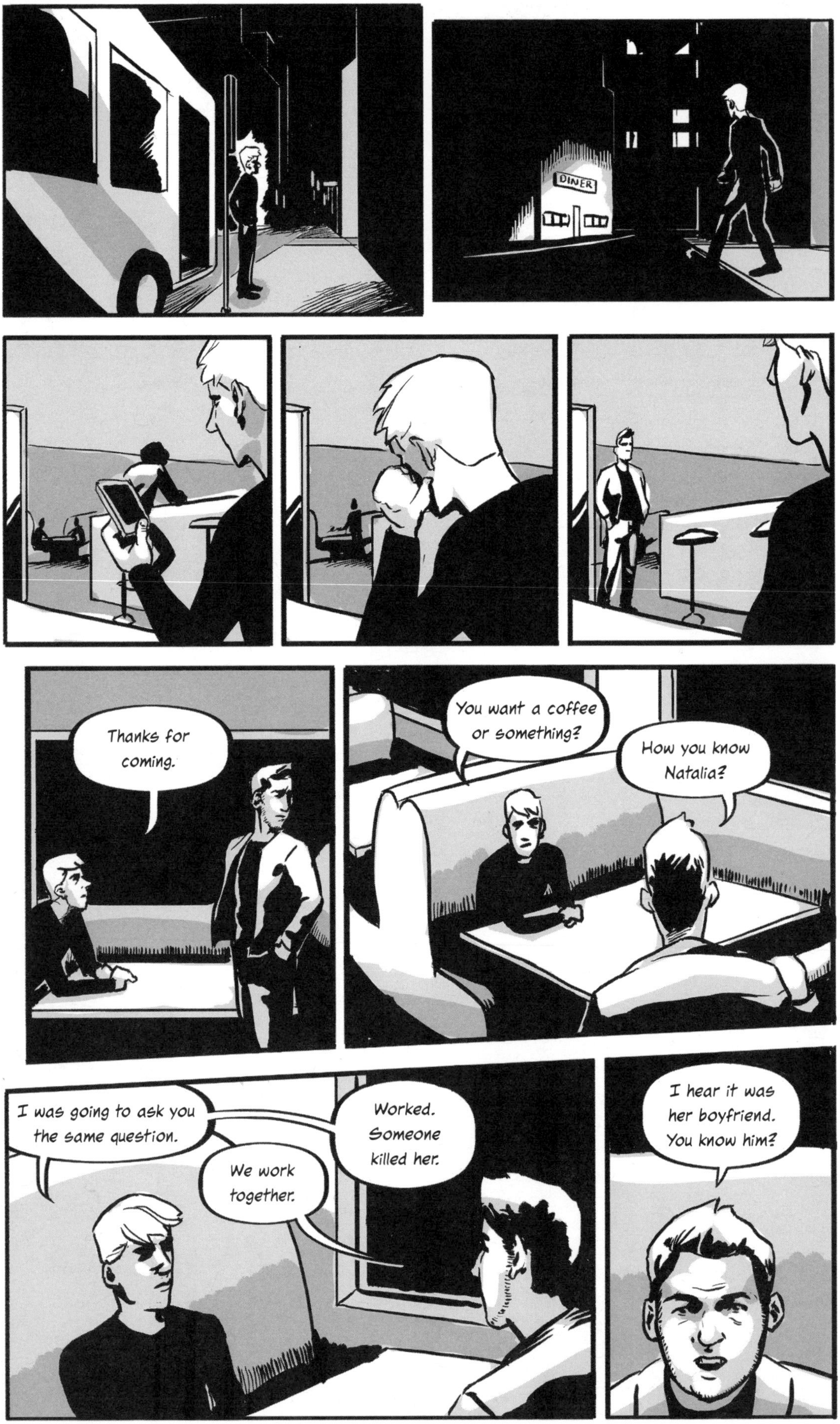
DINER
Thanks for coming.
You want a coffee or something?
How you know Natalia?
I was going to ask you the same question.
We work together.
Worked. Someone killed her.
I hear it was her boyfriend. You know him?

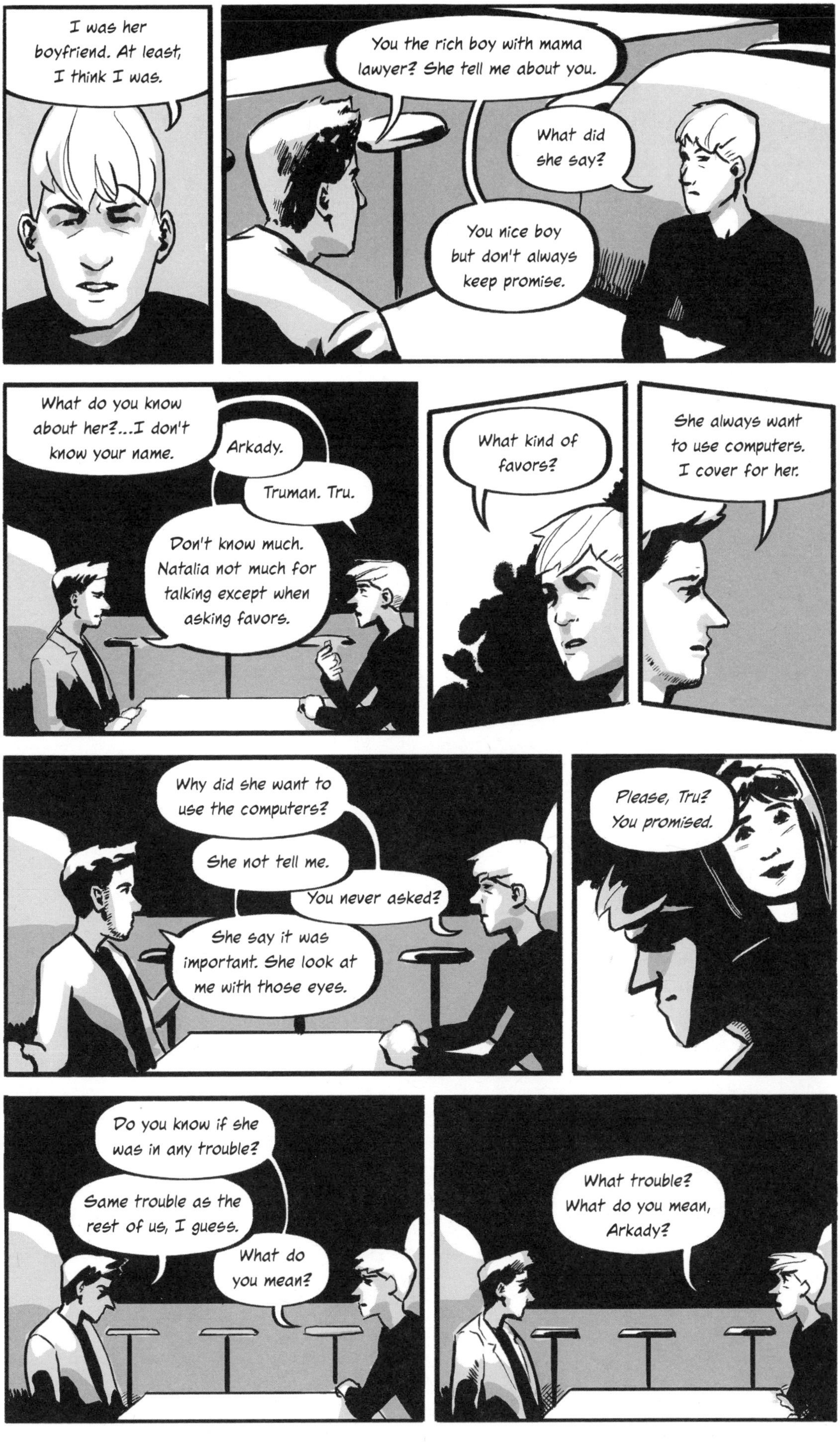
I was her boyfriend. At least, I think I was.
You the rich boy with mama lawyer? She tell me about you.
What did she say?
You nice boy but don't always keep promise.
What do you know about her?...I don't know your name.
Arkady.
Truman. Tru.
Don't know much. Natalia not much for talking except when asking favors.
What kind of favors?
She always want to use computers. I cover for her.
Why did she want to use the computers?
She not tell me.
You never asked?
She say it was important. She look at me with those eyes.
Please, Tru? You promised.
Do you know if she was in any trouble?
Same trouble as the rest of us, I guess.
What do you mean?
What trouble? What do you mean, Arkady?

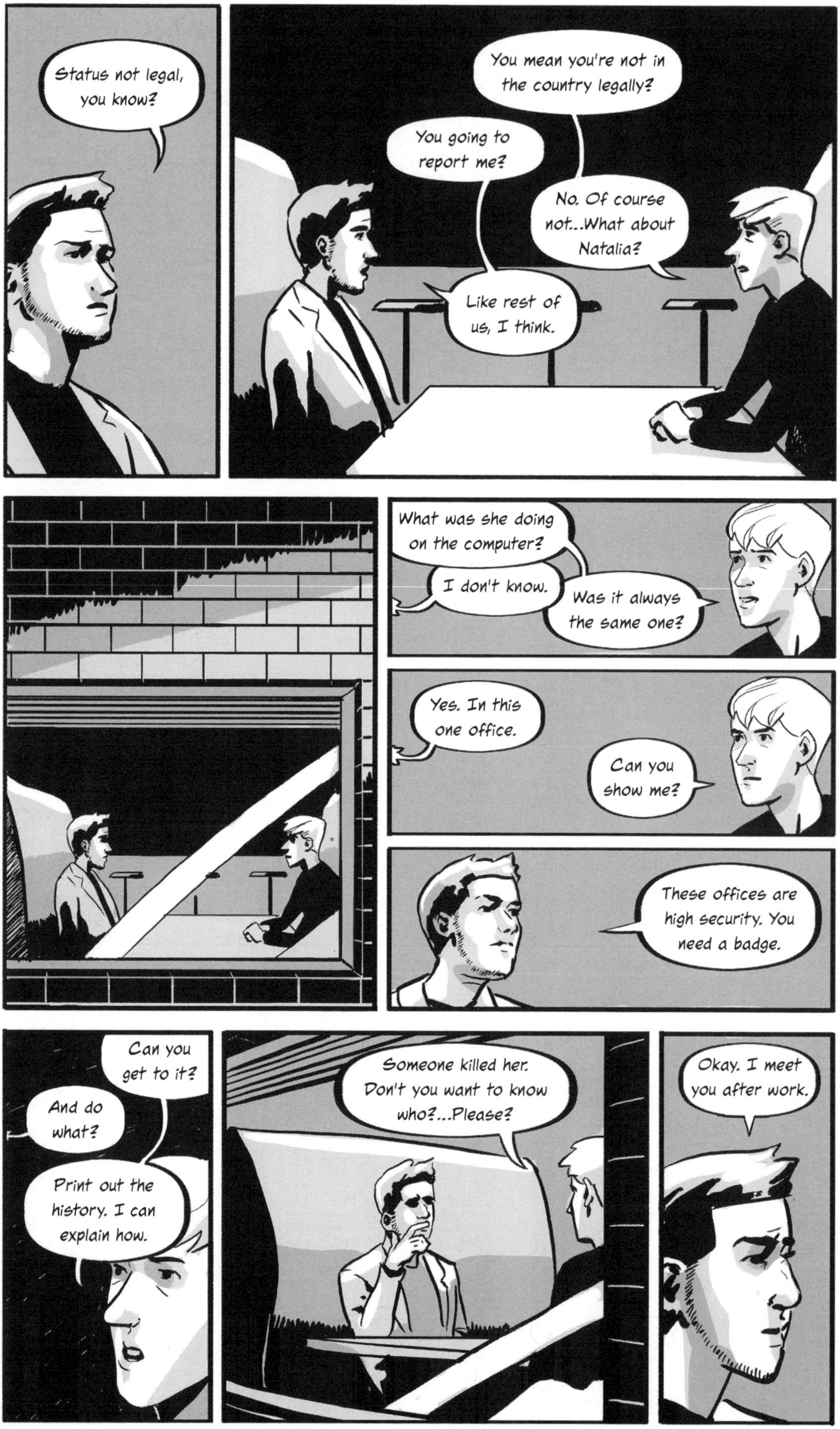
Status not legal,
you know?
You mean you're not in
the country legally?
You going to
report me?
No. Of course
not...What about
Natalia?
Like rest of
us, I think.
What was she doing
on the computer?
I don't know.
Was it always
the same one?
Yes. In this
one office.
Can you
show me?
These offices are
high security. You
need a badge.
Can you
get to it?
And do
what?
Print out the
history. I can
explain how.
Someone killed her.
Don't you want to know
who?...Please?
Okay. I meet
you after work.

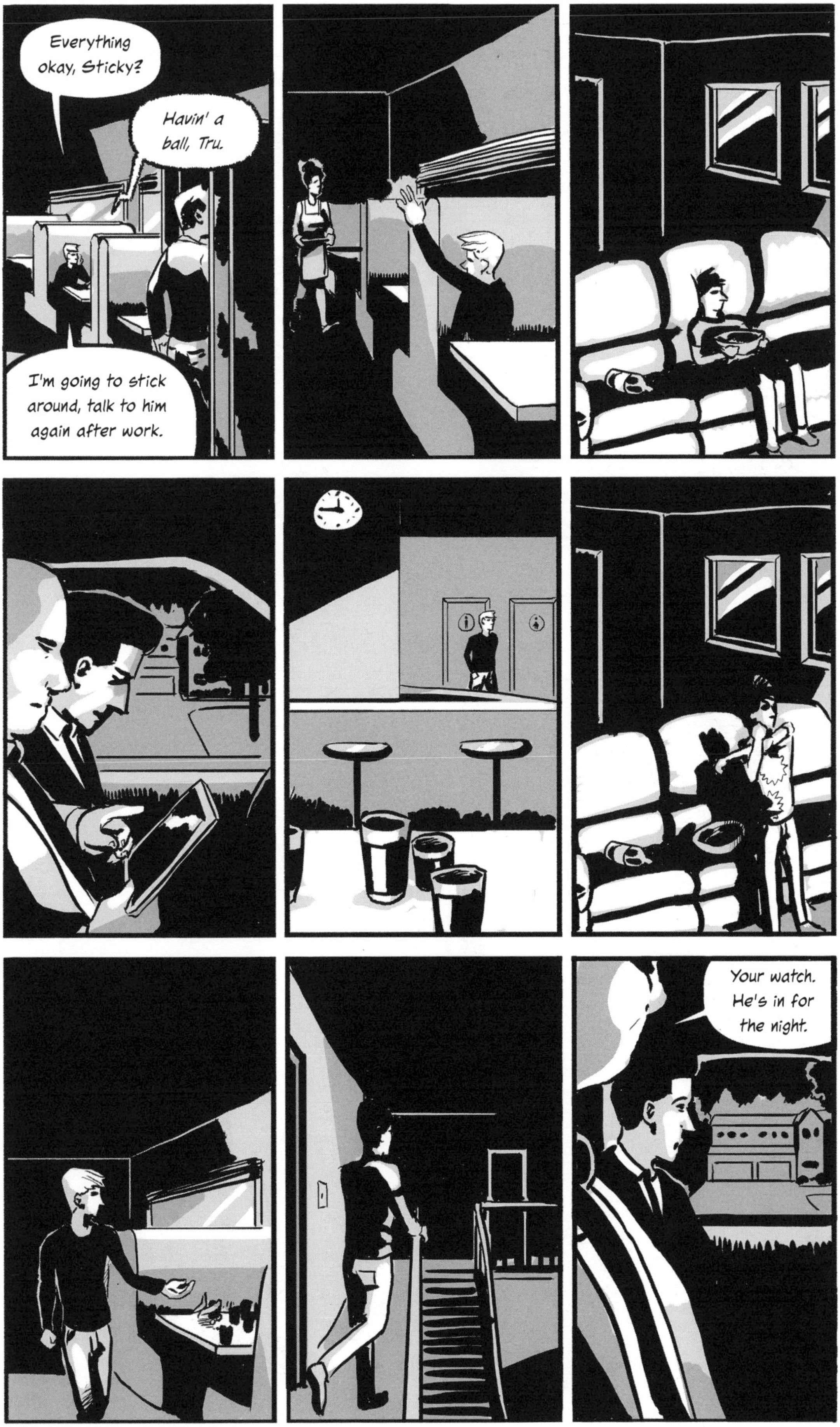
Everything okay, Sticky?
Havin' a ball, Tru.
I'm going to stick around, talk to him again after work.
Your watch. He's in for the night.

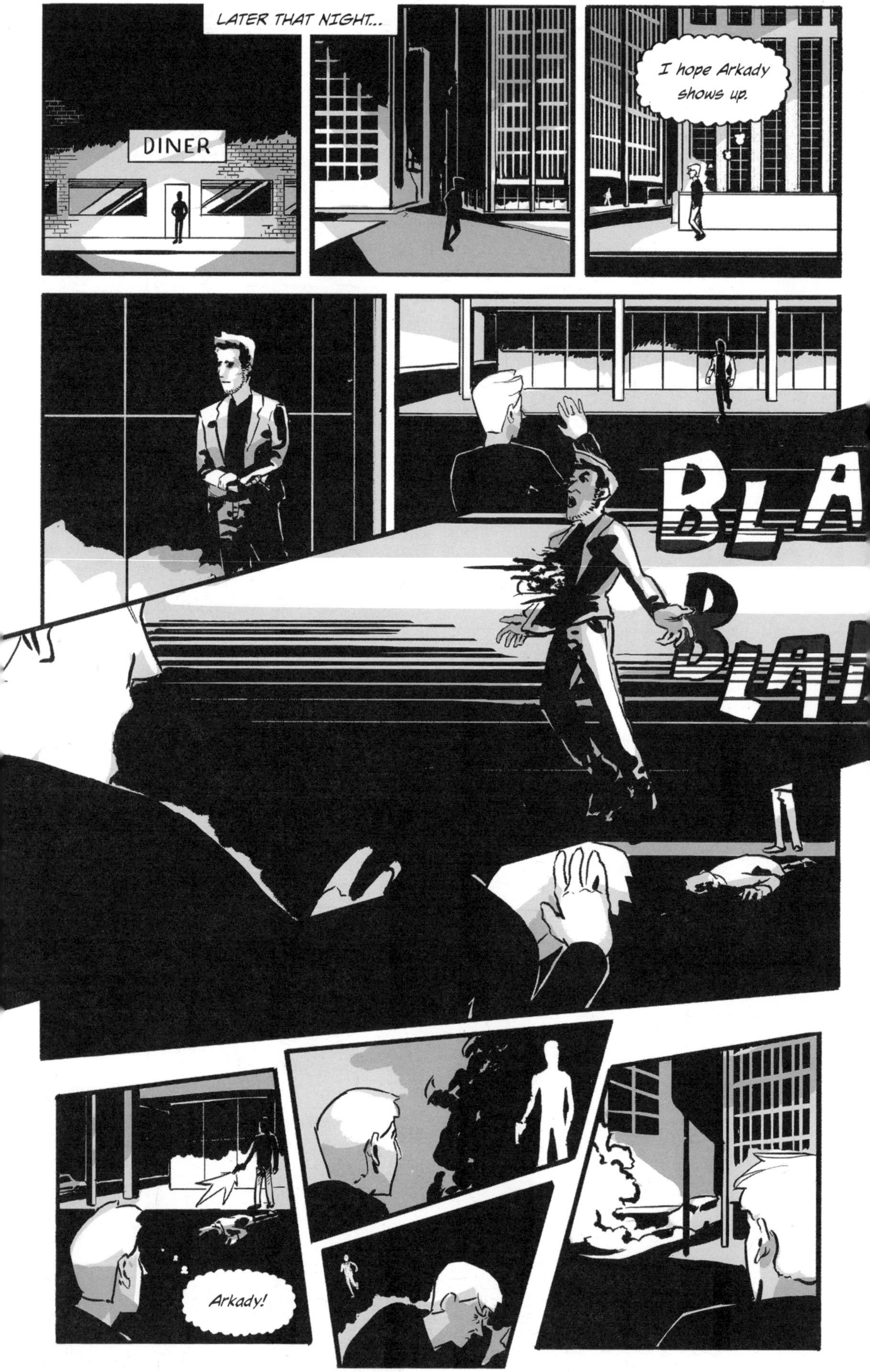

LATER THAT NIGHT...
DINER
I hope Arkady shows up.
BLA
BLA
Arkady!

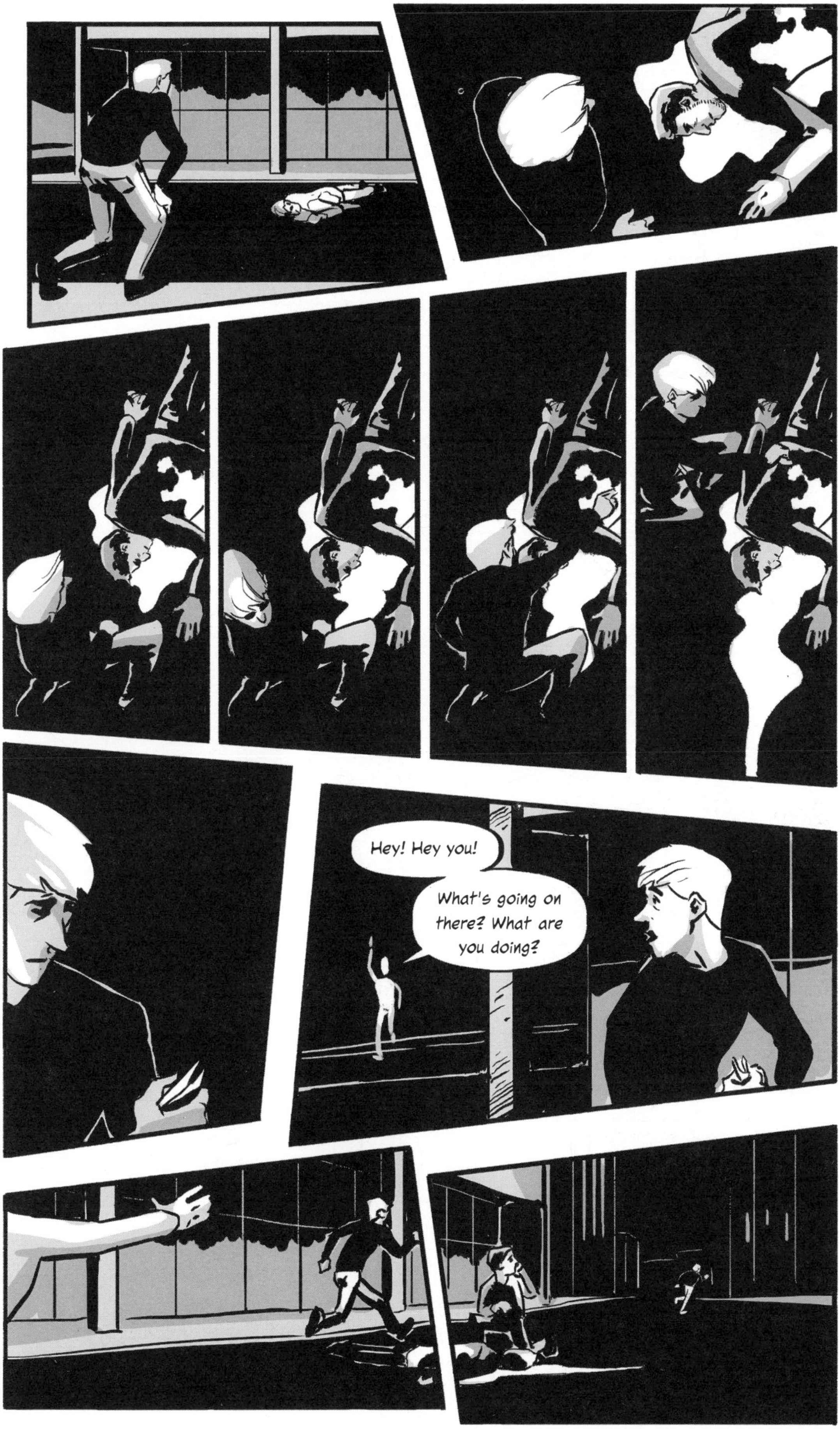
Hey! Hey you!
What's going on there? What are you doing?

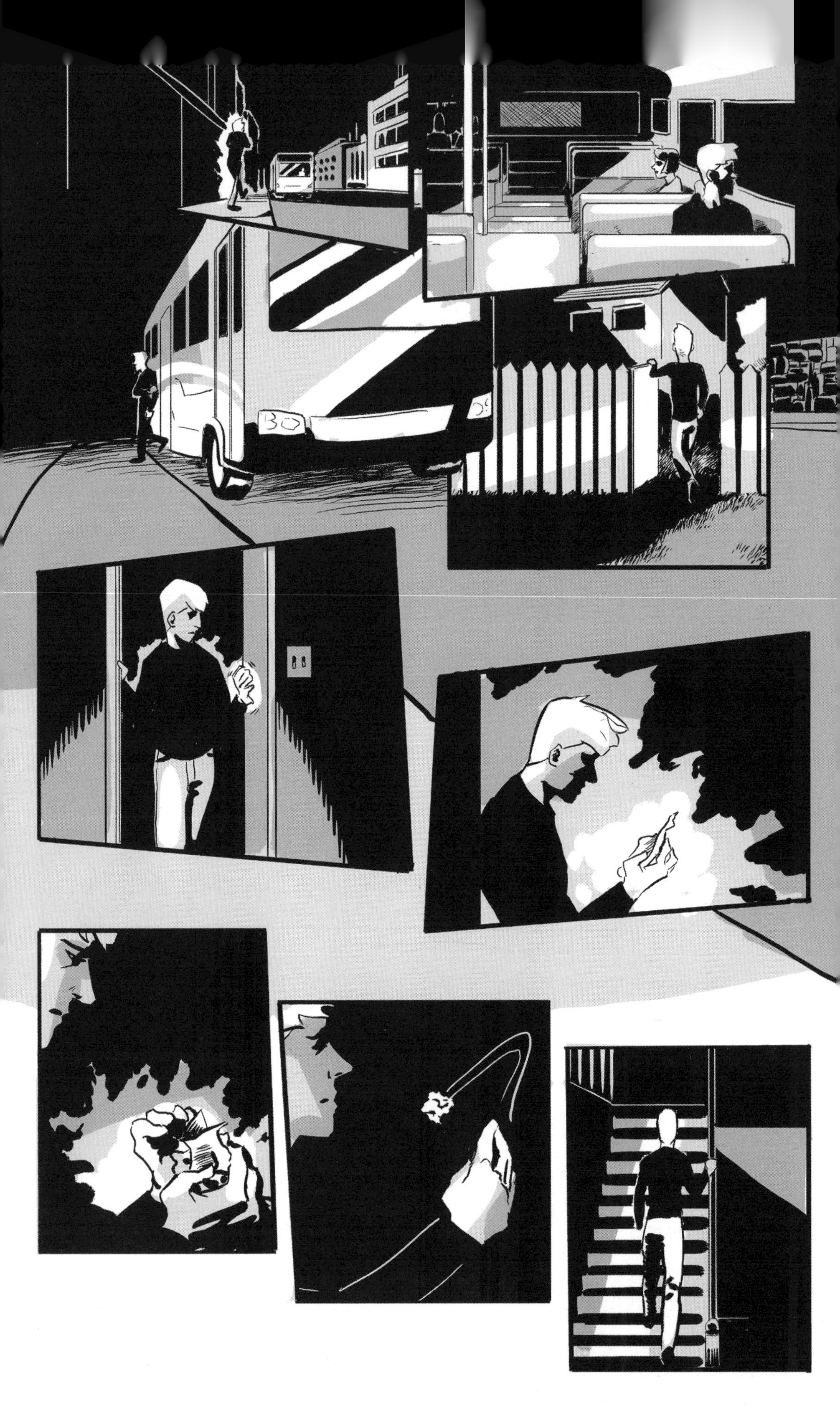
30

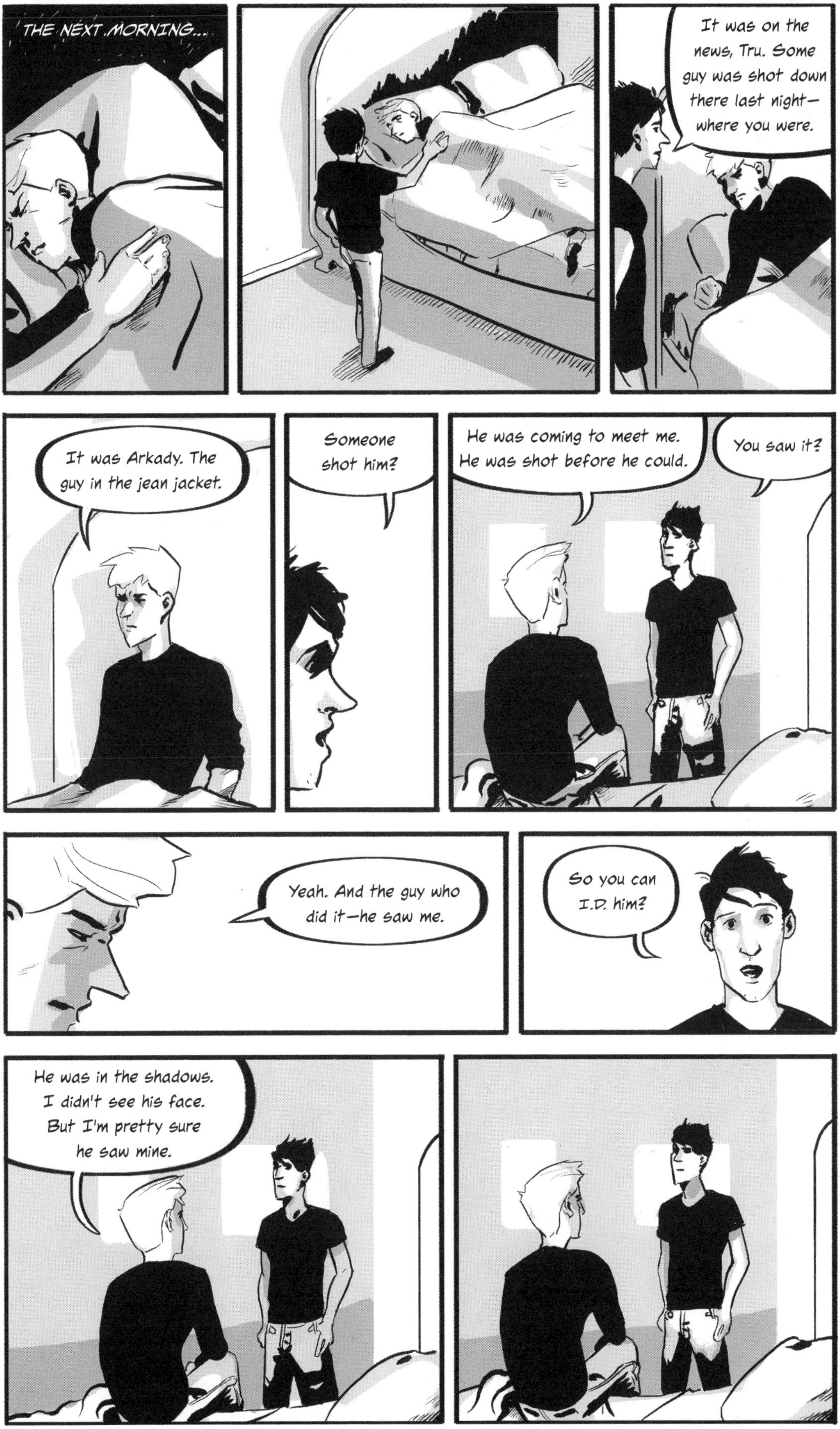
THE NEXT MORNING...
It was on the news, Tru. Some guy was shot down there last night—where you were.
It was Arkady. The guy in the jean jacket.
Someone shot him?
He was coming to meet me. He was shot before he could.
You saw it?
Yeah. And the guy who did it—he saw me.
So you can I.D. him?
He was in the shadows. I didn't see his face. But I'm pretty sure he saw mine.

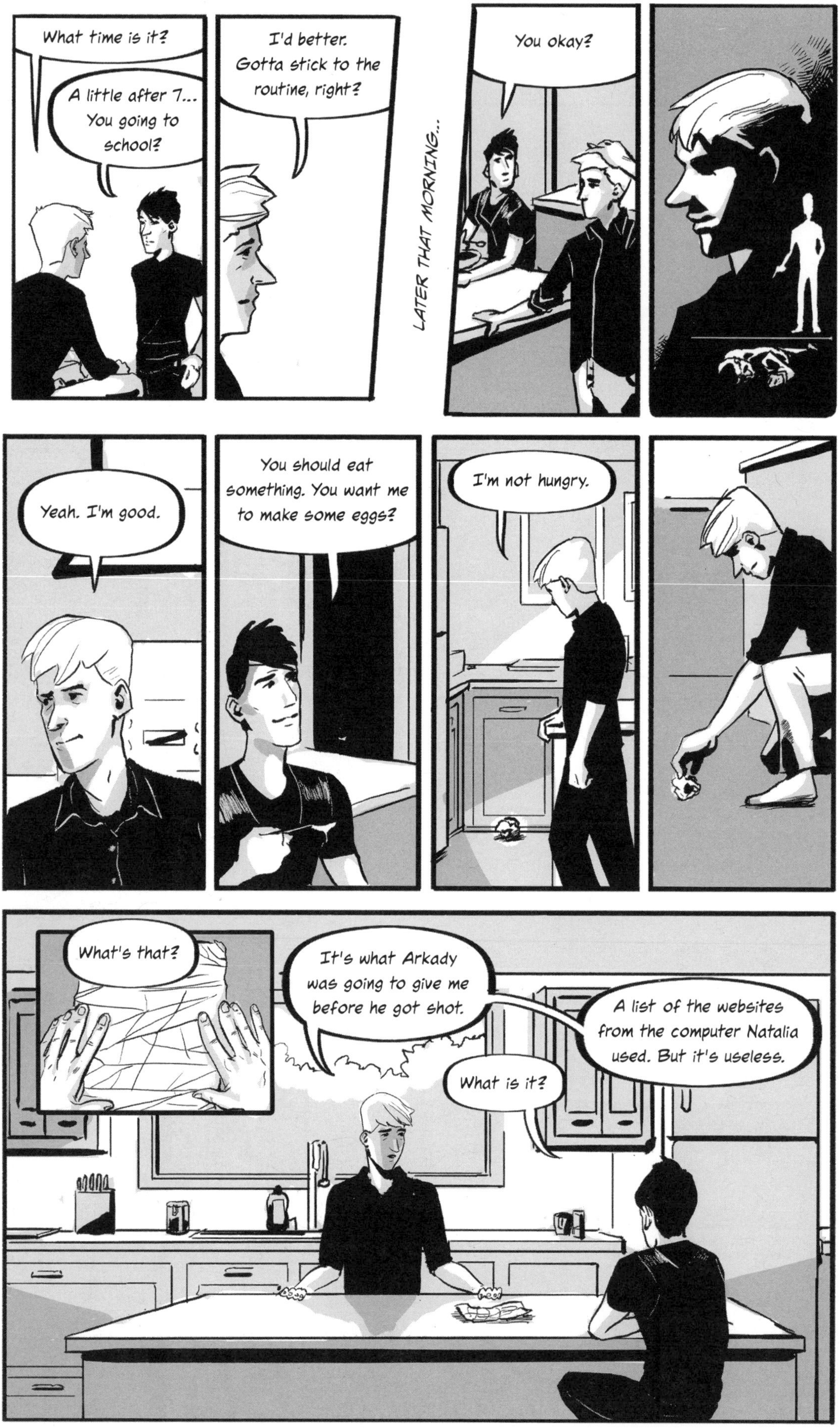
What time is it?
A little after 7... You going to school?
I'd better. Gotta stick to the routine, right?
LATER THAT MORNING...
You okay?
Yeah. I'm good.
You should eat something. You want me to make some eggs?
I'm not hungry.
What's that?
It's what Arkady was going to give me before he got shot.
What is it?
A list of the websites from the computer Natalia used. But it's useless.

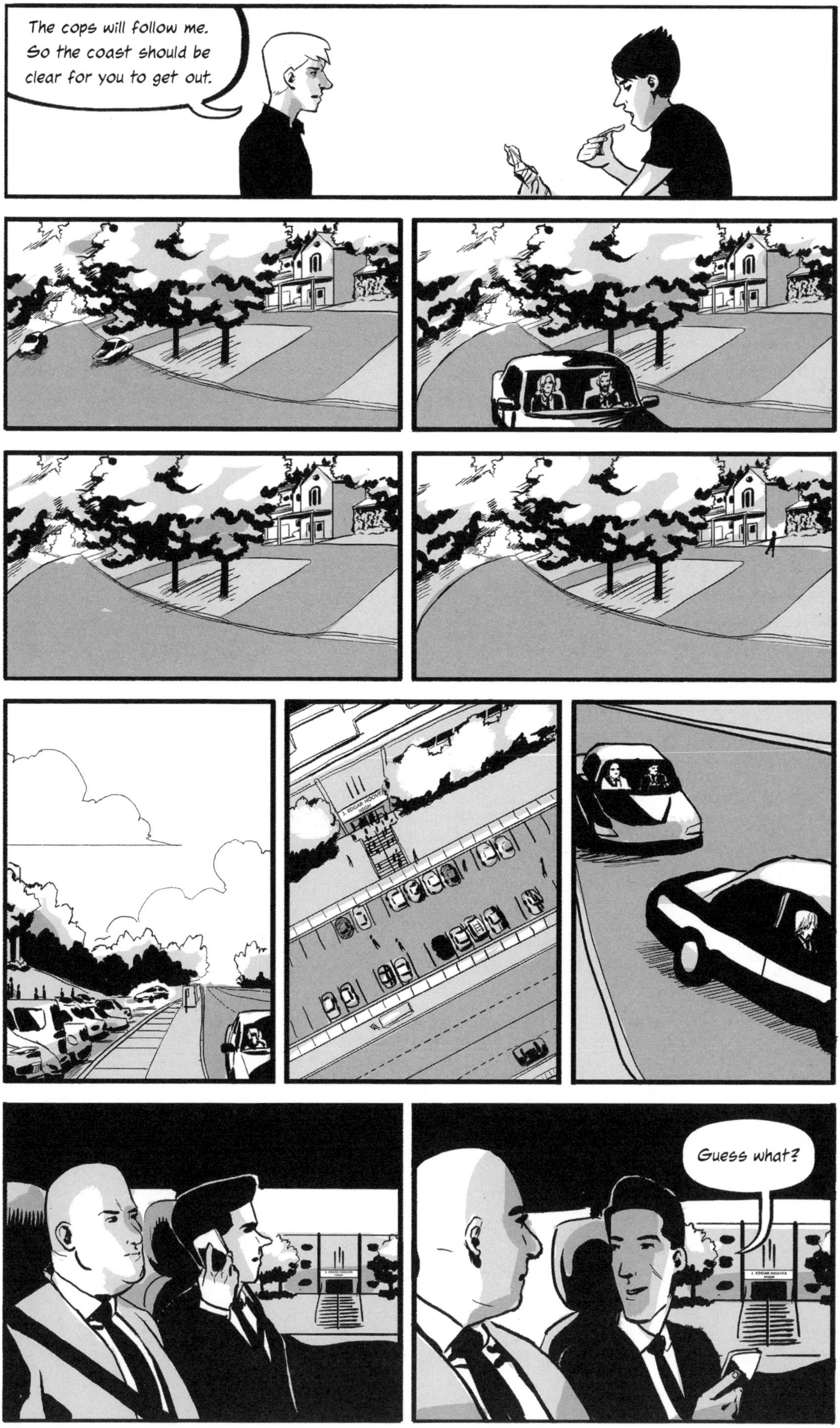
The cops will follow me. So the coast should be clear for you to get out.
J. EDGAR HOOVER HIGH
Guess what?

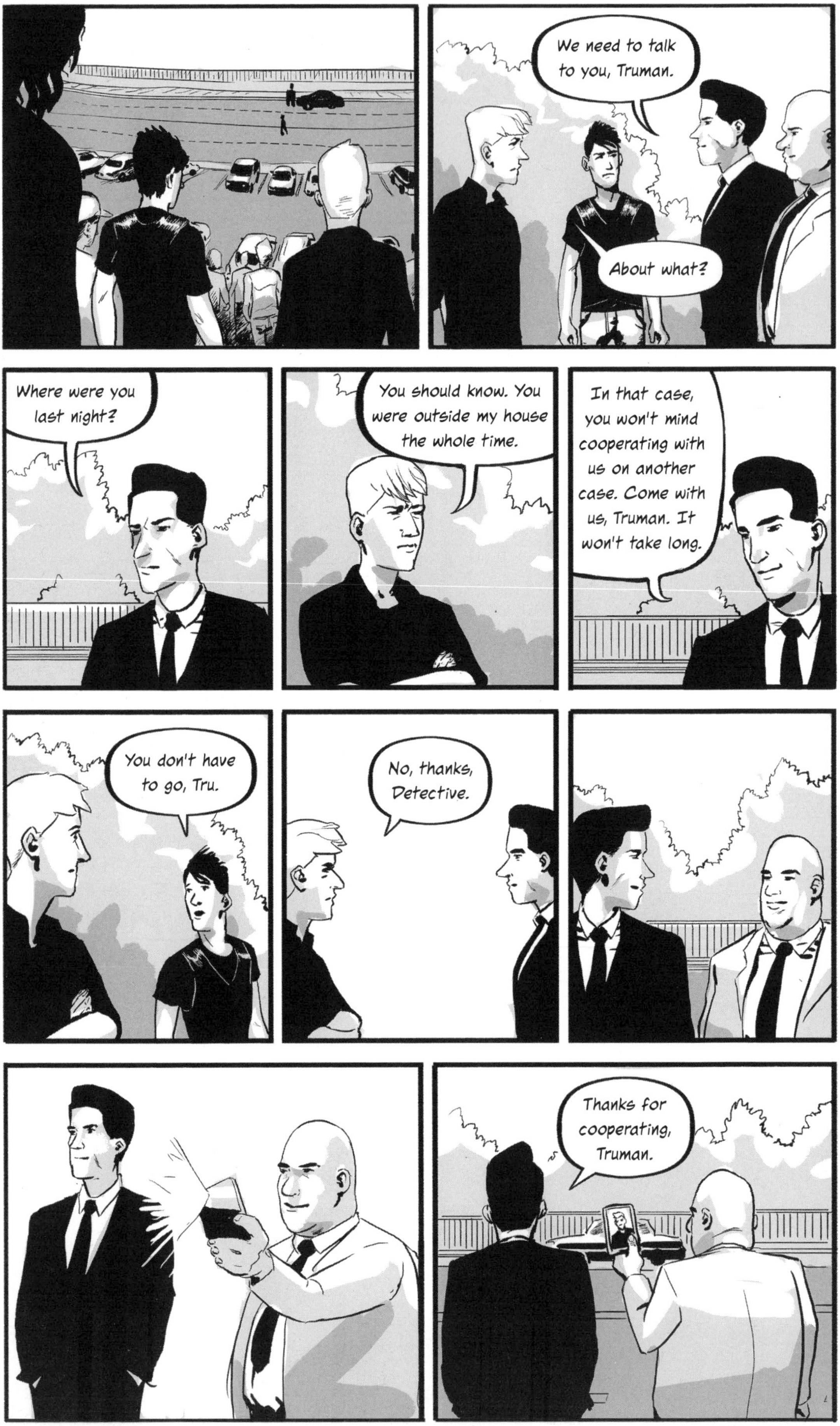
We need to talk to you, Truman.
About what?
Where were you last night?
You should know. You were outside my house the whole time.
In that case, you won't mind cooperating with us on another case. Come with us, Truman. It won't take long.
You don't have to go, Tru.
No, thanks, Detective.
Thanks for cooperating, Truman.

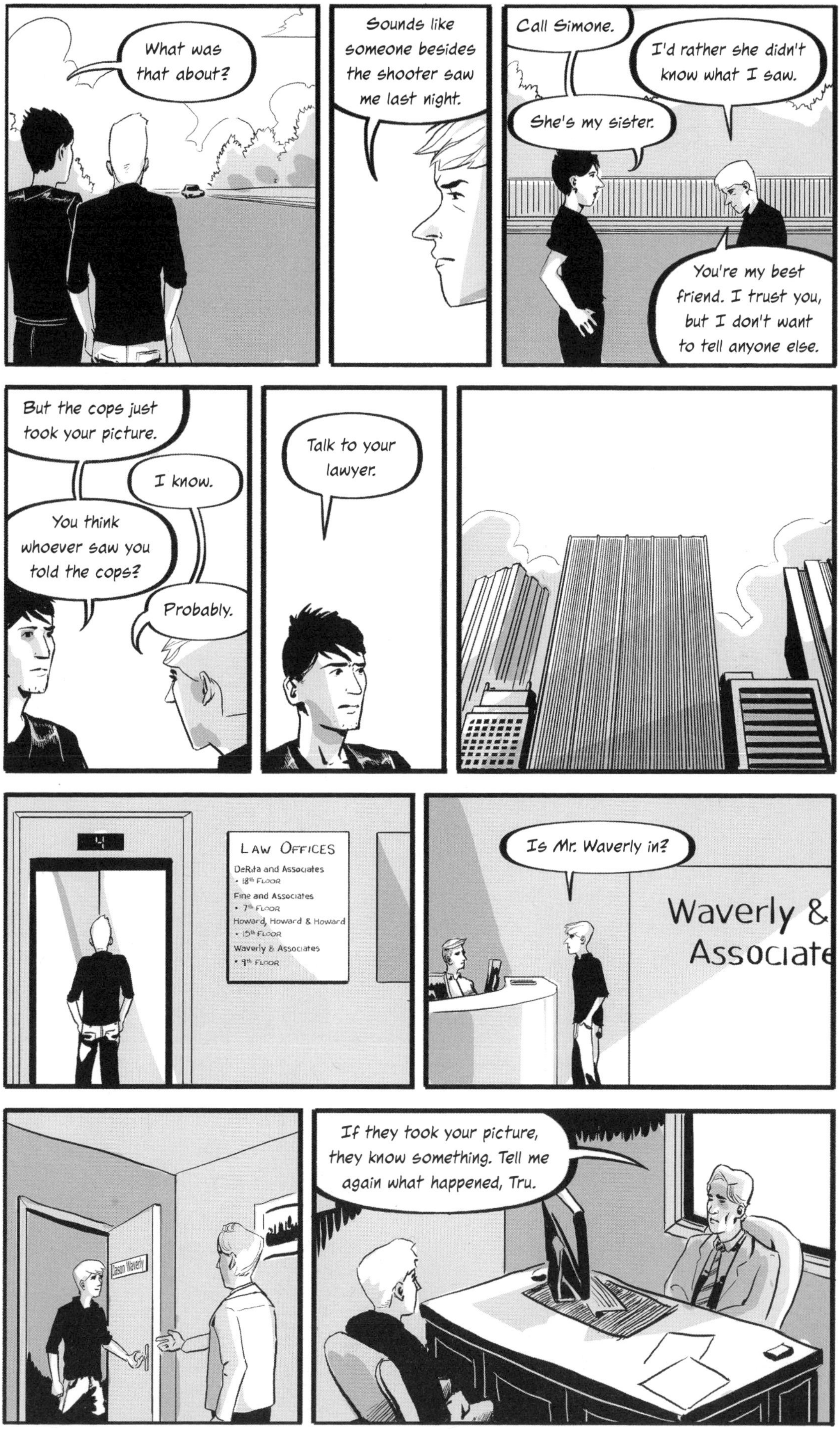
What was that about?
Sounds like someone besides the shooter saw me last night.
Call Simone.
I'd rather she didn't know what I saw.
She's my sister.
You're my best friend. I trust you, but I don't want to tell anyone else.
But the cops just took your picture.
I know.
You think whoever saw you told the cops?
Probably.
Talk to your lawyer.
LAW OFFICES
DeRita and Associates • 18th FLOOR
Fine and Associates • 7th FLOOR
Howard, Howard & Howard • 15th FLOOR
Waverly & Associates • 9th FLOOR
Is Mr. Waverly in?
Waverly & Associate
Jason Waverly
If they took your picture, they know something. Tell me again what happened, Tru.

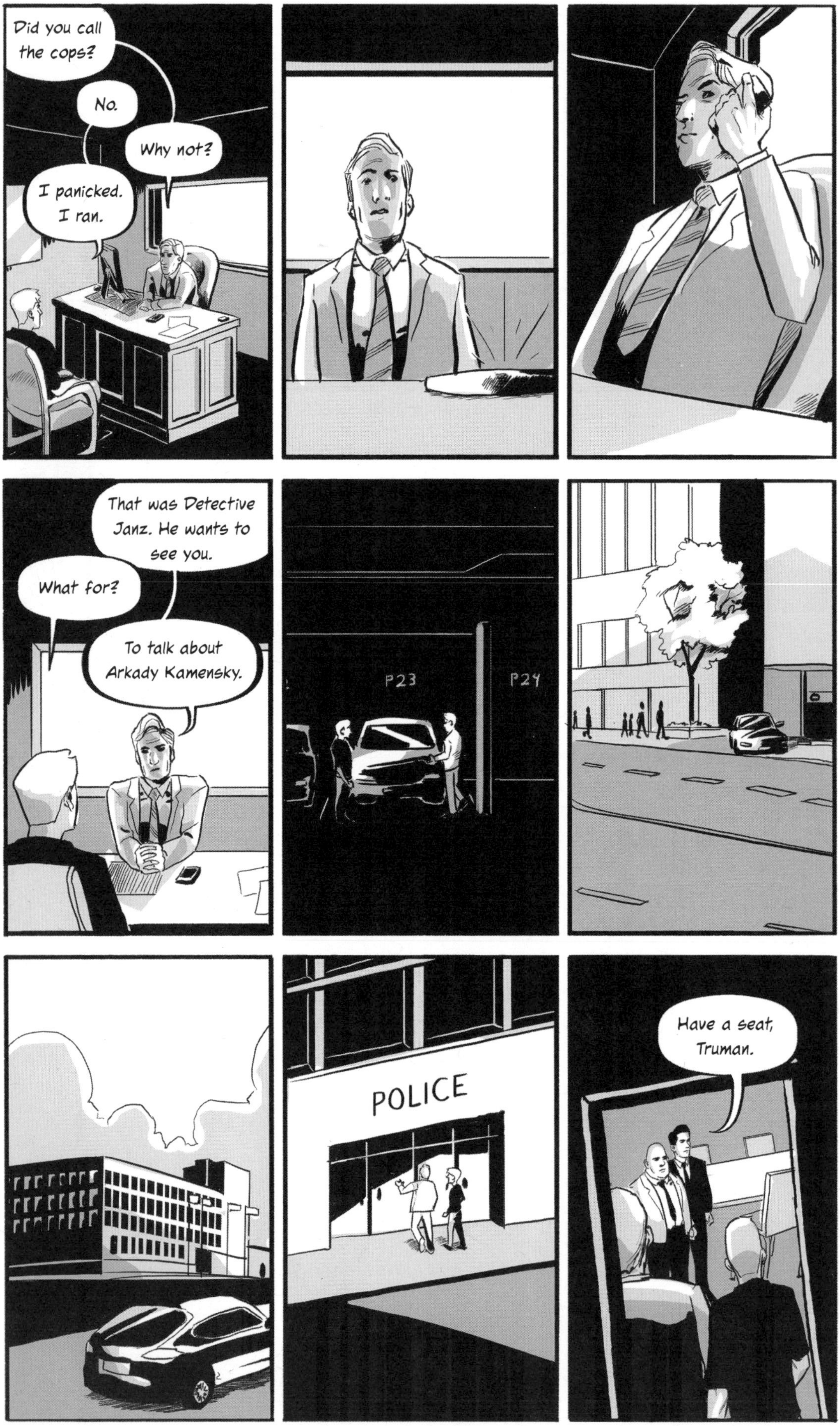
Did you call the cops?
No.
Why not?
I panicked. I ran.
That was Detective Janz. He wants to see you.
What for?
To talk about Arkady Kamensky.
P23
P24
POLICE
Have a seat, Truman.

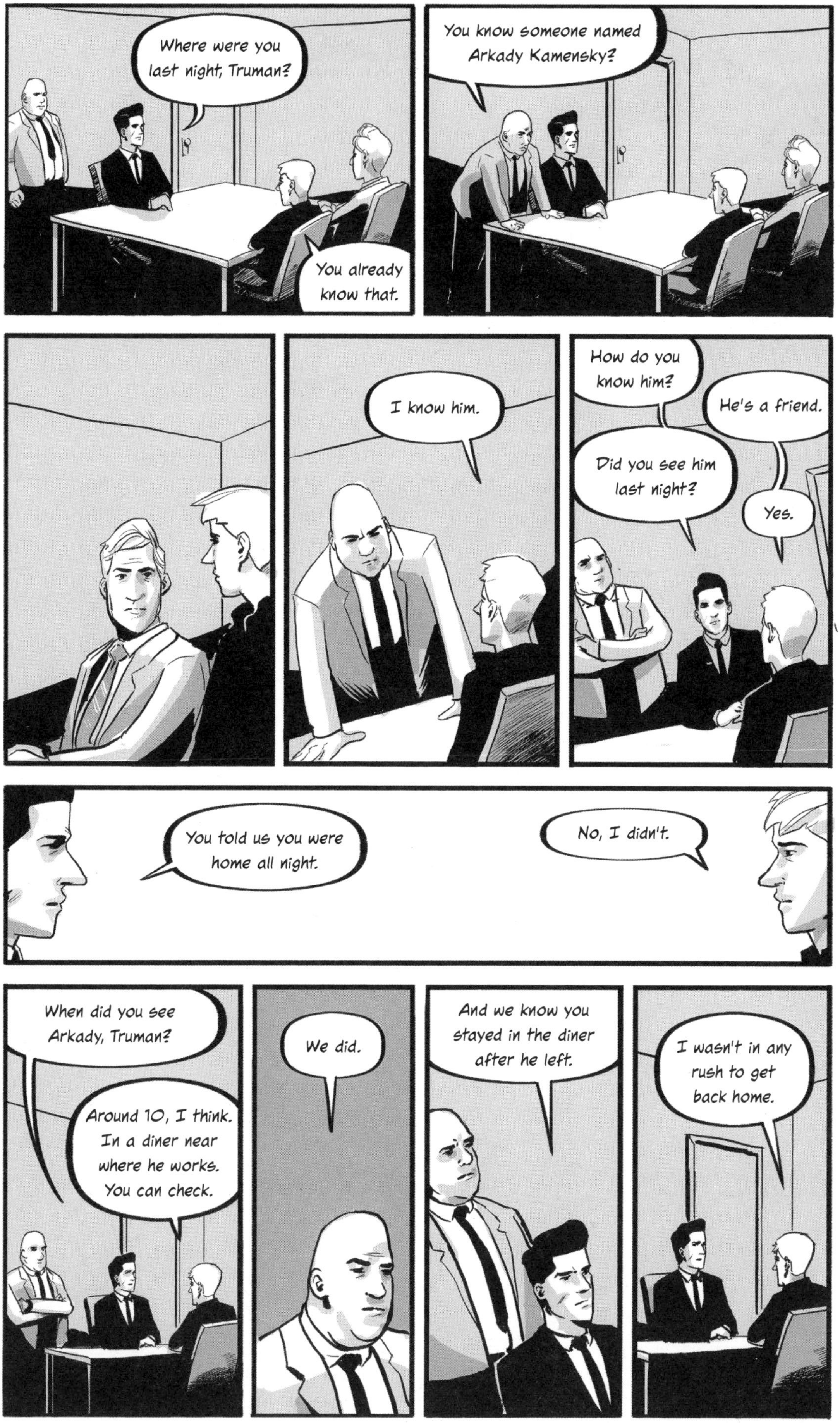
Where were you last night, Truman?
You already know that.
You know someone named Arkady Kamensky?
I know him.
How do you know him?
He's a friend.
Did you see him last night?
Yes.
You told us you were home all night.
No, I didn't.
When did you see Arkady, Truman?
Around 10, I think. In a diner near where he works. You can check.
We did.
And we know you stayed in the diner after he left.
I wasn't in any rush to get back home.

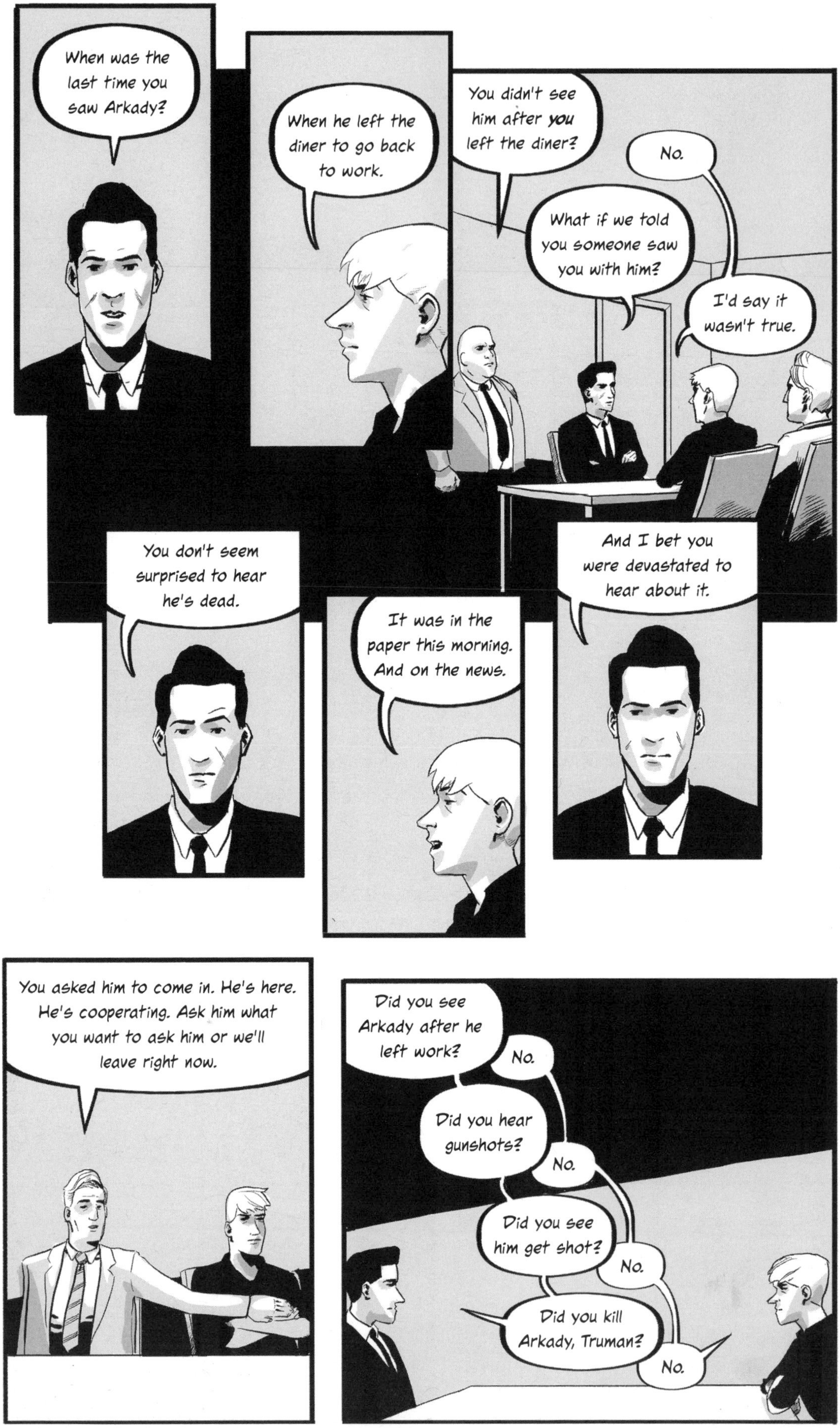
When was the last time you saw Arkady?
When he left the diner to go back to work.
You didn't see him after **you** left the diner?
No.
What if we told you someone saw you with him?
I'd say it wasn't true.
You don't seem surprised to hear he's dead.
It was in the paper this morning. And on the news.
And I bet you were devastated to hear about it.
You asked him to come in. He's here. He's cooperating. Ask him what you want to ask him or we'll leave right now.
Did you see Arkady after he left work?
No.
Did you hear gunshots?
No.
Did you see him get shot?
No.
Did you kill Arkady, Truman?
No.

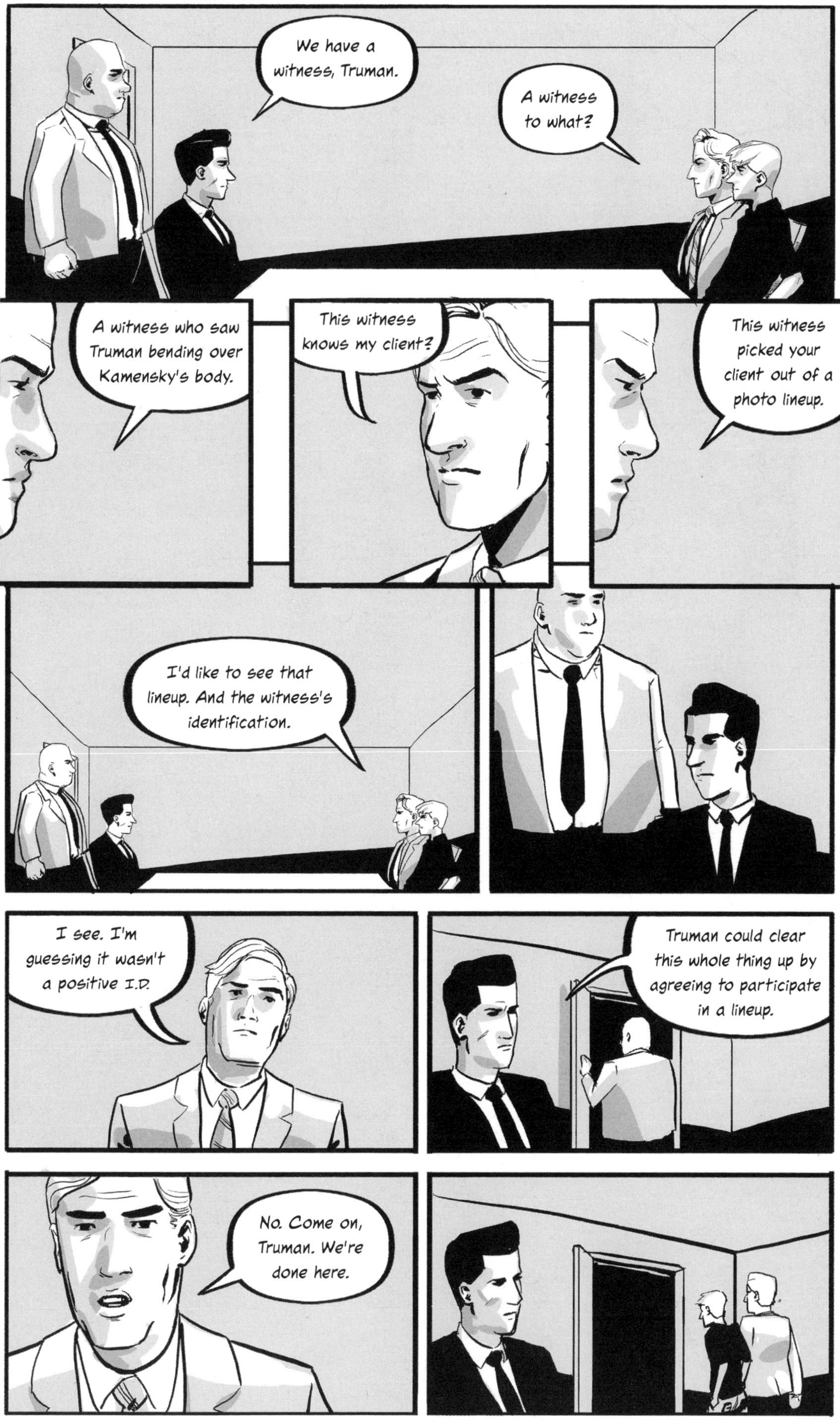
We have a witness, Truman.
A witness to what?
A witness who saw Truman bending over Kamensky's body.
This witness knows my client?
This witness picked your client out of a photo lineup.
I'd like to see that lineup. And the witness's identification.
I see. I'm guessing it wasn't a positive I.D.
Truman could clear this whole thing up by agreeing to participate in a lineup.
No. Come on, Truman. We're done here.

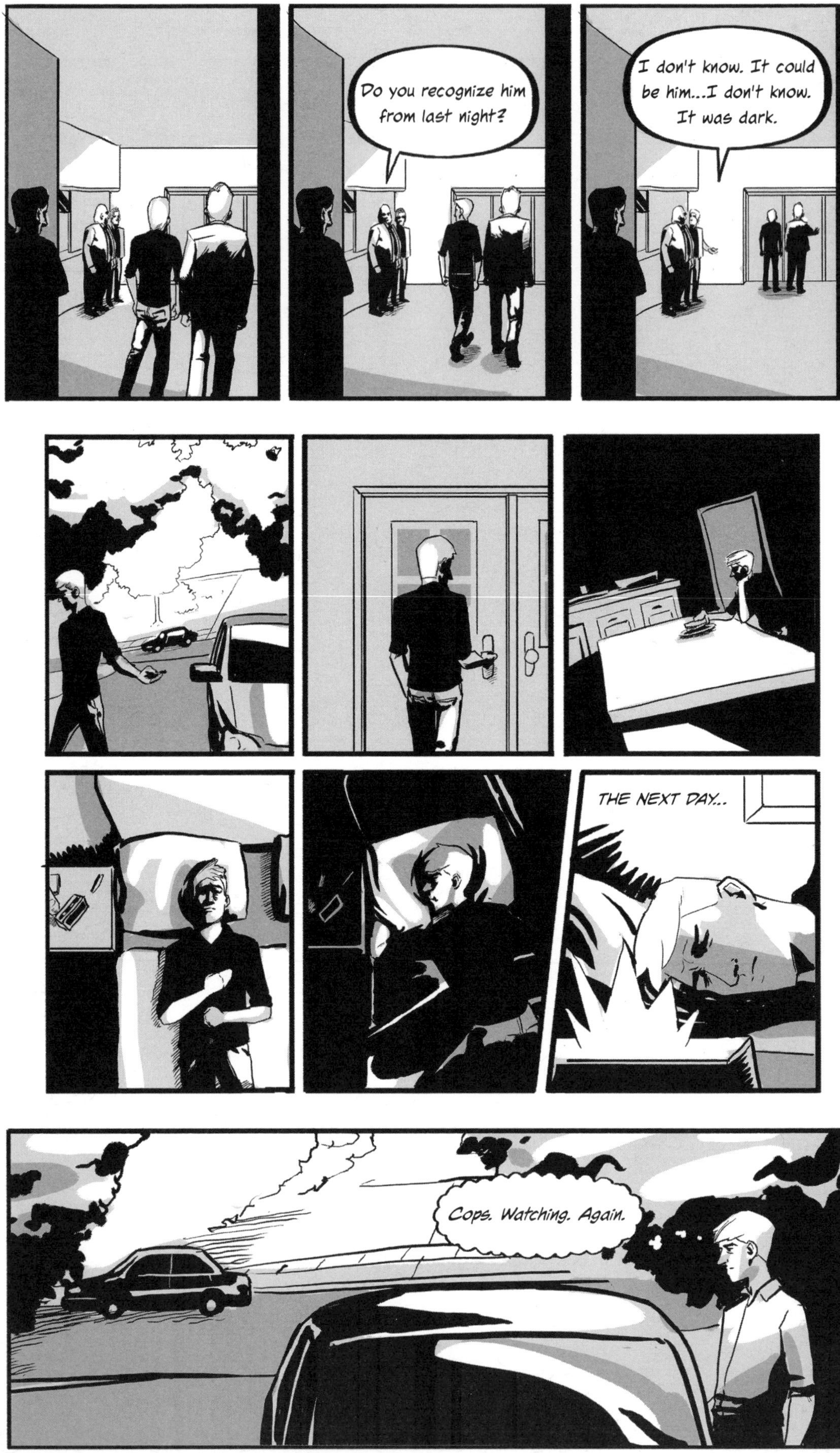
Do you recognize him from last night?
I don't know. It could be him...I don't know. It was dark.
THE NEXT DAY...
Cops. Watching. Again.

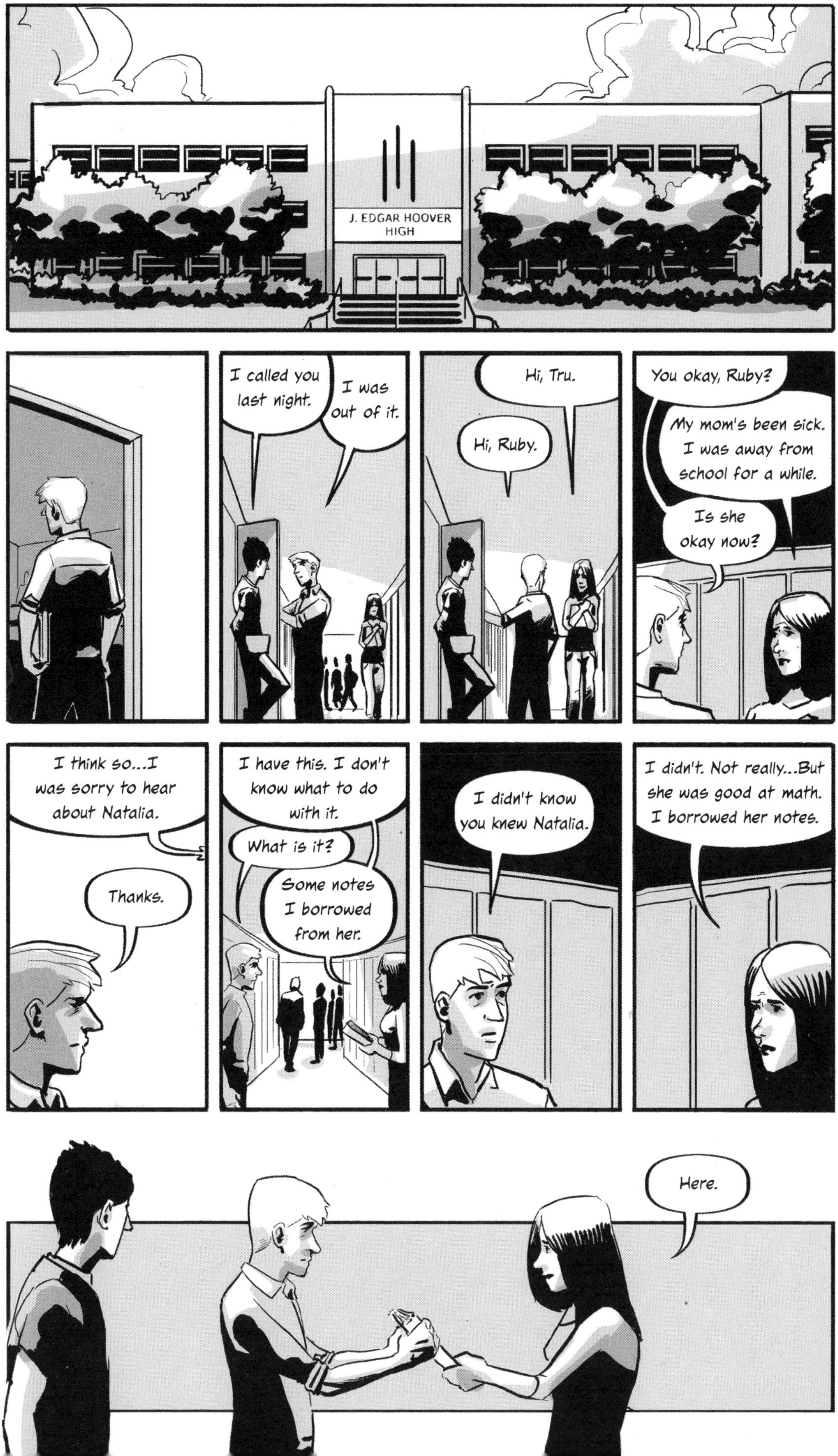
J. EDGAR HOOVER HIGH
I called you last night.
I was out of it.
Hi, Tru.
Hi, Ruby.
You okay, Ruby?
My mom's been sick. I was away from school for a while.
Is she okay now?
I think so...I was sorry to hear about Natalia.
Thanks.
I have this. I don't know what to do with it.
What is it?
Some notes I borrowed from her.
I didn't know you knew Natalia.
I didn't. Not really...But she was good at math. I borrowed her notes.
Here.

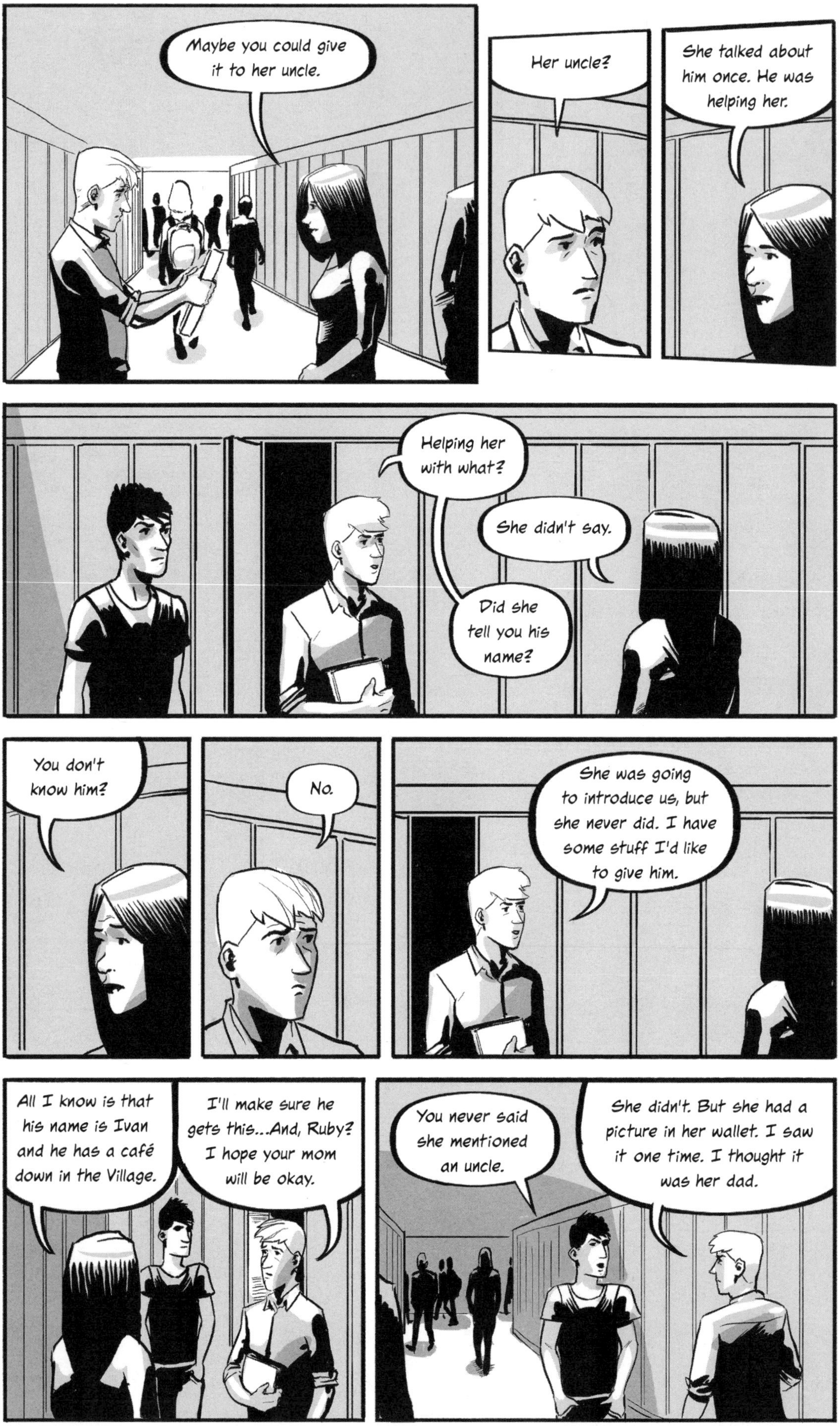
Maybe you could give it to her uncle.
Her uncle?
She talked about him once. He was helping her.
Helping her with what?
She didn't say.
Did she tell you his name?
You don't know him?
No.
She was going to introduce us, but she never did. I have some stuff I'd like to give him.
All I know is that his name is Ivan and he has a café down in the Village.
I'll make sure he gets this...And, Ruby? I hope your mom will be okay.
You never said she mentioned an uncle.
She didn't. But she had a picture in her wallet. I saw it one time. I thought it was her dad.

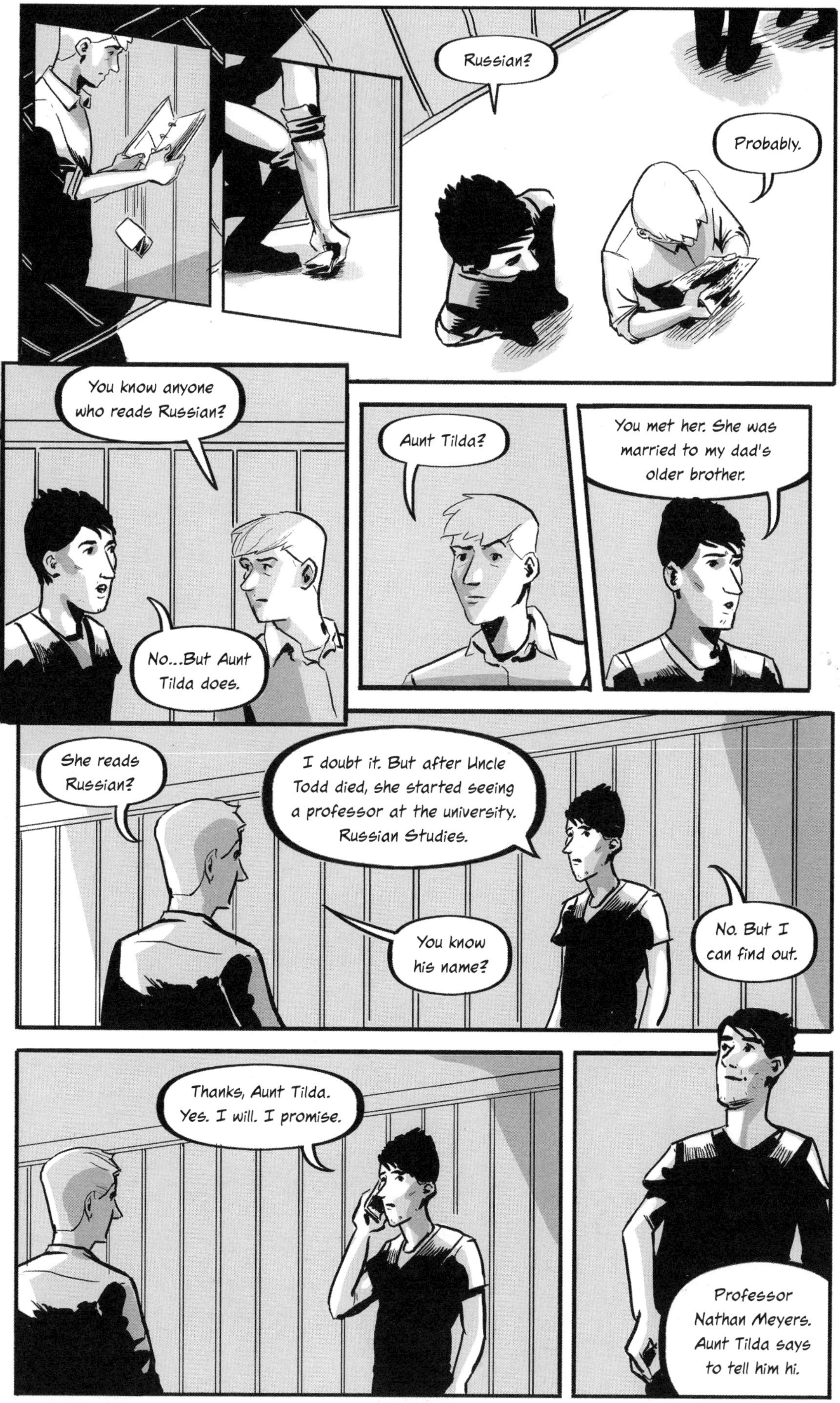
Russian?
Probably.
You know anyone who reads Russian?
No...But Aunt Tilda does.
Aunt Tilda?
You met her. She was married to my dad's older brother.
She reads Russian?
I doubt it. But after Uncle Todd died, she started seeing a professor at the university. Russian Studies.
You know his name?
No. But I can find out.
Thanks, Aunt Tilda. Yes. I will. I promise.
Professor Nathan Meyers. Aunt Tilda says to tell him hi.

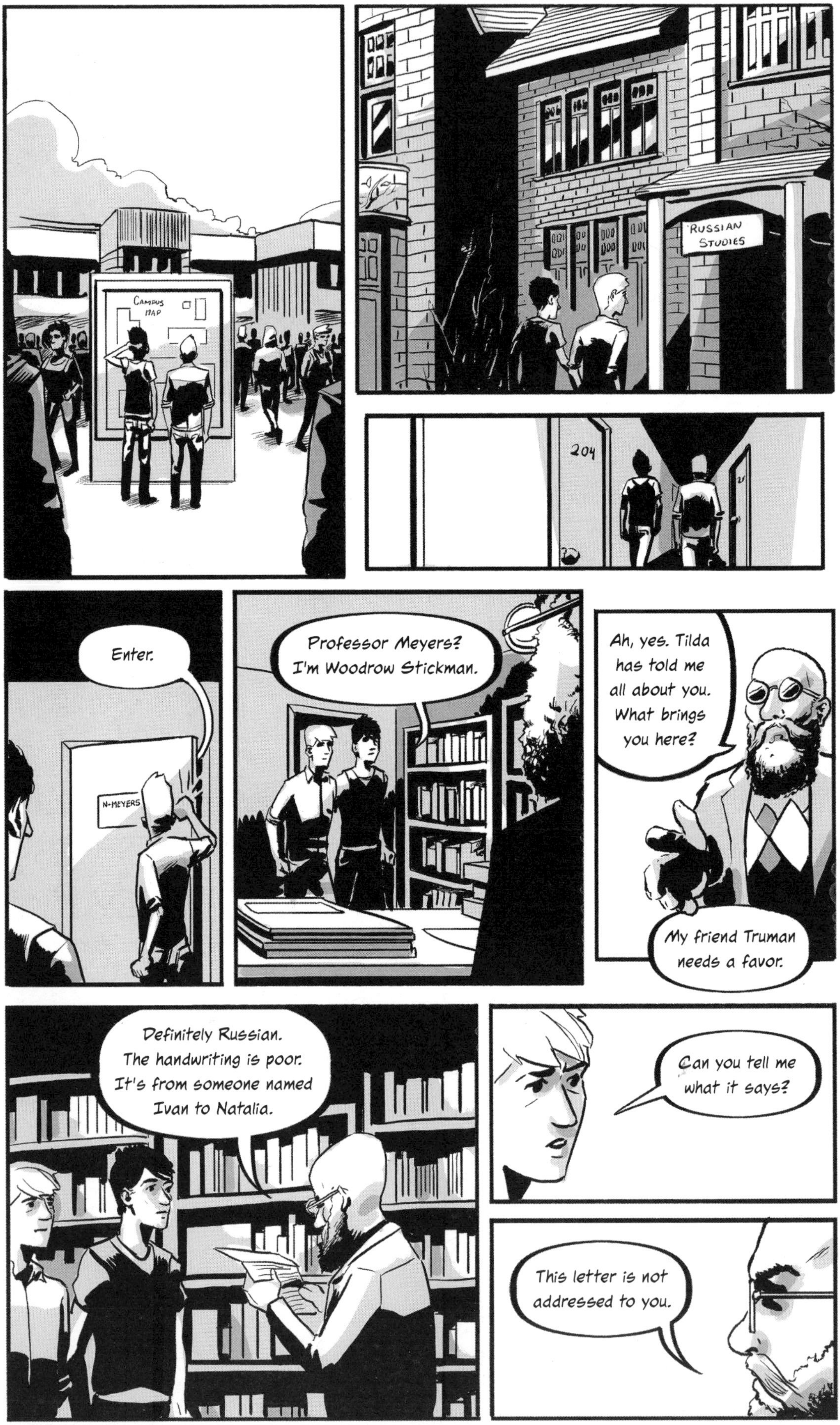

Campus map
Russian Studies
204
N-Meyers
Enter.
Professor Meyers? I'm Woodrow Stickman.
Ah, yes. Tilda has told me all about you. What brings you here?
My friend Truman needs a favor.
Definitely Russian. The handwriting is poor. It's from someone named Ivan to Natalia.
Can you tell me what it says?
This letter is not addressed to you.

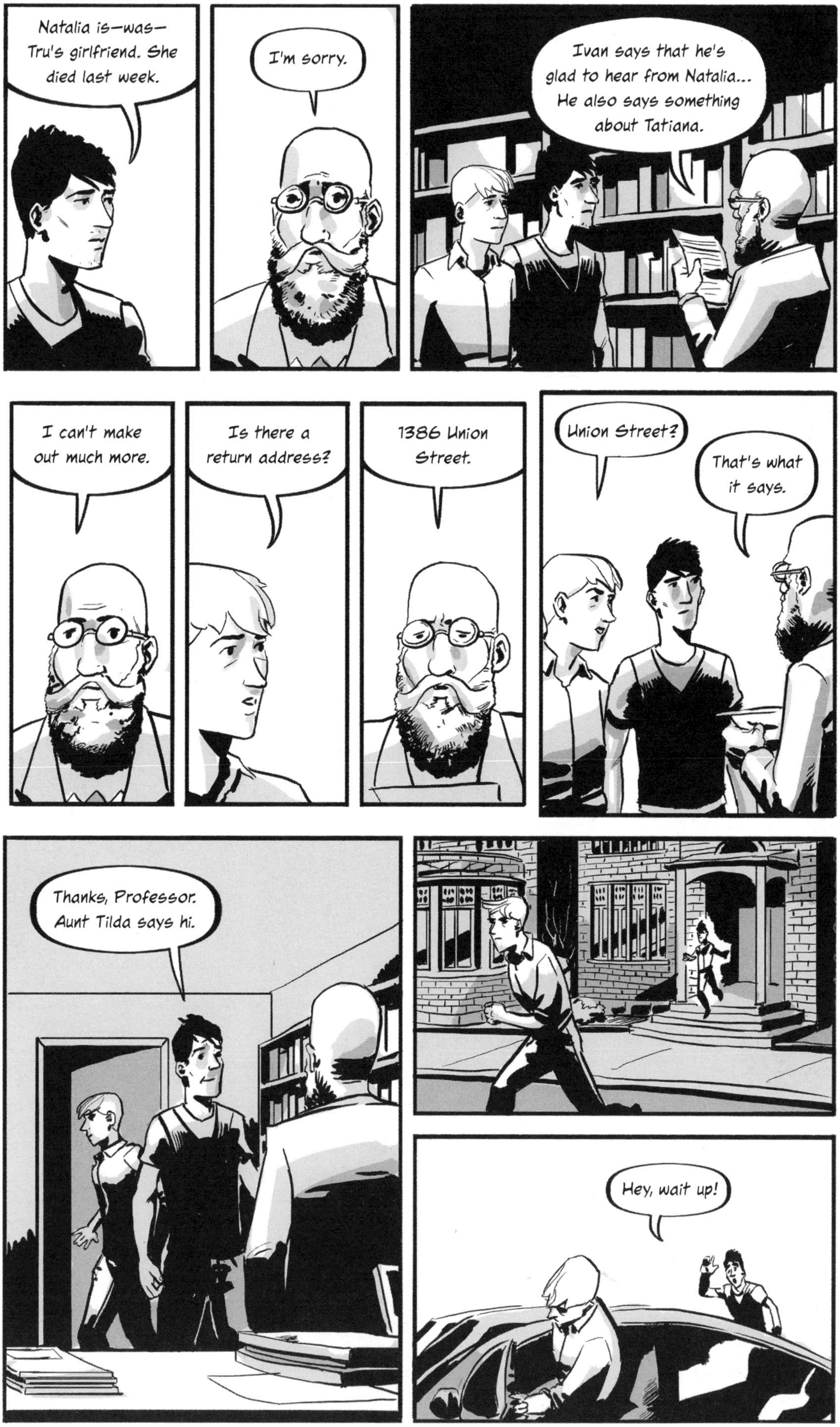
Natalia is—was—Tru's girlfriend. She died last week.
I'm sorry.
Ivan says that he's glad to hear from Natalia... He also says something about Tatiana.
I can't make out much more.
Is there a return address?
1386 Union Street.
Union Street?
That's what it says.
Thanks, Professor. Aunt Tilda says hi.
Hey, wait up!

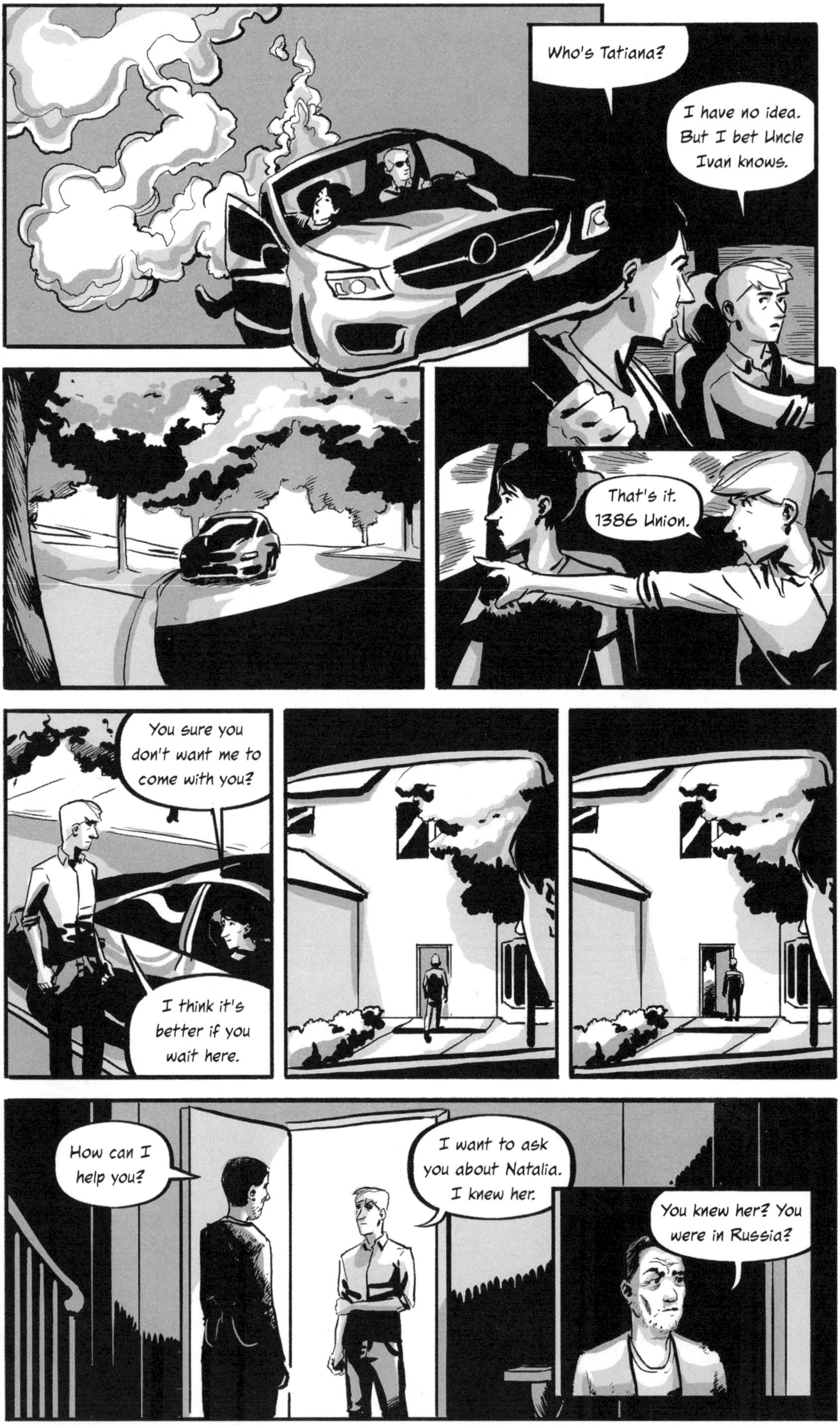
Who's Tatiana?
I have no idea. But I bet Uncle Ivan knows.
That's it. 1386 Union.
You sure you don't want me to come with you?
I think it's better if you wait here.
How can I help you?
I want to ask you about Natalia. I knew her.
You knew her? You were in Russia?

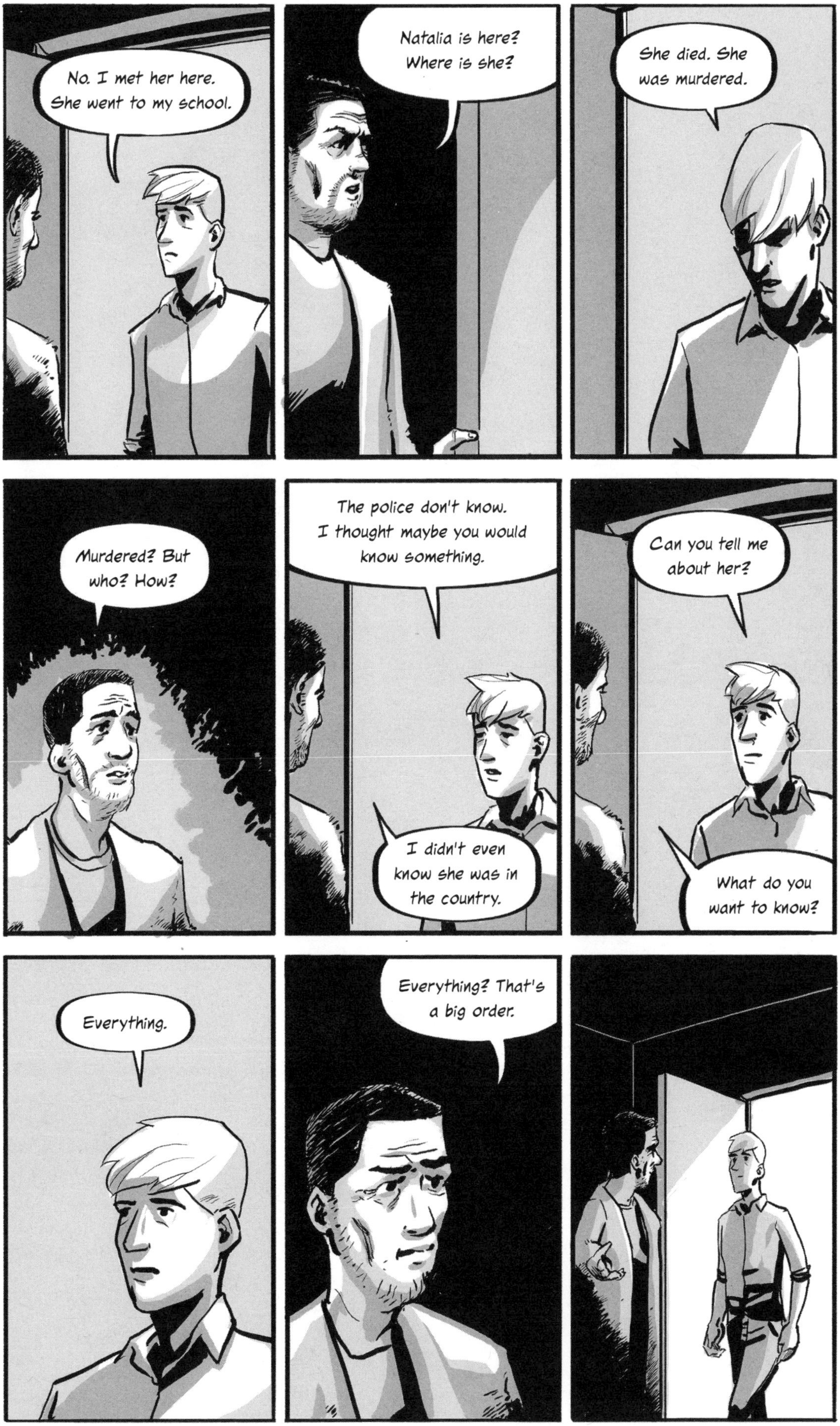
No. I met her here.
She went to my school.
Natalia is here?
Where is she?
She died. She
was murdered.
Murdered? But
who? How?
The police don't know.
I thought maybe you would
know something.
I didn't even
know she was in
the country.
Can you tell me
about her?
What do you
want to know?
Everything.
Everything? That's
a big order.

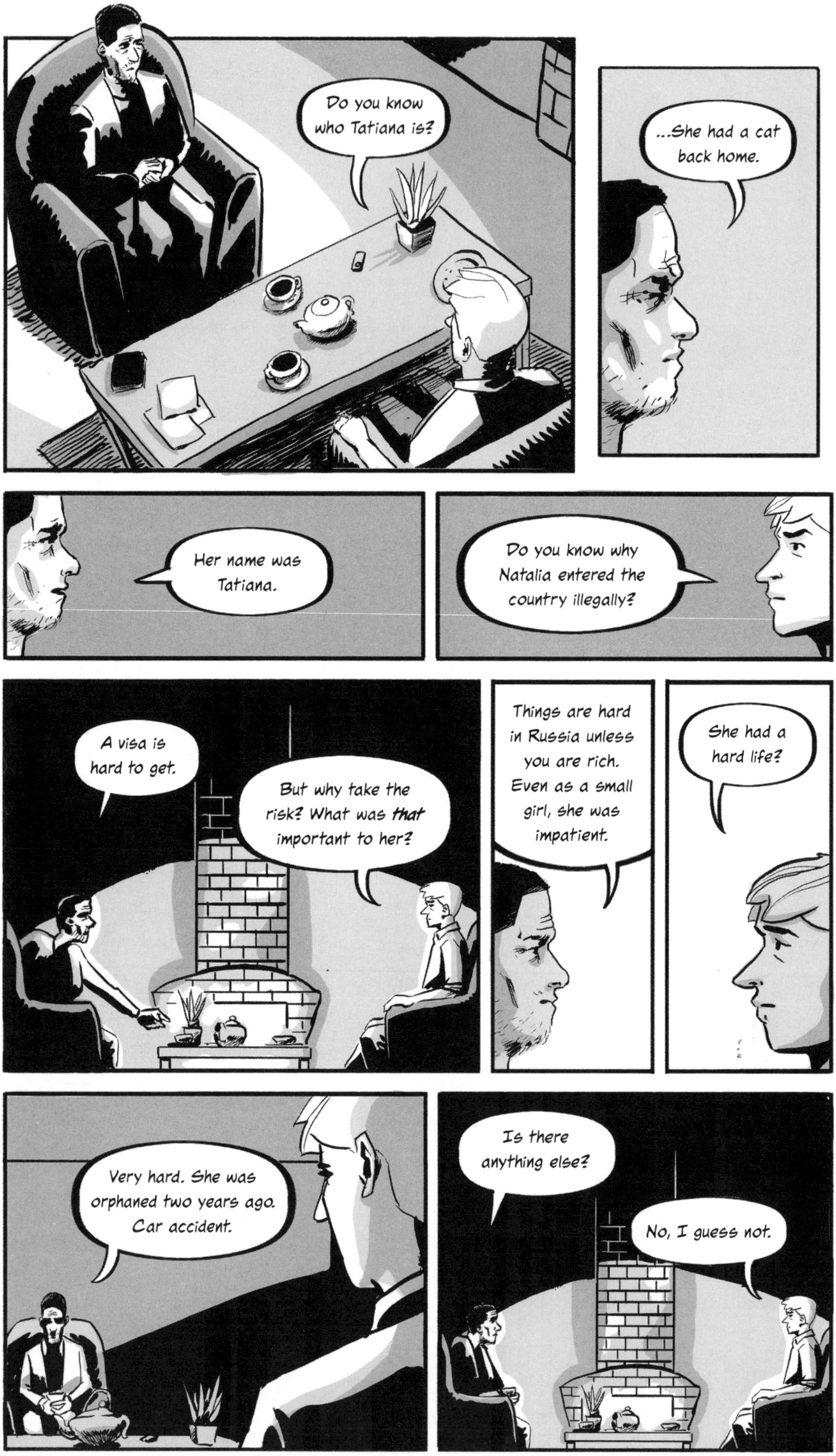
Do you know who Tatiana is?
...She had a cat back home.
Her name was Tatiana.
Do you know why Natalia entered the country illegally?
A visa is hard to get.
But why take the risk? What was *that* important to her?
Things are hard in Russia unless you are rich. Even as a small girl, she was impatient.
She had a hard life?
Very hard. She was orphaned two years ago. Car accident.
Is there anything else?
No, I guess not.

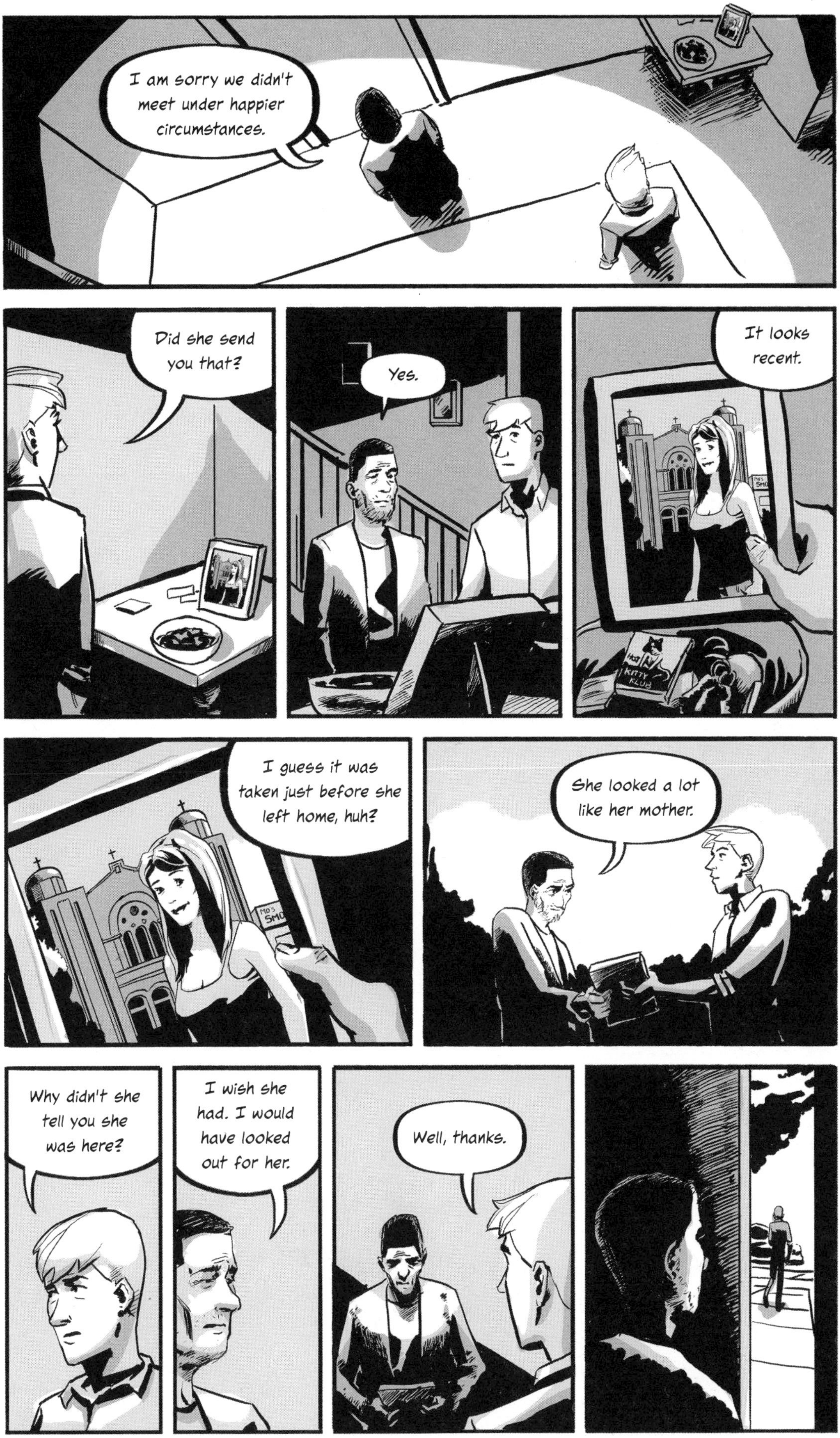
I am sorry we didn't meet under happier circumstances.
Did she send you that?
Yes.
It looks recent.
KITTY KLUB
I guess it was taken just before she left home, huh?
She looked a lot like her mother.
Why didn't she tell you she was here?
I wish she had. I would have looked out for her.
Well, thanks.

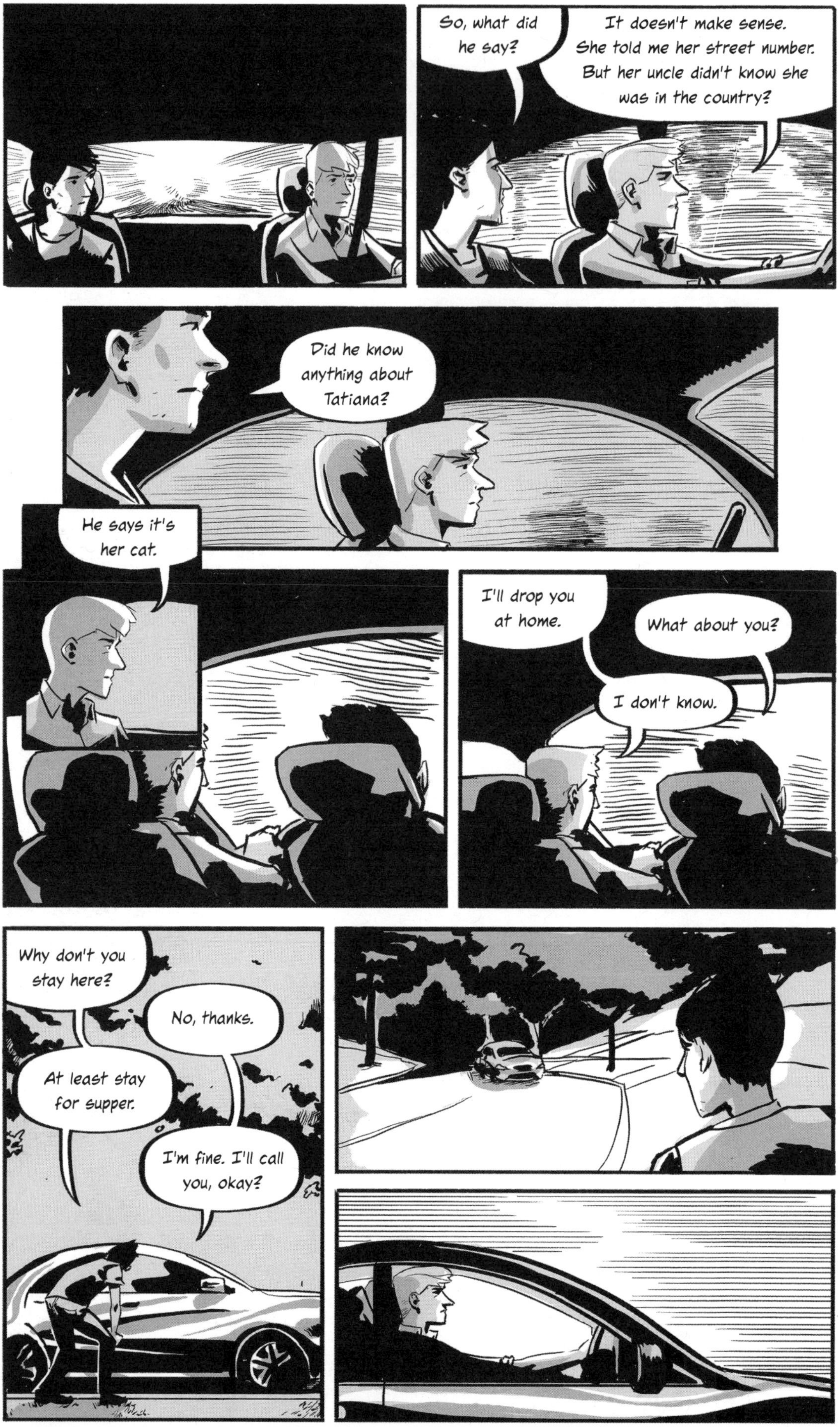
So, what did he say?
It doesn't make sense. She told me her street number. But her uncle didn't know she was in the country?
Did he know anything about Tatiana?
He says it's her cat.
I'll drop you at home.
What about you?
I don't know.
Why don't you stay here?
No, thanks.
At least stay for supper.
I'm fine. I'll call you, okay?

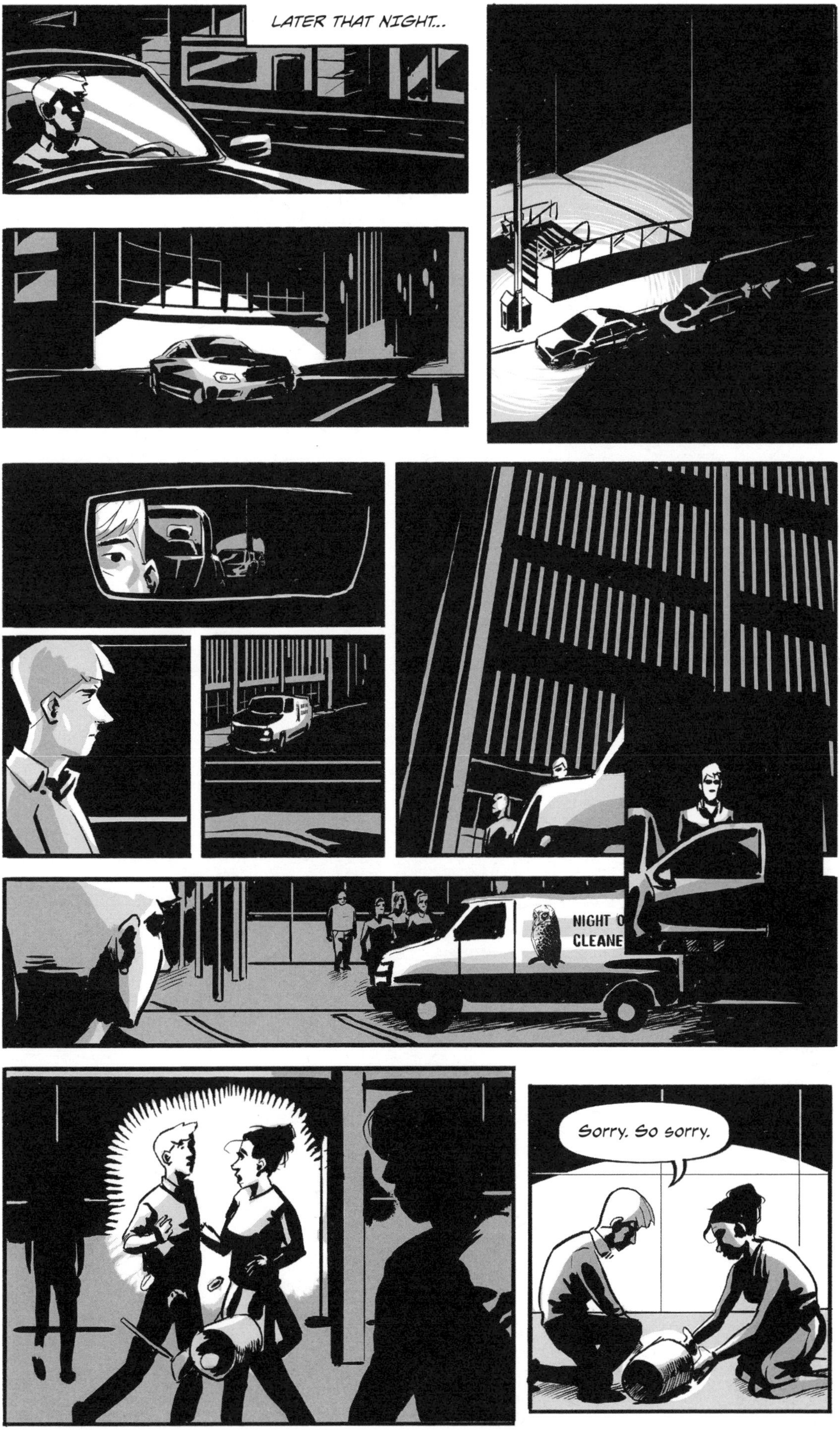
LATER THAT NIGHT...
NIGHT O
CLEANE
Sorry. So sorry.

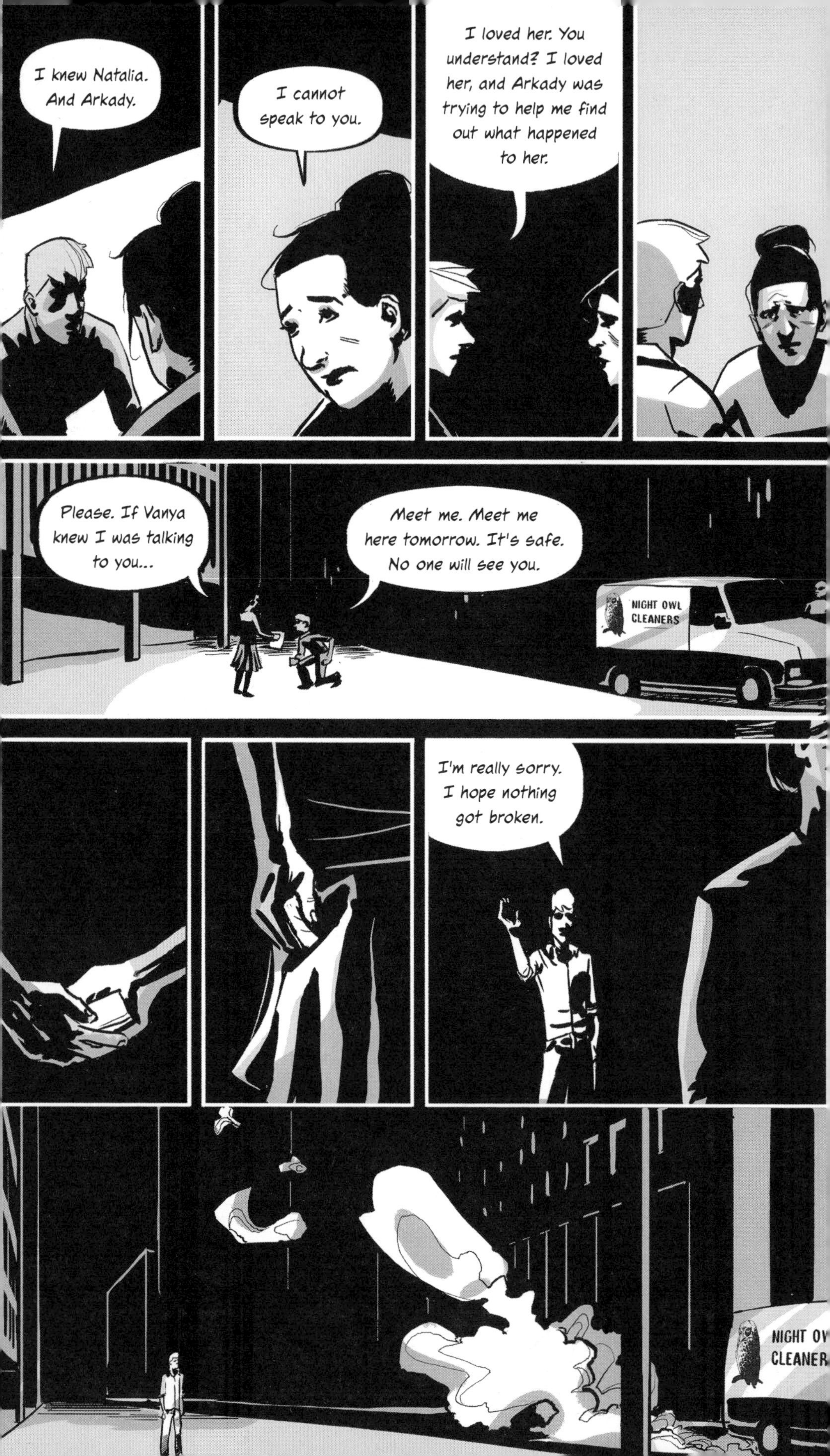
I knew Natalia. And Arkady.
I cannot speak to you.
I loved her. You understand? I loved her, and Arkady was trying to help me find out what happened to her.
Please. If Vanya knew I was talking to you...
Meet me. Meet me here tomorrow. It's safe. No one will see you.
NIGHT OWL CLEANERS
I'm really sorry. I hope nothing got broken.
NIGHT OW
CLEANER

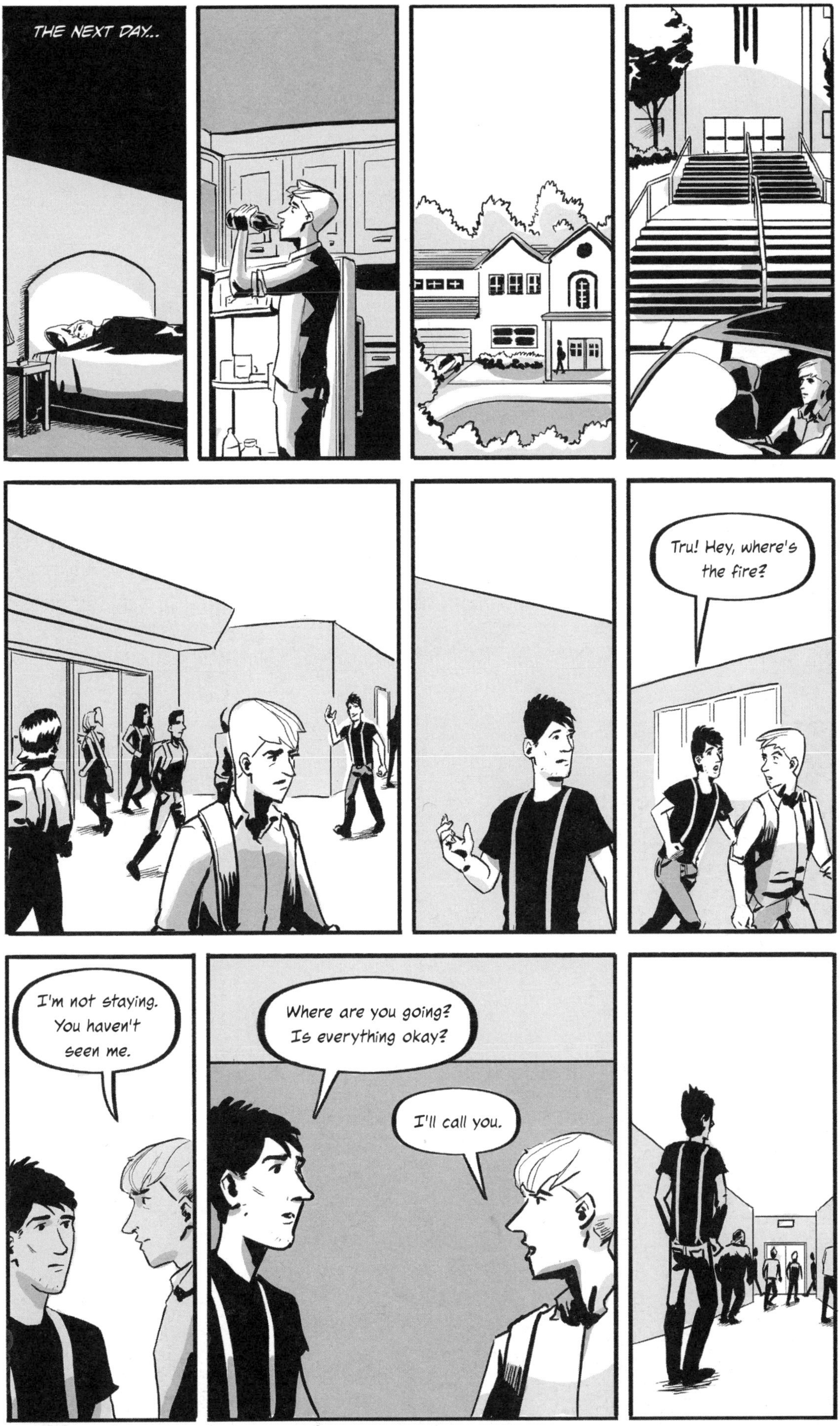
THE NEXT DAY...
Tru! Hey, where's the fire?
I'm not staying. You haven't seen me.
Where are you going? Is everything okay?
I'll call you.

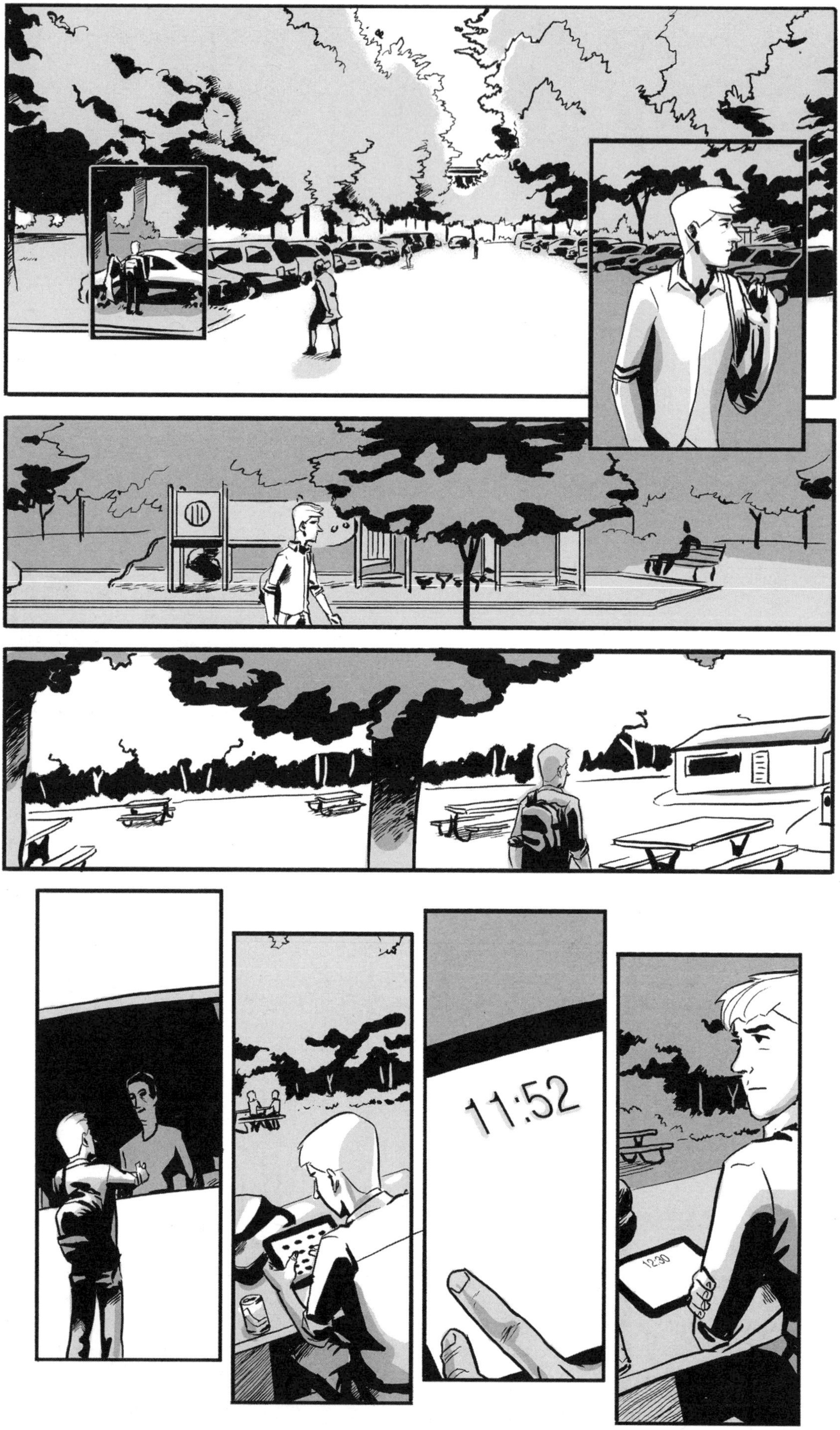
11:52
12:30

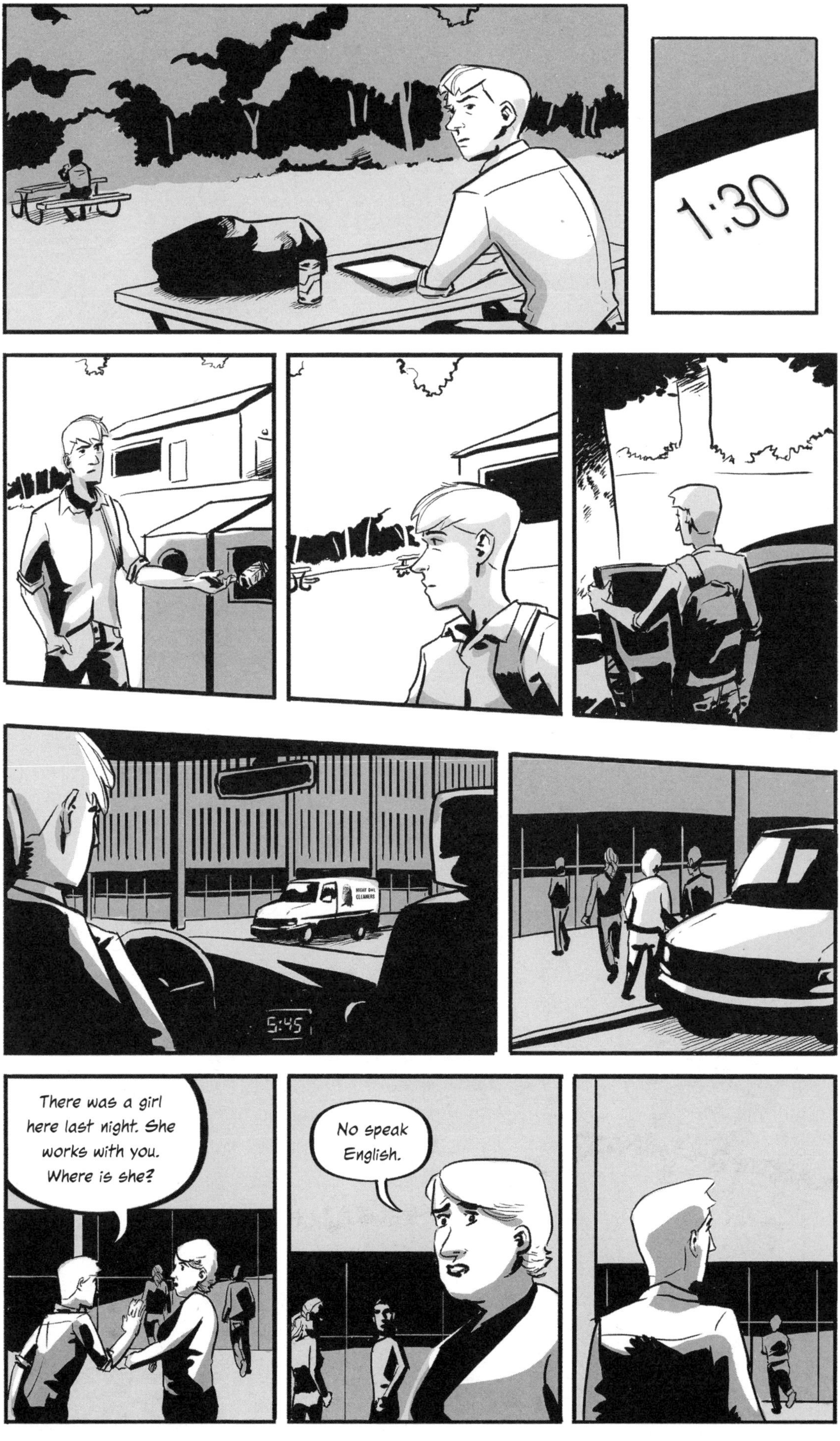
1:30
NIGHT OWL CLEANERS
5:45
There was a girl here last night. She works with you. Where is she?
No speak English.

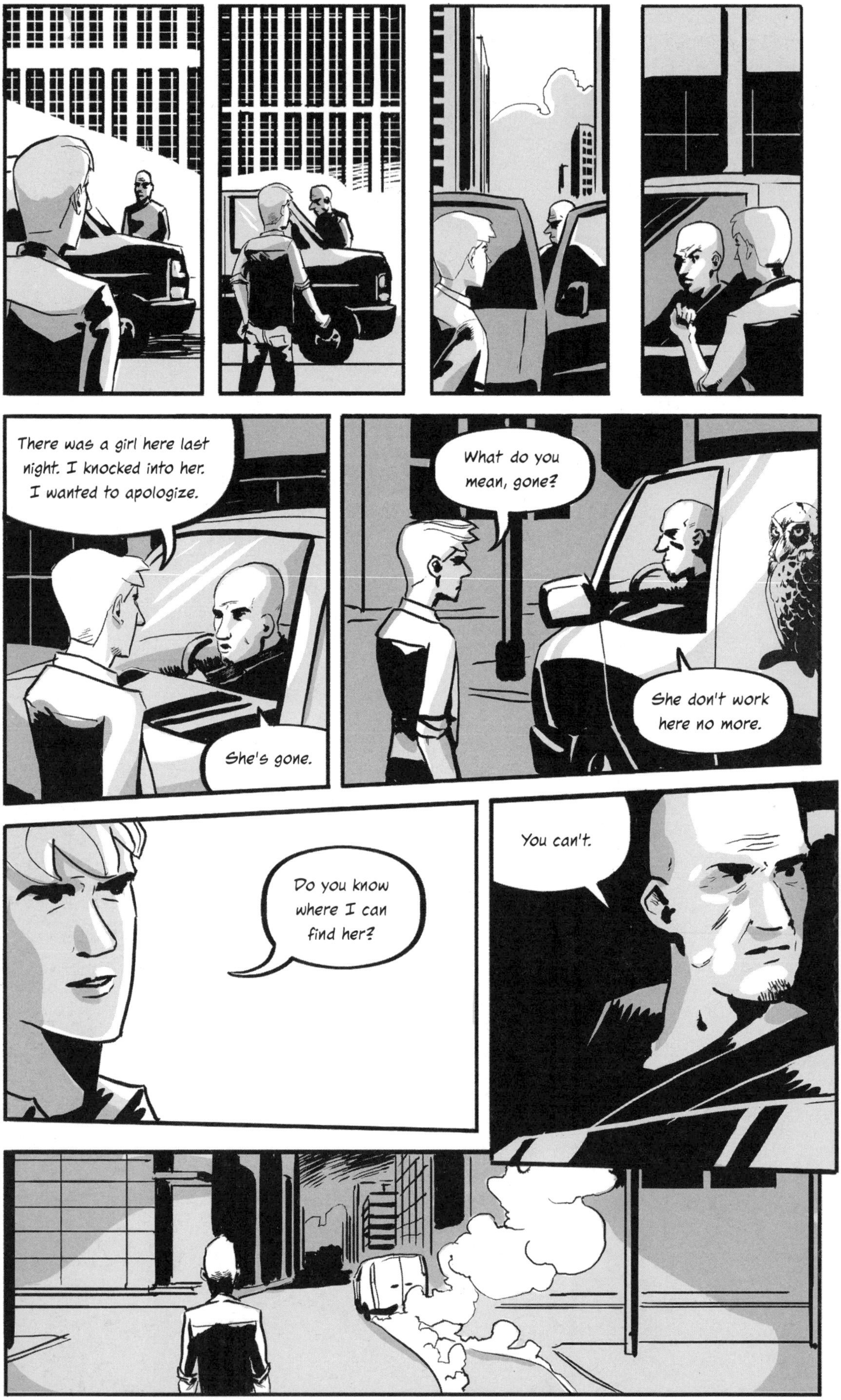

There was a girl here last night. I knocked into her. I wanted to apologize.
She's gone.
What do you mean, gone?
She don't work here no more.
Do you know where I can find her?
You can't.

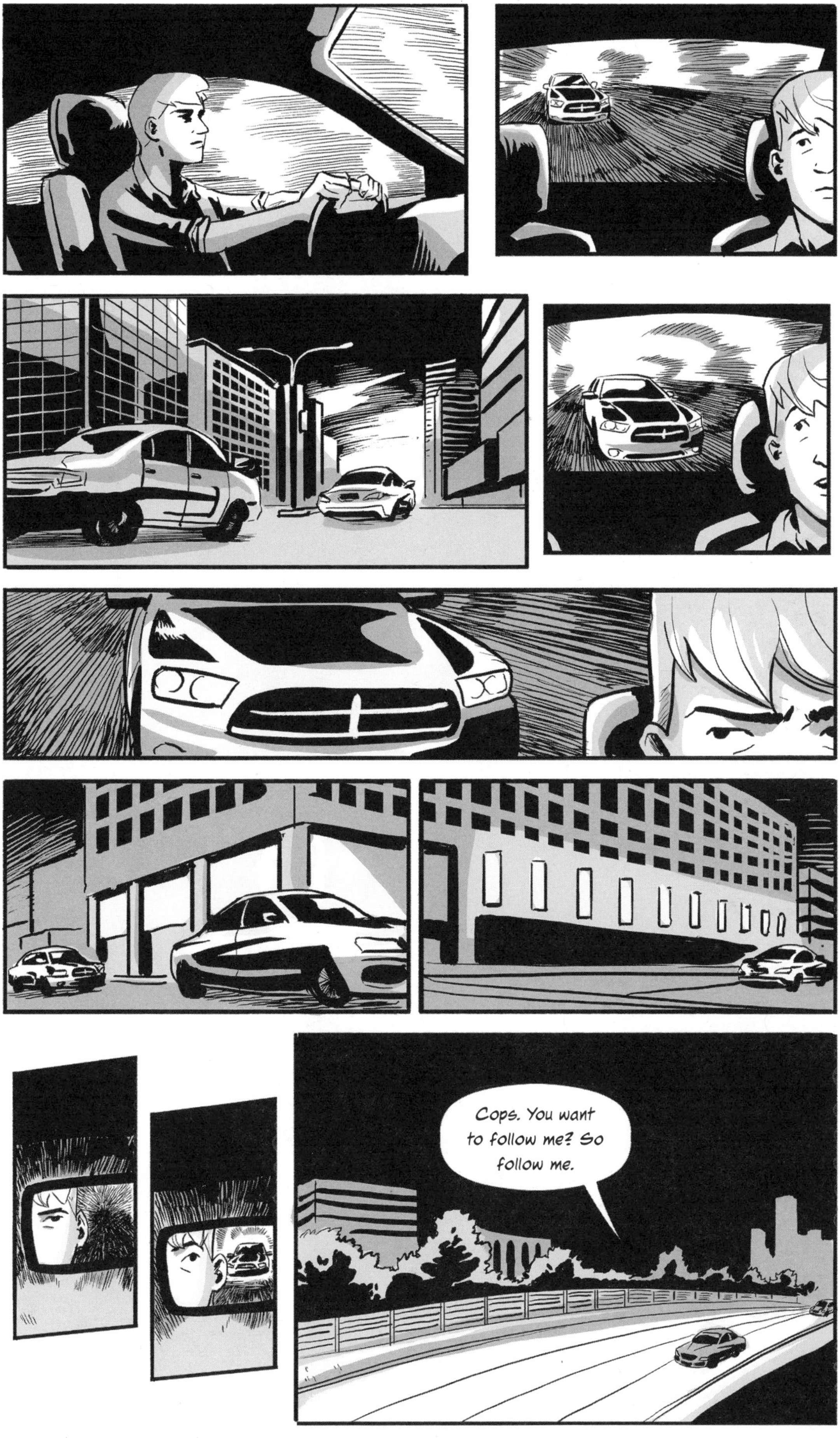
Cops. You want to follow me? So follow me.

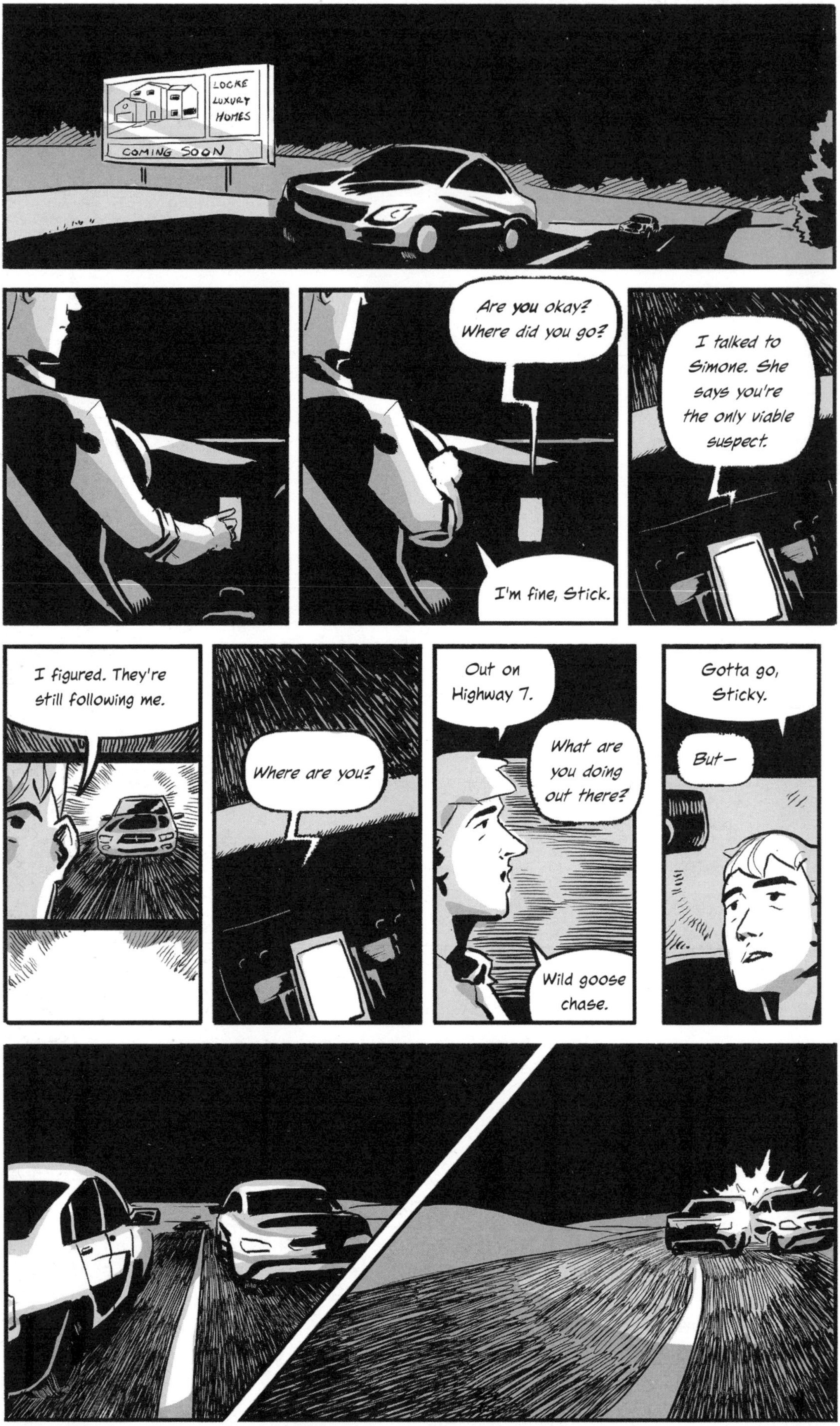
LOCKE
LUXURY
HOMES
COMING SOON
Are you okay? Where did you go?
I'm fine, Stick.
I talked to Simone. She says you're the only viable suspect.
I figured. They're still following me.
Where are you?
Out on Highway 7.
What are you doing out there?
Wild goose chase.
Gotta go, Sticky.
But—

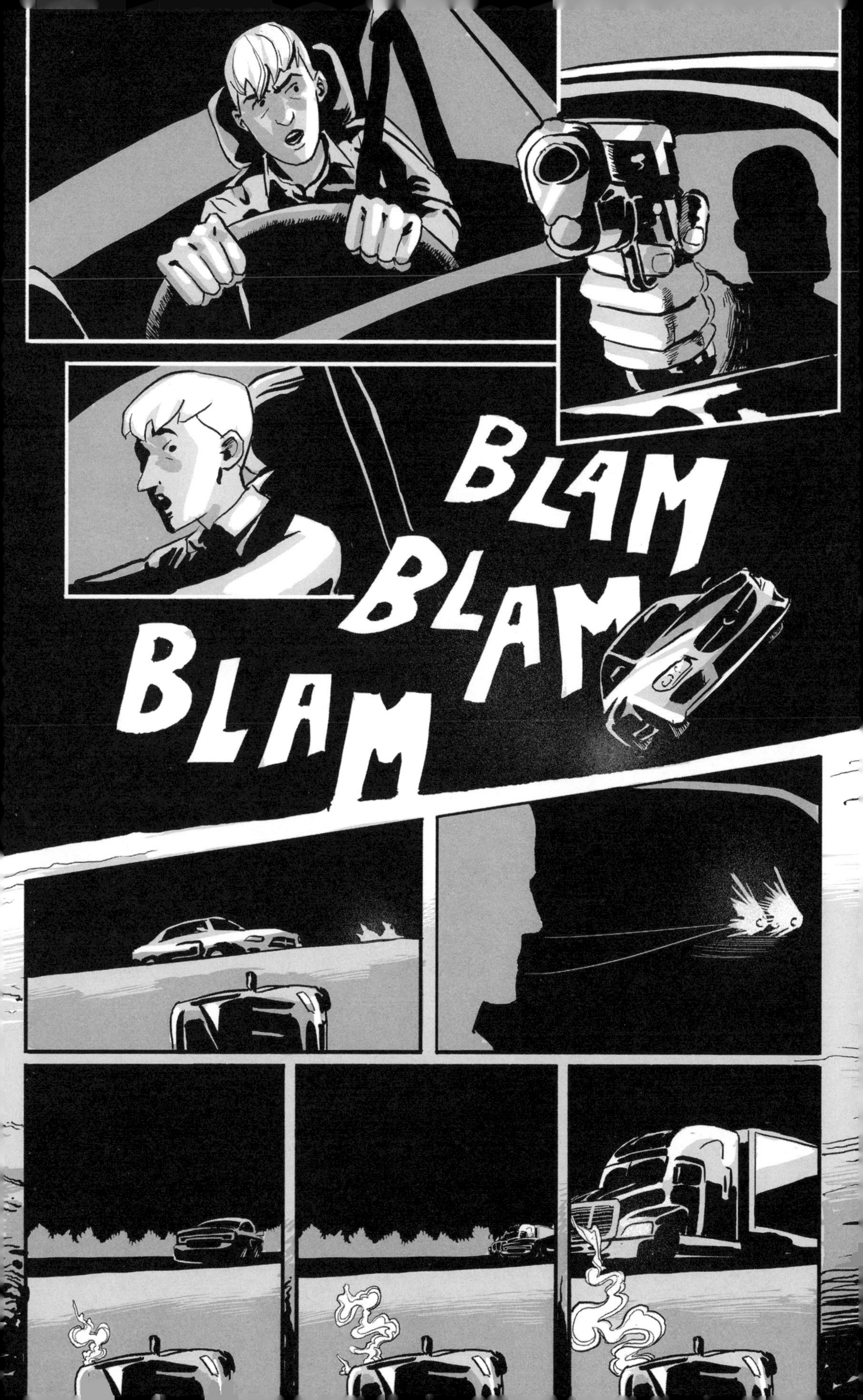
BLAM
BLAM
BLAM

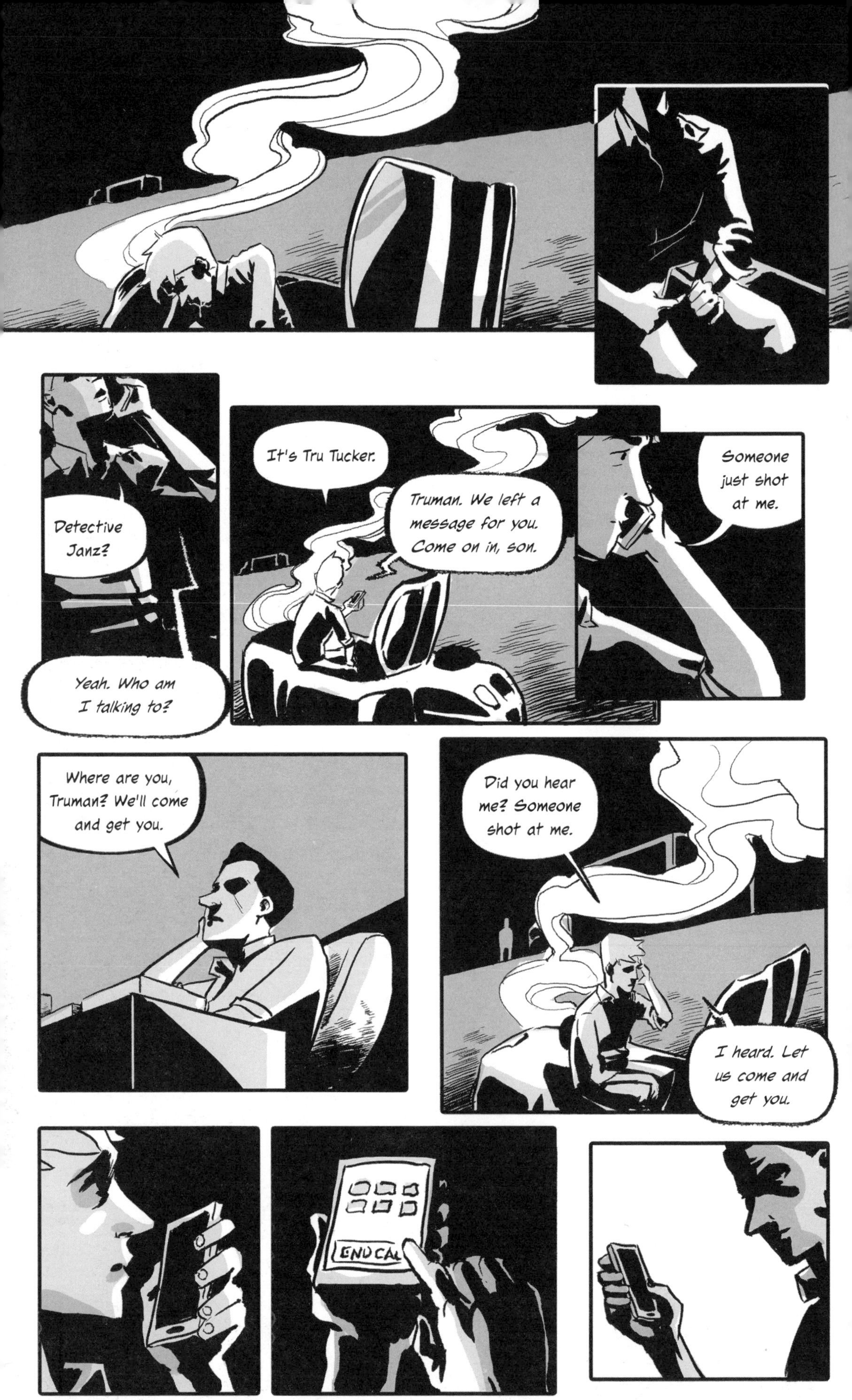
Detective Janz?
Yeah. Who am I talking to?
It's Tru Tucker.
Truman. We left a message for you. Come on in, son.
Someone just shot at me.
Where are you, Truman? We'll come and get you.
Did you hear me? Someone shot at me.
I heard. Let us come and get you.
END CAL

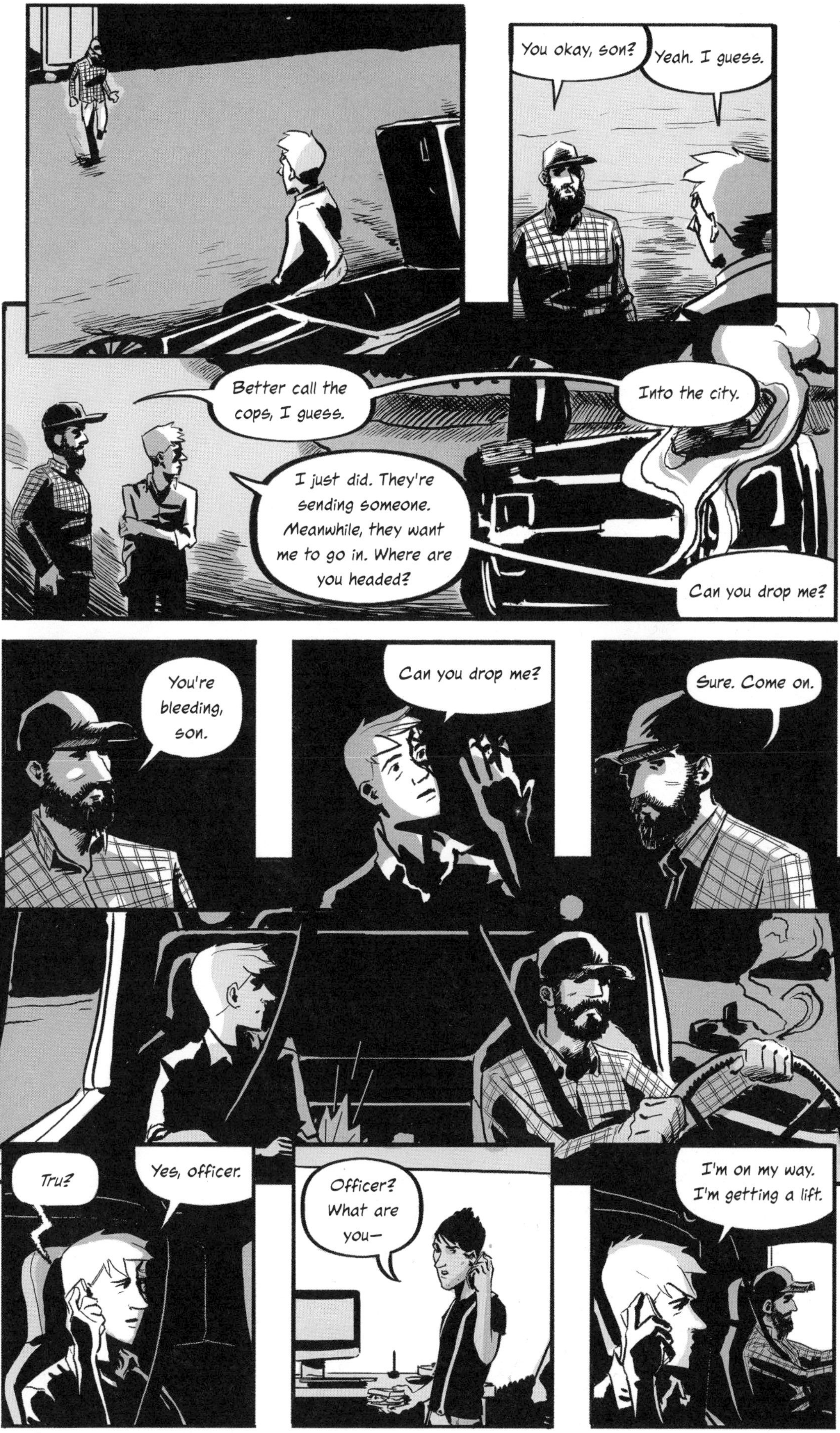
You okay, son?
Yeah. I guess.
Better call the cops, I guess.
I just did. They're sending someone. Meanwhile, they want me to go in. Where are you headed?
Into the city.
Can you drop me?
You're bleeding, son.
Can you drop me?
Sure. Come on.
Tru?
Yes, officer.
Officer? What are you—
I'm on my way. I'm getting a lift.

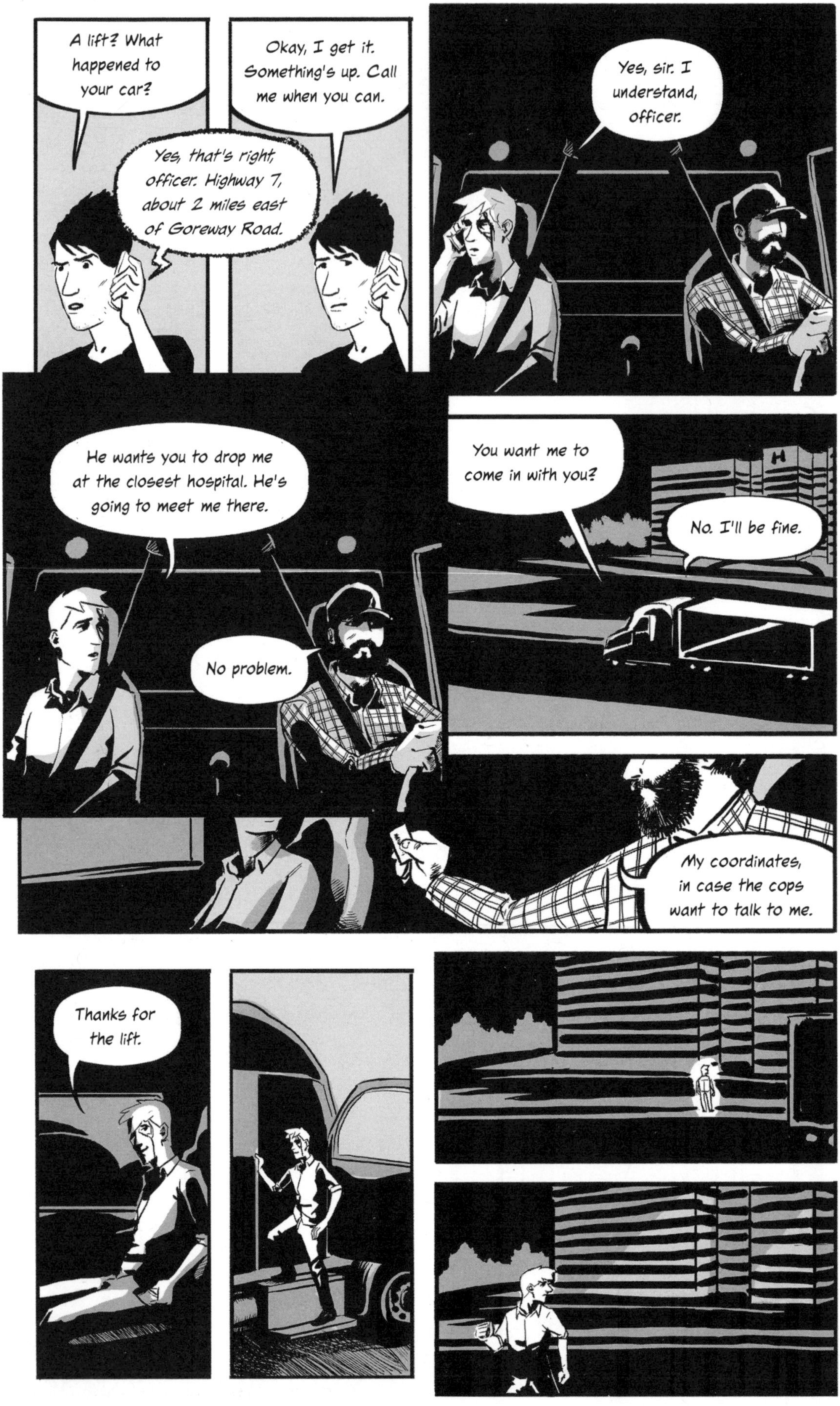
A lift? What happened to your car?
Yes, that's right, officer. Highway 7, about 2 miles east of Goreway Road.
Okay, I get it. Something's up. Call me when you can.
Yes, sir. I understand, officer.
He wants you to drop me at the closest hospital. He's going to meet me there.
No problem.
You want me to come in with you?
No. I'll be fine.
My coordinates, in case the cops want to talk to me.
Thanks for the lift.

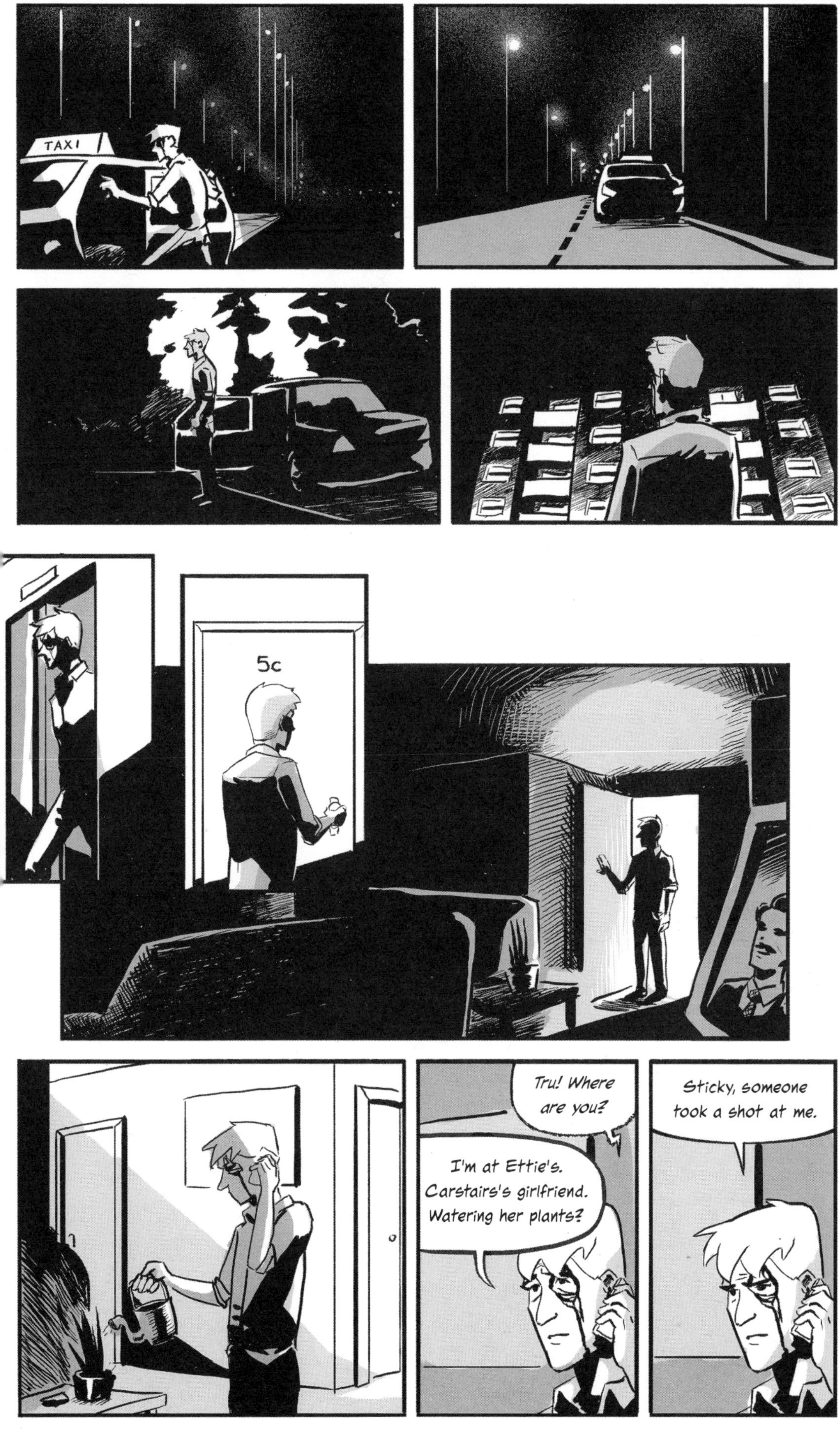
TAXI
5c
Tru! Where are you?
I'm at Ettie's. Carstairs's girlfriend. Watering her plants?
Sticky, someone took a shot at me.

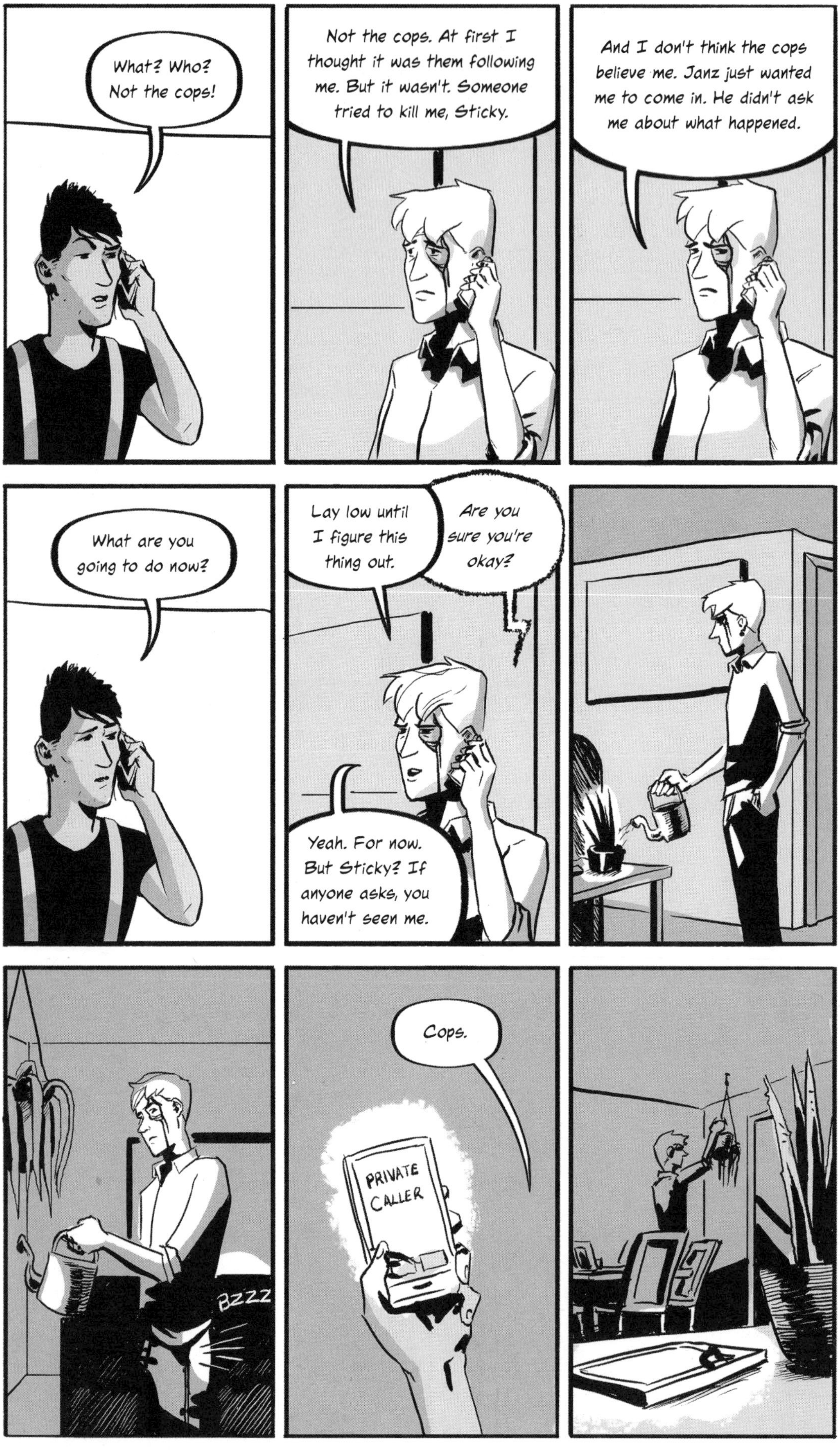
What? Who? Not the cops!
Not the cops. At first I thought it was them following me. But it wasn't. Someone tried to kill me, Sticky.
And I don't think the cops believe me. Janz just wanted me to come in. He didn't ask me about what happened.
What are you going to do now?
Lay low until I figure this thing out.
Are you sure you're okay?
Yeah. For now. But Sticky? If anyone asks, you haven't seen me.
BZZZ
Cops.
PRIVATE CALLER

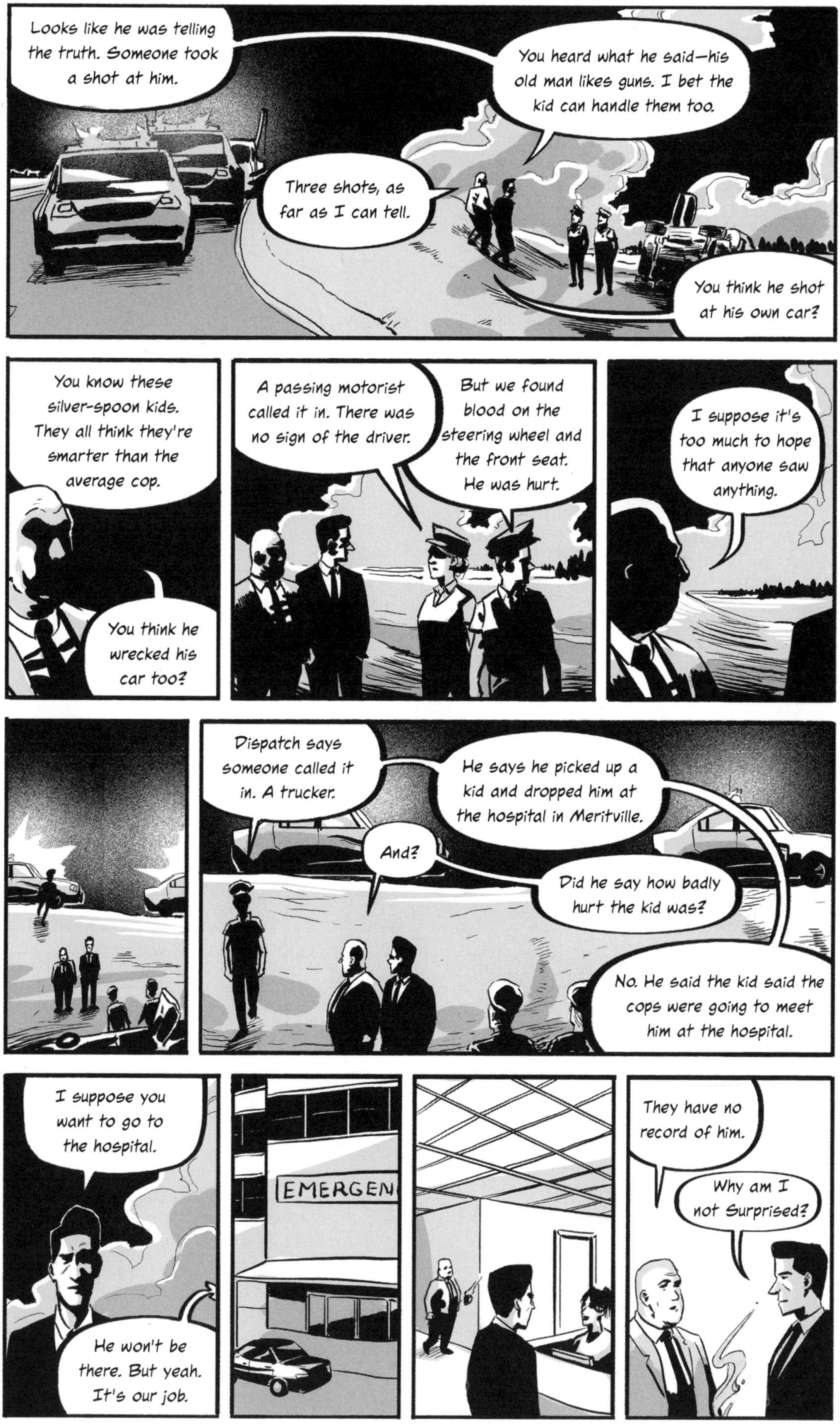
Looks like he was telling the truth. Someone took a shot at him.
You heard what he said—his old man likes guns. I bet the kid can handle them too.
Three shots, as far as I can tell.
You think he shot at his own car?
You know these silver-spoon kids. They all think they're smarter than the average cop.
You think he wrecked his car too?
A passing motorist called it in. There was no sign of the driver.
But we found blood on the steering wheel and the front seat. He was hurt.
I suppose it's too much to hope that anyone saw anything.
Dispatch says someone called it in. A trucker.
He says he picked up a kid and dropped him at the hospital in Meritville.
And?
Did he say how badly hurt the kid was?
No. He said the kid said the cops were going to meet him at the hospital.
I suppose you want to go to the hospital.
He won't be there. But yeah. It's our job.
EMERGEN
They have no record of him.
Why am I not Surprised?

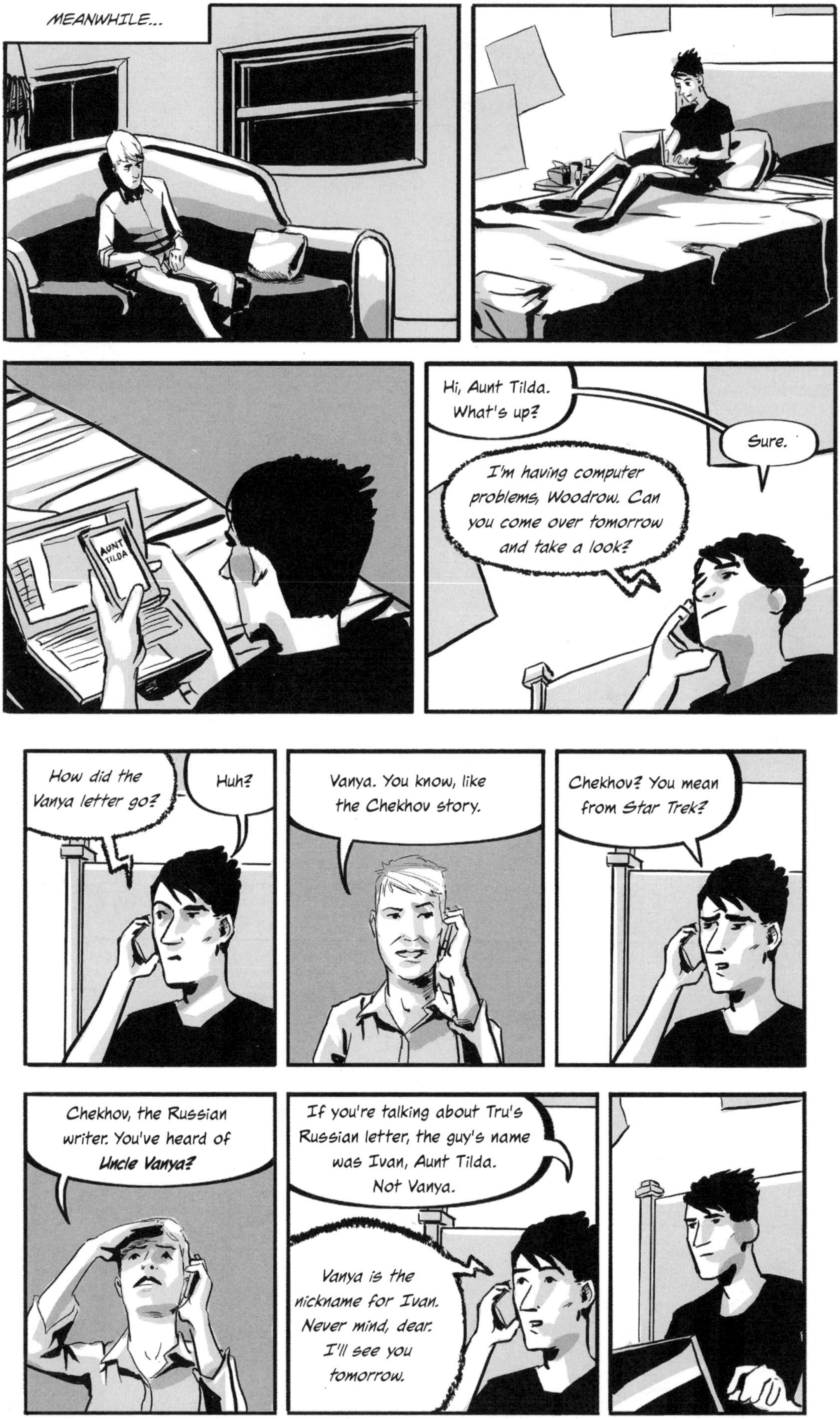
MEANWHILE...
AUNT TILDA
Hi, Aunt Tilda. What's up?
I'm having computer problems, Woodrow. Can you come over tomorrow and take a look?
Sure.
How did the Vanya letter go?
Huh?
Vanya. You know, like the Chekhov story.
Chekhov? You mean from Star Trek?
Chekhov, the Russian writer. You've heard of Uncle Vanya?
If you're talking about Tru's Russian letter, the guy's name was Ivan, Aunt Tilda. Not Vanya.
Vanya is the nickname for Ivan. Never mind, dear. I'll see you tomorrow.

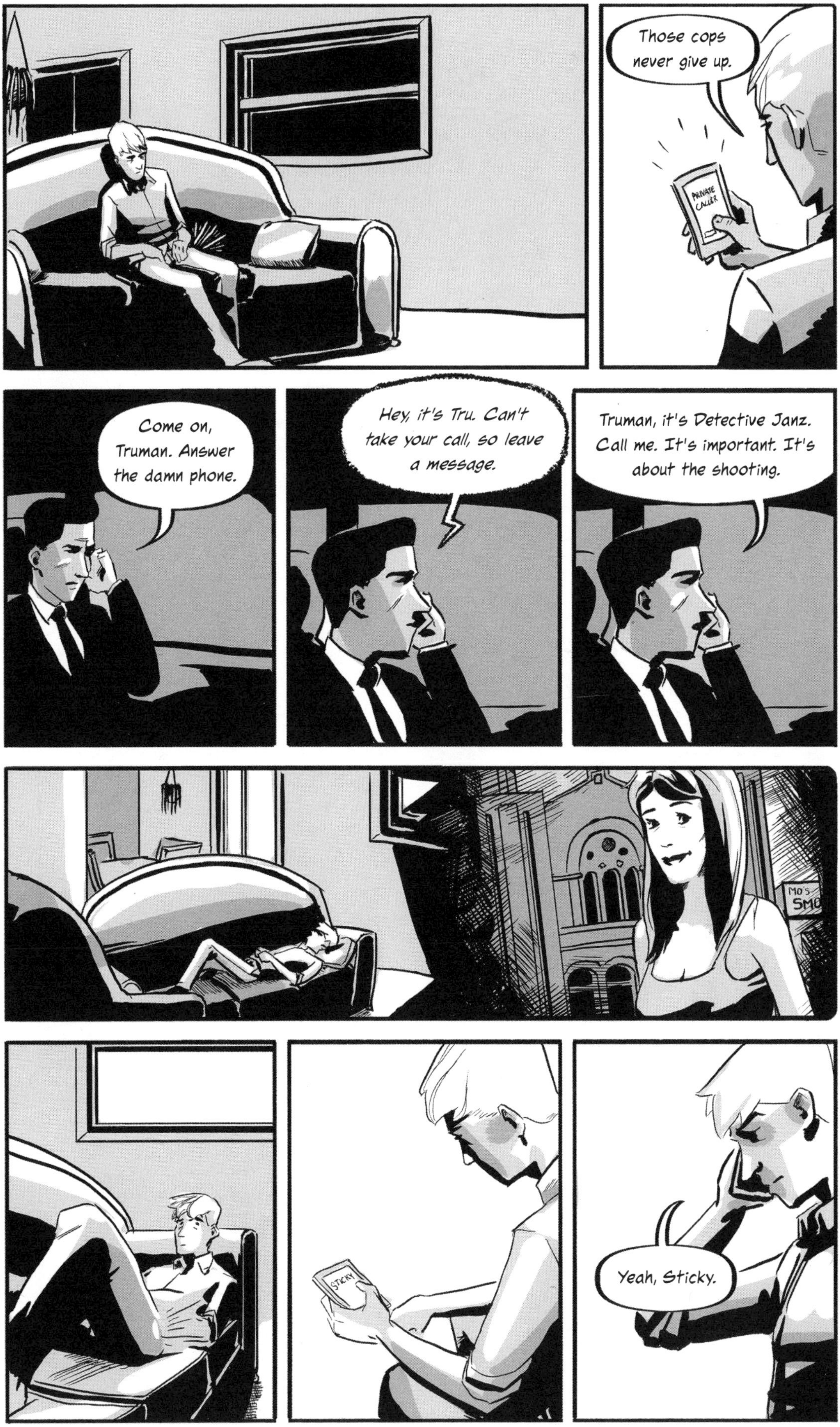
Those cops never give up.
PRIVATE CALLER
Come on, Truman. Answer the damn phone.
Hey, it's Tru. Can't take your call, so leave a message.
Truman, it's Detective Janz. Call me. It's important. It's about the shooting.
MO'S SMO
STICKY
Yeah, Sticky.

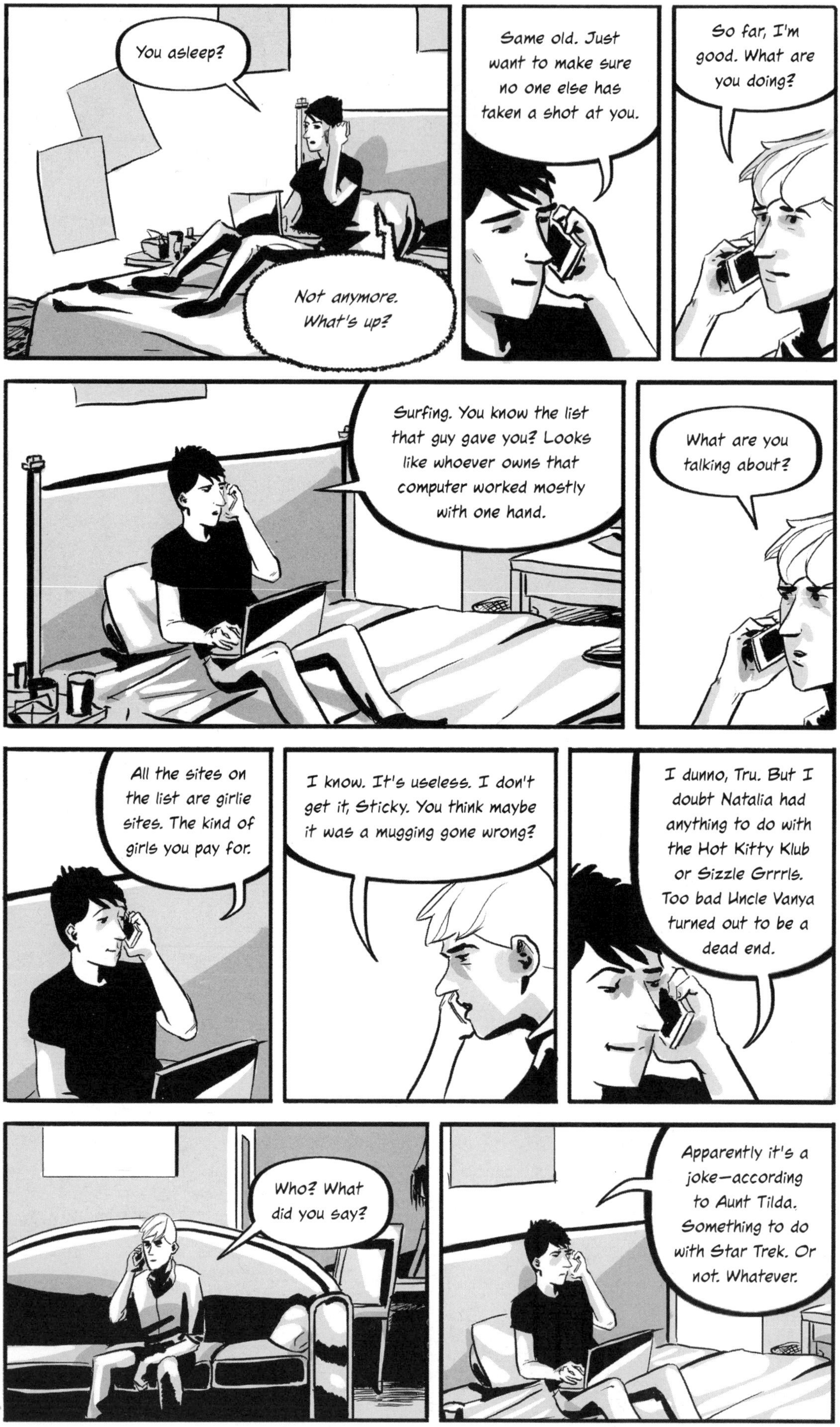
You asleep?
Not anymore. What's up?
Same old. Just want to make sure no one else has taken a shot at you.
So far, I'm good. What are you doing?
Surfing. You know the list that guy gave you? Looks like whoever owns that computer worked mostly with one hand.
What are you talking about?
All the sites on the list are girlie sites. The kind of girls you pay for.
I know. It's useless. I don't get it, Sticky. You think maybe it was a mugging gone wrong?
I dunno, Tru. But I doubt Natalia had anything to do with the Hot Kitty Klub or Sizzle Grrrls. Too bad Uncle Vanya turned out to be a dead end.
Who? What did you say?
Apparently it's a joke—according to Aunt Tilda. Something to do with Star Trek. Or not. Whatever.

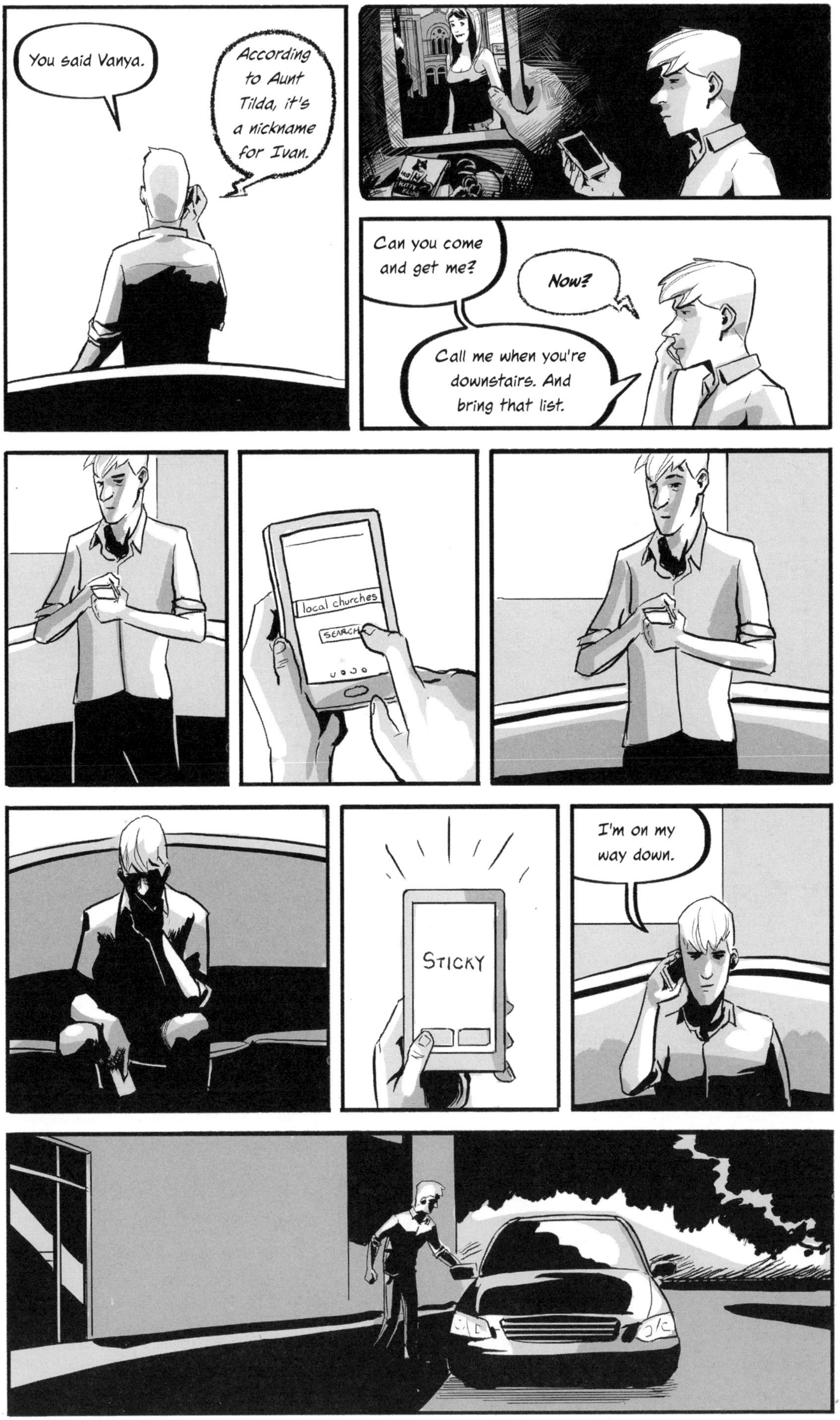
You said Vanya.
According to Aunt Tilda, it's a nickname for Ivan.
Can you come and get me?
Now?
Call me when you're downstairs. And bring that list.
local churches
SEARCH
STICKY
I'm on my way down.

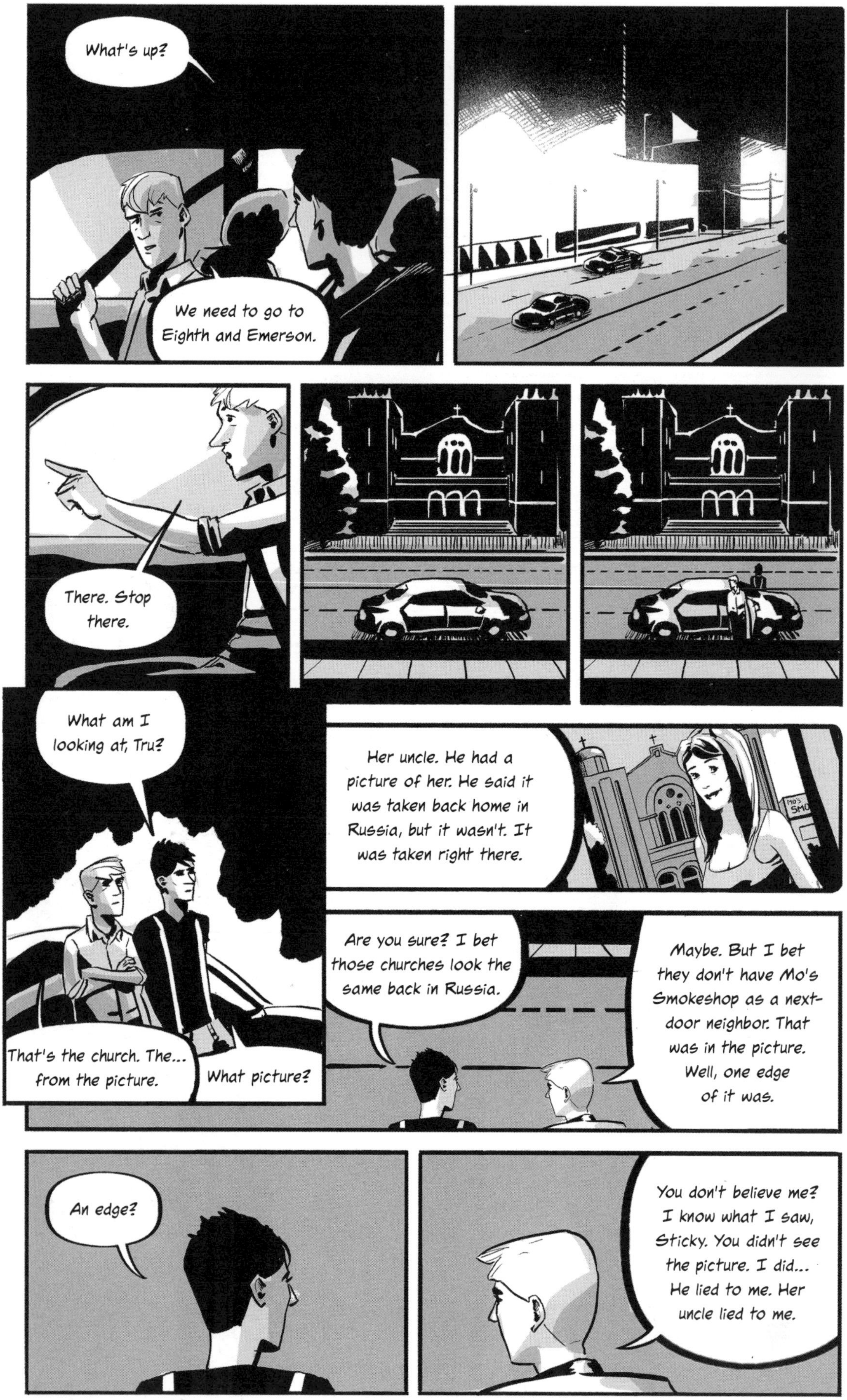
What's up?
We need to go to Eighth and Emerson.
There. Stop there.
What am I looking at, Tru?
That's the church. The... from the picture.
What picture?
Her uncle. He had a picture of her. He said it was taken back home in Russia, but it wasn't. It was taken right there.
Are you sure? I bet those churches look the same back in Russia.
Maybe. But I bet they don't have Mo's Smokeshop as a next-door neighbor. That was in the picture. Well, one edge of it was.
An edge?
You don't believe me? I know what I saw, Sticky. You didn't see the picture. I did... He lied to me. Her uncle lied to me.

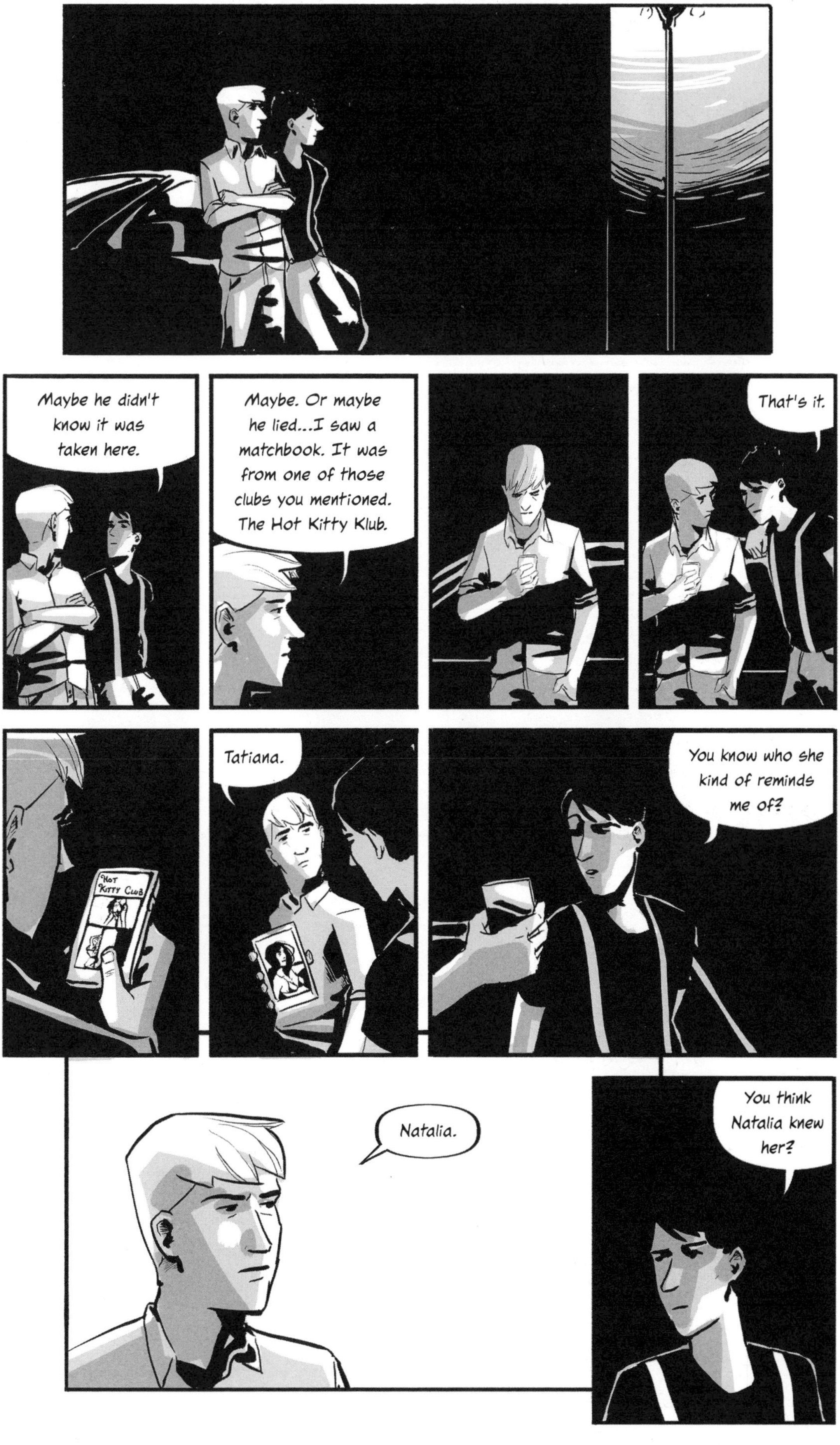
Maybe he didn't know it was taken here.
Maybe. Or maybe he lied...I saw a matchbook. It was from one of those clubs you mentioned. The Hot Kitty Klub.
That's it.
Hot Kitty Club
Tatiana.
You know who she kind of reminds me of?
Natalia.
You think Natalia knew her?

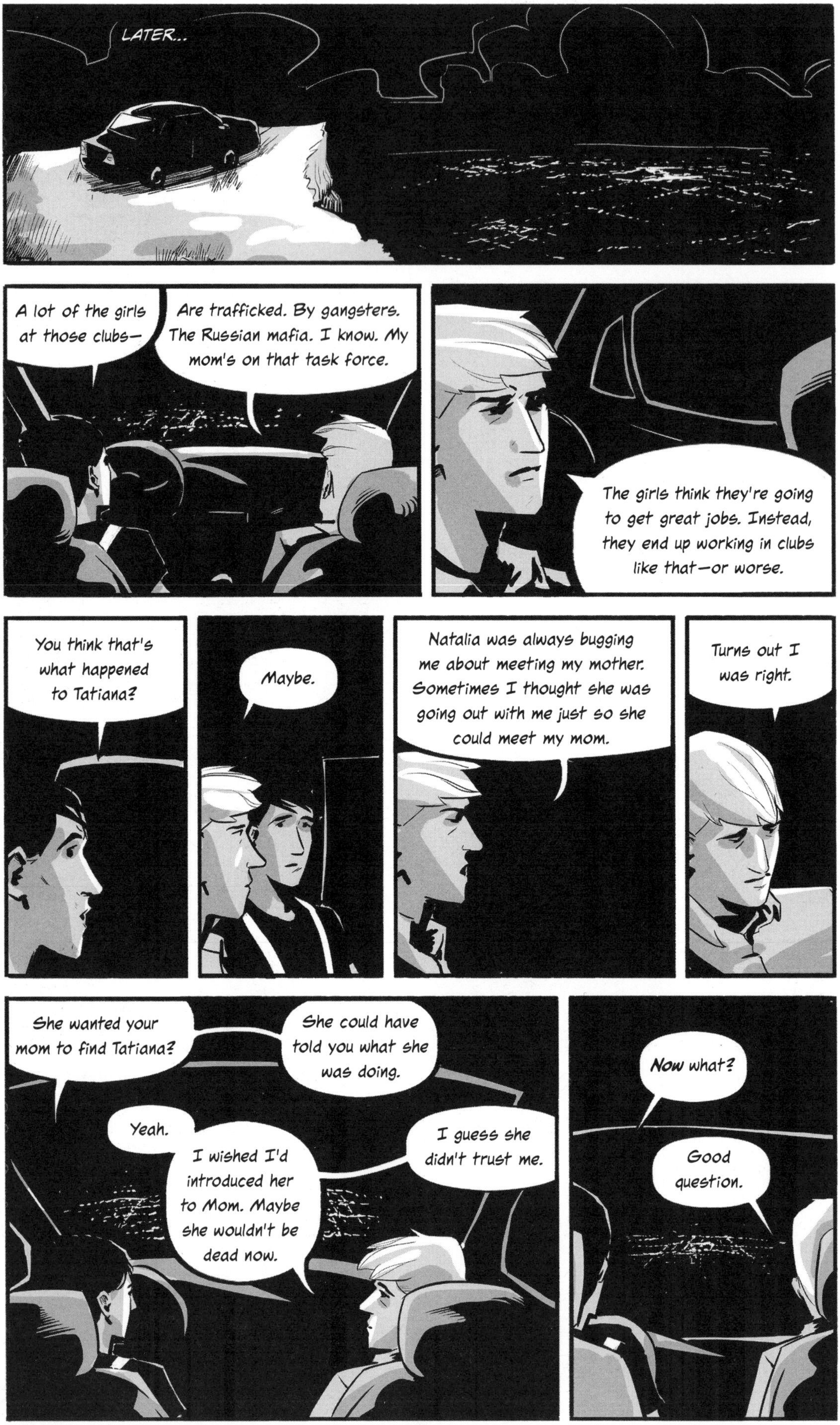
LATER...
A lot of the girls at those clubs—
Are trafficked. By gangsters. The Russian mafia. I know. My mom's on that task force.
The girls think they're going to get great jobs. Instead, they end up working in clubs like that—or worse.
You think that's what happened to Tatiana?
Maybe.
Natalia was always bugging me about meeting my mother. Sometimes I thought she was going out with me just so she could meet my mom.
Turns out I was right.
She wanted your mom to find Tatiana?
She could have told you what she was doing.
Yeah.
I wished I'd introduced her to Mom. Maybe she wouldn't be dead now.
I guess she didn't trust me.
Now what?
Good question.

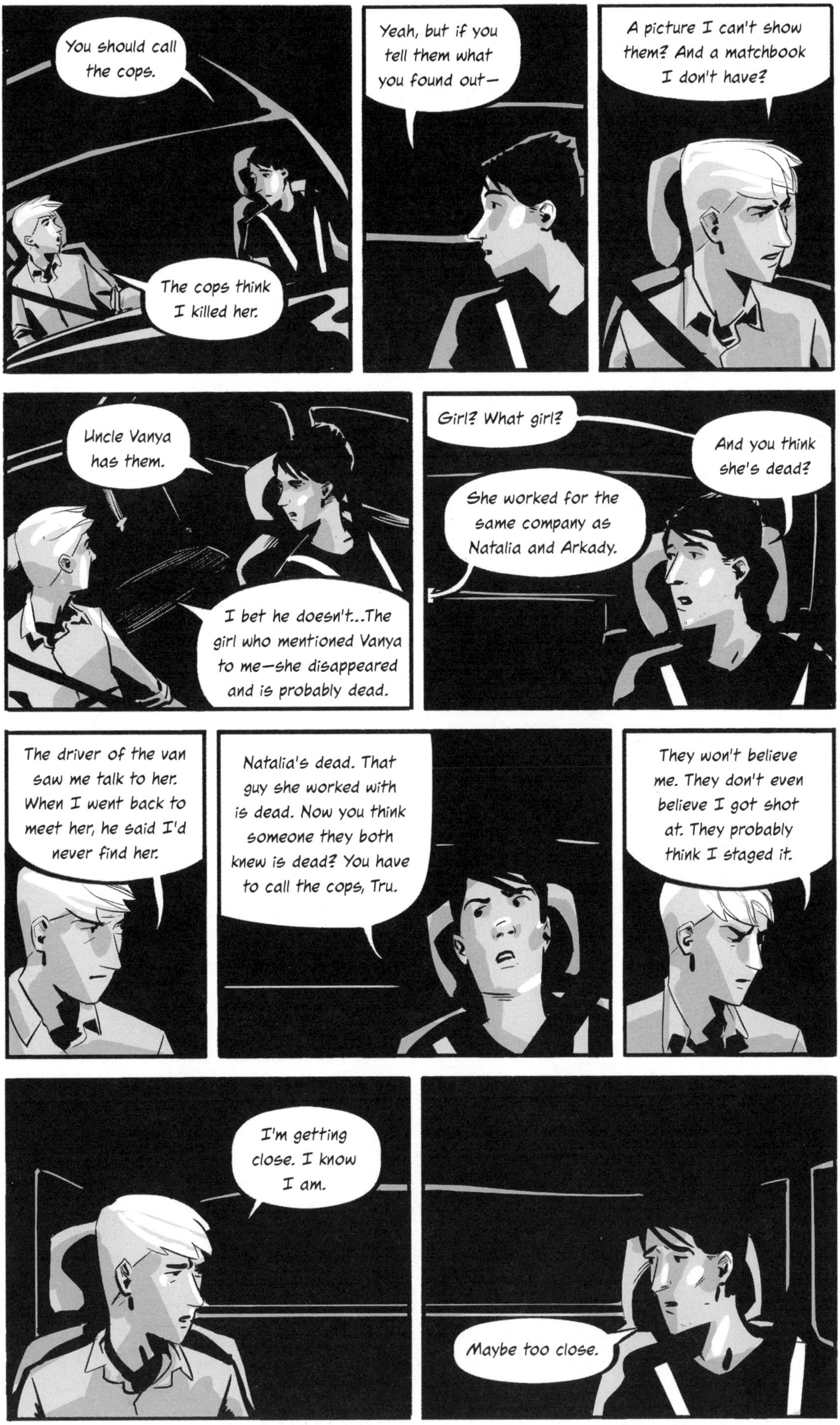
You should call the cops.
The cops think I killed her.
Yeah, but if you tell them what you found out—
A picture I can't show them? And a matchbook I don't have?
Uncle Vanya has them.
I bet he doesn't...The girl who mentioned Vanya to me—she disappeared and is probably dead.
Girl? What girl?
She worked for the same company as Natalia and Arkady.
And you think she's dead?
The driver of the van saw me talk to her. When I went back to meet her, he said I'd never find her.
Natalia's dead. That guy she worked with is dead. Now you think someone they both knew is dead? You have to call the cops, Tru.
They won't believe me. They don't even believe I got shot at. They probably think I staged it.
I'm getting close. I know I am.
Maybe too close.

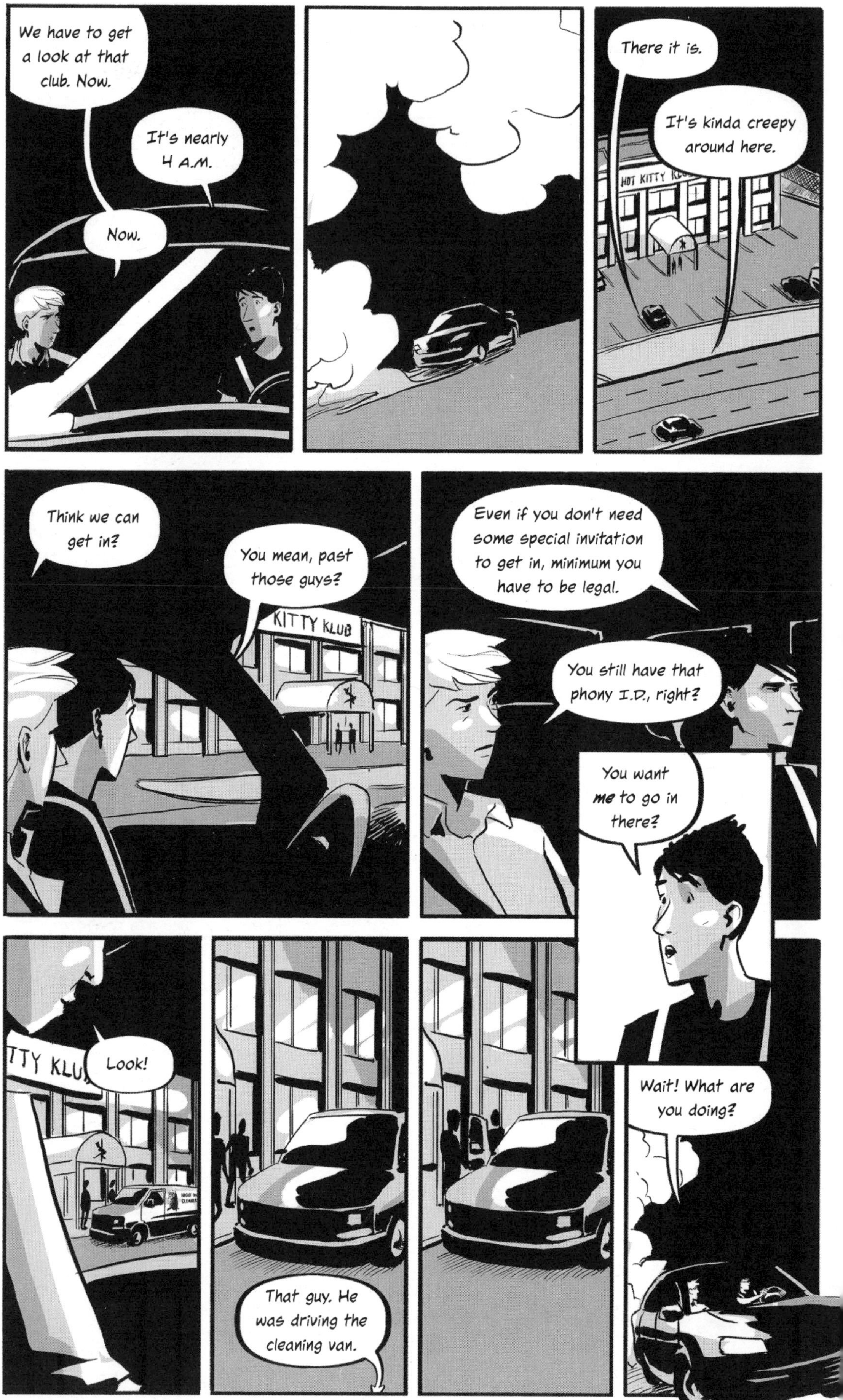
We have to get a look at that club. Now.
It's nearly 4 A.M.
Now.
There it is.
It's kinda creepy around here.
HOT KITTY KLUB
Think we can get in?
You mean, past those guys?
KITTY KLUB
Even if you don't need some special invitation to get in, minimum you have to be legal.
You still have that phony I.D., right?
You want *me* to go in there?
TTY KLUB
Look!
That guy. He was driving the cleaning van.
Wait! What are you doing?

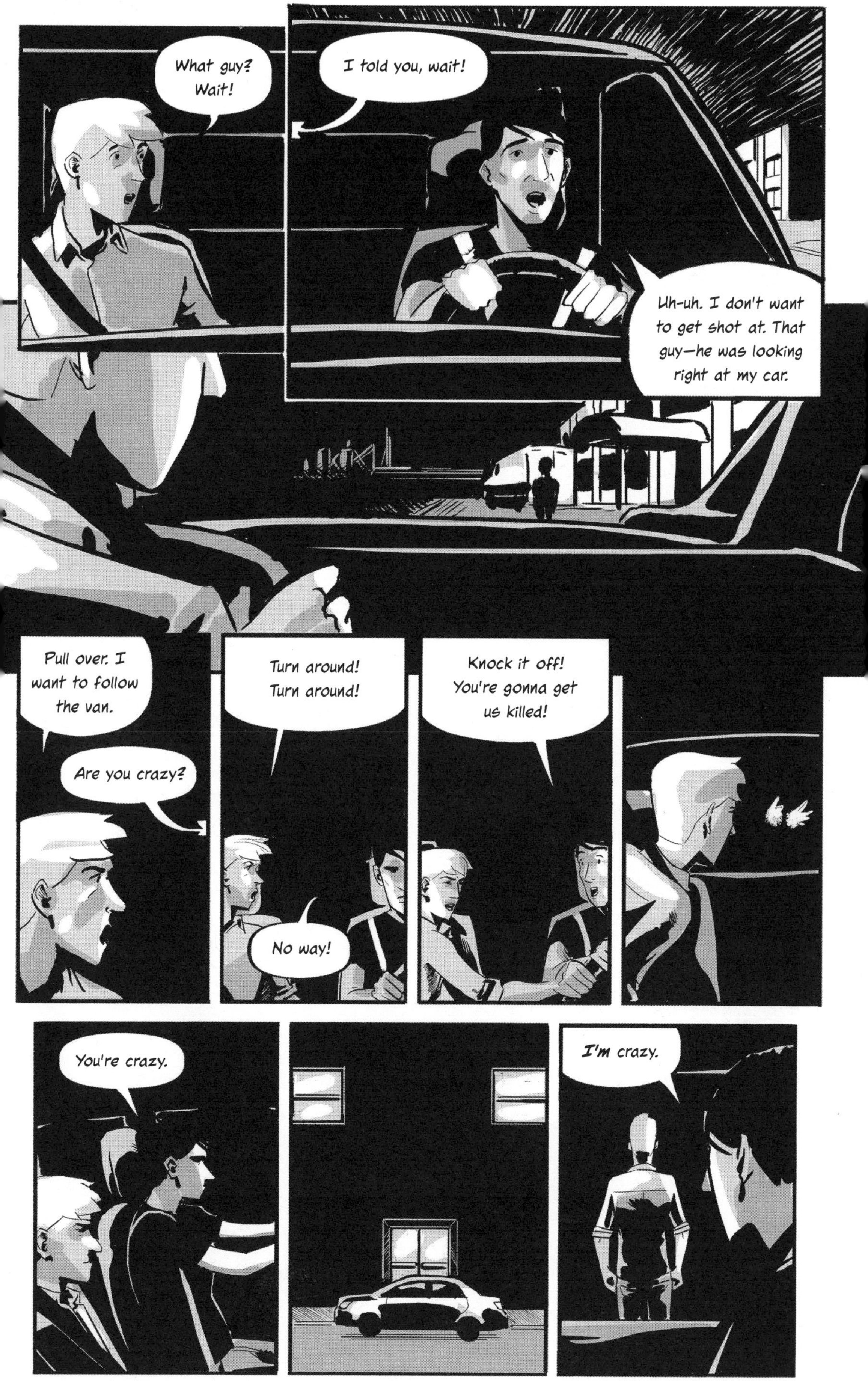
What guy? Wait!
I told you, wait!
Uh-uh. I don't want to get shot at. That guy—he was looking right at my car.
Pull over. I want to follow the van.
Are you crazy?
Turn around! Turn around!
No way!
Knock it off! You're gonna get us killed!
You're crazy.
I'm crazy.

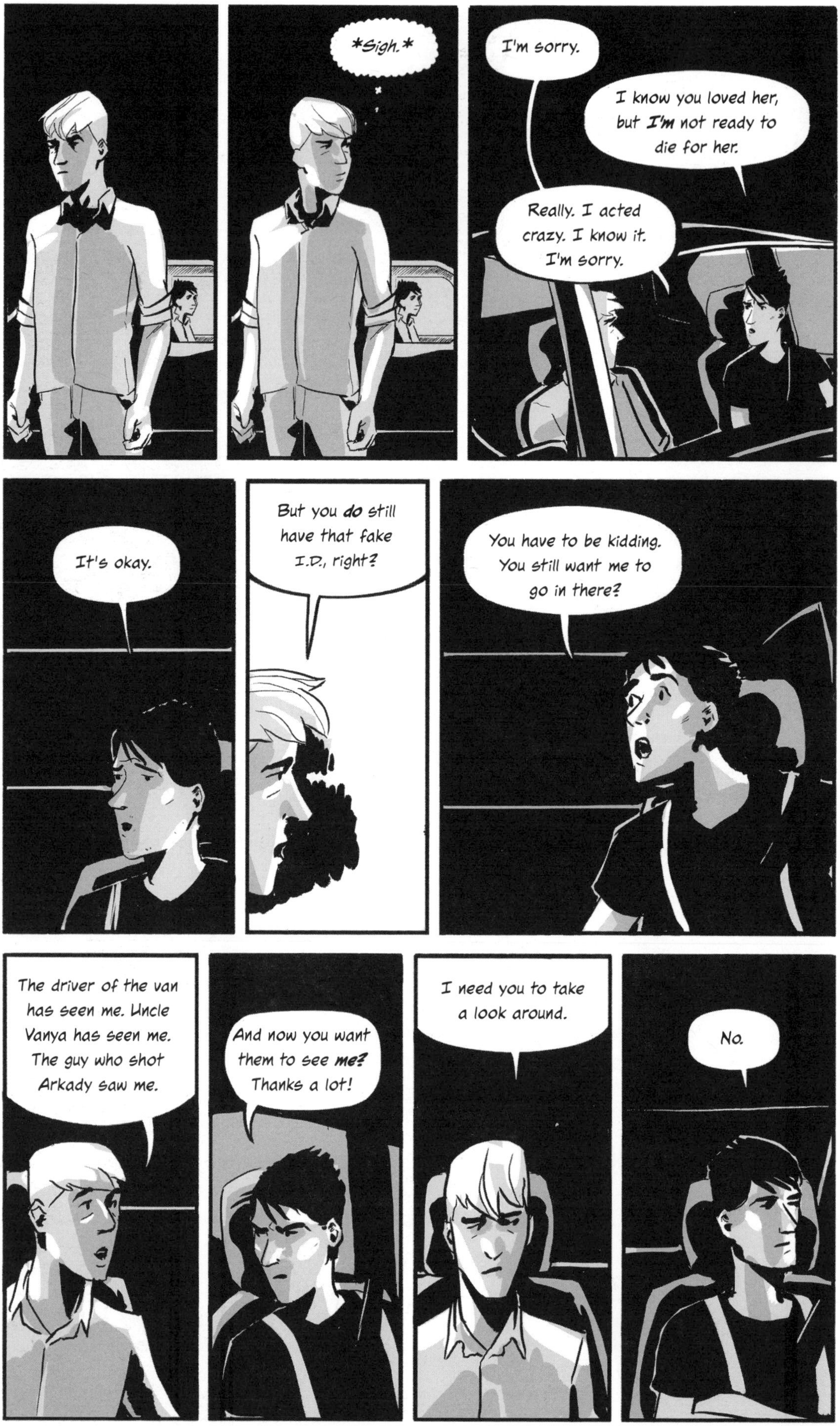
Sigh.
I'm sorry.
I know you loved her, but ***I'm*** not ready to die for her.
Really. I acted crazy. I know it. I'm sorry.
It's okay.
But you ***do*** still have that fake I.D., right?
You have to be kidding. You still want me to go in there?
The driver of the van has seen me. Uncle Vanya has seen me. The guy who shot Arkady saw me.
And now you want them to see ***me?*** Thanks a lot!
I need you to take a look around.
No.

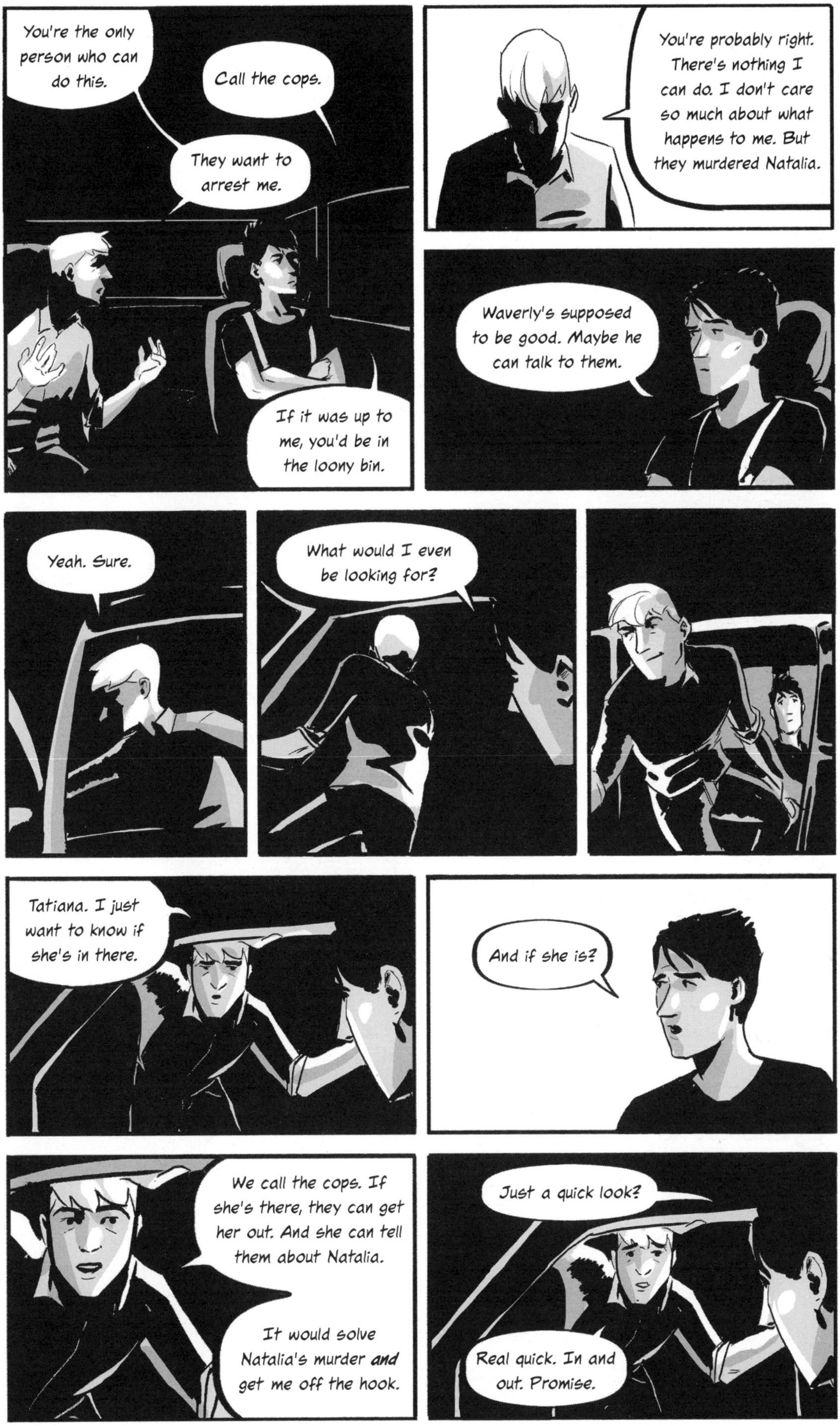
You're the only person who can do this.
Call the cops.
They want to arrest me.
If it was up to me, you'd be in the loony bin.
You're probably right. There's nothing I can do. I don't care so much about what happens to me. But they murdered Natalia.
Waverly's supposed to be good. Maybe he can talk to them.
Yeah. Sure.
What would I even be looking for?
Tatiana. I just want to know if she's in there.
And if she is?
We call the cops. If she's there, they can get her out. And she can tell them about Natalia.
It would solve Natalia's murder **and** get me off the hook.
Just a quick look?
Real quick. In and out. Promise.

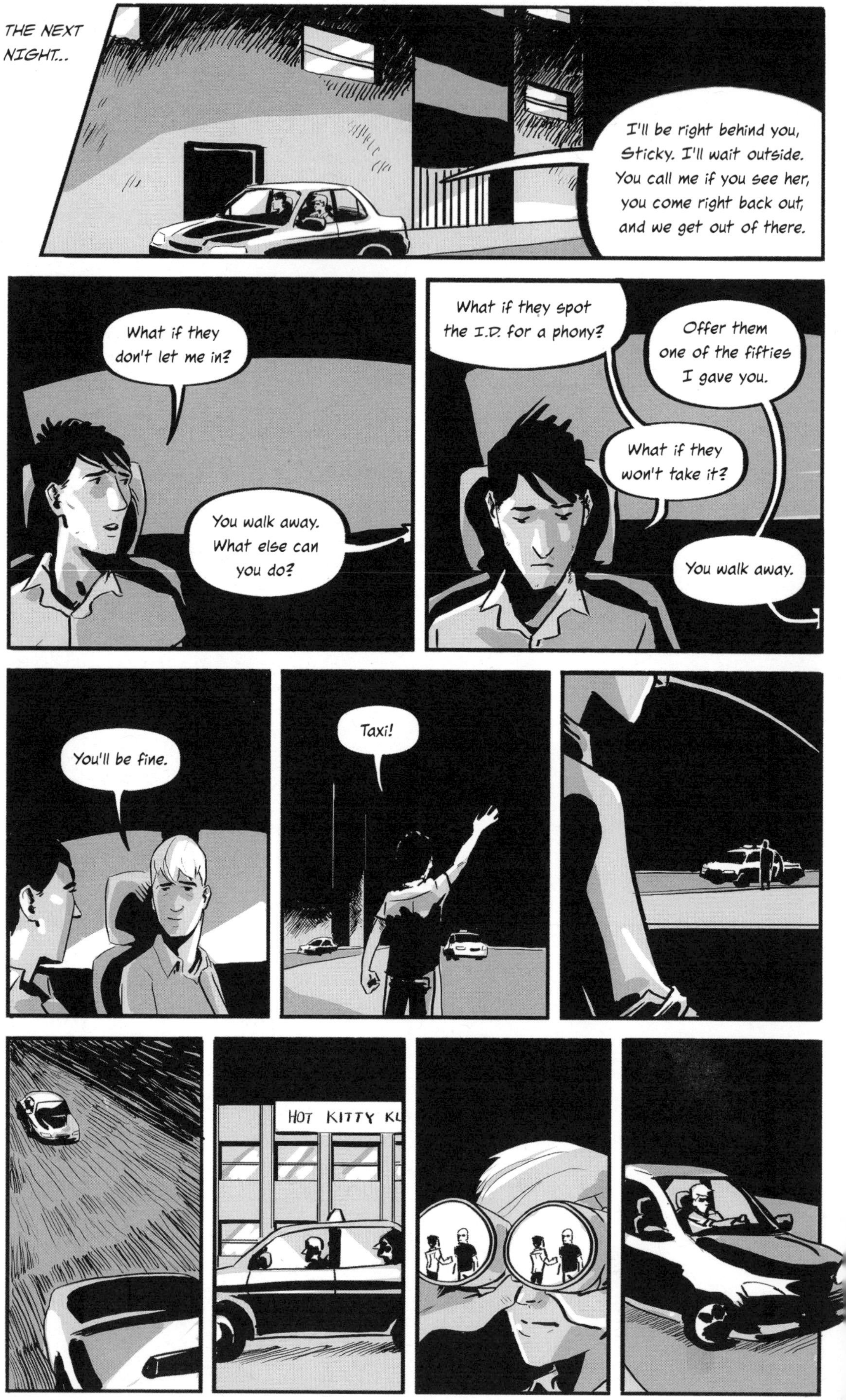
THE NEXT NIGHT...
I'll be right behind you, Sticky. I'll wait outside. You call me if you see her, you come right back out, and we get out of there.
What if they don't let me in?
You walk away. What else can you do?
What if they spot the I.D. for a phony?
Offer them one of the fifties I gave you.
What if they won't take it?
You walk away.
You'll be fine.
Taxi!
HOT KITTY KL

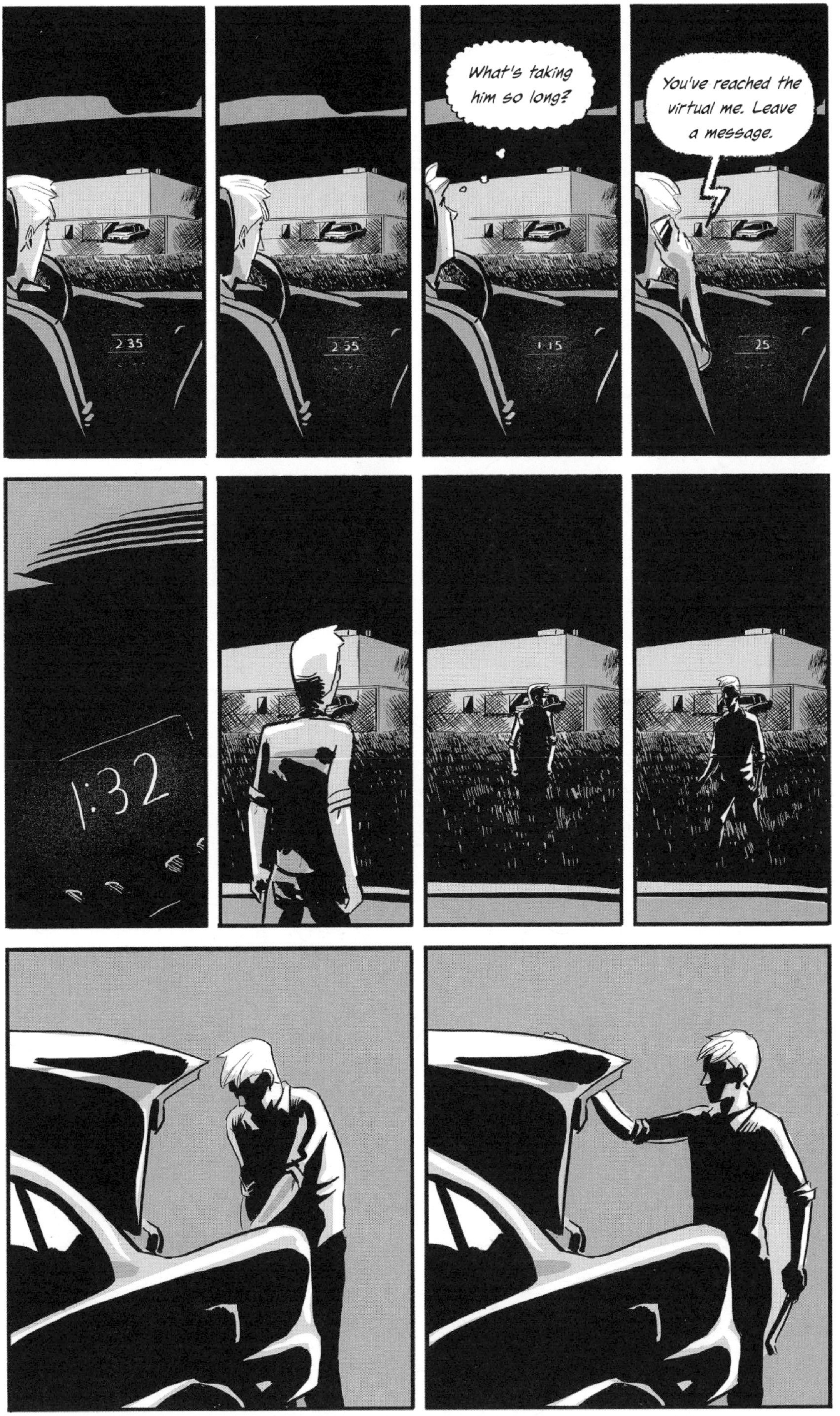
2:35
2:55
What's taking him so long?
1:15
You've reached the virtual me. Leave a message.
1:25
1:32

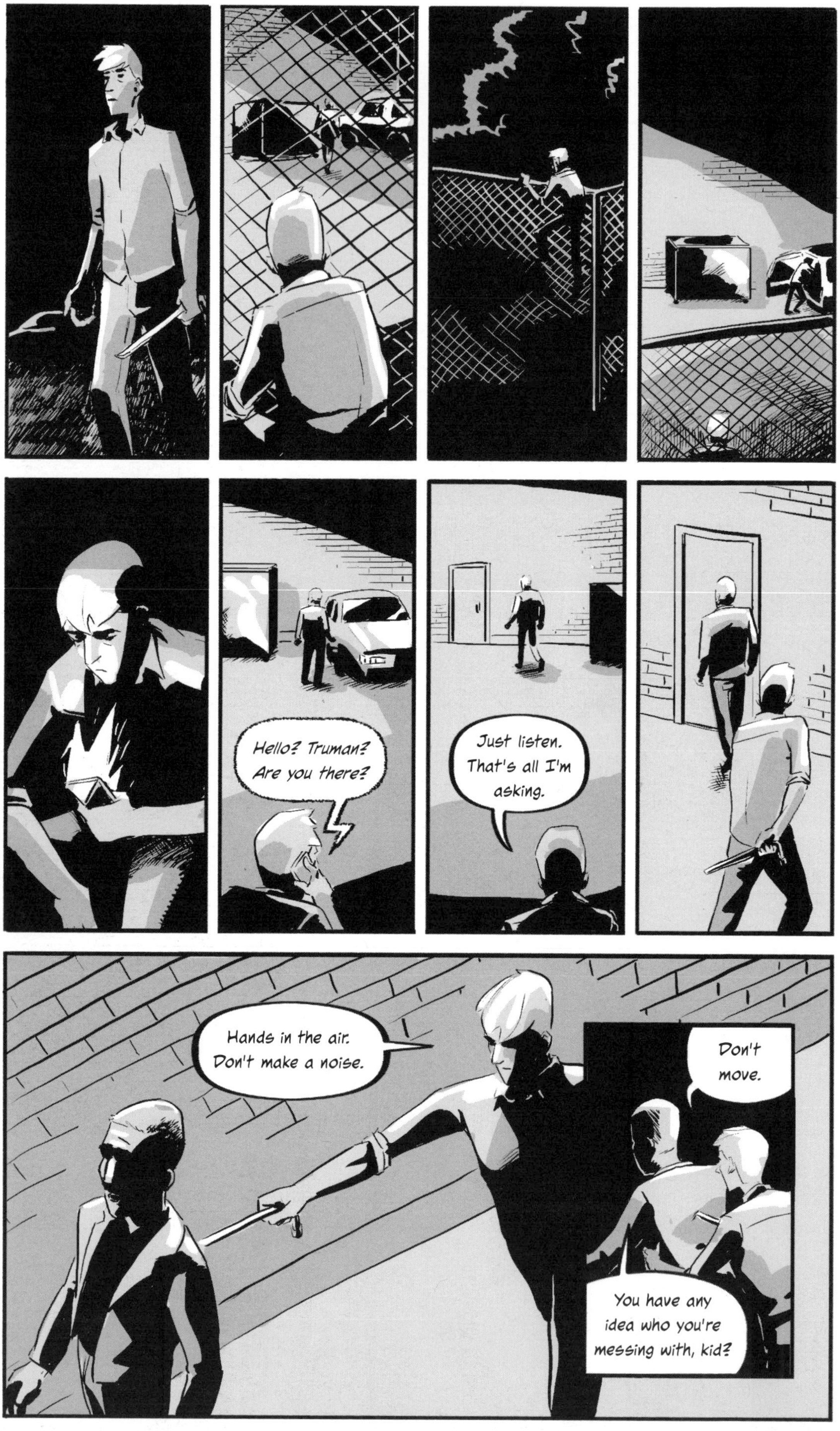
Hello? Truman? Are you there?
Just listen. That's all I'm asking.
Hands in the air. Don't make a noise.
Don't move.
You have any idea who you're messing with, kid?

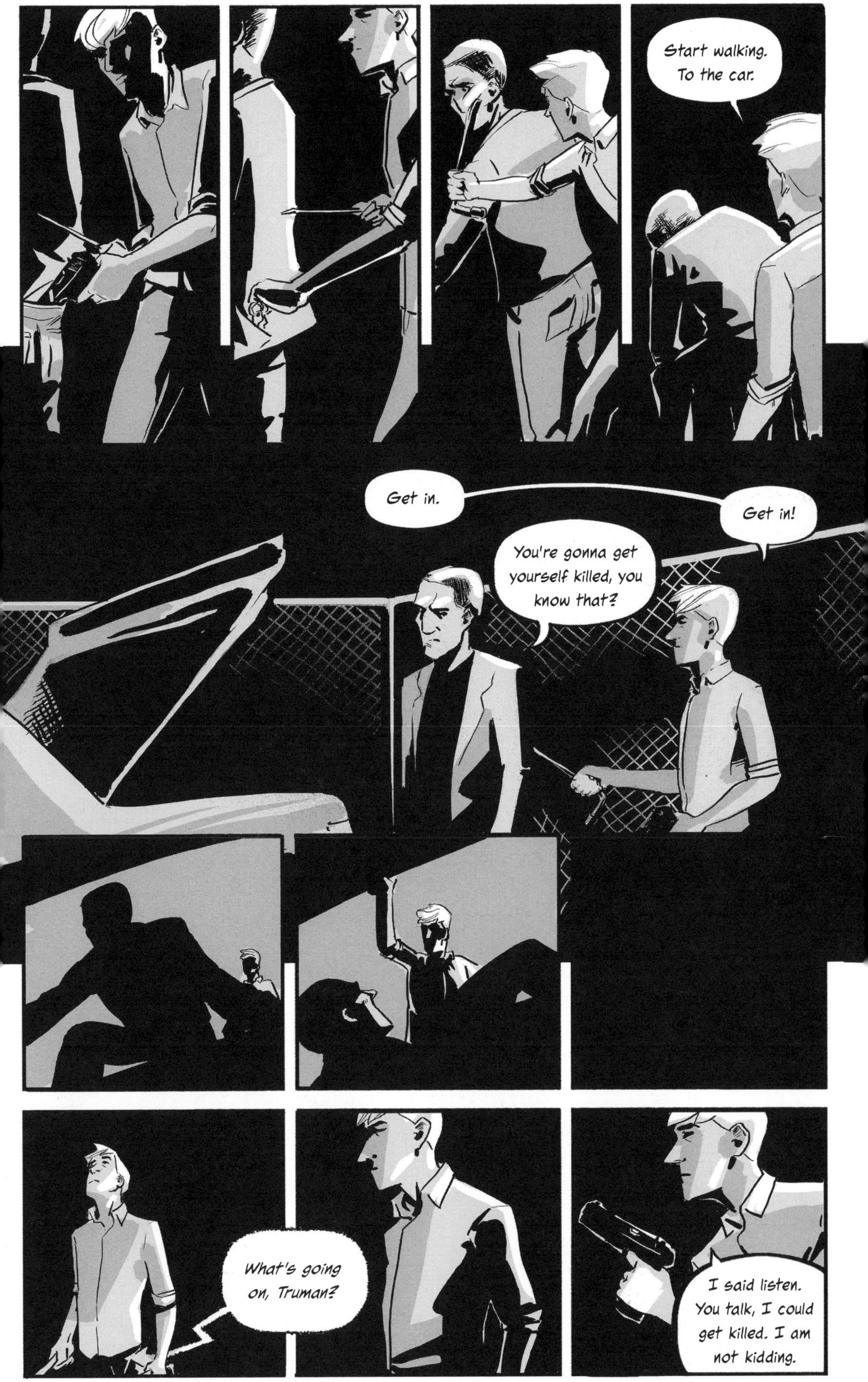
Start walking. To the car.
Get in.
Get in!
You're gonna get yourself killed, you know that?
What's going on, Truman?
I said listen. You talk, I could get killed. I am not kidding.

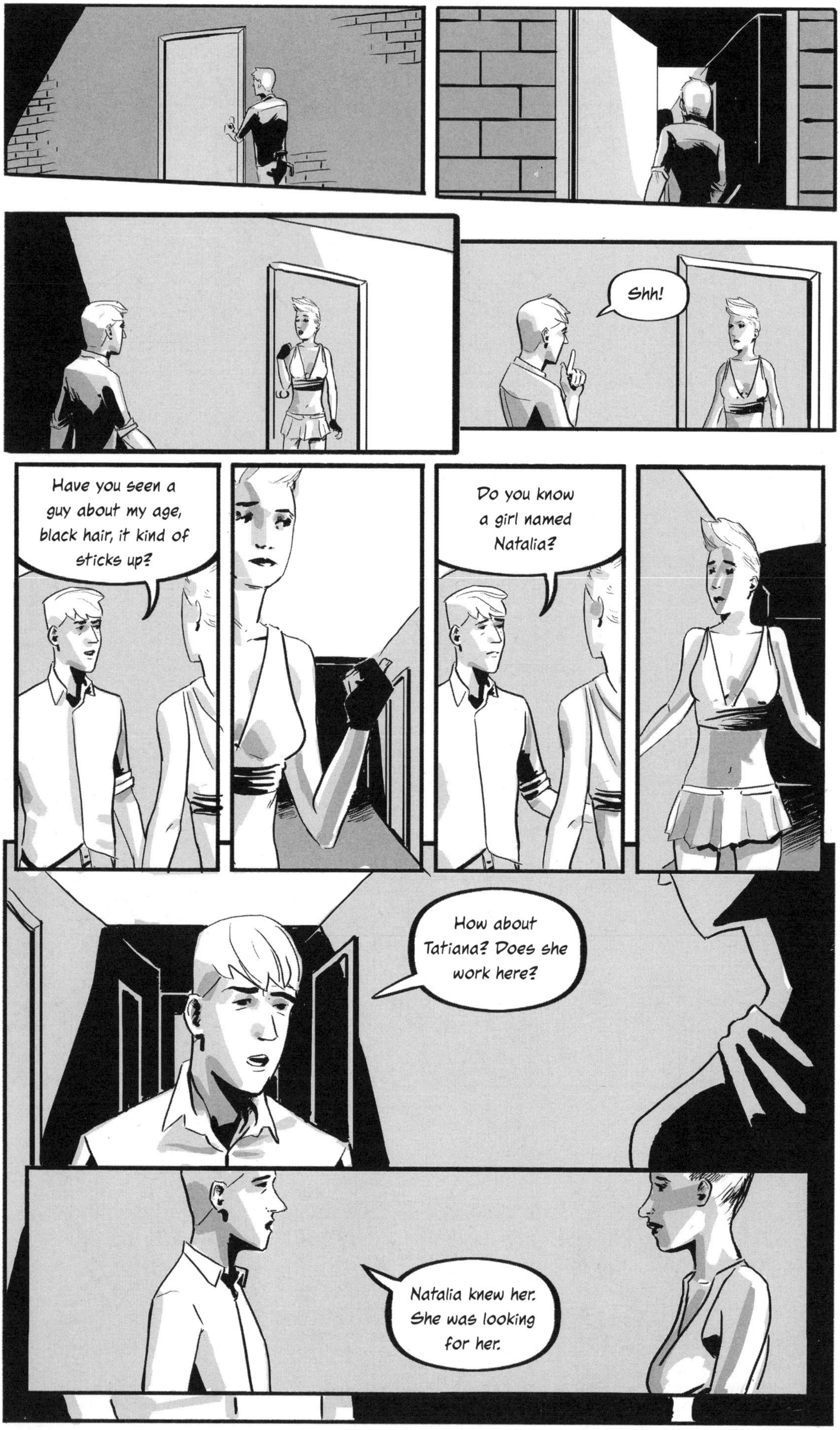
Shh!
Have you seen a guy about my age, black hair, it kind of sticks up?
Do you know a girl named Natalia?
How about Tatiana? Does she work here?
Natalia knew her. She was looking for her.

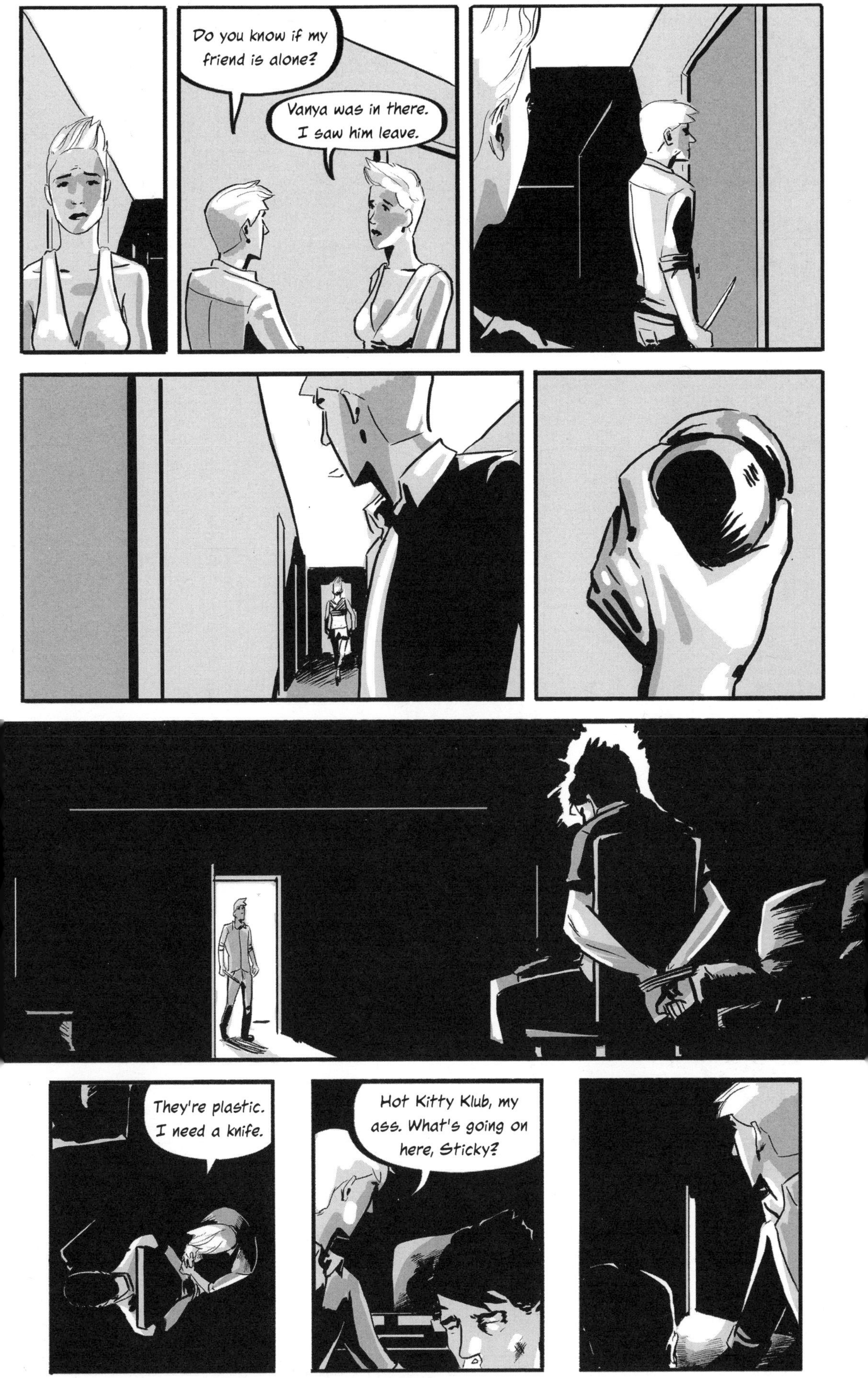

Do you know if my friend is alone?
Vanya was in there. I saw him leave.
They're plastic. I need a knife.
Hot Kitty Klub, my ass. What's going on here, Sticky?

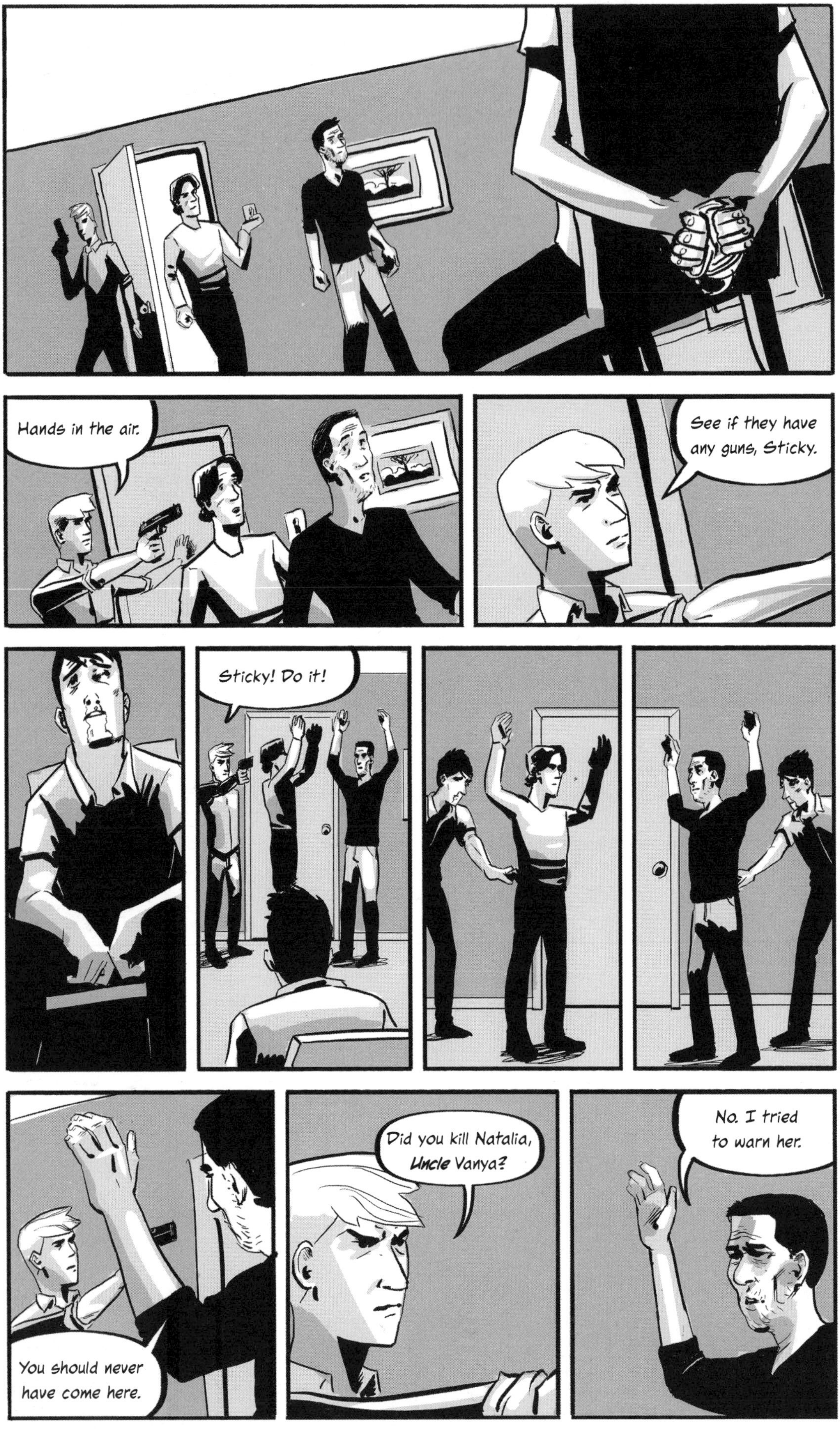
Hands in the air.
See if they have any guns, Sticky.
Sticky! Do it!
You should never have come here.
Did you kill Natalia, Uncle Vanya?
No. I tried to warn her.

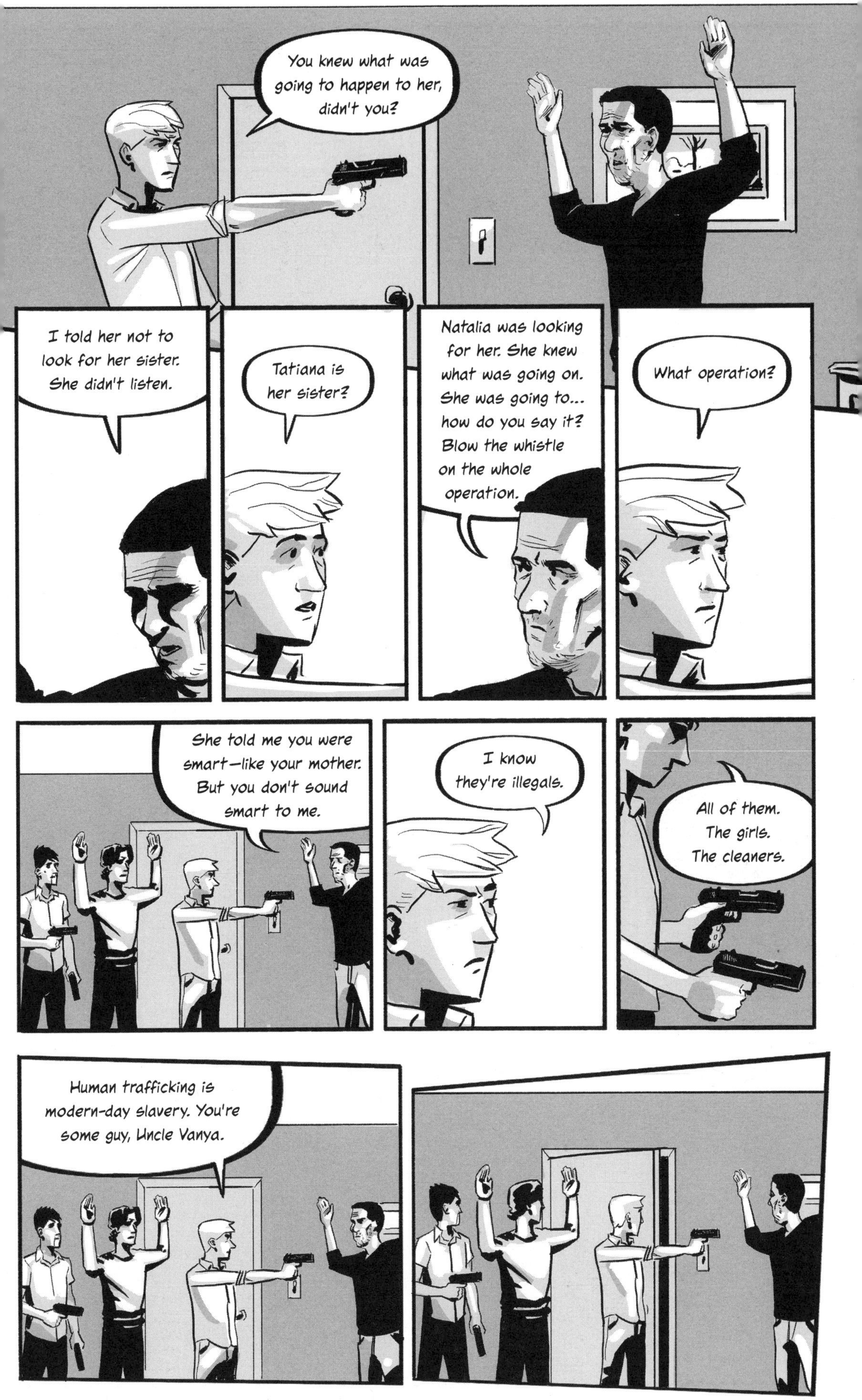
You knew what was going to happen to her, didn't you?
I told her not to look for her sister. She didn't listen.
Tatiana is her sister?
Natalia was looking for her. She knew what was going on. She was going to... how do you say it? Blow the whistle on the whole operation.
What operation?
She told me you were smart—like your mother. But you don't sound smart to me.
I know they're illegals.
All of them. The girls. The cleaners.
Human trafficking is modern-day slavery. You're some guy, Uncle Vanya.

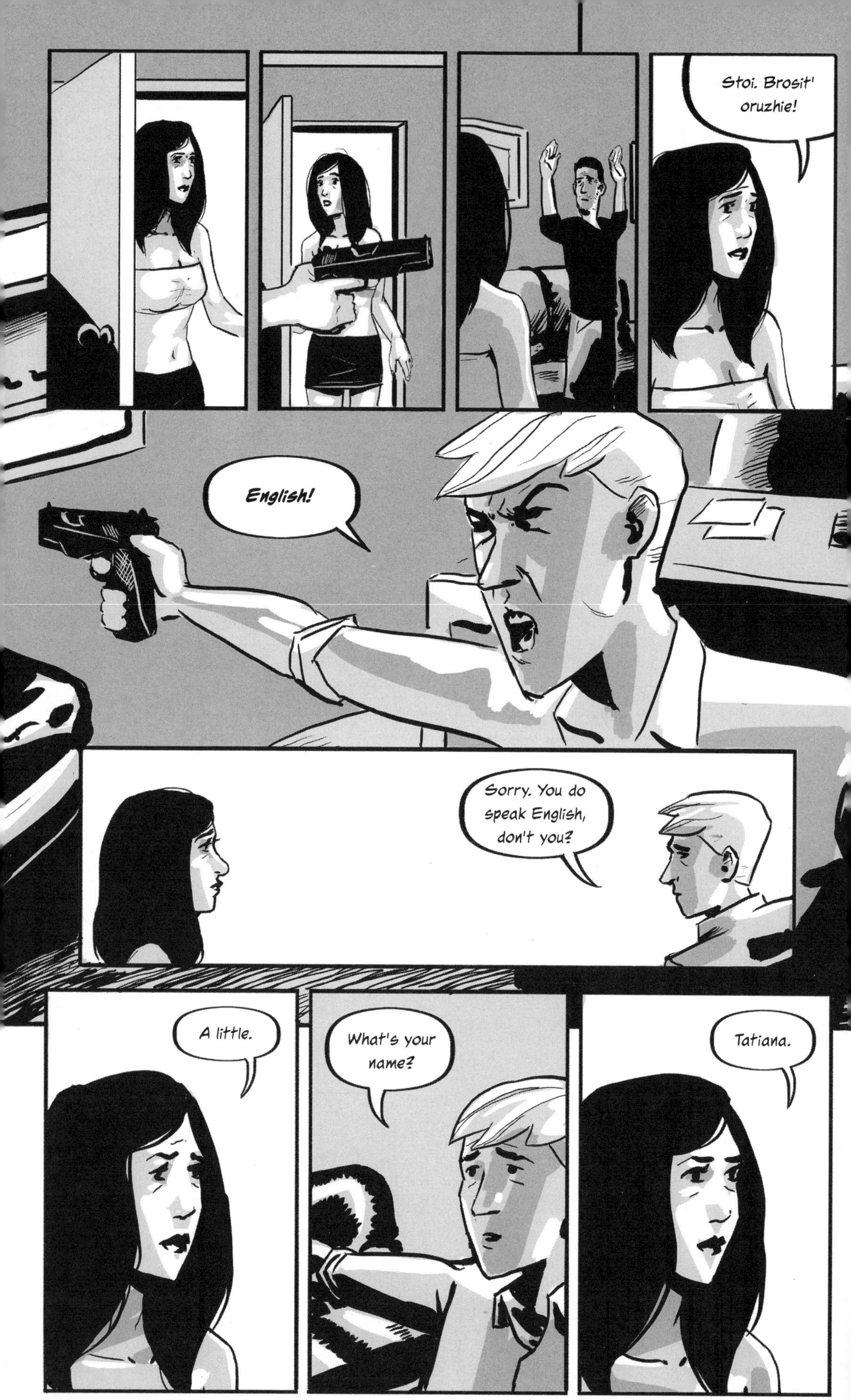
Stoi. Brosit' oruzhie!
English!
Sorry. You do speak English, don't you?
A little.
What's your name?
Tatiana.

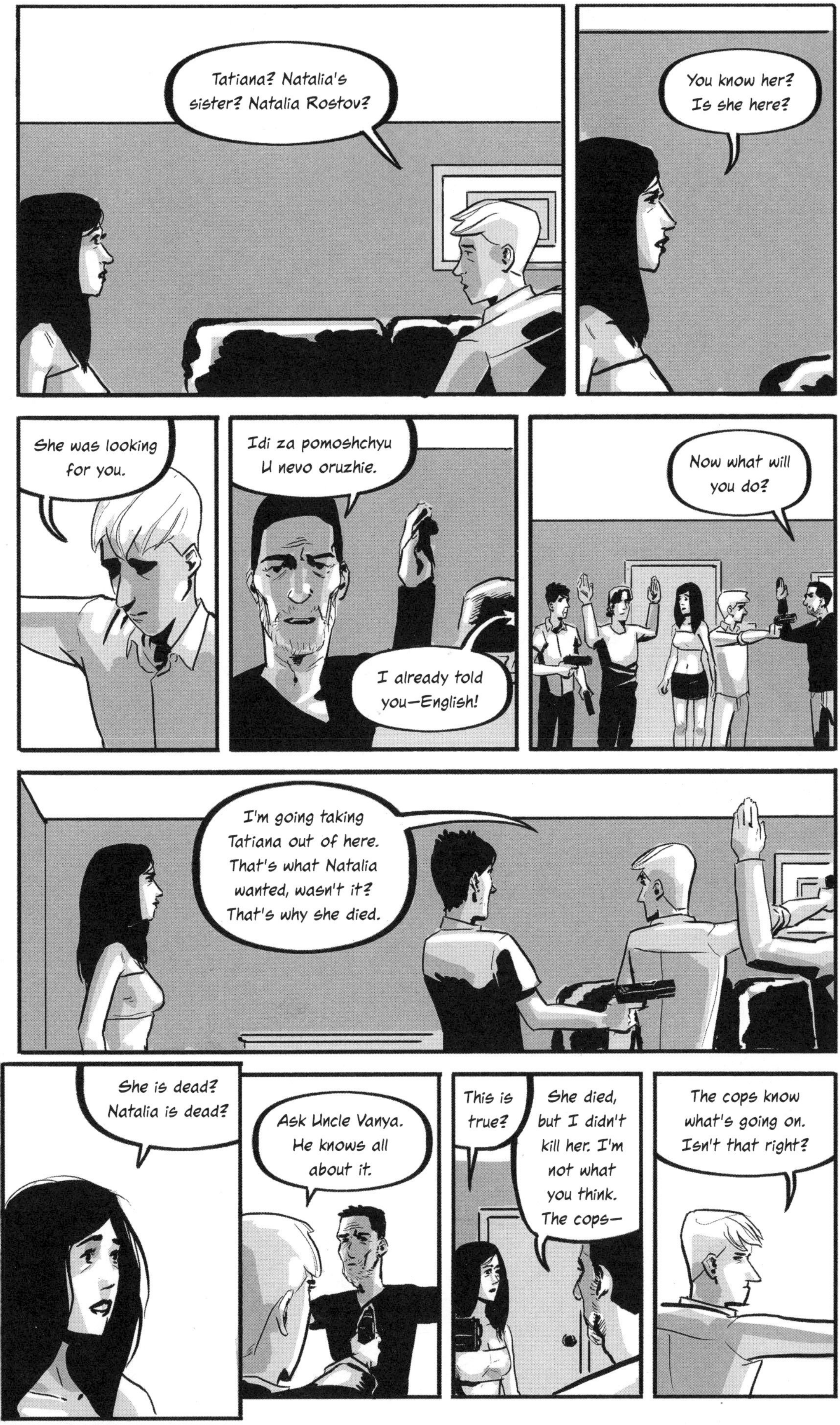
Tatiana? Natalia's sister? Natalia Rostov?
You know her? Is she here?
She was looking for you.
Idi za pomoshchyu U nevo oruzhie.
I already told you—English!
Now what will you do?
I'm going taking Tatiana out of here. That's what Natalia wanted, wasn't it? That's why she died.
She is dead? Natalia is dead?
Ask Uncle Vanya. He knows all about it.
This is true?
She died, but I didn't kill her. I'm not what you think. The cops—
The cops know what's going on. Isn't that right?

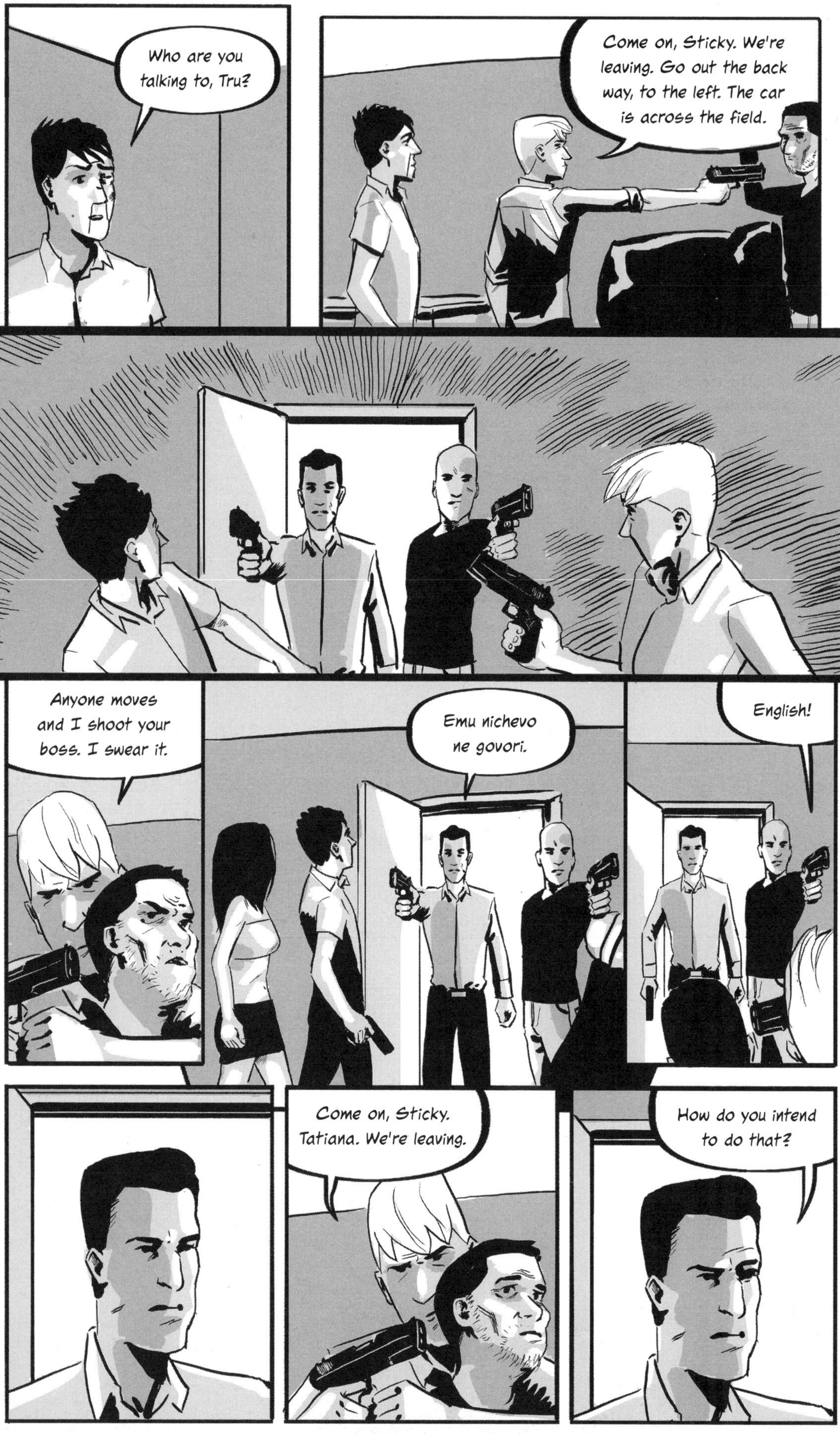
Who are you talking to, Tru?
Come on, Sticky. We're leaving. Go out the back way, to the left. The car is across the field.
Anyone moves and I shoot your boss. I swear it.
Emu nichevo ne govori.
English!
Come on, Sticky. Tatiana. We're leaving.
How do you intend to do that?

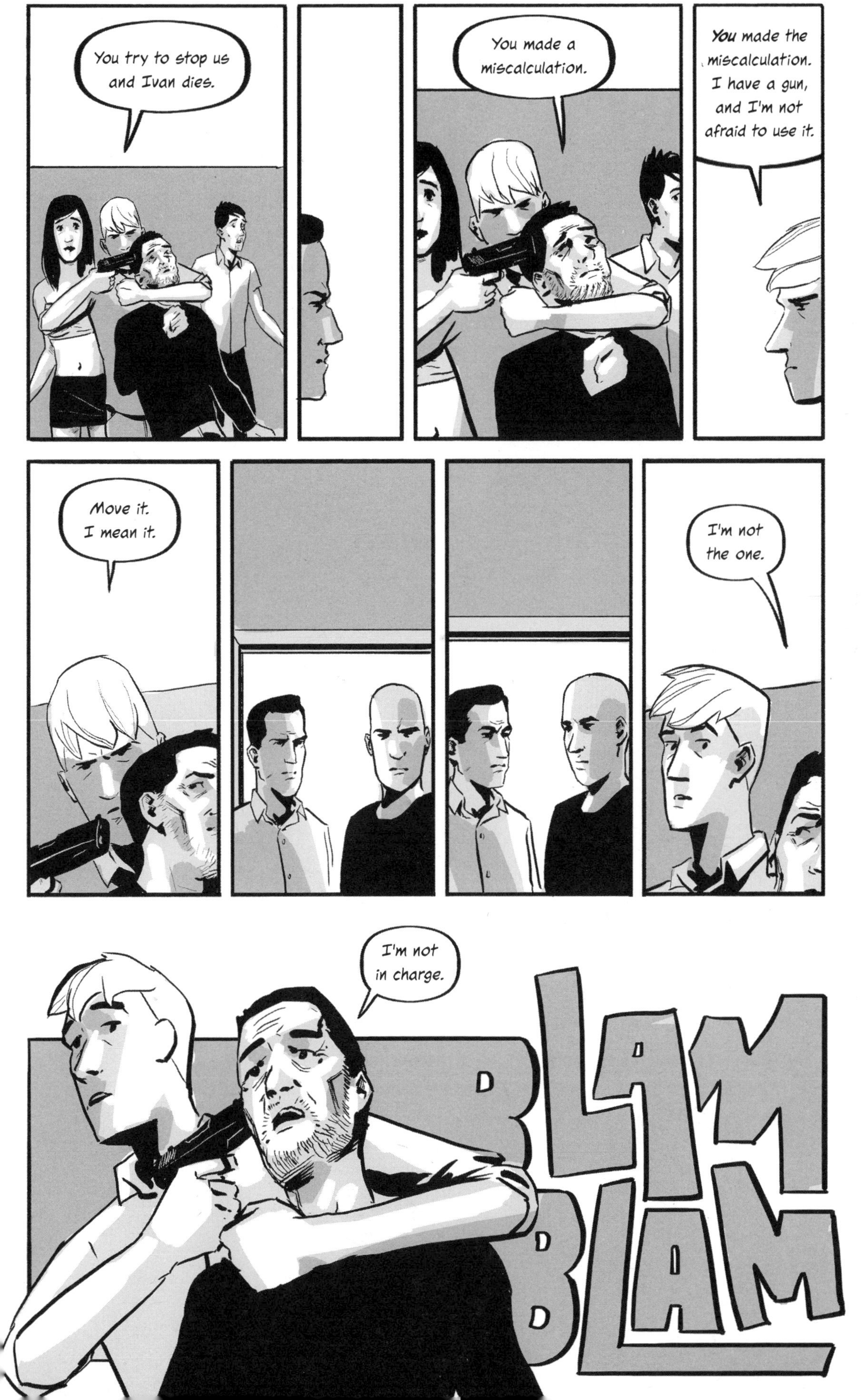
You try to stop us and Ivan dies.
You made a miscalculation.
You made the miscalculation. I have a gun, and I'm not afraid to use it.
Move it. I mean it.
I'm not the one.
I'm not in charge.
BLAM BLAM

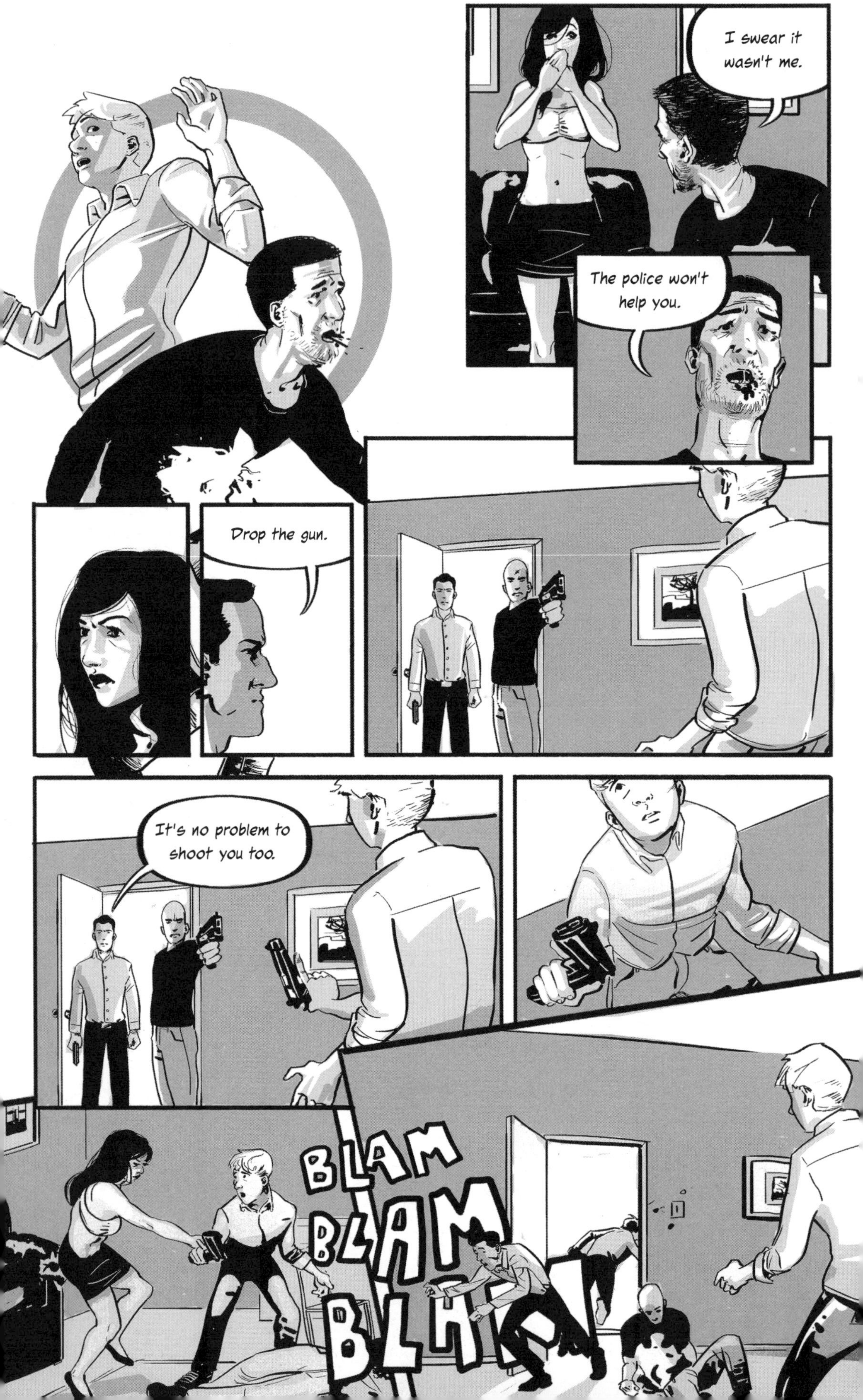
I swear it wasn't me.
The police won't help you.
Drop the gun.
It's no problem to shoot you too.
BLAM
BLAM

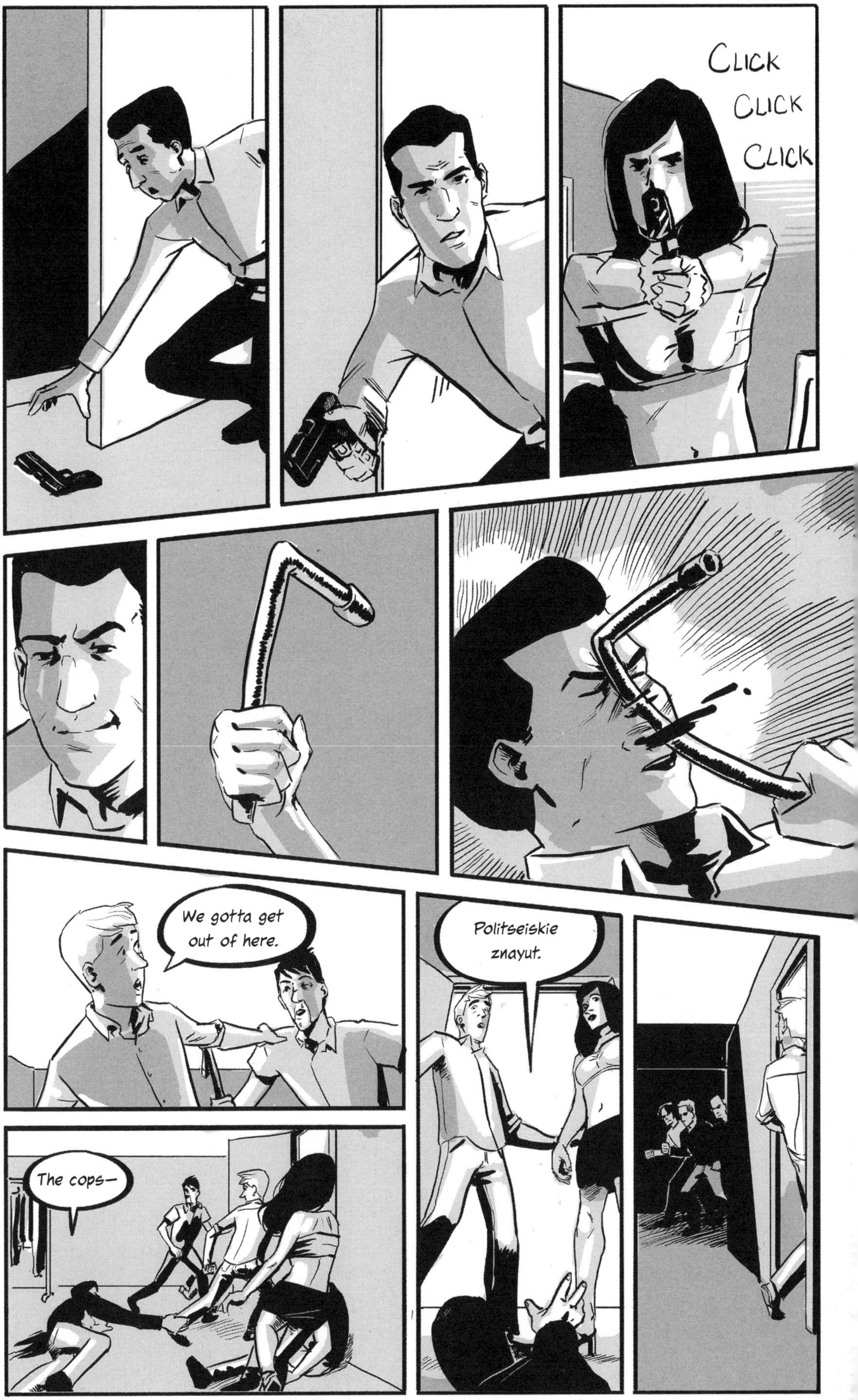
CLICK
CLICK
CLICK
We gotta get out of here.
Politseiskie znayut.
The cops—

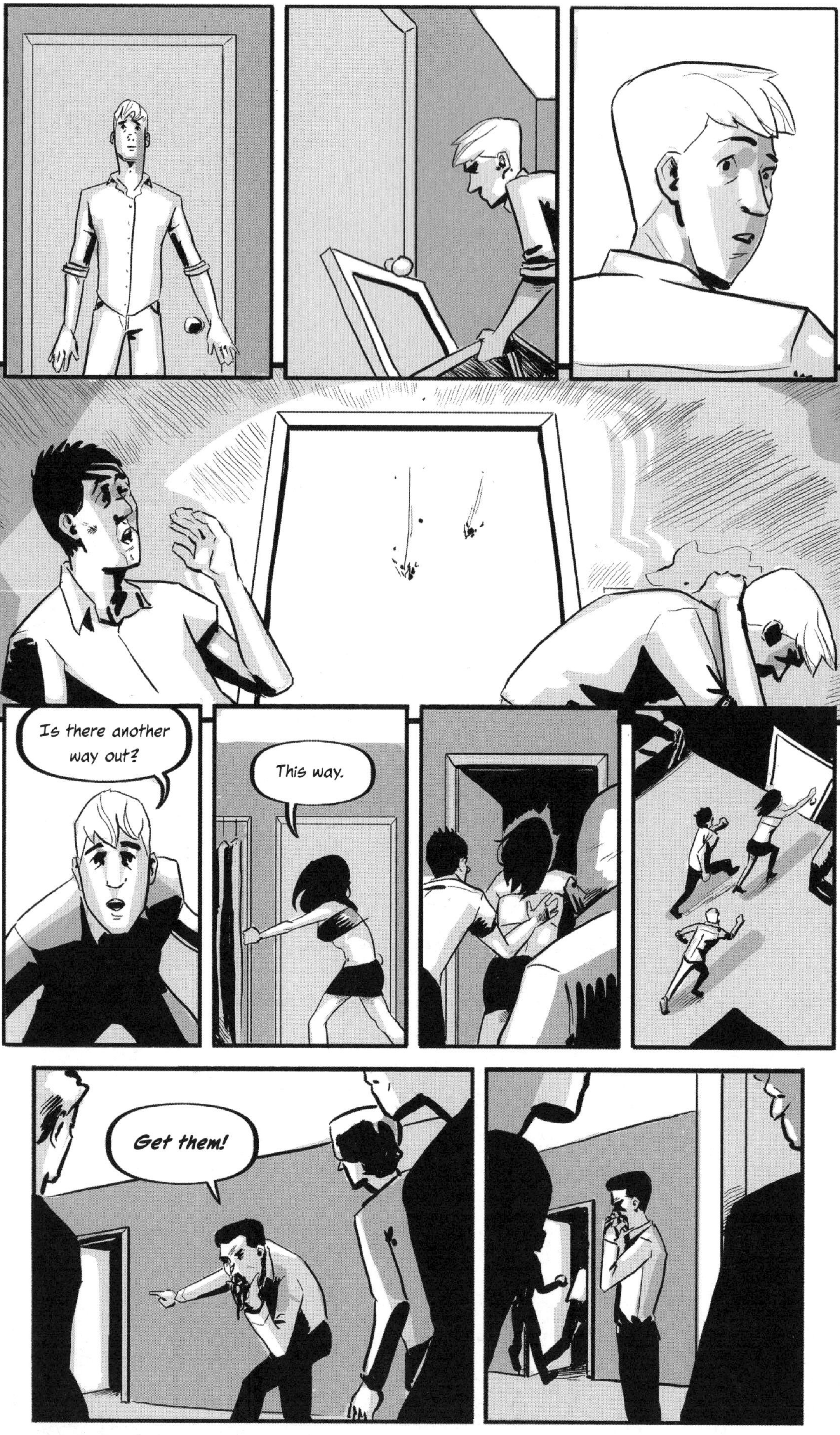
Is there another way out?
This way.
Get them!

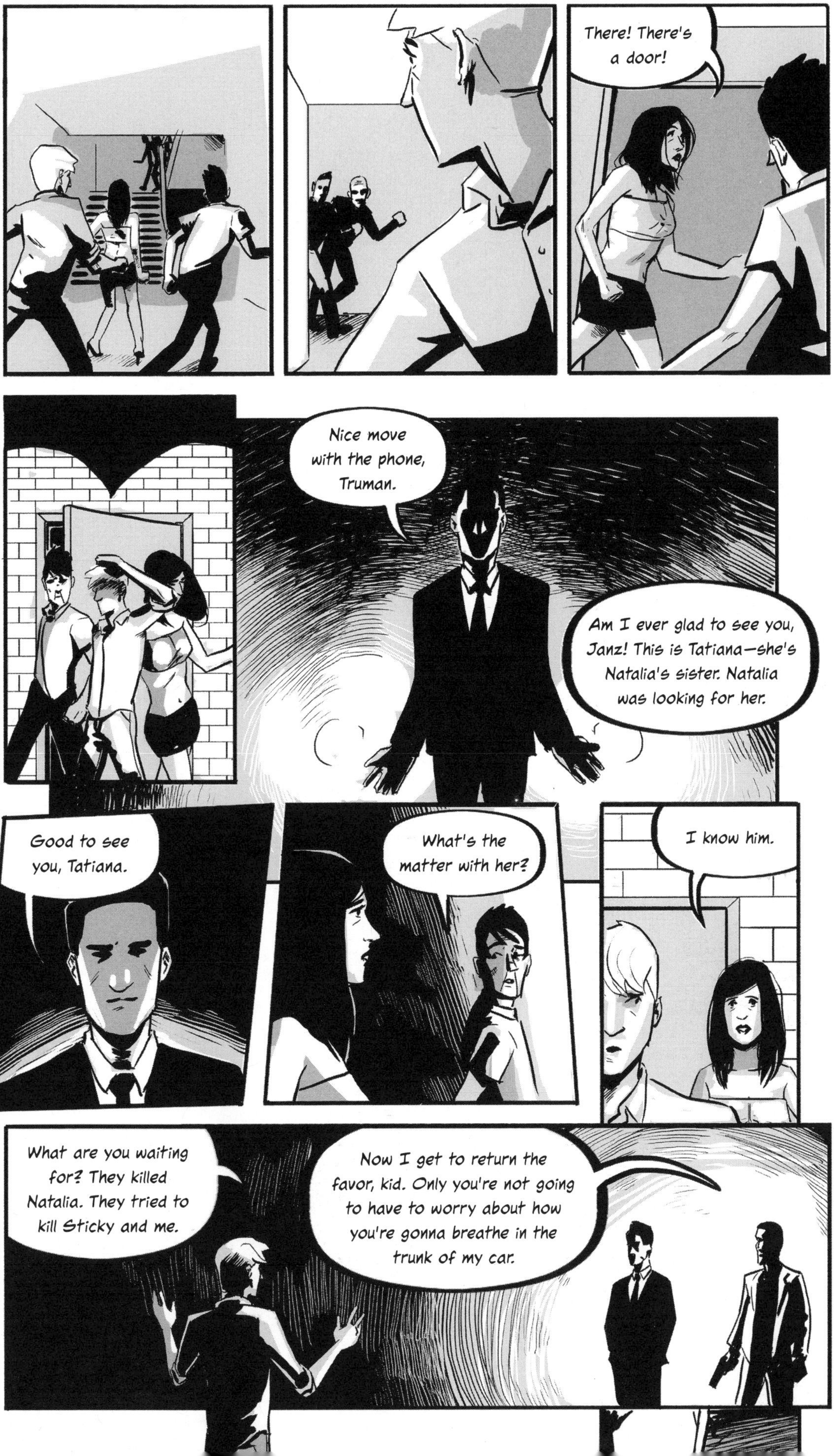
There! There's a door!
Nice move with the phone, Truman.
Am I ever glad to see you, Janz! This is Tatiana—she's Natalia's sister. Natalia was looking for her.
Good to see you, Tatiana.
What's the matter with her?
I know him.
What are you waiting for? They killed Natalia. They tried to kill Sticky and me.
Now I get to return the favor, kid. Only you're not going to have to worry about how you're gonna breathe in the trunk of my car.

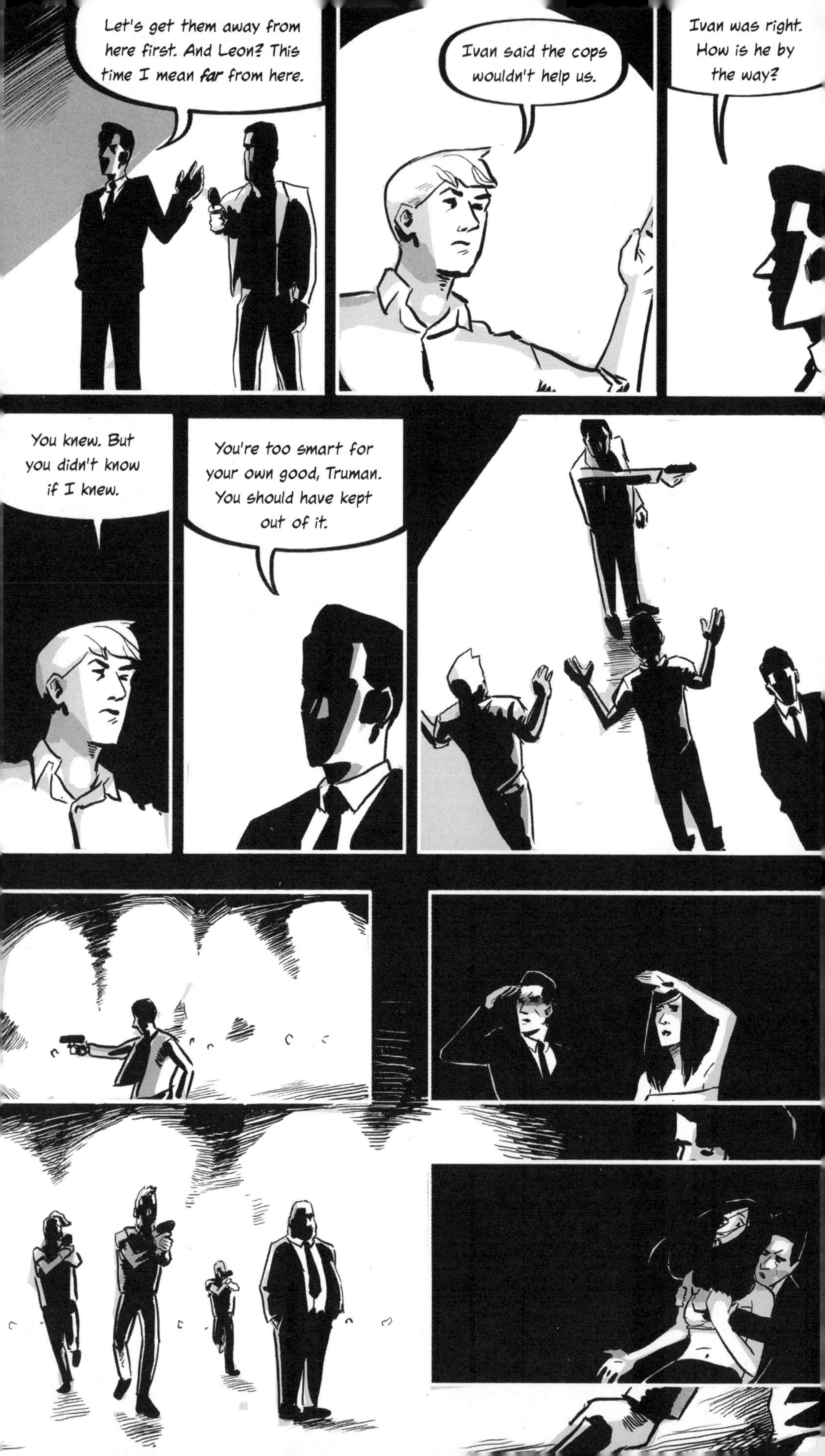
Let's get them away from here first. And Leon? This time I mean far from here.
Ivan said the cops wouldn't help us.
Ivan was right. How is he by the way?
You knew. But you didn't know if I knew.
You're too smart for your own good, Truman. You should have kept out of it.

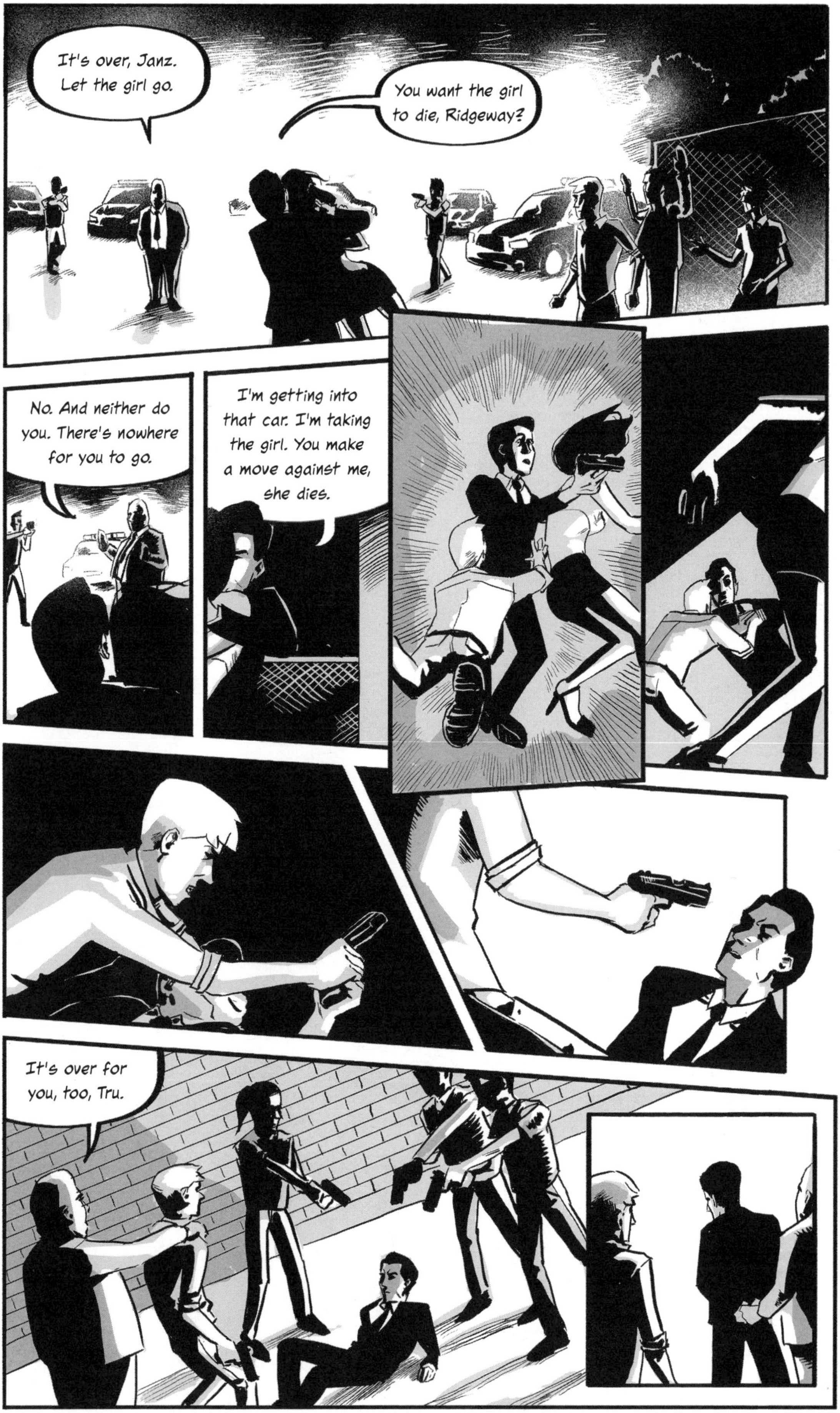
It's over, Janz. Let the girl go.
You want the girl to die, Ridgeway?
No. And neither do you. There's nowhere for you to go.
I'm getting into that car. I'm taking the girl. You make a move against me, she dies.
It's over for you, too, Tru.

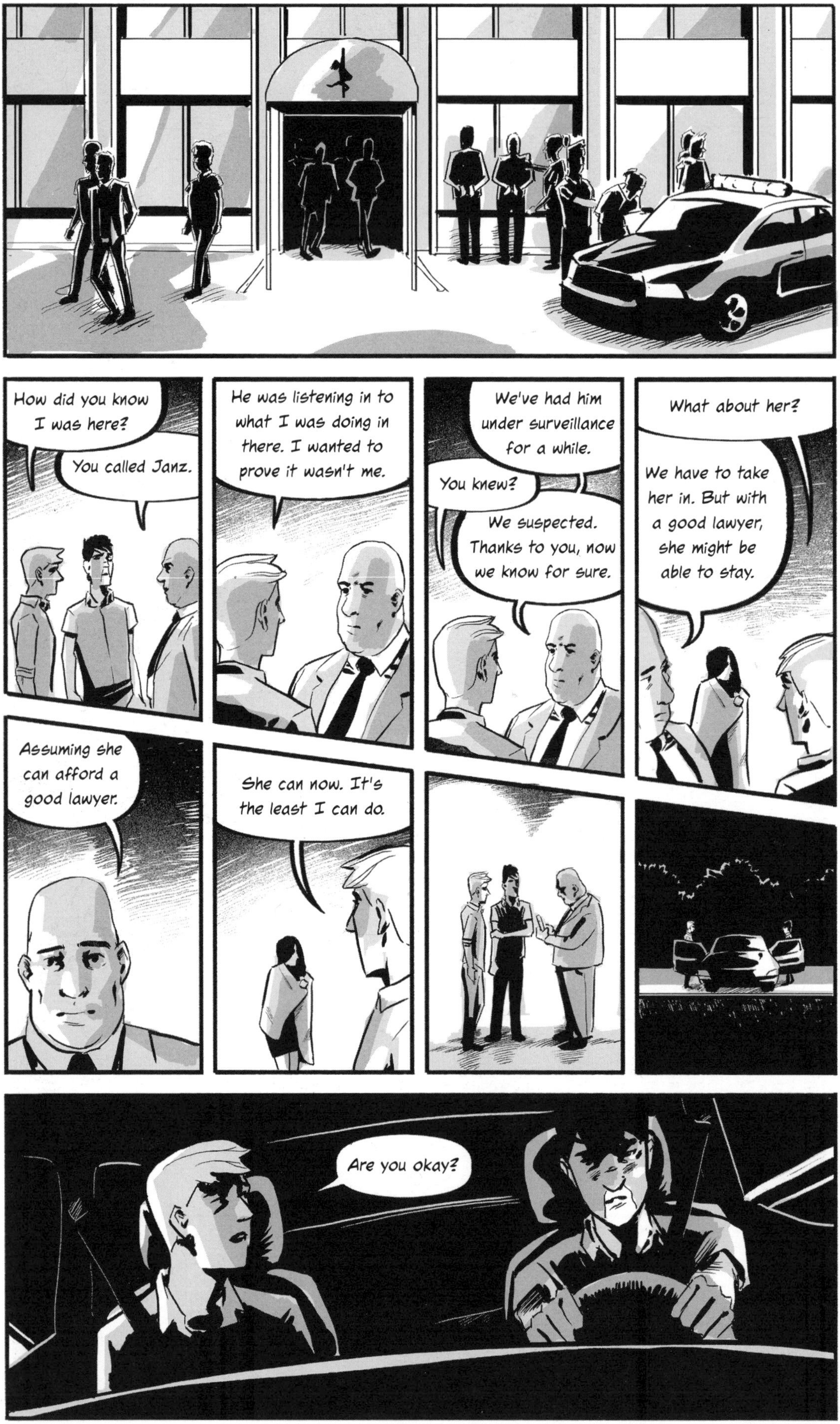
How did you know I was here?
You called Janz.
He was listening in to what I was doing in there. I wanted to prove it wasn't me.
We've had him under surveillance for a while.
You knew?
We suspected. Thanks to you, now we know for sure.
What about her?
We have to take her in. But with a good lawyer, she might be able to stay.
Assuming she can afford a good lawyer.
She can now. It's the least I can do.
Are you okay?

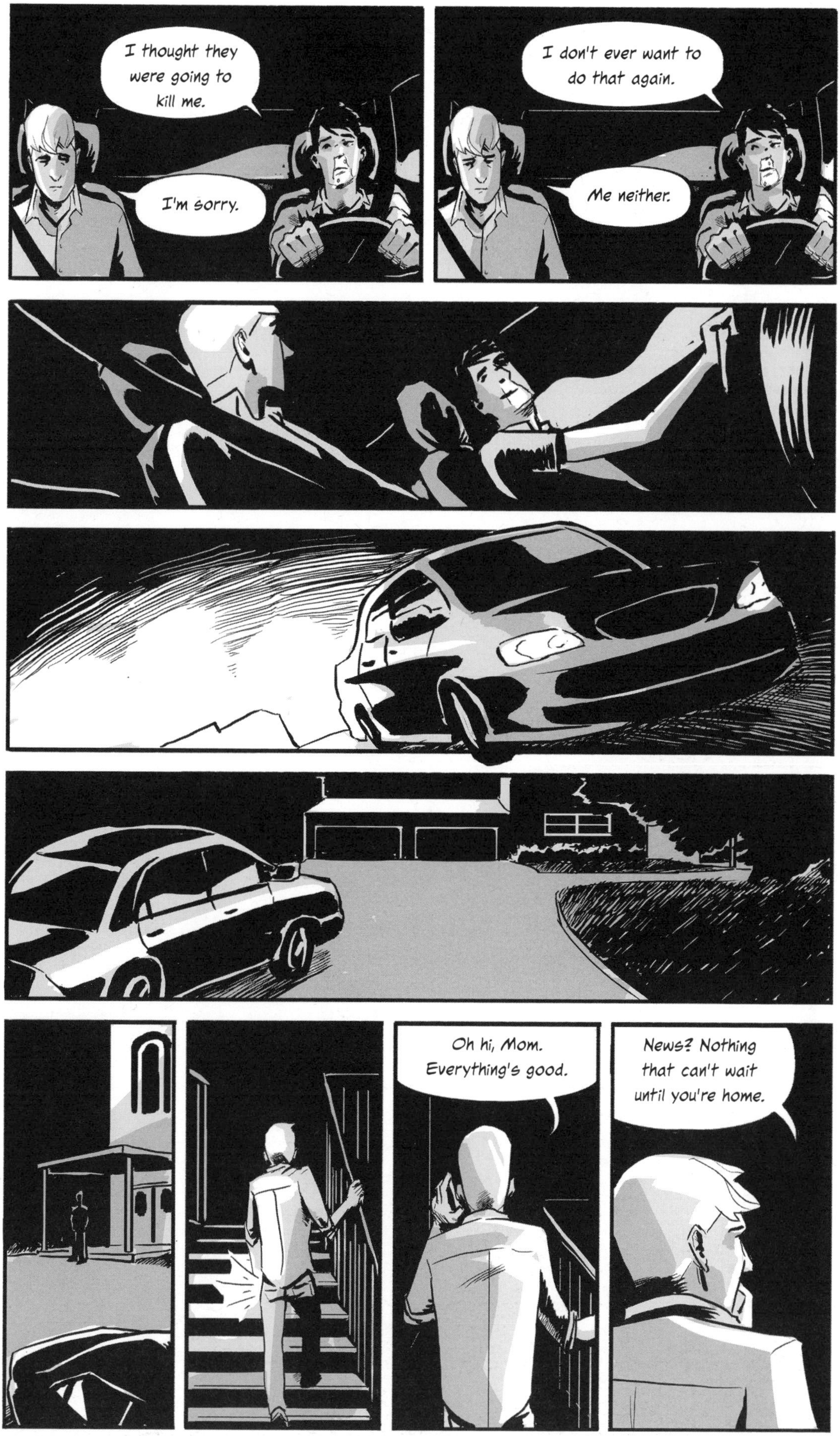
I thought they were going to kill me.
I'm sorry.
I don't ever want to do that again.
Me neither.
Oh hi, Mom. Everything's good.
News? Nothing that can't wait until you're home.

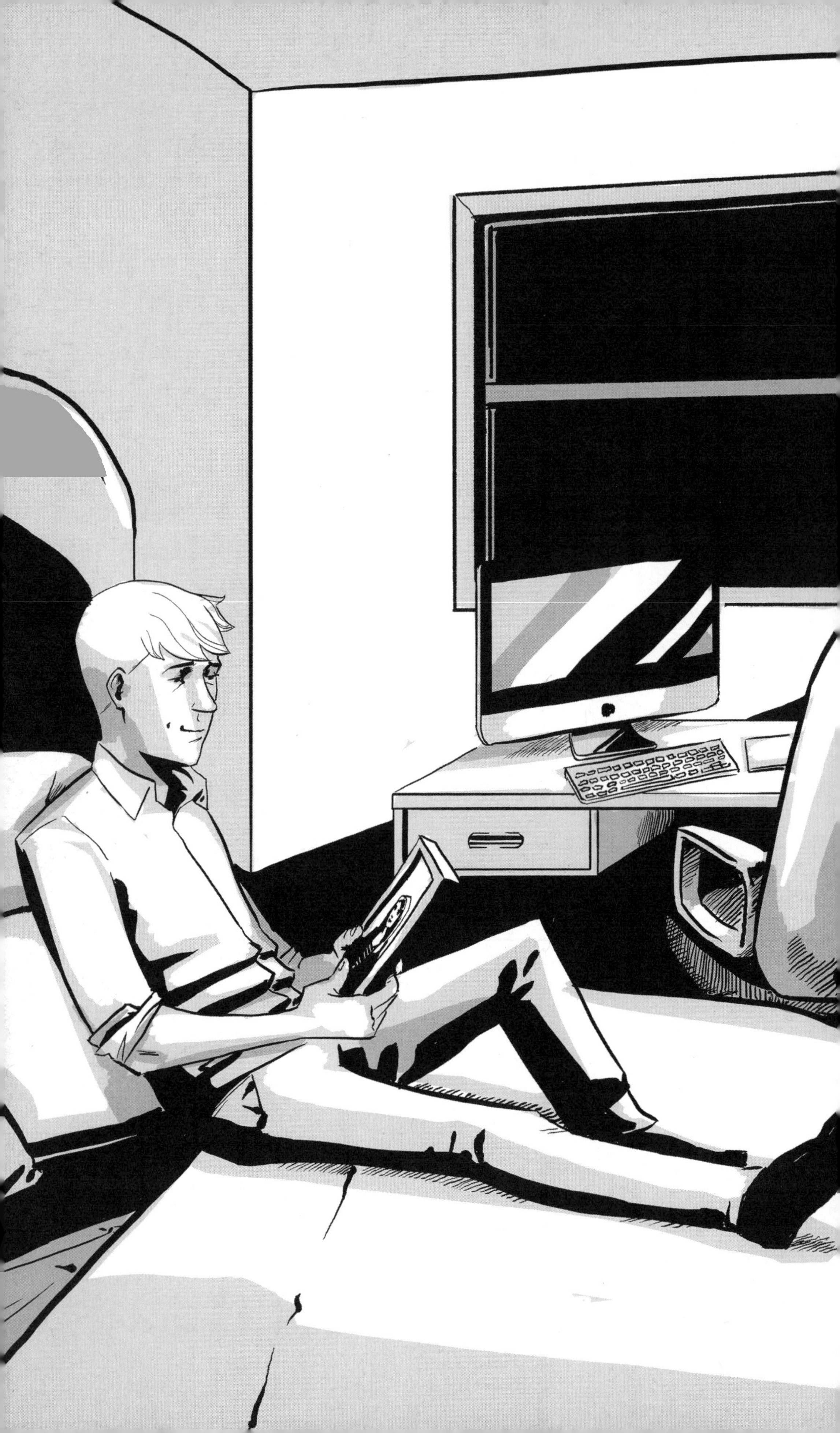

Check out Norah McClintock's first Graphic Novel

A Junior Library Guild Selection

"McClintock…shows her customary concerns with character development, fast and abrupt action, and the effectiveness of showing different viewpoints. Deas' dramatic black-and-white artwork is splashed with a bright blood red spilt across those panels where violence occurs. The story demonstrates the dark power of eyewitnesses who, either through a code of silence or fear of reprisal, don't share information when murder is committed…An effective thriller that raises questions about the complicity of silence on violence."

—*Booklist*

2014 Stellar Award Nominee

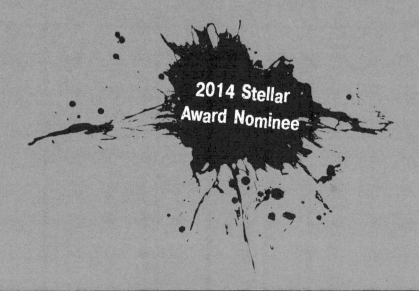

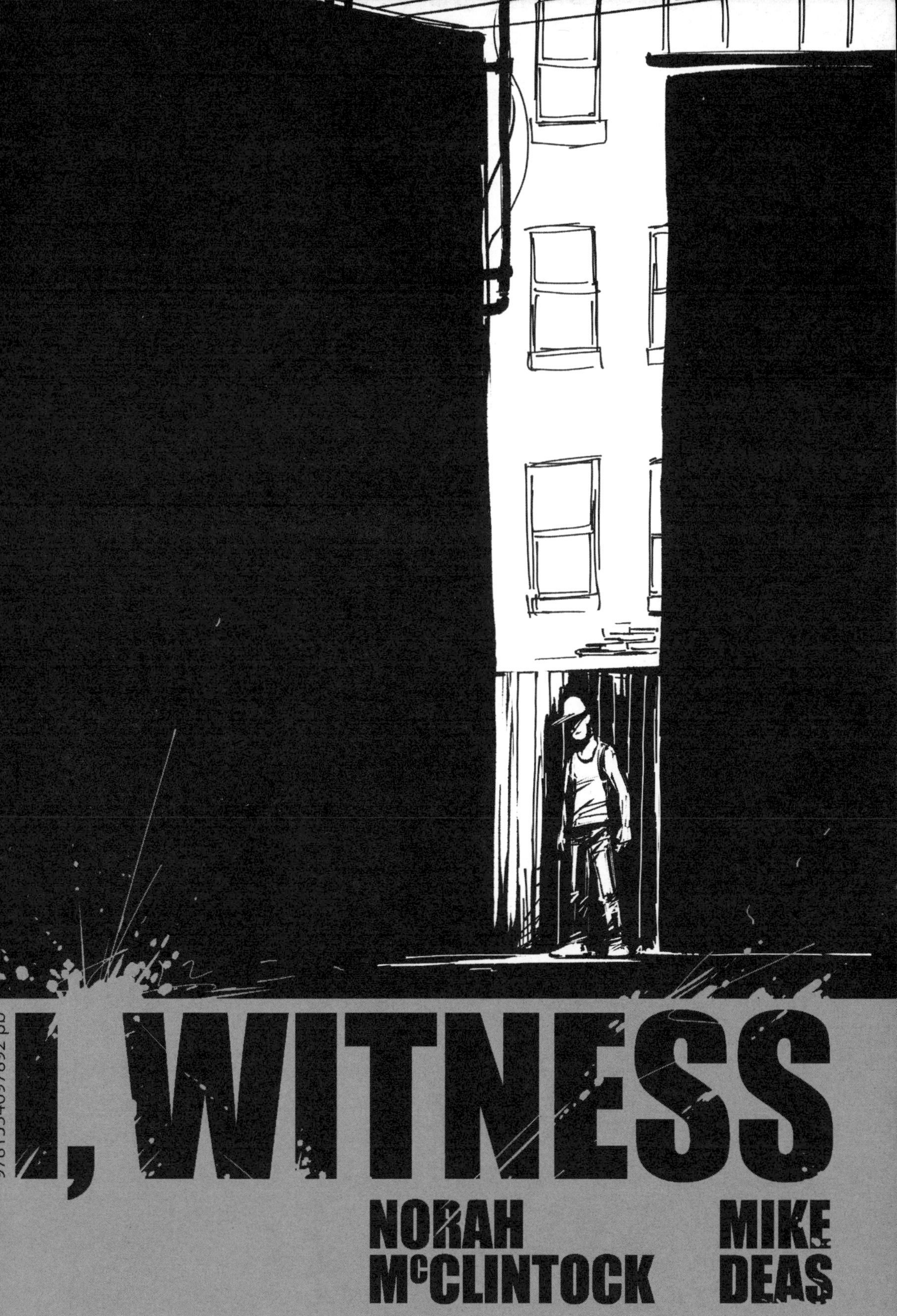

I, WITNESS

NORAH McCLINTOCK

MIKE DEAS